"Funny, steamy, and full of wonderful side characters, this one will hook you from the first page."

—Oprah Daily

"What a joy! *Dating Dr. Dil* is further proof that Nisha Sharma is a mega-talent who can do it all. Anything Nisha Sharma writes is an auto-buy for me."

—Meg Cabot, #1 *New York Times* bestselling author

"This book is rom-com gold: steamy, hilarious fun with tons of swoony, emotional scenes."

—*Washington Post*

"We simply cannot go into spring without a rom-com, and Nisha Sharma has provided us with exactly what we need!"

—Shondaland

"Filled with banter, steam, and Indian culture, Sharma's . . . latest is a charming rom-com. The character development is top notch, and readers will love seeing the protagonists realize that love can be a welcome surprise. . . . This first book in Sharma's 'If Shakespeare Was an Auntie' series is a recommended first-tier purchase."

—*Library Journal*

"Replete with endearing references to Indian, specifically Punjabi, culture. Kareena and Prem are engaging protagonists, and the relationships they each share with their closest friends are fresh and fun."

—*Kirkus Reviews*

T0316088

Also by Nisha Sharma

MARRIAGE & MASTI

A Novel

NISHA SHARMA

AVON

An Imprint of HarperCollinsPublishers

HarperCollins books may be purchased for educational, business, or sales promotional use. For information, please email the Special Markets Department at SPsales@harpercollins.com.

FIRST EDITION

Interior text design by Diahann Sturge-Campbell

Ring © 3djewelry/Shutterstock

Flower garland © ALEXEY GRIGOREV/Shutterstock

Library of Congress Cataloging-in-Publication Data

Names: Sharma, Nisha, 1985– author.
Title: Marriage & masti : a novel / Nisha Sharma.
Other titles: Marriage and masti
Description: First edition. | New York : William Morrow, 2024. | Series: If Shakespeare Were An Auntie ; book 3 | Summary: "The third and final installment in Nisha Sharma's beloved Shakespeare-inspired rom-com trilogy-an ode to Twelfth Night-is the perfect friends to lovers romp featuring an accidental wedding, meddling families, and plenty of sizzling chemistry"—Provided by publisher.
Identifiers: LCCN 2024002746 | ISBN 9780063001183 (paperback) | ISBN 9780063001190 (ebook)
Subjects: LCGFT: Romance fiction. | Novels.
Classification: LCC PS3619.H356636 M37 2024 | DDC 813/.6—dc23/eng/20240119
LC record available at https://lccn.loc.gov/2024002746

ISBN 978-0-06-339811-5

24 25 26 CPI 10 9 8 7 6 5 4 3 2 1

This one is for the single friend in the group of married couples. The odd person out at weddings, parties, and group vacations. Hey, third wheelers, everyone knows that the best love story is saved for last.

She pined in thought,
And with a green and yellow melancholy
She sat like patience on a monument,
Smiling at grief.
—*Twelfth Night*

Indians don't get depressed. They get married.
—Mrs. W. S. Gupta, Avon, New Jersey

FEEBA: Today, we have the honor and privilege of speaking with Mrs. W. S. Gupta, the most popular dating advice columnist in the Indian diaspora community. Mrs. Gupta is ready to share her views on the latest gossip. Welcome!

MRS. W. S. GUPTA: It's a pleasure to join you in the Desi Gup Shup Column, Feeba.

FEEBA: Wonderful! Let's dive right in. As you know, the number of eligible bachelors in the New York, New Jersey region has shrunk in the last year, since two of our favorite Punjabis are out of the running. Any thoughts?

MRS. W. S. GUPTA: If you're referring to Prem Verma and Benjamin Padda, I wish them a happy life. Dr. Dil, or Dr. Prem Verma, ended his heart health TV show and opened a community health clinic before he married lawyer and advocate Kareena Mann. Then there is award-winning chef Benjamin Padda who fell in love with everyone's favorite Desi wedding planner in the tristate area, Bobbi Kaur. Both men showed sound judgment in following their hearts.

FEEBA: Interesting you say "hearts" since love isn't associated with arranged marriages very often.

MRS. W. S. GUPTA: That is a misconception, Feeba. Even the most practical of unions has opportunity for love after marriage. For both Prem Verma and Benjamin Padda, love came first.

FEEBA: Do you think love will happen for the third Punjabi bachelor in the trio of friends, Deepak Datta? He has made the Forbes 30 under 30, and now the 40 under 40 list. He is regularly featured in *Fortune*, the *Wall Street Journal*, and *Business Weekly*. He has been a keynote speaker at multiple international South Asian association events, and he has brought South Asian diaspora entertainment into the forefront of global entertainment. Any thoughts on his upcoming wedding to lifestyle and beauty blogger Olivia Gupta, no relation to you of course.

MRS. W. S. GUPTA: I will say this. He has been engaged to Ms. Olivia Gupta for eight months with no sign of a wedding. There have been no announcements, no save-the-date news, no details about their lives other than pictures from public appearances. If he's so determined to get married, then where is the enthusiasm? Where is the dedication for the bride? Like I've always said: if a Punjabi man wants something, he'll go after it with his whole heart.

CHAPTER 1

Veera

Veera had never been in a shipwreck before.

Well, this was more like a yacht-wreck, but shipwreck was an actual term.

No one said yacht-wreck. Especially not off the coast of Goa.

So there she was: a shipwreck/yacht-wreck survivor.

She looked down at the puffy safety vest she still wore, and with a sigh, began to undo the clasps at the center of her chest. Now that they were back on land, there was no need for it. Or so she thought.

The scene in front of her was absolute chaos.

The seven-star beachfront resort had to set up temporary tents to give local authorities and onlookers some shade. The staff, paramedics, and news crew bounced around like pinballs in an arcade machine going from tent to tent, then from water bottle station back to a different tent. Their constant movement made it difficult for Veera to see the bright aquamarine ocean lapping gently at the soft sandy beaches in the distance. Not that she was sitting around for the view.

Veera desperately wanted to go back to the room and start the long, tedious process of getting replacement credit cards since her bag was now at the bottom of the ocean. Judging by the increasing amount of law enforcement arriving at the scene, it was probably going to be a few hours before they could question her about the accident.

At that moment, Veera's twin sister, Sana, collapsed on the bench next to her. "We have a problem," she said. Her dark hair, identical to Veera's in thickness and texture, curled on the top of her head. It was perfectly tousled and dried thanks to its short length. Meanwhile, Veera's hung down her back in long, tangled, salty clumps.

Everything else about Sana's appearance was equally similar yet different. The septum piercing instead of Veera's nose piercing. The clavicle tattoo instead of her wrist tattoo. The soccer player's build instead of her dancer's body.

Veera had always been so perceptive about her twin. How could she have completely missed Sana's betrayal?

She shifted in her seat to give Sana her back.

"Oh, real mature, Vee."

Veera's shoulders stiffened. "You don't deserve anything more."

"I know you're mad . . ."

"That's an understatement," she said, as she crossed her arms over her chest. Veera was still seething from the news her sister had shared with her minutes before one of the yacht guests decided to light fireworks on the upper deck, tearing a hole through the vessel.

If Veera were a poetic sort of person, she would have appreciated how the wreck mirrored the way that Sana's words devastated her heart.

Veera was not poetic.

Sana tapped her on the arm in an irritating, persistent rhythm. "Come on, Veera. We've spent the last year traveling to all these incredible places. Can you blame me for not wanting to go back to New Jersey?"

Veera had to bite her tongue to keep from snapping at her sister. Of course, she didn't blame her. Who wanted to go back to *New*

Jersey? But that was the plan. That was the only thing that had kept Veera going when her life had imploded almost a year ago.

First, her father merged their family business with a global media empire and created Illyria Media Group, a giant news and financial conglomerate. The Desi version of Bloomberg.

Then, he had fired Veera and Sana, who had been adamantly opposed to the business deal. He claimed their jobs had become redundant and it was important for them to think about getting married and settling down.

And of course, to make matters worse, her best friend Deepak Datta, the intended heir of Illyria Media Group and the man she had fallen in love with, had gotten engaged to another woman. He hadn't even bothered to tell Veera himself that he was seriously considering marriage. No, she had to overhear the news from their mothers while she was hiding in a bathroom stall at their best friends' wedding.

Sana had been the only person Veera was able to count on. That's why when Sana had asked Veera to travel the world with her so they could work on the relaunch of the Mathur Financial Group without their father, Veera sublet her condo, tossed her bags in the back of a taxi, and peaced out of Jersey City.

Now, all the travel, client dinners, hard work, and sleepless nights in foreign countries were for nothing. Veera was back to where she started almost a year ago.

"Say something," Sana pleaded.

"Chutiya."

Sana gasped, the sound loud and dramatic enough to attract onlookers.

"Veera!"

Veera glared at her sister. "You seriously thought that waiting until we were on a prospective client's yacht in the middle of the

Indian Ocean was the right time to tell me that you don't want to go into business with me?"

Sana's expression was a study in guilt. Her perfect complexion was marred by the three little lines that formed between her eyebrows. "I didn't know how else to tell you . . ."

Veera motioned to the fireworks culprit. He was currently being strapped onto a gurney and wheeled into the back of an ambulance. The bright shock of his bleach blond hair contrasted with the red blanket the paramedics had draped over his torso. "Well, you aren't supposed to tell me on some German man's yacht who kept referring to you as Indian-Megan-Rapinoe."

Sana shrugged. "He was strange, yes, but the contacts we met in Portugal a few months ago vouched for him. You also said he was nice when we met him at the bar last night."

"Sana, I think everyone's nice," Veera said. She looked over at the rest of their small group who stood in the distance speaking with the officers on-site.

Why were they laughing? What was so funny about their current predicament?

Veera shook her head in dismay. "Look, can we not talk about this until after we figure out how to get our stuff replaced and get out of here?"

"Yeah, about that . . ."

Her sister's tone was another blow. Veera covered her face with her hands and groaned. "What the hell is it now?"

"Most of my cards are at the bottom of the ocean, too. We can work with our bank, but it's going to be a while before we're flush again. We're supposed to pay the balance on our hotel bill when we check out in a couple days."

Veera shifted in her seat so that she could face her sister now.

"You used to be an SVP of Global Operations at a multibillion-dollar hedge fund and advisory company. Don't you know how to work with international banks here to speed things up?"

"Your eyes are doing that bulging thing again," Sana said, pointedly. "Look, we'll probably be okay, but we need a plan B."

"What does that mean?" Veera asked.

Sana motioned with both of her hands in response.

Veera flicked her in the arm. "Stop it. Just stop doing that and tell me with your words."

"Ouch! Okay, fine." Sana took a deep breath. "Look, we need money."

"Who doesn't?"

"Vee, we need money *now*."

Veera pursed her lips as she tried to understand the edge in her sister's voice. "Wait, are you saying that we should call someone to wire us money?"

Sana nodded, her curls flopping against her forehead. "Mom and Dad would be superhelpful in this situation, but we know we can't count on them." It was hard to miss the bitterness in her voice. The sound was enough to trigger a cascade of memories for Veera.

You were never meant to lead a business of this size, Veera.

I'm doing you both a favor.

The leadership positions you hold are more of a formality.

This merger is for the best.

"I'm not calling them," Veera said. "You can if you want to, especially since you're not going to have to face them anytime soon."

Sana nodded, and the small gesture was enough to twist the knife in Veera's heart.

"I don't want them to think we've blown through our trust funds and our severance packages like vagabonds," she said. "We need another option."

"Do you have any local friends in India from the time you were stationed here for work?" Veera asked.

"No," Sana replied. "Not anyone who I would want to find out that I'm in trouble. What about your friends? Kareena . . . Bobbi?"

Veera felt a pang in her chest. Kareena and Bobbi weren't just her friends, but her college roommates who became her soulmates. They were both in committed relationships now and living their happily ever afters. Veera would've thought of them the moment the rescue boats brought her onshore. She would've texted them and said that she was okay, and she couldn't wait to see them to share the whole story.

But over the last year of traveling, she'd learned how to be brutally truthful to herself. And if Veera was being honest right at this moment, she'd gotten used to their absence. Even before she'd left for her trip, they hardly had time for her, save for a brunch here and there.

Being the third wheel was lonely.

Asking for help as the third wheel was impossible.

"I can call Kareena in theory, but it's like four in the morning over there," Veera said slowly. "She never answers her phone this early."

"What about her husband? The doctor? He must be available for calls."

"Doubtful."

"Okay. Can you try Bobbi?" Sana asked. "Her events probably don't end until four in the morning."

Veera shook her head and could feel her hair tangling together as one solid mass. "Bobbi is in California right now with Benjamin.

Based on the last text she sent in the group chat, she's on vacation. There isn't a snowball's chance in hell that either of those two are picking up the phone."

Sana shifted on the bench and rested a hand on Veera's shoulder. Her gaze remained rock steady as she focused on Veera's face. "We may have to call him."

"Call wh— Oh no. Nope, no way. Absolutely not." Her pulse jumped at the very thought of him. He was the one man she'd tried so hard to forget for the last year, and she'd do anything to keep him out of her life for as long as possible.

"He owes us, and you know he's probably at his desk working already," Sana continued.

"I'll just wait until I can get ahold of someone. I still have my phone in my pocket, so if I have to go through my address book one name at a time, I will."

"It's going to take time to wire us money, Vee. He can move quickly."

Veera could feel panic clawing at her throat. She tried to stand once, then twice, but Sana kept yanking her back down in her seat. Her grip was stronger than Veera's ability to run away.

"I am not calling Deepak Datta," Veera said. "Do you know how humiliating it would be to ask him for money? Even if we're just requesting a small loan, Dad would find out! We would be validating his belief that we aren't responsible enough to be leaders in Illyria Media Group."

"You and Deepak were so close once," Sana pointed out. "He'll understand and keep it from our parents."

"I rarely talk to him now since he's engaged," Veera said. The pain still felt so fresh even after all this time. But Sana was right. Before the merger, Deepak and Veera had been close. He was just as important to her as Kareena and Bobbi were. They met at a cocktail party when Kareena and Prem were just starting to date and bonded over business. As their friends partnered up, Veera and Deepak met for lunch a few times a week. Then he'd asked her to join him for a lecture at Columbia University. After that, weekly lunches became dinners and movie marathons until they were constantly in each other's daily lives.

He'd text her news articles first thing in the morning, and she'd respond with cat memes. He'd wish her good night before bed, and she'd respond with market reports and projections.

Her phone had been silent for quite some time, though.

Sana's hand felt warm on her shoulder. "Look, I am not his number one fan. Especially after what he did to you, and then getting engaged to our nemesis—"

"—Olivia is *your* nemesis." Olivia was one of the most popular Desi social media personalities with a shrewd business sense. She and Sana had started to hang out in the same friend group, and for years, they circled and crashed into each other like bucks knocking antlers.

"Deepak is officially our best option," Sana continued.

"You don't know what you're asking," Veera said. She'd been putting her pride aside for years. From the way her father treated her, to the way her community took advantage of her softness and criticized her, knowing that she'd never respond in kind. And then with Deepak.

He'd broken her heart.

Unknowingly. Unintentionally. Carelessly.

"Veera?"

Veera closed her eyes and tilted her head back, until her face was hot from the relentless tropical sun. The sounds of conversation buzzing around her and the sweet and salty smell of the ocean in the distance grounded her. She was so far away from her friends and family in New Jersey, from Deepak in Brooklyn.

"I can't believe you're backing out on eight months of hard work and then telling me I have to call Deepak Datta to ask for money," Veera said with a groan.

"It could be worse," Sana replied. "We could've sunk in that yacht-wreck."

Veera looked back at Sana. "I bet you he and Olivia have moved in together by now, and since Olivia and you have bad blood, there is a good chance that she won't let him help us."

"We'll have to take that risk," Sana said. She patted Veera on the shoulder. "You call; I'm going to see how soon they'll let us get back to our room."

CHAPTER 2

Deepak

> **BUNTY:** Yo . . . you okay? Do you need a hug or something?

> **PREM:** For fucks sake, Bunty. Are you seriously opening with that?

> **PREM:** Deepak, let us know if you want us to swing by today. We know how important this deal is for you to secure your CEO nomination.

> **BUNTY:** Food always makes me feel better. Do you want sheet pan nachos? I'll make you nachos.

Deepak Datta woke at precisely five a.m. every day. He took his vitamin, drank the water he'd left on his bedside table the night before, and dressed for a workout in his home gym. He'd sometimes jog, but jogging in his Brooklyn neighborhood was less like exercise and more like dodging people and cars.

After his workout, he showered, checked the news while eating one of three breakfasts he'd have on rotation, and then he left for Midtown. He usually walked through the double doors of his office building at 7:25 a.m. on the dot.

But today was different. Today felt off the minute his phone buzzed at 3:55 a.m. He rubbed the grit out of his eyes in the darkness of his bedroom and reached for his cell.

Through blurry vision, he checked the screen and bolted into an upright position.

Ninety-seven unread messages. Fourteen missed calls.

The last one had been from his father, which was one of the five numbers that could still reach him even when he'd set his device to do not disturb.

Deepak switched on the light and after scanning the list of names, he decided to open his assistant's message first.

KIM ISHIYAMA: Boss, this is bad.

KIM ISHIYAMA: Have you seen this?

KIM ISHIYAMA: Boss, wake up! I tried calling but it went straight to VM. You have to get in front of this now.

KIM ISHIYAMA: I'm tagging publicity and communications in an email so they can help with a press release.

KIM ISHIYAMA: Boss, now is not the time for you to prioritize self-care.

Deepak clicked on the link Kim had sent over, and his fiancée's face filled the screen. Olivia Gupta had smooth, bare skin, and bright eyes with a soft sheen of tears that he knew she was able to produce on command. Her perfect, angular face was practically poreless, and her husky voice disrupted the quiet of his bedroom.

"Get ready with me to break up with my fiancé, Deepak Datta."

Son of a bitch.

His stomach twisted in knots as Olivia began rubbing a clear gel into her cheeks.

"As some of you know, my mother set me up with Deepak almost a year ago, because she is friends with his parents. When Deepak and I first met, we hit it off. We had some good chemistry, and I knew that he would be the right match for me to help me push my business to the next level."

She switched to dabbing her dark spots with a concealer wand. "He has always been charming and sweet, and just an overall, wonderfully kind person to me, but what I've realized is that he is already married."

"What the hell?" Deepak said.

As if answering his question, Olivia continued. "He's married to his business, and I would never come first in his life." She then held up a glass bottle with her name printed in swirling black letters. "This foundation is magic. My makeup line drops in a few weeks, and I can't wait to share it with all of you! Sign up for my newsletter so you don't miss any of the details. Link is in the bio."

Then, as if she weren't completely ruining his life, she dabbed the thick liquid on her cheeks, chin, nose, and forehead. "Anyway, Deepak is the kind of man who will never put a woman first. Not me, not anyone. I always thought that our business agreement would turn into something more the longer we were engaged but he has barely even *kissed* me. We definitely haven't slept together. And do you know how insecure that makes me? To have every advance coolly rejected for almost a year?"

Deepak rolled his eyes. Their schedules barely aligned, and when they were together, they only talked about business. Unless he had completely misread every conversation, Olivia had never made an advance.

She expertly added mascara, eyeliner, and lashes. "Anyway, by the time you see this, I'll be a free woman. I'm so sorry you'll miss out on all the incredible wedding content I had planned for you, but don't worry. It'll happen. But with the right person. Just not Deepak Datta. That man has all the red flags. He's unavailable, inattentive, and emotionally constipated." Her voice hitched in the exact right moment for optimal impact.

She smoothed on lipstick then smacked her lips. "I'm packing a bag and heading to Europe to see some friends for a month or two," she said. "I won't be posting for a bit, because I just need to take some time for myself."

Her voice dropped in pitch, holding the briefest tremble. "I'm just asking you all to please respect my privacy. Oh, and respect Deepak's, too. Sometimes a man can't help it if he's emotionally unavailable."

The video ended and looped to the beginning. Deepak closed the window, so he didn't have to watch it again.

Kim was right. This was bad. This was *very* bad. Because what most of Olivia's four million followers didn't know was that she was also a member of the Illyria Media Group board. She'd inherited an Illyria board seat from her father after his death and it had transitioned during the merger. Marrying Olivia was supposed to secure his role as CEO at the year-end November board meeting. She was the swing vote.

Now there was a chance that he'd lose his legacy all because of her video.

He propped his elbows on his knees. His chest tightened with anger over the fact that Olivia resorted to her social media platform to put him on blast, but Deepak would be lying to himself if he didn't admit that he felt a wave of relief, too. He'd only said yes to the engagement because he knew that he had to make a personal sacrifice and marry the best match for the company. If he'd chosen a woman for himself alone . . . well, he was picturing an entirely different person.

But love had no place in his reality. He just thought that Olivia understood his position and wanted the same thing he did.

Deepak didn't bother reading the other messages before he called his now ex-fiancée.

Her face filled his screen once more, but this time, she was in full-glam, sitting in what looked like an airport lounge. The buttery brown leather of the headrest behind her contrasted with her dark curls.

"Hi, Deepak," she said with a sigh. Her brilliant, deep brown eyes looked wary.

"Olivia, what's going on?" he replied softly.

She had the decency to look guilty. "My social media consultant wasn't supposed to post the video until after you and I had a chance to talk, but she made a mistake, and I'm so sorry that you had to find out this way."

Deepak slipped out of bed and began pacing his room from entryway to balcony doors. "I thought we were on the same page. I didn't realize you were so unhappy . . ."

She chuckled, and the sound was humorless. "Are you being serious right now?"

His pacing faltered. "Why would I joke about this?"

"Deepak, after eight months, I don't know if you even like me as a person."

"Ah, excuse me?"

"Do you even *like* me?" She lifted a champagne flute to her lips and sipped. The tasteful engagement ring that he had purchased for her was no longer on her finger. "I know that you want to marry me because I'm on the board. Because our fathers were friends before Daddy died, and we come from similar backgrounds. I want to marry you because you can fund my businesses. But there has to be more than that between us."

"Olivia, of course I like you," he said, evading her comment about wanting something more from their relationship. "I wouldn't have said yes to our engagement otherwise."

Olivia held up her fingers in front of her phone camera and began to tick them off one at a time as she listed his transgressions. "You never show me any affection or appreciation unless it's for the cameras. You don't ask me about my job, or the things I like to do. You don't text me just to check in unless you're confirming plans. You never share anything about yourself. I haven't even met your friends yet, and we've been together for almost a year."

"I thought you wanted to take things slow," he said.

"There's slow and there's molasses slow." She shifted in her seat and the leather creaked. The sound echoed through the phone. "I sent you wedding venues over a month ago, and you refused to get involved at all. On Monday, you were supposed to pay the wedding planner's deposit. When you forgot, that was the last straw for me."

Deepak pinched the bridge of his nose before he remembered that was something his father was fond of doing. He dropped his hand to his side.

He wished Veera was here. She always knew exactly what to say to help him with moments like this in his life. She'd cock her head and lean in to listen to what he'd have to say. Her eyes would darken, and she'd have a look of intense concentration on her face as if he were the only person who mattered. Then she'd pat him on his arm, and her sunny smile would ease the tension around his heart.

Their friendship was short, but it was the most meaningful one he'd had other than his longtime brotherhood with Prem and Benjamin.

"Deepak, are you even listening to me?"

He blinked and refocused on Olivia's irritated expression. "Olivia, as a friend—"

"I'm not your friend, Deepak," she snapped, her voice hardening. Then she looked around, as if making sure no one could hear their conversation. Her glossy, plump lips set in a thin line before she spoke in a soft, even tone. "I'm supposed to be more than that. Look, aren't you tired of the once-a-week dinners, too? Of the kisses on the cheek, and the polite goodbyes? Are we going to live the rest of our lives like we're our great-grandparents who just stay together because it's what's expected of us? I refuse to be a fucking cliché when I've spent my career fighting against clichés."

The word *cliché* flashed in Deepak's head like a Vegas marquee.

Cliché.

Cliché.

Cliché.

How had they gotten eight months into an engagement without acknowledging how fundamentally different they were from each other? He'd sacrificed everything for his family's company. And if that meant making a marriage work with someone he didn't love, with someone who didn't love him in return, he'd do what he had to. But it looked like Olivia always expected hearts and roses from him.

She was right. This wasn't working at all.

And now, as he clenched his phone in front of him, watching the dispassionate, almost irritated look on Olivia's face, he knew there was no chance in going back. Her video made him seem like a callous, unloving asshole, because that's exactly what he was.

He sat on the edge of his mattress, feeling the knots tighten in his shoulders.

"Olivia, I'm so sorry. But I wish we had this conversation *before* you blasted it everywhere."

"Deepak, I asked you to choose our future, the one that our parents wanted us to have, that we're *supposed* to have, dozens of times before." She tilted her head, as if listening to an announcement before she drained her champagne flute and stood. "I'm sorry, but I have to go. That's my flight. I've already sent the ring to your assistant. You should get it along with a few other gifts you've bought me."

"Wait, wait, wait," he said, feeling the desperation crawling up his neck. "We started this together because of the board. I hired you for the newspaper, and we supported each other for years. We always had the company in mind from the beginning. I hate to ask this, but will you be back in November?"

Her expression fell. "After watching my video and hearing me rant just now, that's really what you're asking me? If I'll make it back to New York to vote you in as CEO?"

"I've never lied to you," he said. "I've always said that the board vote is my priority."

"No. No, you haven't lied about that," she said quietly. "Maybe I was in the wrong for failing to listen to what you were telling me."

Her solemn expression was an indication that he'd screwed up again. He turned to face his bed and really wished he could lie back down and pretend this nightmare was over.

"Have a safe flight, Olivia," he finally said. "I'm sorry that this didn't work out."

She rolled her eyes, then hung up on him.

"*Fuck*," he groaned. He needed coffee if he was going to try to diffuse this situation.

In the dark shadows of the early morning, he crossed his bedroom then passed the sitting area and out into the hall. His town house was five floors, but he rarely went anywhere beyond the first two levels. He walked down his stacked stairs, passed his empty and meticulously designed living room and dining room, then entered his kitchen. He turned his lights on low and made his way over to the open shelving where his interior designer had arranged his mugs on tiny brass hooks over his built-in coffee station.

His phone buzzed just as he put a mug under the dispenser spout of his built-in single-serving grind-and-pour-over coffee machine.

Without looking at the screen, he pressed it to his ear and answered.

"Yes?"

"Beta, you've shit your pants, haven't you?"

His father's gruff Punjabi was as callous as it had always been when he was in a foul mood. And when his father was in a foul mood, it usually meant that Deepak was on the receiving end of some of the strangest profanities.

"Papa, in my defense I didn't even know Olivia was feeling this way until I watched the video."

"And whose fault is that?"

"Mine," he said, as the machine groaned and sputtered. The smell of rich, ethically sourced organic coffee trickled into his mug. "To be fair, we had a business arrangement more than a relationship from the start."

Deepak heard a loud creak, and he knew his father was leaning back in his ancient desk chair in the home office close to the kitchen. His shocking white hair was most likely sticking up in odd angles and a steaming cup of chai was sitting at his elbow. His mother was most definitely still asleep, but in a couple hours, his father would make a second pot of chai and take it up to bed to her like he'd done for over thirty years.

"Olivia's vote is important," Deepak's father said, interrupting his thoughts. "Half of the new Illyria board think you don't deserve the position because of nepotism. The other half are only willing to support you because of me. Your marriage was supposed to establish you as a stable, reliable bet."

Deepak stood again and began to pace.

Assess, address, reevaluate.

As the COO, he'd succeeded by mobilizing those three simple words, no matter how large or small the project. That's what he had to do here, too.

"My successes speak for themselves," he said.

"Oye dafa ho ja, you and your success. Nothing is ever fair in business. And now Olivia's video will appear on all the mainstream news channels. What are you going to do?"

Deepak tried to think of a response.

Assess, address, reevaluate. Assess, address, reevaluate.

"Papa, is the board going to be angry about my bad press, or the fact that their best option for CEO is a single thirty-five-year-old?"

There was that long, heartfelt sigh again. The same one that he'd inherited. "Beta, maybe you should listen to your heart, to your instincts on this one, na?"

Deepak bit back another curse. How could his father even suggest that he be emotional about something so critical to the media conglomerate that he started? This was not the man he grew up with. This was not the fearless leader who taught him how every relationship can shape the way he conducted his business.

His phone pinged with another incoming call, and he squinted at the screen. When he saw Veera's name, he froze.

What the hell?

It had been months since the last time he'd talked to Veera on the phone. Their relationship had diminished to a weekly text or gif. She'd send him the random picture of scenery, and he'd text her pictures of bagels. They used to communicate at least twice a day. The thought of hearing her voice pulled at him until he knew he didn't want anything else in that moment.

"Dad? I got to go."

"I expect you to have a solution to this before the workday begins," his father said. "I'm still responsible for the company, and this doesn't just affect you."

Deepak didn't bother answering before he connected to Veera's call. With his mug in hand, he crossed to the kitchen island.

"Vee? Are you okay?"

"Yeah." Her voice was like icy cool rainwater in a desert heat. The tension in his shoulders melted at the warm familiarity. "Hey, Deeps. How's it going?"

"Did you see the video?" he asked, as he pulled out a stool.

There was a long pause. "Video?" Veera asked. "What are you talking about?"

"Olivia's video."

"Your fiancée? No, why, what happened? Oh my god, is she pregnant?"

There was a thin threadiness in Veera's voice that sounded almost like panic.

"No, quite the opposite actually," Deepak said, chuckling. He didn't know that he could laugh at this moment of crisis. "I wonder if I should be offended at how panicked you sound at the thought of me having a baby. I'd be a great dad, thank you very much."

"Of course you would," she said, and her agreement was so immediate, her faith in him unwavering despite the time and distance between them. He looked down at the swirling black liquid in his mug and cleared his throat.

"If that's not why you're calling, what's up?"

Great. He sounded like he had all the damn time in the world instead of a massive PR crisis on his hands. Olivia was flying out, his father was asking for a solution, and the board was definitely going to be pissed.

Veera was on the line.

"So, I'm in Goa with my sister," she said slowly. "And there was a bit of a boating mishap . . ."

"Mishap?" He had just picked up his coffee, and the hot liquid sloshed over the rim as he placed it back on the counter. "Are you okay?"

"Yeah, we're totally fine," she said. "And I normally wouldn't ask this of you because I know how busy you are, but both Sana and I lost our wallets in this . . . mishap. We'll have to get our cards replaced but we don't know how long that's going to take. We don't want our parents to know because, well, for obvious reasons."

If his relationship with his company, with his father, was complicated, then Veera's was downright hostile. "How much do you need?" he asked.

"We don't exactly know?" she said. "We're supposed to check out of our rooms on Sunday. Look, I'm sorry for asking, and I have no idea how you'd even wire it to us at this point."

Something about the way she spoke had the gears in Deepak's brain clicking into place. He stood and crossed to the windows that overlooked the deserted street below. The soft light from the streetlamps cast a golden glow on the worn sidewalks. In less than two hours, there would be a steady flow of pedestrians.

"Where are you staying?" he asked.

Veera named one of the top resorts in Goa. He'd always wanted to visit but never had the time.

How long had it been since he was in India? As ironic as it sounded, India was the perfect place to hide from the press for a few days. His assistant could reschedule some meetings for him, and he'd handle whatever he could remotely.

And this way, he could spend time with the one person who always knew exactly what to say when he felt lost. He'd comp her entire damn hotel bill for saving him from his current nightmare in return.

Veera rambled on for another few minutes before Deepak cut her off.

"I should be able to catch the next flight out."

There was a long pause, before Veera spoke again. "Excuse me?"

"I'm coming to Goa," he said, as he left his mug and spilled coffee on the counter and retraced his steps back to his room. "Do I need bug spray?"

"Do you need . . . okay, is this your attempt at making a Bunty-like joke? Because he does it better than you."

Deepak grinned as he stepped into his walk-in closet and pulled his carry-on out of the base compartment of the wall unit before he answered. "It's been too long, Vee. I'll be there soon."

Then he hung up and called his assistant to help secure a ticket while he began to fill packing cubes with focused determination.

Yes, he thought. Seeing one of his best friends was exactly what he needed before he figured out the rest of his life.

Indians don't hear music when they fall in love. They hear the sound of their parents' satisfaction.

Mrs. W. S. Gupta
Avon, New Jersey

CHAPTER 3

Veera

BOBBI: Hello, from sunny California! I wish we did more girl trips when we were single. Is that lame to say?

KAREENA: Not lame. I feel the same way. When can we all get together for brunch? Veera, when are you coming back? We miss you!

VEERA: I'll be back by Monday! Miss you, too. A lot has happened.

VEERA: Also, I think it is my duty to remind you that we used to make fun of people who were attached to their partners the way you two are right now.

VEERA: Consider this my "you both are being ridiculous cut it out" message.

BOBBI: That's fair.

KAREENA: You know what? We deserve that.

"I know that it doesn't feel right," Veera said in Hindi. Her voice was as soothing and gentle as she could make it. "But that's only because men have told you not to trust your instinct."

The woman in the police uniform sat across from her at the greenish beige metal desk. Her fingers trembled as she touched the files in front of her, shifting them from left to right, then back again. She looked so distraught that Veera's heart went out to her. But it was important to understand financial independence because financial abuse was such a common problem in their community both in India and in the diaspora.

"I make more than he does, you know," the officer said in English.

"That's because you're a strong, self-sufficient woman," Veera replied. "I know that I'm the American Desi coming here and talking about money in a way that is so different from what you're used to, but that doesn't change the truth: you have the right to control your money."

"You said that yesterday, too," the woman replied. "Right after I questioned you about the accident."

Veera nodded. "That's because it's true."

Officer Fernandez had been so kind when verifying their story and citizenship, so Veera tried to pay her back the only way she knew how: by giving her advice about money.

She took a notepad that sat the edge of the woman's desk and retrieved a pen from the cupholder before she clicked the release button for the pen tip.

"I'm going to give you some resources," Veera said, and she began to scribble the names of YouTubers, books, and classes that helped women understand economics and savings from a beginner's level. "When you take your one-hour lunch, watch one of the videos, or read one of the books on your phone. You don't have to tell anyone you're doing it if you don't feel safe. Then, think about opening a bank account where you put some money away so you're not giving your whole paycheck to your husband."

Officer Fernandez gaped at Veera, her cheeks turning an ashy color. "You want me to *hide* money from my husband?"

"If he doesn't understand how important it is for you to have control over your finances, then yes," Veera said firmly. "You think he's hiding money from you, right?"

"Well, yes—"

"I normally recommend open communication about money," Veera replied. "But if you think that he'll react badly, and you don't feel safe, then you have to take precautions to help yourself. Think of it this way: our mothers used to tuck gold away in small silk pouches underneath stacks of saris for emergencies, right? Same concept."

Officer Fernandez cocked her head. "I don't know what could happen that—"

"I don't mean to scare you, but what if your husband is in an accident? You don't want to move in with your parents again, right?"

Officer Fernandez balked, her eyes bulging. She shook her head so hard that her beret almost fell off.

"That's what I thought," Veera said. She tore off the top sheet of the pad and held it out for Officer Fernandez. "Put this in your desk. No one has to know."

Officer Fernandez wobbled her head side to side, the signature yes head shake that Veera had seen members of her community do since she was a baby. Then the woman folded the paper in half and tucked it in her top drawer. "Thank you, Veera-ji," she said in her accented English.

"Mention not," Veera replied, speaking in the same accent to make the officer smile. "I appreciate how nice you've been to me and my sister."

"And now it's time for you to go," a deep, familiar voice said from behind her.

Even after all this time, Veera could identify that voice as quickly as she could identify her twin's. She sat up, her spine ramrod straight. The hair on the back of her neck prickled, and she had to bite her lower lip to stop from shivering.

Good god, the precinct was a hot and humid eighty degrees and here she was shivering.

She hadn't heard that voice in so long, but it still had the same effect on her as the first time she heard it. It was deep, the tone crystal clear, and vibrating with confidence.

Officer Fernandez stood, the legs of her heavier metal chair scraping across the tile. "Mr. Datta. We received your call. We have finished speaking with both Veera Mathur and her sister. I believe Sana Mathur has already left."

"Thank you. Veera?"

Veera braced herself to see Deepak for the first time in almost a year.

Like that did any good.

She slowly turned around, and when their eyes met, she was breathless all over again. Just like the moment she'd first seen him in her best friend's foyer.

He looked tired in his wrinkled suit that had seen better days. His towering height and lean build were the same, along with his penetrating stare that focused on her like she was the only person in the room. His hair was slightly disheveled, and his mouth was set in a thin line. A soft, gentle scruff had formed on his chiseled jaw.

"What are you doing here?" she blurted out. It was the only question that came to mind. For months now she'd imagined how they'd cross paths again. She'd left New Jersey with her chin up, tears in her eyes, as a lovesick puppy who had been ignored for too long. She planned on returning as the cool, sophisticated businesswoman with a global client base who just completed a trip around the world. Unlike the woman he used to know, Veera would wear ruby red lipstick, drink fancy wine that didn't come in a box or a can, and act aloof and standoffish.

Reality was a cruel bitch. Instead of the perfectly poised, confident Veera persona she'd crafted in her mind, here she was, standing in a police precinct in Goa with frizzy hair at her temples and damp palms.

In fact, she was pretty sure that every gland in her body was sweating.

"I stopped at the hotel first, but Sana told me that you were at the police station," Deepak replied. He rolled his shoulders, the only sign of discomfort from the heat. "So here I am."

"We really could've managed," she said.

"Except you asked for my help."

Right, she thought. And if anyone found out that she was in a yacht-wreck, and there was bad publicity for the Mathur family, it could potentially impact Illyria Media Group. Her parents were on the board, after all, and Deepak was Chief Operating Officer. He was next in line for CEO once his father retired. Rumor had it that the announcement was going to come any day now.

"I'm so sorry to drag you into this," Veera said.

He motioned to her crisp linen pants and tank top. Her hair she'd tied in two French braids. Her toes and nails were painted a hot pink and they peeked out from her brown leather sandals she'd picked up in Italy. "You look good, Vee. Relaxed. Not at all like you've been in a yacht-wreck."

"I prefer the term shipwreck."

One thick black eyebrow winged up in surprise.

"What is it?" Veera asked.

He didn't take his eyes off her as he shook his head in one slow, easy movement. "Never mind," he said. "Are you ready to go?"

Veera turned to Officer Fernandez who was watching their interplay. "Will you call me if you need any help?"

The officer wobbled her head side to side in a yes gesture.

"Great. Thank you!" Going on instinct, she held her arms out and hugged the other woman. "Don't forget those resources," Veera whispered in her ear. Then with one last wave, she squared her shoulders and faced Deepak.

"Okay, now I'm ready," she said when she stood a foot away from him. She could see the depth of the tired lines around his mouth now, the soft smudges under his eyes, and hated that she'd worried him enough to convince him to fly halfway across the world to see her in person. He was probably busy planning a wedding and running their fathers' company.

She owed him big-time.

When Deepak just stared at her, his hands tucked in his pockets, his watchful gaze tracing the outline of her hair, her sweaty forehead, and her heated skin, Veera shifted side to side. She needed to get back to the hotel, to her room so she could process seeing him again, so all the sadness that she'd ruthlessly tied inside of her heart didn't burst free.

Except Deepak didn't move. His assessment of her was hard to read, and she wondered if it was because he was judging how casual she looked.

"Is everything okay?" she said, as coolly as possible.

Deepak reached out with an index finger and tapped the tiny gold hoop in her left nostril. "You changed your jewelry."

"Yeah," she said. "In Amsterdam."

"Your hair is longer, too."

She tugged on the end of one of her French braids. "I was going to cut it, but I wanted to find a different stylist than the one I had before I left for my trip."

Deepak touched the hand that was twirling the end of her hair and turned it over so he could see the inside of her wrist. His thumb brushed over the tiny, printed lettering. "Veera?"

"Yes?"

"Why do you have a wrist tattoo that says 'paneer'?"

She shrugged. "I got a tattoo. We were in Japan and had too much sake. I told the artist that I really like cheese. Sana has a clavicle tattoo that says 'cash money' in Punjabi."

Deepak nodded. His grip on her wrist tightened and he tugged. She tumbled forward straight into his arms.

As if no time at all had passed between them, Veera's arms wrapped around Deepak's waist on instinct, while his cheek rested on the crown of her head. She closed her eyes and felt the soft fabric of his shirt and suit coat lapel against her skin, the hard lines of his back under her fingertips, and his breath against her hair. He was warm and solid and real.

At one time, they'd had so many quiet moments together, so many laughs and conversations until two in the morning. They'd shared text messages and heated arguments in front of his TV. They'd worked together, argued about their passions, made plans, and talked about future moments when their lives were inextricably tangled.

But right now, they held each other in the hot, humid Goan air, and Veera knew that running away hadn't helped her forget those memories after all.

The twine she'd used to keep her feelings locked in her heart began to fray, and she held her breath as one by one the strands snapped until she was drowning with love for a man who didn't feel the same way about her.

She moved to pull away, but he tightened his hold on her back.

"Missed you, Vee," he said, his voice gruff and thick. It grated against her soul, raw and abrasive.

For a moment, she let herself go. Veera fisted her hand in the shirt at the small of his back and burrowed into the rich scent of his cologne. "Missed you, too, Deeps," she whispered. "Missed you, too."

CHAPTER 4

Veera

Veera, Sana, and Deepak had all convened at the outdoor beach-front bar at the hotel. The patio was covered by a thatched roof with wide fawn-shaped ceiling fans, and tables angled to face the sand and the crystal-clear water.

Instead of focusing on the scenic view or enjoying the soft instrumental music filtering through discreet speakers hidden behind clusters of coconut shells, they stared at the small phone screen situated between three half-empty glasses.

"Sometimes a man can't help it if he's emotionally unavailable."

Deepak stopped the video from replaying, then flipped his phone face down in the center of the table. "So Olivia's 'get ready with me' video is why I am now hiding here in Goa with you," he said.

He leaned back in his chair, and despite the fact that his position as CEO was now a tenuous one, he looked so much more relaxed than he had when he arrived. His button-down shirt was open at the neck, and his board shorts fell to his knees. He even wore a pair of sunglasses that he propped on top of his damp windswept hair.

Sana let out a low whistle and slid her mango margarita across the table toward him. "She's cruel but I don't think I've ever known her to be that evil."

"You know each other?" he asked, as he waved off her margarita offer.

"Unfortunately," Sana said. She folded her arms on the table and leaned forward. "We had the same friends in college and ran into each other. Consider yourself lucky that she left you."

"Sana," Veera chided. "That's not nice."

"Well, it's true," she said. "Olivia is the most dramatic person you'll ever meet. She once decided to stop speaking for a whole semester because her brother was kicked off the football team, and she was protesting. The best semester of our lives."

Veera could tell that her sister was about to say something unkind about his relationship to Olivia, so she delivered a quick, swift kick to her twin's leg.

"Ouch," Sana yelped.

"What is it?" Deepak asked, bending down as if he were checking for an intruder. "What happened?"

"Nothing yet," Veera said, glaring at her sister.

Sana rolled her eyes. She didn't care if she hurt Deepak's feelings. A part of her still resented Deepak for keeping his COO title at Illyria Media Group after the merger. He was the heir apparent to the business that Sana always thought she also had a claim to. Veera knew that her sister had joined them for drinks and acted with a modicum of civility because Veera asked her to, but it was clear that she was still bitter.

Sana motioned to the half-empty glasses on the table. "I'm going to need to keep drinking if we're going to continue to act like one big happy family. Anyone need a refill?"

Both Veera and Deepak shook their heads.

"Suit yourself," she said, turning toward the bar, leaving Deepak and Veera sitting in silence.

"She still hates me, doesn't she?" Deepak asked when Sana was out of earshot.

Veera shook her head. "I think hate is a strong word."

"Then 'loathe' is probably more accurate."

She didn't respond. They both knew the truth.

Most of the pavilion was empty in the late afternoon with beachgoers back in their bungalows or rooms getting ready for a long night out. The ocean breeze was cooling under the tropical sun, and Veera relaxed into her seat, despite the fact that she was sitting across from a man who awakened every nerve ending, every quiet desire in her soul.

Veera thought that the ocean could be a balm to her sore, beating heart. She'd already tried the Eiffel Tower in Paris, Christ the Redeemer in Brazil, and Mount Kilimanjaro. The breathtaking views on her trip had allowed Veera the space to lose herself in something bigger than her problems. But they were just waiting for her when she was finished running away.

India was supposed to be the Mathur sisters' last stop. They would connect with a few investors, and then go back to the States where they were licensed so they could open up their business in New York. Now that Sana had backed out of their plan, Veera would have to face her demons by herself.

Starting with Deepak.

She knew his patient, steady eyes were still trained on her profile, even as she accepted that his interest in her wasn't romantic. She was never going to be the perfect match for him. Not when he wanted someone compatible for his business, too.

"Where did you go?"

Deepak's deep, smooth voice sliced through her thoughts like a cleaver. She turned to look at his beautiful face, defined against the sunlight.

"I'm just thinking how surreal it is that we're both in Goa," she said absently. "I was sure that the next time I saw you would be at your wedding. If I was invited, that is. With Olivia and Sana's beef, that was probably debatable."

His brow furrowed. "I wouldn't have let that happen. You're important to me. I'd want you to be there."

But not important enough.

"Once someone gets married," she said patiently, "they become a part of a unit. Olivia's opinion would've mattered."

"You and I are a unit," he said stubbornly. "We're friends."

"With a very complicated work history now," Veera replied softly.

This time his jaw ticked. "I'm sorry for what your father did to you and your sister, Sana. But we were ready to hire you back in a heartbeat in a different department."

"Despite family relationships, Sana and I earned our positions in Dad's company. We didn't need Illyria's pity hire. No, we were going to earn our way back—" Veera stopped when she realized that Sana and she were no longer a "we."

Deepak leaned across the table until they were inches apart. "Vee, you are one of the smartest people I know. You would've never been a pity hire."

She tried to smile at him but couldn't meet his eyes. "It doesn't matter now. I'm supposed to be back stateside in a few days. That was the plan. Sana and I were going to start a business together. Mathur Financial Group, redux. But now she wants to consult full-time. She has no intention of returning to Jersey."

"Which means you're starting that business on your own," he said. He sounded so sure, so confident. As if there was no question in the world that she could do it. The faith in her was a blissful familiar warmth Veera always felt around Deepak.

She itched to reach out and tuck the stray curl off his forehead and cup the softness of his smooth, shaven cheek. Just for a moment. Instead, she placed her hands under her thighs. Sitting on them was the better alternative than touching what didn't belong to her.

"I'm not sure what I'm going to do," she finally said. "What about you? Any plans on responding to Olivia's video with a press statement?"

"Still working on it," he replied ruefully. "No one knows I'm here, including our friends, so hopefully the next few days will give me a chance to figure out how I'm going to save my candidacy."

Veera knew that she didn't have a right to ask, that she shouldn't interfere, but she couldn't help herself. She leaned over the table. "Why didn't you tell me when you first decided to marry Olivia? After we became friends, you used to tell me everything, but I found out at Prem and Kareena's wedding when I overheard our moms talking in the bathroom about it. Then there was the press release."

His eyebrows shot up almost to his hairline. "You never told me that."

"Considering my job insecurity a week later when the merger began, I didn't exactly have time."

He leaned closer to her and twisted one of her stray curls around his finger and tugged ever so slightly. "I didn't mention Olivia because I didn't want to disappoint you."

She gaped. "Disappoint *me*?"

"Your opinion matters, and I knew even then that marrying Olivia was very much a . . . business decision. I didn't think you'd approve."

"No," she said. "No, I probably wouldn't have." She didn't add that her reasons for why she thought they didn't belong together were purely selfish on her part.

Before Veera could urge the conversation into more neutral territory, Deepak tugged on her curl again. The warmth of his hand was so close to her cheek that she had to fight the urge to lean into his touch.

"Now can I ask you a question?" he asked.

"Mm-hmm," she said.

"It's been eight months since you left to travel the world. Did you think about us?"

"*Us?*" Her heart began to pound hard enough that she was afraid he'd see the thrumming at the base of her neck. She felt like he'd slowly reopened the wound that she'd worked hard to seal shut after all this time.

"I'm glad you valued our friendship," she said, then sat back in her seat.

He frowned at her, then cocked his head. "I value you—"

"I brought shots!" Sana said, as she placed a small tray down between them. There were six small shot glasses in various hues arranged in a circle. She plopped down in her chair and immediately placed two glasses in front of Veera, then another two in front of Deepak.

"You can't be serious," Veera said, blandly. "We're not twenty-five, Sana."

"No, which is why this is going to hurt so much more in the morning. But, hey, I think we could all use some mind-numbing liquid courage. That's what people do in Goa, right?" She lifted one glass and cleared her throat. "To almost dying in a yacht-wreck!"

Deepak glanced at Veera, then at the drinks. "What the hell," he said, as he lifted his shot glass. "To potentially losing my chance at CEO and my legacy."

Veera looked between the two of them and knew that she was outnumbered. Maybe this would help cauterize her heart wounds. She picked up one of the glasses and held it up. "To wasting eight months traveling around the world only to not have a job, a lover, or a family."

Deepak and Sana stared at her, their mouths gaping.

In her defense, it was technically their idea to toast. She tossed back the shot and felt the burn of the subpar liquor slide down her throat.

Sana and Deepak finally drank their shots, and they all turned their glasses upside down on the table.

Then Sana handed out the second shot glass. In the distance, a group of hotel employees were walking across the sandy beach toward the water's edge. They carried large parts of a mandap with them that they were most likely going to set up for a sunset wedding. Veera had been at the hotel long enough to see a few small, quiet elopements occur on the same makeshift platform.

"To the bride and groom getting married today!" Sana said, lifting her shot glass in the direction of the mandap construction.

"To rejoining the marriage market!" Deepak said, holding up his glass, too.

Veera thought about their toast, then held up her glass as well. "To updating my LinkedIn profile!"

She was met with stares again, but she didn't care. She downed the shot in one burning gulp. When the familiar numbness began to seep through her blood, the floating sensation that took some of the weight off her shoulders, she embraced it wholeheartedly.

The man she'd fallen in love with was here, not because he wanted to help her when she called . . . but because she was a convenient place to hide from his problems. The sister she'd trusted hadn't wanted to travel with her so they could go into business. And her best friends back home, the found family she'd loved since they were in college, had no idea what was going on in her life anymore.

So if she fell into another shot glass or two to help feel just a bit disconnected from the world, even if it was just for one night, she was going to embrace the moment with open arms.

She stood and shouted in the general direction of the bar, "More shots, please!"

Indians Abroad News

Indian weddings that don't include families and friends, colleagues and neighbors, are often a sign of shame. Remember that, parents, when you are fighting with your children over your guest list.

Mrs. W. S. Gupta
Avon, New Jersey

CHAPTER 5

Deepak

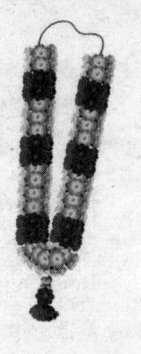

> **KIM ISHIYAMA:** Boss? You aren't answering your phone. I have a lot of requests coming in from the communications and the publicity teams. They're sounding feral.

> **KIM ISHIYAMA:** Boss? I'm fearful for my life.

> **KIM ISHIYAMA:** Boss? I work really hard, but I need to feel appreciated, and when you ignore my text messages, I am not appreciated!

There was something incredibly dangerous about being here with Veera.

Eight months.

Eight months of limited contact.

Eight months wondering how she was doing and who she was with.

Eight months of *cordiality*.

He'd given her space when she'd first left because that's what she'd wanted from him. It wasn't until he heard her voice again that he realized how much he needed her.

Deepak knew that was a selfish thought. It was no wonder she looked at him with disgust. He had been engaged less than twenty-four hours before, and now he was asking about their relationship. Veera was so sensitive to other people's feelings that she probably thought his line of questioning was disrespectful to Olivia.

"We almost got locked inside," Veera said, her words stumbling over each other as she tried to tell him a story about a museum in Paris. She waved an empty shot glass like a conductor. "We were so scared, but then we heard a wedding march, and we knew we weren't alone."

"A wedding in a museum?"

She nodded. Clumps of hair were coming loose from her braids now, and she looked beautiful drunk and disheveled, with flushed cheeks and shiny eyes. She was a picturesque postcard sitting in front of a brilliant orange twilight that hovered over the beach in the distance.

She jabbed her fork in one of the fried paneer cubes on a hot tava platter and waved it in sync with her shot glass. "It was a beautiful ceremony. Right, Sana?"

Sana stood at the edge of the pavilion next to their table, watching the wedding set up in the distance. "It was scary," she said. "My worst nightmare."

"The wedding on the beach or the wedding in the museum?" Veera asked.

"Obviously the museum," Sana said. She motioned toward the sand. "The beach wedding looks amazing."

Deepak looked around her to the mandap. The hotel staff had worked fast in building something from nothing. The small platform was now draped in flowers and sheer fabrics, with string lights hanging all around the base. A priest and his assistant, both dressed in mustard yellow tunics and red dhotis, were assembling the pyre in the center of the platform and arranging fruits, flowers, rice, and ceremonial objects around the base.

"Have there been a lot of beach weddings since you got to Goa?" Deepak asked.

"A ton," Veera and Sana said in unison.

Veera sighed dreamily. "It's always so beautiful."

The bartender arrived with more shots, and before Deepak could say no, Veera took all three glasses off the tray. "Thanks, Peter."

"You're most welcome, ma'am."

"Maybe we should all stop for the day," Deepak said. He knew he was sliding into alcohol bliss and one more drink would definitely teeter him over the edge.

"Maybe you should drink more," Sana said. Then picked up a shot and handed him one.

"I think I've drunk enough," he said, and his laugh was a little loose, a little too free and he knew he spoke the truth.

Veera leaned forward, glassy gaze and all. "I'll tell you what. For every shot you take, we'll answer any question about the last eight months."

His hand stilled on the glass. "Any question?"

"Yup! I know you're nosy and want to know everything about everything," Veera said with a giggle. He felt it like seltzer bubbles tingling his nose, and he wanted to gulp up the sound.

"Oh, I'm not playing this game," Sana said. She tossed back the shot and then spun in a wobbly circle to face the beach. "I'm going to check out the wedding." She started her slow descent across the sand.

When Sana was halfway to the mandap, Veera tapped his fingers with her own. "What do you think? You and me?"

Deepak knew that the temptation was too great to pass up with Veera. If he could get a free pass to ask her whatever he wanted, he was going to take it, even if that meant he'd have the mother of all hangovers the next day when they were supposed to travel back stateside.

Taking a deep breath, he tossed back the whiskey, closing his eyes and shaking his head while he heard her clapping. "Question!" he said.

"Answer!" she cheered in response.

"Why did you stop calling me, or taking my phone calls?"

Damn it, that wasn't supposed to be his question.

Veera made a sickly sweet *aww* sound. "I'm so sorry if you needed me, but I was on an adventure. I wish you could've done this trip with me, but you were getting married to another woman. *And* I needed to figure out what to do next. Next? Next is a funny word."

He didn't bother commenting on her hiccups. Instead, he tossed back the second shot and let it settle into his bones. His stomach churned with the mix of food and liquor, but he was feeling so relaxed now. Like he was at zero gravity. "If you aren't going to open your own business when you get back, what are you going to do?"

"I can't tell you," Veera said in a conspiratorial whisper.

"Why not?"

"Because I really don't know. I don't know what I want to do for the rest of my life."

He didn't laugh even as she covered her mouth to giggle again. He felt like his reactions were slower; everything was hazy, but even in his current state one thing was still crystal clear: he was part of the reason why she was without a job in the first place. Maybe if he'd advocated for her, fought hard to ensure she had a position at Illyria Media Group before her father could step in, they wouldn't have this distance between them.

A piercing whistle cut through the air, and Deepak turned to see Sana waving at them frantically to come meet her in front of the mandap.

Veera scanned the beach, then let out a startling shriek and clapped her hands when she spotted the woman wearing a bright red sari in the distance. "The bride and groom are here! Let's go sit with Sana!"

She was out of her chair and kicking off her sandals next to the table. Then she stumbled onto the beach and raced across the sand. Her arms flailed in a windmill gesture, her braids swinging over her shoulder. "Come on, Deeps! Let's go watch!"

Deepak grinned, and he knew that he probably shouldn't be smiling at how happy Veera looked on her way to crash a wedding, but she was so fucking cute.

He turned to Peter who was already at their table ready to clear their collection of empty glasses. "Peter, can you put all this on my card? I'm going to a wedding."

Peter wobbled his head side to side. "Yes, sir."

"Oh! Tip. Shit, sorry." Deepak turned to look at Veera who was almost at the mandap, then pulled out his slim billfold. He removed an American hundred-dollar bill and pressed it to Peter's chest. "Thank you!"

Then he was off, following Veera across the sand, toward the sunset and the beach mandap where an older couple stood waiting to step onto the platform. Both Sana and Veera had approached the bride carrying a tiny bouquet of impatiens tied together in gold string. They spoke with animated gestures.

"You'll be fine, I promise," Veera said. "I'm sure they speak English!"

"But it's more about the *rituals* that I want to get correct, dear," the woman replied. She adjusted the pallu of her red sari. "I don't know what's expected of me."

The groom wore a simple cream kurta and possessed a full head of shocking white hair. He stepped up to his bride's side and rested a hand on her shoulder as if agreeing with her concerns.

Veera glanced back at Deepak. "Hey! Come meet Debby and Manfred."

Deepak tried to think sober thoughts as he walked the rest of the distance to Veera's side. "Hi," he said.

Was that his voice? What had happened to his voice? Why did he sound like he was a talk-show host?

"Hello," Debby said. She eyed him up and down, then blushed as she patted her platinum blond coif, pinned back with flowers and decorated jeweled tikka that dipped like a teardrop to the center of her forehead. That was when Deepak noticed the massive diamond glittering on her finger.

Weird, Deepak thought. *Did they already have the wedding?* He held his hand out to shake, and Manfred was the first one to take it. "Pleasure. Debby and I are from Munich renewing our vows."

"Oh! Congratulations on your wedding." When Manfred pumped his hand with enthusiasm, Deepak almost buckled under the strength of it.

For a guy who looked to be hitting seventy, Manfred sure as heck had strength.

"We're sorry for the intrusion," Deepak said. "Good luck up there!"

"Oh no, you're not intruding at all," Debby said. "If we're being honest with you, we're nervous. We got married at a church in Goa decades ago, and we always regretted not doing a traditional

Hindu wedding, too. That's why we're renewing our vows by having a Hindu ceremony. But now I feel out of sorts."

"We felt out of sorts on our wedding day, too," Manfred said, pulling his wife close. "But look how that turned out. Happiest years of my life. We have four daughters and a slew of grand-children."

"Aww," Sana said, pressing her hands to her chest. "You really do look wonderful. Both of you. You'll be *fine*. My sister and I have seen a million of these this week and they're a piece of cake. Just follow the motions, and you can do it."

"But you speak the language," Debby said, motioning with her impatiens.

"Not Sanskrit," Veera said. "Or Konkani."

"Not a word," Deepak added, then leaned against Veera's side before he toppled over. Her body felt warm and soft against his.

Tingly.

"It's really simple to follow along," he continued. "Throw the rice, throw the water, get tied together by a scarf, walk around the fire seven times, repeat words the way they sound to you to the priest, mangalam, et cetera, et cetera, and you're Hindu married. You'll have quite a few cultural variations, and the order of things will be different, but that's the basic gist."

"Oh, you two are married!" Manfred said motioning to both Deepak and Veera.

Sana burst out laughing. The sound was more like a cackle on the wind.

Veera kept shaking her head, so Deepak pressed his hands on the sides of it to get her to stop, before turning back to Manfred and Debby.

"All three of us have been to enough weddings to know the rules," he said.

"We could explain a wedding in our sleep," Veera added. Her words were starting to slur.

"I wish we'd seen one before we do it ourselves," Debby said.

"Want us to show you?" Sana asked, her glassy eyes widened as she pointed to the mandap. "We can get up there and do a quick trial run for you to walk you through it."

This time it was Veera who laughed, but the sound coming from her throat was warm and sweet. Deepak smiled and looked down at her just as Debby responded.

"Oh, my goodness, would you? Just like our warm-up round. We have the mandap for three hours, but we were told we could get a shorter version for thirty minutes if we wanted."

"Get the shorter version," Deepak, Sana, and Veera said in unison.

Debby's smile brightened even more. "That's perfect then!" She shoved her bouquet at Sana. "We'll do a short warm-up with two of you, then you can watch Manfred and I renew our vows. After that, we'd like to treat you all to dinner to celebrate."

"Oh, not me," Sana said, as she held her hands palms up, swaying left and right, as if she were in a game of dodgeball and the flowers were the ball. "If I were part of your warm-up ceremony, I would either have to fake marry my sister, or fake marry a man, and I prefer women." She pointed to Veera. "But my twin here would be more than happy to help you."

Deepak watched as Veera's eyes went wide. Then he realized exactly what was happening. The alcohol turned in his stomach.

Veera protested first. "I don't think—"

"Sana, don't even—"

"Please?" Debby asked, as she pressed the flowers against Veera's chest before she could dodge the bouquet, too. "I'm really nervous." The bride-to-be batted her lashes.

Deepak saw Veera's expression soften. "I want to help, but Sana is the one who—"

"What's the big deal?" Sana said, as her words slurred at the edges. "We're doing this for a good cause." She grabbed Deepak's arm in a viselike grip before she nudged him and her sister toward the mandap. "Debby needs us, guys!"

"We need you!" Debby called out.

"It won't be fake because this is a *real* mandap," Veera managed to say. Then she repeated the word *mandap*, giggled, and lifted the blooms to her face so she could smell them. Her eyes closed, and her shoulders lifted and fell with pleasure.

"Just do it for the couple," Sana called from the base of the mandap steps. "It's not like either of you are in a relationship." She chortled at her own joke.

Deepak stopped to give her the middle finger when he caught the pandit's eye. He immediately tucked his hands behind his back.

"This mandap is so pretty," Veera said with a soft sigh. She looked up at Deepak, her eyes bright and beautiful. "I mean, it can't hurt, right? I'd hate for Debby and Manfred to be nervous during their vow renewal."

"Veera," he said, and for some reason her name felt thick on his tongue. "We can't do this, and you know it."

It would be too real.

"I know you'd never want to marry me," she said. "I understand."

"What? That's not true—"

She looked up at him with a drunken smile. They were so close, standing side by side. "You know what? I think we should do it. It's just to make them feel more comfortable. If I can't have a happily ever after myself, the least I can do is help others get their happiness."

The nausea grew stronger. Did she really believe that she wasn't going to get a happily ever after? He wished he could tell her right there in front of everyone that he would do everything he could to help her achieve all her hopes and dreams.

"Vee, wait—"

"Excuse me, Pandit-ji?" Veera said, tapping the shoulder of the older man who was eating shards of fresh coconut and golden raisins from a small plastic baggie. Veera pointed to Deepak and then herself. "We need to show the bride and groom what the ceremony looks like."

Veera then pointed to Debby and Manfred who were sitting on the sand now in front of the mandap as if they were getting ready to watch a show. Sana sat behind them, whispering in their ear. She held up two thumbs.

"You married?" the pandit asked.

"Fake married," Veera replied.

"*Fake* married?" The pandit's accent hardened the sound of "fake" so that it echoed like a drumbeat in Deepak's head.

"Never mind, Pandit-ji, we'll just go." Deepak touched Veera's arm, but she pulled away.

"Please?" she asked. Then she turned to Deepak. "Give me your wallet."

"What? Why?"

She didn't bother asking again and instead reached in his back pocket to remove the billfold. Before he could stop her, his limbs too sluggish to do much more than register her hand on his ass, she'd removed his last hundred-dollar bill and handed it to the priest.

"Fake marriage, please."

The priest looked at the bill, then at Veera's face. "Konkani?"

"Ah, Punjabi if you know it."

He pinched the plastic baggie of coconut and raisins closed and dropped it into a small box he'd tucked in the back of the mandap. He motioned to his assistant who quickly plucked the bill out of Veera's hand.

"We do two marriages now," he said. "This one a Punjabi wedding. Sit."

"This Punjabi wedding has to be fake," Deepak corrected; his words felt thick in his mouth. "We're just showing Debby and Manfred how it's done. We're the *warm-up*."

"Sit," the priest said again, his voice so cutting that Veera and Deepak had no choice but to collapse in the seats facing the small pyre. The priest's assistant draped a red cloth over Veera's head, and handed Deepak a string of beads that he was to keep with him until he had to tie it around Veera's neck.

This feels wrong, Deepak thought. And yet at the same time, when he turned to see Veera at his side, looking back at him with flushed cheeks, he felt happier than he had in a long time.

They were on tiny stools sitting on a raised platform in front of a sparkling aquamarine ocean and orange sky. Their clothes were inappropriate, and their parents weren't there, but they were together. At all the parties they had attended for business, at the wedding festivities for their friends, and even when they were out to dinner on their own, Deepak had always felt excited to just be with her.

The alcohol continued to set in, and Veera seemed to quiet down. Her giggles subsided and her expression became solemn as the pandit began reciting mantra after mantra.

The Jaimala ritual was next, and they took turns draping garlands around each other's necks. Veera giggled when Deepak sniffed the flowers, and he delighted in the sound.

Then the marriage pyre was lit, and the pandit's chants grew louder. Sana's cheers faded into background noise, along with the soft hum of conversation from the real bride and groom.

Deepak and Veera were then given fistfuls of uncooked rice to throw into the fire. The kernels stuck to his damp palm, but he did what he was told.

The pandit stood in his line of sight. "Repeat after me."

Deepak nodded, and swallowed the lump in his throat. He recited the words that he was told to recite, then Debby was asked to help tie a piece of cloth that draped over his shoulders and Veera's head.

When they stood for the seven circles around the fire, Deepak knew in the back of his whiskey-addled brain that this was real. This was all real and there was no coming back from it. But Veera wasn't looking at him anymore. She kept her eyes fixed on the fire, or on their audience as Sana explained what the priest was doing as if this was still a fake wedding. She was smiling at Debby and giving her a thumbs-up.

"The first phera!" the pandit shouted, and then pointed for Deepak to lead Veera in the circle around the fire. He chanted the words symbolizing their unity.

I promise to always make you happy and take care of you.

They finished the round, and then the priest shouted, "The second phera!"

Deepak could feel sweat trickle down the back of his neck, the whiskey sour in his stomach, gurgling as his knees shook, and he began the slow journey around the pyre with Veera at his back. He could feel her trembling, standing so close to him. The vibrations were subtle through the cloth that tied them both together.

We will seek our strength and courage from God and stand by each other's side. We'll support each other forever and always.

"Third phera!" the priest said, and Sana, Debby, and Manfred cheered.

They took the steps together, and Deepak felt his resolve harden.

"Fourth phera!"

"Fifth phera!"

Thank you, dear wife, for being my best friend.

The translation of the mantra shared by the pandit had Veera stumbling at his back, but Deepak reached an arm around and held his hand out for her. Her palm was damp, too, but she linked hands with his.

"Sixth phera!"

You fill my heart with so much happiness.

"Seventh phera!"

We belong to each other, forever and always.

Then it was over, and they were told to resume their seats. Deepak's head was swimming, and now he couldn't look in Veera's direction. Even when he was told to tie the mangalsutra around her neck, a symbol of their union, he avoided touching her any more than he had to.

The minute the clasp on the mangalsutra closed, the pandit let out a surprising yelp.

"I now pronounce you husband and wife!" he said.

Sana, Manfred, and Debby cheered from their spots on the sand.

"Kiss the bride!" Manfred called out, his thick German accent as clear as the stars in the darkening sky.

"No!" the pandit said, his voice sharp. "We don't do that here. You may shake her hand."

Deepak automatically extended his hand to Veera and shook before she burst out laughing like they'd just done the most hilarious prank in history.

This is what it would be like if they actually got married in real life, he thought. They would laugh and cheer and celebrate because he would be so damn happy to call her his bride.

This is what it would be like if he hadn't fucked up their lives so royally when he got engaged to someone else.

When he didn't fight for her to stay, to work by his side as his equal in the company that should've belonged to both of them.

When he didn't wait for eight fucking months to see her again.

"That's how you get married in a Hindu ceremony!" Veera said, breaking his trance. She tugged off the cloth from her head and quickly untied the knot that connected her to Deepak.

He sat there stunned, his head filled with an alcoholic daze as it dawned on him that he had actually gotten married. This was it. This was the real deal. In front of God, and family.

Well, sort of family, because he was sure Sana still wanted to murder him.

But his bride. Damn, how had it taken eight long months to realize that he'd asked the wrong woman to marry him? That the uncomfortable ache in his chest whenever he thought about Veera was because he wanted to *be* with her? That he genuinely found her funny, and brilliant and beautiful?

Getting married instead of asking her for a date was probably the wrong way to approach this, especially with the history between them, but he didn't regret this for a moment, as complicated as it made their relationship.

In Deepak's heart, Veera was now officially his wife.

"Are you guys ready?" Sana said, an arm draped over the bride and groom each.

"Yes!" Debby said. She looked glowing. Happy. "Will you three watch and help us?"

This time Deepak found himself responding. "Sure," he said. "Let's get you married, too!"

There were more cheers as the pandit and his assistant reset the mandap, doused the fire, and built a second one for Manfred and Debby's ceremony. Then Deepak was sitting in the sand with his bride while Peter brought them drinks from the bar.

Deepak's brain grew fuzzier as he drank and danced with Veera. He and Manfred got the hotel to open the jewelry store so they could buy Veera a sparkly diamond that made her sigh. Manfred acted as her uncle and put her chuda on her wrists, the set of red bangles a symbol of her marital status.

Then they danced together some more before Deepak followed Sana and Veera to their suite in the early dawn. He was barely able to stand, and he squinted through double vision to untie Veera's braids for her. The last coherent memory he had was of pouring water down her throat along with four aspirin before curling up on the soft mattress behind her. There was no point in going back to his own room when this was exactly where he knew he belonged.

CHAPTER 6

Veera

Text messages from two years and three months ago:

VEERA: Hi, it's Veera! Great meeting you last night.

DEEPAK: Hey, I was just thinking about our conversation. Great meeting you, too. I'm always thrilled to drink whiskey with a woman who knows her daaru.

VEERA: I only know whiskey because it's the thing my dad and I have in common, so it's been a part of many awkward father-daughter moments.

VEERA: Sorry, that was weird.

DEEPAK: Not at all. As a Punjabi, whiskey was my rite of passage into adulthood. Thankfully, I didn't mind. I wish my friends were able to enjoy the selection at the party, though. They love whiskey as much as I do.

VEERA: Sorry they disappeared on you.

DEEPAK: No big deal. The advice on the tech investment portfolio was incredibly helpful. Would you be interested in meeting up for lunch this week? Our offices are close. I really want to get your take on ethical lending.

VEERA: My specialty! Yeah, happy to meet. Tuesdays and Thursdays are my best days right now. Either one work for you?

DEEPAK: I'll make it work. Tuesday at one?

DEEPAK: Honestly, I wanted to support Prem by going to this party with him. I guess meeting you was my gift for being a good friend.

VEERA: That's really sweet of you to say.

VEERA: Sorry, I have to run to a meeting, but Tuesday works for me!

Veera's first thought before she opened her eyes was that she wanted the gods to take her right then and there and save her from her misery. Her head throbbed, a steady pounding that intensified as sleep faded into awareness. To make matters worse, her eyes burned behind closed lids, and her stomach roiled with what little was left in it after she'd puked most of the contents the night before.

She unglued her tongue from the roof of her dry mouth as she slowly lifted her head off the pillow in an attempt to sit up. Why was she so warm? She was usually freezing.

Then a hand slid over the curve of her hip and onto her abdomen. The touch was firm and possessive.

She froze before shifting ever so slightly to look down at her stomach. Her vision cleared in the pale morning light filtering through the small gap in her curtains to see a large masculine hand with long, tapered fingers.

There was a thin gold band on the ring finger.

Veera shifted her hips and felt a very noticeable hard erection at the curve of her ass.

"Sorry." The rough, deep timbre of Deepak's voice was like an electric current through her body. He shifted his hips back. "It's . . . morning."

She reacted before she could think through her next steps and rolled right off the bed and onto the floor.

"God damn it," she shouted as her knees sang in a fresh wave of pain. Her stomach pitched and she had to focus to keep from throwing up into the bedside table drawer.

"Veera! Shit, are you all right?" Deepak said. She looked up to see his disheveled hair sticking up in all directions. He was shirtless, and his hard lean body loomed over her like a cruel, tempting joke that said, *look but don't touch.*

In all the time she'd known him, she'd never seen his naked torso. Now that she was faced with all that gleaming, muscled skin, she was grateful for her ignorance.

It would've made the miserable pining so much worse.

Once her stomach settled, her desire warred with absolute humiliation.

"What are you doing in my bed?" she finally croaked.

He scratched his day-old scruff at his jaw. "I think I fell asleep here after our wedding last night."

"Wedding?" she choked. Veera stumbled to her feet. She looked

down at her sleeveless, thin, cotton nightie to make sure all the important parts were covered.

"We got married last night," Deepak said, as he sat back on the bed and leaned against her headboard. He retrieved a bottle of water from the side table and chugged half of it before dropping his head back and closing his eyes.

He looked like he was in just as poor shape as she was, despite his cheery voice.

"You mean our *fake* wedding," Veera said. She wanted desperately to sit down, to ease some of the hangover aches and pains, but she was afraid of getting too close to Deepak again in their current state of undress. She'd want to reach out and touch, and touching was not allowed among friends. Even fake-married friends.

"Technically it was a real wedding," Deepak said. "The pandit did a full religious ceremony. As Hindus, it's as real of a marriage as we can get."

"Nope," Veera said. "Nope, no, no, no, no, no."

He cocked his head to the side. His brow furrowed as if he were realizing what had happened, too. "Yes."

"Deepak, we did not just get married for real."

"I hate to break it to you, but unless you've converted, that was a real wedding. For Americans, it's more about the legal paperwork. But for us? This was it. Culturally, and religiously, our souls are now together for seven lifetimes, wifey."

Deepak squinted, then mouthed the word *wifey* as if he were trying it out again. He shook his head.

"I'm sure there is a religious ceremony for *divorce*, too," she said.

"Maybe." Deepak scratched the scruff on his jaw. The bristles made a rasping sound that caused goose bumps to race down her arms. "Wow. I'm married to Veera Mathur."

There was a sharp knock, and Veera was grateful for the brief intrusion. She glanced one more time at Deepak's naked chest and stumbled across the room to open the door.

Her sister stood on the other side with a food tray in both hands. Her hair was wet from a shower and slicked back off her face. Her eyes were bloodshot, her cheeks ashy, but she was smiling and dressed in a polo and board shorts. It was the same outfit she preferred to wear when she was traveling.

"Hey, sis."

"Where are you going?" Veera asked.

"It depends." Sana looked over Veera's shoulder at Deepak. "Hey, brother-in-law."

"Hey, sister-in-law," he responded and saluted her with the empty bottle of water. He glanced over at Veera, that confused, unsure expression still on his face.

"Stop it, both of you," Veera shouted. Her head rang from the sound of her own voice. "There was no *real* wedding."

Sana sailed past her into the room and placed the tray on the bed. "Technically, it was a proper religious ceremony by a priest done with traditional Punjabi rituals. That makes it real."

"Exactly," Deepak said, as he pointed a finger at Sana. His eyes focused on the gold band, and he looked down at it, turning his palm over back and forth as he examined the ring.

"God will understand if we all call it fake," Veera replied.

"I don't think that's how that works, Vee," Sana said. She picked up a cup and handed it to her. "Hangover cure."

Veera didn't hesitate in bringing the chai to her lips and drinking as quickly as she could without scalding her tongue. The warm, richly spiced milk tea with turmeric and extra ginger settled her stomach. The piercing pain in her skull began to fade to a dull throb.

Sana reached across the bed to hand Deepak the second cup. "I would've let you newlyweds sleep in, but we have a small problem that you should know about."

Newlyweds. Veera had to still be in a daze, a dream, to be called a newlywed. She looked down at her hands and that's when she noticed the short stack of red bangles on her wrists. Her chuda, a gift given by an uncle, which symbolized a newly married woman.

Then she saw the giant solitaire diamond that was the size of a brick on her finger. It was so sparkly it rivaled the sun. She would've probably noticed it first if she hadn't been staring at Deepak's chest.

Dear god, the ring was beautiful. It was exactly what she would've wanted if she were getting married for real. She tilted her hand back and forth to see the sparkle and rainbows from the pristine clarity and cut. Its weight felt magical on her hand, like this one particular ring was always supposed to belong to her.

"What kind of problem?" Deepak said, crashing through Veera's awestruck thoughts. He motioned toward her sister with his cup. "Sana, I don't think I can handle any more problems. Do I need to be completely sober? Because I'm not sure if I am quite yet."

"You don't have to be sober, and I think it's something you can handle," Sana replied. She pulled out her cell phone from her back pocket and handed it to her.

"Spotted in Goa," he read aloud. Then he squinted and brought the phone inches in front of his face. "Deepak Datta, recently ditched fiancé of lifestyle and beauty blogger Olivia Gupta, was seen Thursday evening with the daughters of Malkit Mathur, former CEO of the Mathur Financial Group."

Deepak stared at the phone, then glanced up at Veera who met his gaze. His expression was stunned.

Haunted.

"There is a picture of the three of us drinking shots yesterday."

"It's fine," Veera said, even though she felt the sick dread pool in her gut. "I'm sure it'll just blow over. I'm not newsworthy, and Deepak, your fame will die down, too."

"Not likely," Sana replied, as she took her phone back from Deepak. "The person who saw both of you drinking probably saw you get married, too."

Veera could feel a cold sweat at the base of her neck. "That's a really big assumption that you're making, Sana."

Deepak sat forward in her bed. "Vee, as much as I should disagree with your sister on principle—"

"Hey!"

"I think she has a point. It's possible we were seen. I can't take chances and assume anything but the worst, because my position with the board is already shaky."

Veera turned on her sister, careful not to drop her chai. "This is your fault. You're the one who demanded that we help Manfred and Debby."

"And you're the one who said you'd help them!" Sana shot back. "We may still be drinking like we're twenty-five, but we're old enough to take responsibility for our own actions, Veera."

"Hey now, that's my wife you're talking to," Deepak said.

"Zip it," both Sana and Veera said in unison.

"Fine," he said and held one hand up in surrender as he sipped his chai.

Veera had to turn her back to him. He still hadn't taken the time to put a shirt back on, and he had a small smattering of chest hair that trailed down the center of his abdomen toward the waistband of his shorts. On top of that, he was calling her *wife*.

If Veera didn't think the world was cruel before, she sure as hell thought so now.

"I'm sorry for my part in your complicated mess," Sana finally admitted. She took Veera's chai, sipped, and handed the cup back. "To be honest, I didn't realize the priest was going to actually get you married in a full Hindu ceremony until you two started walking around that fire. By then it was already too late."

"It's still not legal," Veera said to her sister, her voice sounding suspiciously shrill. "Why are we making a big deal out of this when it's not even legal?"

"Because we're in India, and we're Indians and legal doesn't matter when there is a traditional Hindu ceremony. In the eyes of every Hindu god, you're about to spend seven lifetimes together."

Damn. Veera sat at the edge of her bed, her cup gripped tightly in her hands as she tried to remember all the details from the night before. She'd been so swept up in the drunken fantasy of getting married to Deepak that she hadn't been able to think clearly about the consequences. She looked down at her ring again, her thumb brushing over the edge of the cool diamond.

"Don't look like that, Vee," Sana said. "Instead of lying low, and being on defense, I have an idea. That's why I'm dressed in my travel clothes." She motioned to her outfit.

Great, Veera thought. She knew her sister was up to something the minute Sana put her polo shirt on.

"What's the idea?" Deepak asked. He was now checking his phone that he must've left on the side table. His brow furrowed. "It looks like the picture of us is starting to make its rounds on a few of the other gossip sites, so at this point, I'm willing to try anything."

Sana's eyes sparkled as she stepped forward and gripped Veera's shoulders.

"Vee, I think you should stay married."

"*What?*" Veera said.

"Yes. I mean—*what?*" Deepak added.

Veera turned to glare at him, and he had the audacity to look sheepish.

"Sana," Veera said. "Why in the world would we stay being fake married?"

"Because it accomplishes both of your goals," Sana said. "I had this epiphany in my hangover shower this morning." She ran her hands through her damp hair and gestured to both Deepak and Veera. "Deepak needs to prove that he is a dependable, stable choice for CEO of Illyria. That's why he was going to marry Olivia."

Deepak raised his hand. "Olivia is also an Illyria Media Group board member. She inherited her seat from her father who was my dad's best friend. She's the swing vote."

Veera looked over her shoulder at Deepak and gaped. Had he really agreed to marry Olivia because she was so crucial to winning board votes? Was that the only reason that he'd chosen her as a wife? "Deepak, why didn't you tell me?"

"It wasn't exactly a decision I was proud about," he said.

Sana waved a hand in front of Veera's face, cutting off her spiraling thoughts. "You may not have a board vote, but there are still Mathur Financial Group members who would support you. And if Deepak can pretend that he had to leave Olivia because he wanted to be with you, then his reptation is salvageable."

"What's in it for Veera?" Deepak asked. "It sounds like she gets shafted in the deal."

Sana glared at him. "Of course, she doesn't get shafted, you ass," she said. "This whole plan is because I want to support my sister, not cause her more harm. I'm trying to help her, not you. Obviously."

It was Veera's turn to wave a hand in front of Sana's face. Her eyeballs were burning, and she really wanted to crawl into a dark hole right now. "Just tell me the rest, Sana."

Sana cupped Veera's cheek in a fleeting touch of comfort. Her expression softened, and like when they were children and someone had hurt Veera's feelings, Sana was right there in front of her, telling her that it was going to be okay, and she would kick some ass in retribution.

"With Deepak's name," she started, "you'll be able to access some of your older client base. You can either work for them or do something on your own."

Veera did not like where this was going. She stepped away from her sister's touch. It was no longer comforting, no longer safe. "I don't need to be fake married to accomplish my career aspirations. That's sexist."

"But wouldn't it be easier with some help? You can either go back to your old job, or you can open up your own business, just like we planned. You won't have me—"

"—but you'll have me," Deepak said from behind them. He was still leaning back against the headboard, the sheet pooled in his lap.

Sana pressed both her palms together, as if in prayer. "By joining forces, you both will be unstoppable. Deepak gets a wife that he *likes*—"

"That's true."

"—and Veera gets the support she needs."

"Right," she said, slowly.

This whole situation was way too risky, way too dangerous to decide between one heartbeat and the next. It required careful consideration and planning. It required a list of pros and cons, the same type of list that she wrote with her best friends when they had a major life pivot.

Veera desperately wished she could talk to Kareena and Bobbi right now. She felt like they would know exactly what to do in this situation.

Except she hadn't been the most present friend over the last year. It would be unfair of her to call them now after all this time and ask them for help. She was on her own.

No, that wasn't true. She did have *one* friend she could talk to.

"Deepak," she said, as she looked down at the swirling steaming tea she cupped in her palms. "Thoughts?"

He cocked his head to the side, as if assessing her in her cotton Indian nightie. "If I get the CEO position, you'll have the option to come back to work for me, no questions asked. No one would even think twice if you were hired again since we're married. I can also give you a small business loan to start your own company. As my wife, your future clients would expect that I'd be your first investor."

She hadn't thought of it that way. That pretending to be married to Deepak meant that she had access to capital. She could go back to work as if nothing had changed at all, or she could open up a business and focus on what she was truly passionate about. Ethical lending, microloans, and minority-owned businesses.

"Won't everyone assume Deepak's just saving his ass?" she asked.

"Please," Sana said. She waved a hand in dismissal. "We come from one of the most romantic cultures in the world. Our people would be ecstatic at the thought that Deepak didn't sleep with Olivia because he was secretly still pining over you. We can pitch this as a whirlwind love affair where Deepak finally felt free enough to be with the woman he always wanted."

"Sana has a point," Deepak said. "We just have to make sure we have the same scripted story about our relationship." He put his cup aside, got off the bed, and picked up his discarded shirt off the floor. At least he was wearing shorts that were modest enough to limit her wild imagination, Veera thought. She watched as he slipped his head through the hole and covered up inch by gorgeous inch of creamy skin.

When he turned and caught her staring, she blurted out, "What about Olivia?"

Sana raised her hand. "That's where I come in. As long as Deepak still helps you, I'll work on getting Olivia back to the States so that she can participate in the vote."

"How are you going to do that?" Deepak asked. "She's not answering her phone, and no one knows where she is."

Sana combed her fingers through her hair, and the cocky expression on her face was the same one that had made countless people fall in the past. "I heard through the rumor mill that Olivia is up in Scotland spending some time with mutual friends. As long as you protect my sister, Deepak, I'll make sure you get your vote at the November board meeting even if I have to drag her by her extensions onto a plane headed for New York."

Veera rubbed her hands over her face as Sana and Deepak continued to talk strategy, as if their plan were as simple as picking a restaurant for dinner or participating in a snorkeling expedition. There were so many things that could go wrong. This was a fake relationship they were talking about.

Veera read romance novels. She knew that someone always found out the truth.

Except you had a real wedding ceremony, Vee. The giant rock on your finger and the red bangles are proof that there is nothing fake about the setup.

Her subconscious irritatingly refuted each and every one of her concerns. She and Deepak didn't hate each other. Her feelings for him were exactly the opposite of "hate" even after all this time. But what happened when he was voted in, and Olivia was back?

Would she ever be able to reclaim the life she'd built for herself then?

Veera couldn't think about this anymore. She needed a clear head and some Advil before she made any more decisions.

"I'm going to take a shower," she said over the sound of Sana and Deepak's bickering. "An epiphany shower."

She strode into the adjoining bath and locked the door behind her. With the lights off, Veera stepped under the hot heavy spray of the showerhead. She closed her eyes and let out a shuddering breath.

Holy shit, she was married. She was a married woman. She watched as the steady stream of water trickled over the bright red bangles, over her ring that she neglected to take off. Then she sat on the shower bench and stared at the solitaire and matching wedding band that continued to sparkle in the dark.

She could guess Deepak's reasoning for agreeing to something as chaotic as a fake relationship. He'd always been willing to do anything to get what he wanted.

But was she strong enough to do the same? Would going along with this whole story, even if it was for a few months, help her gain independence and contentment?

When the water began to cool with her spiraling thoughts, she stepped out of her shower, brushed her teeth, washed her face, and braided her hair. She slipped on a cotton sundress that she retrieved from her suitcase and debated removing the chuda and ring but decided to leave them on. A chuda was a sacred symbol that acknowledged her religious match.

If she could honor it just a little bit longer, she thought.

A few minutes later, she walked out into the common living space.

Deepak was sitting on the couch. He'd also freshly showered and shaved, even though his bloodshot eyes matched hers. She smelled pine and musk as she walked passed him and nearly sighed in pleasure.

"Advil's on the table," he said. "Want me to order you some more chai?"

Veera shook her head. "Where's Sana?"

"She's looking at flights," he said. Then he crossed the room until he stood inches from her. In a move so uncharacteristic of their friendship, he took her hands in his. She looked up at him, wide-eyed as his thumbs brushed the inside of her wrists and touched the stack of red bangles she'd chosen to leave on.

"Veera, we can just forget about Sana's plan," he said quietly.

"You don't think we can pull it off?" she said.

Deepak chuckled, and the deep rumbling sound was so close she could almost feel the vibrations against her heart. "If anyone could pull it off, I think we can. But I am the one with the publicity disaster on my hands. If someone finds out about the wedding, I'll handle it. You and your sister don't owe me anything. Regardless, I'll help you any way you need when you're back in the States—"

"I'll do it," she said before she lost her courage. She turned her hands over in his and squeezed his fingers. "I'll be your fake wife. As long as you agree if either of us are done pretending, then we stop all this. We'll reassess after the board meeting in November."

Deepak hesitated, his jaw clenching. "Fine," he said. "I can agree to that."

"I mean, this has to end, right? Once I get my life back, the one I had before . . ."

"Riiight," he said, the word drawn out, as if he were debating whether that was the right response she was looking for. "But for now, you'll do it?"

Veera nodded. "To be honest, it's not the most insane thing I've ever done. Sana and I used to switch places all the time as kids, and we got into way worse situations."

"Oh yeah?" Deepak said. She saw his shoulders relax as his pale face brightened with a smile. "Did you ever get caught?"

"Nope," Veera said. "But it was superawkward when I once sent her to tell this guy that I wasn't really into him, and the next day, his sister was professing her love for me."

Deepak grinned. "See? If you didn't get caught after that, then we'll be fine."

Veera slipped her hands out of his. "As long as we promise to always put our friendship first, we just might be able to pull this off."

Deepak grinned. "We're *married* friends," he said. "Now we can eat at all the restaurants, and I have to pay for it."

"Oh, look at that, I'm already seeing the bright side."

He pulled her in for a hug and dropped a friendly kiss to the crown of her head. His hands were firm, his hold was respectful, and his voice, the silky-smooth timber, inspired a quiet confidence. "You and I will make a great team, Vee. I'm so sorry that our parents never saw your value, but I promise I always will."

Veera burrowed into his embrace for one brief moment. She hoped that he was right.

GROUP CHAT

DEEPAK: Hey, Veera and I have something we need to talk to you all about.

VEERA: Yeah, we sort of got married.

KAREENA: WHAT!?

BOBBI: Without us??

PREM: Holy shit

BUNTY: Are you joking!?

DEEPAK: We're flying back now. We'll explain everything when we're stateside.

* * *

GROUP CHAT: Deepak

PREM: What is going on?

BUNTY: How could you get married without telling us? And if we're going in order of engagement, you should've waited for me and Bobbi first.

DEEPAK: Wait, you two are engaged?

BUNTY: Well, not yet, but we got together first.

DEEPAK: You're a fool.

BUNTY: I'm not the one engaged to Olivia Gupta one moment and married to Veera Mathur the next. I feel like we're missing a LOT of context here.

* * *

GROUP CHAT: Veera

KAREENA: The last text we get from you is about some yacht you planned on taking with a bunch of German investors, and now you're married to Deepak?

BOBBI: Are you okay? I know you've been grieving with all the changes in your life, but we did not expect you to bounce back like this.

VEERA: I still don't know if I made the right decision, but I promise we'll clear it all up when we get home.

KAREENA: We can't wait to see you. We missed you so much.

BOBBI: And we love you and just want you to be happy. If that means marrying a man who doesn't deserve you, and giving him another chance, we'll support you.

KAREENA: And we'll collectively roast and hate him if you want us to do that, too.

* * *

FAMILY CHAT: Deepak

DAD: You've never made me so proud before.

DEEPAK: Really? You're not upset? Mom hung up on me after I told both of you.

DAD: Why would I be upset after you saved me from paying for a ridiculously expensive wedding? Of course not! Your mother is crying in the kitchen, though, so she may need some time. Congratulations, beta. I can't wait for you to bring our new daughter-in-law home. I've always loved Veera.

* * *

VEERA: Hi, Mom, there is something I have to tell you. I tried to FaceTime but it says your line is busy.

MOM: You're married!???????

VEERA: Wait, how did you find out?

MOM: Deepak's mother texted me! You know, an important religious responsibility we have as Hindu parents is to get our daughters married. It's our dharma. We have so many things to do! We need to hire a priest, and finish all your ceremonial rites.

VEERA: I don't think that's necessary, especially if that means I have to spend time with Dad. I don't want to talk to him.

MOM: This grudge you have against your father is childish, Veera.

VEERA: Annnnd we're done. We'll have a dinner party back in New Jersey after we're settled. We can do whatever ceremony things you want to do right before the dinner party, but I don't want to see Dad yet. Like I said, I'm not ready. I deserve an apology from him, and until he's ready to admit that he hurt us, I refuse to forgive him.

CHAPTER 7

Deepak

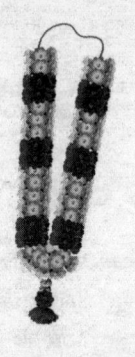

Faking marriage as a non-Indian person would've required little to no effort on Deepak's part. But he *was* Indian, which meant that both he and Veera had a lot of cultural and religious ground to cover to make sure that their story was believable.

With the hotel's support, they were able to stage wedding photos in designer bridal outfits. Because in their drunken haze they had already purchased wedding bands and a red chuda bangle set, they didn't need much more jewelry other than Veera's mangalsutra. After some debate and coaxing on his part to get her to spend his money, she'd chosen a simple black-and-gold beaded necklace with three large solitaire diamonds in a grouping that rested against her collarbone. It replaced the beads that the pandit had given Deepak to use during the ceremony. When Deepak helped her put it on for the first time in front of the small oval table mirror in the jeweler's storefront, their eyes met and the reality of what they were doing slammed into him like a semi.

They didn't talk about it after he finalized the purchase.

The night before they flew out, four mehndi women arrived at the suite to cover Veera's hands, arms, feet, and legs in intricate designs. They took pictures at every stage, documenting the entire process. Veera slept with the mehndi carefully covered and bandaged. When she woke in the morning, staff from the hotel arrived to help her remove the bandaging and rub an oil into her skin to preserve the color.

Now that they were on the plane headed toward New York, Deepak couldn't stop looking at the rich dark red mehndi on Veera's hands as she twisted the champagne flute between her fingers. The designs swirled in paisleys and floral swoops from her fingertips to the center of her forearm. The five-carat diamond ring that matched the solitaire shape of her mangalsutra necklace glittered in the overhead light of the first-class cabin seat. They had a full-size flat-screen TV, two luxury recliner chairs, and access to a full bar cart at their disposal, yet all he could focus on were her delicate hands with deep red staining all of her fingertips.

Even now, he was so sure she was going to back out. With all the attention he knew that she didn't want, there was a very real chance he would have a runaway wife on his hands.

Deepak leaned against the center armrest that divided their seats. "Are you okay?" he asked. "You've been gripping that same champagne flute since we took off."

"You mean the one from the bottle that you conned our flight attendant into handing over?" Veera said blandly. "You don't have to tell everyone that we're newlyweds who eloped in Goa, you know."

He grinned. "I don't have to, but it's good practice. And you and I both know that's not what's bothering you."

She shrugged, and it was such a soft, delicate familiar movement. "It's not. I was just thinking about how difficult it was for me to say goodbye to Sana when she flew out to the UK."

Her twin. Deepak had watched the tearful farewell at the airport. Their bond was something he'd never understand.

"Haven't you been with her every day for like eight months?" he asked, as he leaned against the center console.

"Yeah," she replied. "But she's my sister. I'm still mad at her for pulling out of our business plan. I could've spend the last eight months building a new career. But I'd rather be mad at her while she's . . . I don't know, with me." She twisted the flute in her hand again, and her ring sparkled.

Deepak wanted to ask Veera about her plans for the business, but she was focused so intently on her drink. Three little lines marred the center of her eyebrows as she turned to look out the small porthole to the night sky.

Every instinct in Deepak told him to loop an arm around her shoulders and pull her close. To press a kiss to the crown of her head and tell her it was all going to be okay. As a friend, he wouldn't have hesitated to do just that, but now, things were different.

Deepak had thought about her romantically once before early in their relationship. He'd quickly ignored his attraction when she'd called him a friend out of respect for her feelings. Then, she had become his safe space, the person he turned to when he needed help figuring out all the complicated details in his life. Before his engagement to Olivia, Veera was the person he texted when he heard something funny, and she was the person he went to when he needed to rage about work. More importantly, she was the one woman he'd wanted to spend all his time with.

Their friendship hadn't stopped him from noticing how beautiful she was. How her joy was guileless and gorgeous.

Their wedding was like a release valve, and now all he could think about was how he'd hurt Olivia and wasted time with Veera.

The only problem was Veera was definitely not on the same

page as him. She'd kept her distance and was suspiciously quiet since they decided to follow through on their plan.

Which meant that he had to convince her that, together, they were a perfect fit. That their relationship could be more than just a business arrangement.

Deepak tried to sniff her as discreetly as possible so he could get more of the soft sweetness of her hair. "Vee?"

"Mm-hmm?" she hummed absently as she adjusted the chuda on her wrist.

"I think we need to talk. Maybe we should establish some rules for our relationship."

Her eyes went wide, and she shifted in her seat so she could look at him. "Rules?"

"Rules," he said. He had to hold back his smile. "The last few days have been hectic, establishing our story, but when we land, we should know exactly what we have to do to sell our romance to everyone in our lives."

"Okay," she said, shifting in her seat to increase the space between them. "That makes sense. Should I take notes?"

An image of Veera sitting on his desk with a notepad flashed in his mind. She had a habit of chewing on the cap of her pen and tilting her head, which exposed the long line of her neck. What if she took notes behind his desk? Would she put her heeled feet on his desk pad, and—

Nope, no, he was not having his first real dirty fantasy when there was nowhere to hide.

"I think we can just talk," he said, as he shifted in his seat.

"Okay." She lifted the flute to her lips again and drained the glass. When she put it back on the tray, she turned to him, her expression serious. "Where should we start?"

"With our housing situation."

Surprise lit her eyes. "I sublet my apartment and was planning on renting something until the sublet was over."

"We're married now, remember?" he said. "The expectation is that we live together. My town house is huge. If you want your own space, you can have the entire guest floor to yourself. I rarely go up there."

Her expression went dreamy. "I really do love your house," she said.

"You do?"

"Of course," she said, then sighed.

He'd never thought of his town house as anything but a place to sleep, but he remembered the first time she'd come over for a movie night.

Deeps, this is where you live? Why have we been bumming around the city in lecture halls and restaurants when we could've done takeout and Lord of the Rings *on your big cushy couch?*

He smiled at the memory, his fingers automatically crossing the space between them to touch her red chuda. When she shifted restlessly, he pulled away, curling his fingers into a fist. "If you like my house, then you should move in," he said.

"Fine, but I should pay rent. This is still a fake marriage."

Deepak bit back a smile. "The house is completely paid for. I'm not going to take your money."

"I can cook?"

"I have meals delivered on a schedule."

"Okay, what about keeping the space clean? I know you're a neat freak."

"And I know you don't have it in you to keep a place clean," he retorted.

"Hey!"

"Veera, I've seen your apartment, remember? Your shit is every-where. Don't worry about it, I have a cleaner, too."

She pursed her lips, and his gaze zeroed in on her nude-colored lips coated in a thin layer of gloss. He wondered what it would be like to kiss her. He was attracted to her, but did they have physical chemistry?

"Kissing," he blurted out. "Uh, public affection."

Veera smirked. The soft tension in her seemed to melt from her slender frame. "Kissing? Really? Deepak, we're Indian."

"Yeah?"

She motioned toward him with a wave of her hand. "So kissing is the last thing that anyone is going to expect from us in public."

"Okay, but I am in the news all the time. What if we have to really sell it that we're physically intimate?"

"Yeah, I don't think that's necessary," she said.

"We don't want to be taken off guard, do we?" he replied smoothly. "We have to consider all scenarios here, Veera."

Her fingers twisted together, and he watched as the mehndi designs flexed. "Fine, I guess we can kiss in public."

Deepak knew he was pushing his luck, but he had to know. "We should practice."

Veera gaped at him, then she let out a snort, and a high-pitched giggle.

"Okay, not the reaction I was expecting."

"How did you think I would react when you said that we should *practice*?" Veera replied. Her giggle morphed into a laugh, and for the first time since he'd landed in Goa and seen her again, she had uninhibited joy in her eyes. His stomach clenched at how beautiful she looked when she smiled. Had he always taken her for granted? Taken *their relationship* for granted? He'd been such a fool.

"Look, it's probably been a while since either of us have had a proper kiss," he started.

"Speak for yourself," Veera said.

"Wait . . . who have you been kissing?" Deepak said. Of course, she would have had every opportunity, but that didn't mean he liked it. Did she see someone regularly? He bet whoever had the privilege of touching her didn't know what they were doing. They probably said they were six feet in their dating profiles, but they were four inches shorter in reality. They were most likely a podcaster, too.

His stomach turned as his imagination ran wild. How could Veera even consider dating a podcaster?

Veera patted him on the arm as if she knew exactly what she was doing to him. "I was too busy trying to convince people to give me their money to kiss anyone. But kissing is like riding a bike. A little wobbly at first, but we'll be fine."

"Oh, I mean if you're bad at it, you can just say so . . ."

Veera gaped at him. "I'm not a *bad* kisser," she said. "I'm a great kisser. I mean, I've never had any complaints."

"Neither have I."

She gave him a bland look. "Do we need to pull up Olivia's video again?"

"Ouch, but fair. Look, all I'm saying is that we shouldn't have our first kiss in public. That's a recipe for disaster. People will definitely question us."

Veera rolled her eyes, then drained her champagne glass, and put it on the small ledge next to the TV where it was out of her way.

Before Deepak realized what she was going to do, Veera gripped his head between her palms, pulled him forward, and planted a kiss directly on his mouth. She made a loud smacking sound, and then let him go.

He fell back in his seat and burst out laughing. Even though the wonderful, tingling feel of her mouth on his had his heartbeat thumping faster in his chest, the quick, brazen move was so out of character for Veera. She delighted him.

"There, now we've kissed," she said. She brushed her hands against her thighs and went to settle back down in her chair. He heard the slight hitch in her breath and saw the rise and fall of her shoulders.

"Not so fast," he said. He gripped her arm and tugged her out of her seat until she tumbled into his lap.

Before she could say another word, he cupped the back of her neck and pulled her forward until her mouth landed on his. This time the kiss wasn't playful and friendly. His eyes drifted shut as his mouth fit against hers like a perfect puzzle piece snapping into place. Her lips parted in surprise, and he opened with her. When her tongue grazed his, he heard the softest, sweetest, most delicious sound and swallowed it.

Oh god.

The earthy scent of her mehndi-stained hands cupped his face as he gripped her thigh and shifted her closer. Their mouths slanted over each other and Deepak was consumed by her. Then her fingers sunk in his hair, and he urged her to open for him again by pressing a thumb against her chin. When she gasped at the focused, firm brush of his tongue, he stopped and pulled back. Their eyes met, and hers went wide as she realized their predicament. Their breaths were shallow as she leaned against him, and his hand clenched on her inner thigh.

Wow. Just . . . *wow.*

When Veera climbed off his lap, she nearly banged her head against the ceiling of the plane and stumbled back into her seat just as someone knocked on the door of their cabin.

"Come in," he said after shifting to adjust his dick.

The flight attendant opened the door and smiled at both of them. "It's our newlyweds! I'm so sorry to disturb you, but would you like to order dinner?"

"Can we get a minute?" Veera said, her voice a bit thready. "I just finished the delicious champagne you sent over, and I haven't looked at the menu. I'm so sorry about that, Lisa."

Their flight attendant smiled. "That's no problem at all, Mrs. Datta. I'll come back in a few moments."

When the cabin door closed again, Deepak smiled at her, praying that his voice sounded normal. "Mrs. Datta. It has a nice ring to it, don't you think?"

Veera's eyes narrowed on him. "You kissed me."

"I did."

"Like *really* kissed me."

"Yup." He couldn't keep the satisfaction from his voice. "Now if we do it in public, we'll know what to expect, right?"

There was something about the way that Veera watched him that had him shifting in his seat again. It was a mix of heat and something dangerous.

"Look, if you'd like to try it again until you're comfortable—"

"No, thank you," she said. Then she tried to remove the menu from the small card slot against the wall. Her fingers trembled so it took her a few tries before she was able to yank it free. "It's not like it was special enough for a repeat or anything."

Then she turned away from him and busied herself with the dessert list.

Deepak could only laugh again, and despite all the chaos that awaited them back in the states, he was so happy to have Veera at his side.

"You're a brat, you know that?" he said, as he retrieved his own menu.

"Thank you," she said primly. Then she tapped him on the arm. Her bangles clinked with a musical chime. "Hey, their TV has all the *Lord of the Rings* movies."

"I'll watch if we skip *The Hobbit*," he replied. "The last time you made me sit through that one, you wouldn't stop comparing it to the book."

Veera gaped at him. "That was almost two years ago! You still remember that?"

"Our first movie marathon? How could I not?"

"Fine," she said. "No *Hobbit*. But it feels wrong, Deepak."

"Pretend you've already watched it, and you'll be fine."

At that moment, Lisa returned to take their order. Then as Veera settled in, Deepak enjoyed the movement of her bridal mehndi hands, the wedding ring that sparkled, and the relaxed smile on her face for Legolas. For the first time in way too long, they slipped into their familiar companionship that had become an important part of his heart.

The rest of their complicated relationship could wait for New York.

The public engagement, separation, and marriage of Mr. Deepak Datta can tell us a lot about today's generation and their views on love.

Some are excited to find the right match.

Some feel comfortable by themselves.

And some are only interested in the right match if it serves a greater purpose.

The question for all of us is what greater purpose is Mr. Deepak Datta trying to obtain by bringing former employee of the Mathur Financial Group, and estranged daughter of Malkit Mathur, into his plan?

Mrs. W. S. Gupta
Avon, New Jersey

CHAPTER 8

Veera

> **SANA:** Wait, you're moving in with Deepak?

> **VEERA:** Yeah, it makes the most sense since we're married and all.

> **SANA:** I don't think that's a good idea. I mean, you had feelings for him, and this could go south.

> **VEERA:** Gee, thanks for your vote of confidence. Glad that you think I'm not mature or strong enough to not fall apart if I'm in close proximity with a man that YOU ENCOURAGED ME TO STAY FAKE MARRIED TO.

> **SANA:** Ugh, fine. I just want what's best for you. I feel like I let you down and Deepak can help you, but I'm worried if you get too close personally.

> **VEERA:** I can make my own decisions, Sana. I'm holding up my part of the plan and you just need to focus on yours.

As they deplaned, Veera clutched her phone after she reread the last few messages she'd received from her sister. Maybe Sana was right. She shouldn't have let this fake marriage plan get this far. It almost felt like pretend when she was dressing up and taking pictures in Goa. It was fun to have her mehndi done and to pick out shiny jewelry. But when Deepak kissed her, the deep, intense focus of his lips and the brush of his tongue devouring her in a way she'd never felt before, she began to understand how badly this could wreck her.

Her brain worked overtime as she tried to figure out how to talk about boundaries and barriers as they snaked through the customs line, and Deepak's fingertips periodically caressed the small of her back. She couldn't find the words to tell him she was scared. That she didn't want them to forget that they are not supposed to treat their fake marriage as real.

Even as Deepak's driver helped them with their bags and ushered them toward the waiting vehicle, she tried to formulate her argument.

She slid into the back of the car and took in the luxurious interior. It smelled of lemon-scented leather wipes, and the seats were soft and deep. They pulled out of the airport parking lot, and through tinted windows Veera smiled at the familiar steel bridges and scaffolding, the congested traffic and pedestrians as they navigated toward Brooklyn.

No matter where she'd traveled to, there was nothing like New York City.

Veera worried her diamond ring and wedding band with her thumb, and it slid in a circle. Hopefully the city would be kinder to her this time around.

"If you give me the keys and the information for your storage unit, I can have a few movers empty it out for you and put your things in my garage," Deepak said after almost ten minutes of silence. "It doesn't make sense for you to pay for storage when I have so much space."

She glanced at him across the bench seat. "It'll be such a pain in the ass to move my things again when we're done with our . . ." She glanced toward the front of the car at the driver, then back at Deepak. "We'll figure it out later."

"Okay." He said it so coolly, but she caught the subtle clench of his jaw. His eyes remained glued on his phone as he continued to respond to messages.

Veera realized that she couldn't read Deepak anymore, which made their whole plan so much more difficult to navigate. Since they met again in Goa, something was different, and she wasn't sure exactly what it was. If she wasn't careful, Sana's warning could be her reality.

The car pulled up in front of his brownstone twenty minutes later, and she sighed at the beautiful brick face and wide front steps that led to a glossy black front door. As much as she missed her small Jersey City apartment, Deepak's town house was her dream home.

Veera got out on the sidewalk side and rounded the back to take her bags. Deepak put a hand on her arm.

"Richard? Can you roll our bags into the garage? I'll come down and grab them later."

"Yes, sir," their driver said. He was a slender, middle-aged man with a crisp black suit that felt so appropriate for Deepak's employment. Just as he collected the bags on the sidewalk he stopped and motioned at Deepak. "Your friends. They're waiting for you upstairs."

Deepak looked at Veera, then back at Richard. "Friends?"

"Yes," Richard replied. "Your security team alerted us, and

since one of the gentlemen was the same fellow who used to live with you every other month, they were cleared to enter."

"Bunty," Deepak said with a sigh. He looked down at Veera. "Looks like they're ready to ambush us."

"Oh," she said. There were no other words that came to mind. It had been so long since she'd seen Kareena and Bobbi. She used to be with them a few times a week, and now she'd gone almost a year without having them in her home, or across from her at a dinner table.

All the hesitation, confusion, and hurt feelings she'd felt when it came to her relationship with her best friends faded to background noise at the thought of seeing their beautiful, bright faces again.

"You're not scared to see them, are you?" Deepak asked.

"Of course I am," she replied, as she bounced on her heels.

He grinned, his flash of white teeth. "I don't know, it looks like you're scared."

"You're being a nagging husband," she muttered as Deepak laughed and put in the door code to let her inside. She kicked off her shoes at the front entrance, then quickly walked up the first flight of stairs to the main floor. The ceilings were over ten feet high, and to the left was a large kitchen designed like a picturesque French farmhouse space with wide countertops, open shelving, and a massive expensive range with chrome knobs and handles.

To the right was the living room and a fireplace that was big enough to stand inside. Above the mantel was a flat-screen TV that rivaled most movie theater screens. The deep, buttery leather sofas were arranged to face the screen with a low, wide coffee table in the center.

At the moment, Kareena Mann and her husband, Dr. Prem Verma, as well as Bobbi Kaur, and her boyfriend, Benjamin Padda, were sprawled over the sofas, speaking in soft, hushed tones.

Veera dropped her tote bag on the expansive dining table that separated the kitchen and living space. With her heart bursting at seeing the people she loved, she shouted, "I'm back!" and held her arms wide.

Kareena and Bobbi shrieked and vaulted off the couches. They tackled Veera in the softest, warmest hugs, and she held on as tight as she could, reveling in the feeling of being loved by her chosen family. No matter what happened, she knew that she was loved.

"I missed you two so much," she whispered, and she heard Bobbi sniffle first. Then Kareena. Then she was sniffling, too, and they were all holding each other, hearts beating, eyes squeezed shut, remembering this moment. Veera had so many regrets over the last year, and her biggest one was having to let go of Bobbi and Kareena.

Thankfully, they had full lives now. They had partners that took up space and time.

Bobbi and Kareena began talking at once as they touched her chuda, examined her mehndi, and shrieked over the size of her diamond ring. Their gentle and supportive hands made her feel the weight of her new jewelry, of the significance of the gold, the red, and the diamonds that were supposed to only be for real Desi brides.

Bunty's voice boomed in the background. "Dude, should we be crying, too?"

Deepak's distinctive voice followed. "Shut up, Bunty."

"Are you going to tell us what happened?" Prem asked.

"She hasn't been in the U.S. in months. Let her have this moment."

And that's when Veera knew it was time to share their secret. She slowly extracted herself from the group hug and looked over at Bunty and Prem who stood to the side, next to Deepak.

"We're not really married," she blurted out.

The room went ominously quiet. Veera looked back at Deepak and was grateful when he held out a hand for her. Together, they stood in front of their best friends and waited for their reaction to the truth.

Bunty was the first one to speak. "I think we're going to need some food for this." He slipped his phone from his back pocket before firing off a text message.

"And while we wait for the food, we should sit down," Bobbi added. "I have a feeling this is going to take a while."

VEERA AND DEEPAK SAT on the coffee table facing their friends who reclaimed their spot on the couches. Then when the food arrived from Bunty's new restaurant, Rani's, a luxury Indian cuisine hot spot in Carroll Gardens, they moved to the dining table. It was a solid thirty minutes later before they were able to answer all their friends' questions. The remnants of fragrant biryani, soft fluffy bhature, flaky, crispy samosas, and a mix of curried vegetables and meats sat between them. Veera was still picking at her food when Prem finally spoke.

"What are you going to do now? For the months before the board meeting, how are you going to use your marriage as a publicity stunt?" He was the most practical out of Deepak's friends, Veera thought. He'd also had his own public relations disaster when he first met Kareena as the famed Dr. Dil on the heart health Sunday morning TV show. He'd since retired his Dr. Dil moniker and ran a South Asian health clinic in Jersey City, but that didn't take away from his experience that was coming in handy now.

"We hadn't really thought about that quite yet," Deepak answered. He turned to Veera, a questioning expression on his face.

She had no idea what she was supposed to say. Why couldn't just being fake married be enough? It was always enough in the movies or books. But no. She was Desi, which meant that things were just a tad bit more complicated.

"I wish we had our whiteboard," Kareena said with a sigh. "Remember when we used to use it to draw diagrams of our first dates? Now we're talking about fooling the New Jersey and New York Indian community. We've moved on to bigger and better things."

"Kareena, I was just thinking the same thing, but it looks like we'll have to manage without it," Bobbi said. Even though she was dressed in high-waisted jeans and a collared button-down shirt, she controlled the table like a businesswoman. "Deepak? Veera? If you're going to make this work, you have to follow the chain of command and meet people in order of importance. First up is a public appearance together with the rest of the board."

"Right," Veera said. "Of course." *Thank god for Bobbi*, she thought. Her friend was one of the best event planners on the East Coast. If anyone knew about formality and tradition, it would be Bobbi.

"Before you meet the board," Kareena started, "you should probably visit Deepak's parents' home. You need their support, and if they're excited, everyone will be excited."

"That's a good idea," Deepak said. "I think my parents would appreciate some time with both Veera and I together." He took out his phone, and from her position next to him, she saw that he opened up his messaging app and sent a quick note to his assistant, Kim.

"Wait, don't text Kim," she said and tugged on his sleeve.

He looked up from his phone. "Why not? She knows my father's and my schedules. It'll make things easier if—"

"This is not business," Veera said. "Text your mother, Deepak. I've only met her a few times, but even I know that she'll be insulted if you don't go to her directly."

"Veera has a point," Prem said. "Always go through the moms for marriage stuff."

"What about your family?" Bunty asked Veera. "Do you want to—"

"No," Veera said. "Bobbi, you can loop my mom in on stuff, but my father is not to be involved. We're still no-contact." She swallowed the hard lump in her throat. Truthfully, she'd had a lot of therapy while she was traveling. She'd talked about her father until she was exhausted, and now, she barely felt sadness when his name came up. But that didn't mean she was willing to sacrifice her boundaries for him.

The room became quiet.

Deepak pressed a hand to her lower back, and the warmth of his touch, the pressure of his fingers was oddly soothing in the moment.

"So we're good?" Deepak said.

"Ah, excuse me?" Bunty said, as he knocked on the dining room table. "I think you're going to have to do more than meet the board and your parents. You have about two and a half months to really sell your story. According to my mother and her WhatsApp group, Mrs. W. S. Gupta is casting doubt."

"Of course she is," Deepak murmured. The irritation in his voice had Veera raising an eyebrow at him. He shook his head.

"Guys?" Bobbi said. Her eyes went wide, her face brightening like the sun peeking out of fluffy clouds. She laced her fingers together and leaned over the table as if she were conspiring like an auntie. "We should host a reception!"

"Oh my god, so smart," Kareena said.

"That could work," Prem replied.

"You could use Rani's," Benjamin said. He winked at his girl-friend. One by one excitement took over their faces like they were infected with the thrill of a Desi celebration.

Veera held her hands up in the shape of a T. "Wait a minute, are you seriously using us as an excuse to have a party?"

"Yes," they all said in unison.

She collapsed back in her seat. "Well, at least you're honest."

"Have you thought about what you're going to tell people when they ask how you got together?" Benjamin asked.

Deepak leaned forward on his forearm, and Veera smelled the whiff of aftershave and cologne. "We're going to tell everyone that Veera was consulting for me on a project."

"What project?" Prem asked.

"Ethical lending," Deepak replied quickly.

Veera jerked in her seat and turned to look at him. "What?"

"It's the last big project you launched at Mathur Financial, right? You're an expert. We don't have ethical lending as a core business service at Illyria Media Group, so why don't we say you're helping me launch a new initiative?"

Deepak remembered her passion project. But then again, he had always been incredibly attentive to anything business related. "I can do that," she said slowly. "I don't know if I want to go into business for myself or go back and get a job yet, but for our story, I think it works." She hoped she could have a part of her old life back, but her father had made sure that was impossible. She just needed time, a little more time to decide. If she could hide away for a while and think about what she wanted for herself, maybe she'd be able to start a business or work for someone who appreciated her.

"You still need a party," Prem said. "With open bar. And you should tell Kareena's aunties so they can spread the word."

"Send them your wedding pictures," Bobbi said. "They'll forward them on the WhatsApp information train so quickly that even Olivia will hear about it. Wherever she is."

"Oh, I don't know if telling the aunties is a good idea," Veera said. "Don't forget that I was the one who was responsible for wrangling them when they wanted to interfere in your love lives. I know what kind of chaos they can create."

"It's not meddling," Bobbi replied. "It's just information sharing."

"Bobbi's right," Kareena said. "You need people to know about your marriage from a reliable source, not through speculation. Everyone will pay attention to a WhatsApp text. More importantly, they'll disperse the news quickly if you make the message a truly atrocious graphic with red italicized font." She opened a WhatsApp chat that was titled "Aunties" and held up an image.

The heading, in red italicized font, said *Eat five almonds every morning to increase your IQ by fifteen points.*

Bunty held up his phone. "Oh, I got that, too."

"Me, too," Prem added.

"Okay, I get your point," Veera said. "But what pictures would we even send?"

Deepak was already shoving his phone in front of her and scrolling through a dozen professionally shot images that they'd staged at the resort. "This is exactly why I wanted the photos," he said. "Personally, this one is my favorite." He stopped on a picture of both of them on the beach. They were holding hands while standing on a rocky platform that jutted out into the water.

Her red-and-purple lehenga complemented the brilliant hues of the Goan sunset. Veera remembered the soft, weightless feel of the fabric as the wind and the waves billowed below her feet. She only wished she could have brought the lehenga home with her. They had borrowed the outfit from the designer who was still finishing it for a new collection because they couldn't find something off the rack, or as the designer called it, ready-made. Deepak, on the other hand, wore a tailored black suit with a tie that matched her outfit. They were laughing together, and she remembered the question he'd asked her to loosen her up.

What music video do you think we'd look good in right now? I think Enya.

Enya? Seriously? Some Punjabi folk song with a disco beat. The singer's head would be floating in the corner of the screen while we posed like we were Jack and Rose in Titanic.

Now that was romance, she thought. Well, in a really twisted, messed-up kind of way.

"Kareena, I'm going to text this to you. Can you share the picture with some copy?" Deepak asked.

Kareena was already on her phone, tapping at her screen. "You got it," she said.

Deepak looked back at Veera; his voice lowered as he leaned closer to her side. "Okay with you?"

"Yeah," she said. "I guess . . . let's do it."

They ironed out a few more details for the reception, and for Deepak's meeting with the board on Monday.

When their eyes met every time Deepak asked her for her opinion, Veera had to work hard at reminding herself that he was just protecting a lie, and it had nothing to do with her heart.

She looked down at her mehndi. The color was a dark burgundy now. There was a belief that the darker the mehndi was on the bride, the more the husband loved her. Veera wondered what other traditions were full of shit.

As their friends talked over one another, planning a reception that was so overwhelming she wanted to crawl into a hole and burrow like a gopher, she continued to twist her diamond ring and prayed that she was doing the right thing.

CHAPTER 9

Veera

Text messages from two years and one month ago:

DEEPAK: Hey, weird question.

VEERA: I always say, the weirder the better.

DEEPAK: Good.

DEEPAK: There is this lecture at Columbia I want to go to. It's a leadership seminar. A bit of a snooze fest, honestly. It's just that I don't want to go alone, and our friends are yet again busy.

VEERA: When is it?

DEEPAK: Ah, today? You free?

VEERA: Pathetically, I am. My plans included watching cat videos, reading a romance novel, and wearing a snuggie all day.

DEEPAK: Yikes, no competition. The snuggie wins.

VEERA: But I need the exercise, and I'd feel bad if you were standing in a corner alone with, like, your red Solo cup. Let me know when you want to meet.

Veera realized that she wasn't prepared for marriage. There were no classes on it in college, no rule book for relationships that told her in a step-by-step process what she was supposed to do as a South Asian woman marrying a South Asian man. She was sort of ejected into a whole new world.

Kind of like adulthood. No one had prepared her for that, either. One day, she just had to learn how to write a check and stand up to manspreaders on the subway. Hopefully, she'd learn about marriage the same way.

She looked at the chaos in Deepak's guest bedroom and let out a frustrated huff. She'd only been at the house for one night, and it was already a mess. After their group meeting, she'd realized that she needed a few things from her storage unit after all. Then, she'd made the mistake of asking Deepak, Prem, and Benjamin for help. They neglected her specific instructions to grab the box that read "winter clothing" and instead brought in everything she owned, including her favorite armchair and her small sofa that was currently positioned in her en suite sitting area.

She was now forced to think of Deepak's gorgeous home as her home, too.

If she could just make sense of it all. Maybe coffee would help. Deepak's fancy coffee machine made the best coffee she'd ever tasted and that would most likely get her through her morning plans to organize and unpack.

"Veera?" Deepak called from the hall. "I'm going to head to the office. Do you have everything you need?"

"No, you're not allowed in here!" she shouted when she heard his footsteps approaching her room. She flung herself in the doorway before he could step inside.

He stopped inches from her, his eyebrow twitching when he took in the mess over her head. "Wow, um, okay."

Veera took a subtle sniff, settling into the lush smell of his aftershave he'd used on the sharp underside of his jaw. He was dressed in another one of his delicious charcoal suits that he loved. The lines of the outfit fit to perfection.

"Vee, what happened?"

Shit, he's talking about the room, right? I think he's talking about the room.

"I know you hate disorganization, but I promise by the time you get back from work, you won't have to look at any of this. It'll all be put away and color coded just the way you enjoy it."

He smiled. "You and I both know that's not going to happen, but I appreciate you trying." He glanced at his watch and his expression faded to a grimace.

"What time is the board meeting?" she asked gently.

"Eight thirty. After the press release, along with all the responses from the WhatsApp auntie group, I have a feeling this is not going to be a friendly meeting."

"It's better than the alternative," Veera said.

"Which is?"

"Ignoring your public breakup and convincing the board to trust a single Desi man."

Deepak nodded. "Maybe I'll lead by asking them to our wedding reception."

Veera reached out to touch his tie, then pulled her hand back before she made contact. "Are you going to tell them today that I was consulting for you?"

He nodded, then in an unfamiliar gesture, Deepak brushed a strand of hair off her neck.

She had to bite back a shiver. The casual touch was friendly, that's all. She had been contemplating the same type of touch with the tie.

"When we see my father and my mom on Friday," he continued, "you can tell Dad about your consulting work then."

"Great," she said, letting out a deep breath. "I'll work on a pitch this week. With the very little time I have to prep, I'm just going to have to hope your father likes an earnest pitch." Veera acted on impulse and patted him on the shoulder. "Knock them dead . . . uh, husband."

"We're going to have to work on that," Deepak said. His chest rumbled under her lingering fingertips. "Is there something in Punjabi you can call me instead?"

Veera grinned. "You know Punjabis prefer to swear at each other as a sign of love."

"True," Deepak said. Then he took her hands in his and turned them so that her palms were facing upward. Her mehndi was still a dark burgundy and would probably stay that color for another few days before it began to fade.

Veera's breath hitched as his thumb smoothed over her wrist tattoo that was artfully incorporated into the designs. Her red chuda clinked as he nudged them out of the way. Then she waited, as he paused at the small Hindi script right below the tattoo.

It was his name.

One of the age-old romantic customs in a Punjabi Hindu ceremony was to hide the groom's name or initials in the mehndi design for him to find before the first wedding night was over. She'd agreed to it out of a fantasy, wistfulness, really. But now she wondered if it was the right decision.

Before she could pull away, Deepak leaned down and pressed a kiss right over his name. The soft pressure of his lips left a lingering imprint on her skin. Her pulse jumped, and his thumb delicately traced over its beat.

Then he stepped back and winked at her. "See you tonight, wifey."

The gesture was so uncharacteristic of him that she immediately felt her cheeks heat in response. She was still holding her wrist where she'd felt his lips when she heard the soft ding of the alarm letting her know that the front door had opened and closed three floors below her.

Veera turned around and faced her room with her fists propped on her hips. She was tempted to just dive on top of her pile of clothes in the middle of her bed, pull out the latest romance novel that she had downloaded, and read so she could get out of her head. She needed to shut her brain off, to decompress after all the madness.

"Marriage is like adulting," she said to herself. "You can do this."

The queasiness that hadn't gone away since the moment she'd gotten fake married grew stronger as she began organizing her things in the en suite bathroom first. She thought about Bobbi and Kareena who had been so helpful. Then she thought of her sister whom she'd texted the night before.

It was probably late afternoon where Sana was.

Even as she thought of her sister, her phone pinged with an incoming message. She picked it up and turned on speakerphone.

"Twin-tuition?"

"Yup," Sana said. "What are you doing, Mrs. Datta?"

"Ha ha," she said. "Just tell me you have some good news."

"Good and bad," Sana said slowly. "I talked to Mom. She was asking all these probing questions about you and Deepak."

Veera froze. "Oh my god, please don't tell me you—"

"I didn't tell her," Sana said quickly. "She thinks your marriage is very real. Then she asked me where I was, and I said that I was going to see Olivia."

Veera sank to the edge of her bed, then picked up a discarded sweater. She squeezed it between her fingers like a stress ball. "What did she say?"

"She didn't say anything really. Our conversation was quick because I had to hang up. I was heading back to England, and the station called for my train."

Veera felt like she was experiencing a serious case of whiplash. "Wait a minute, what happened to visiting Olivia in Scotland?"

"She's now with friends in Manchester. I just arrived this morning."

"Sana, you have to make this work, otherwise Deepak may lose his chance of securing the CEO position. Get Olivia to come back for the board vote. Please."

"I know, I know," Sana murmured. "But maybe this is a good thing for him. We were literally fired because we were his competition."

"He works really hard for Illyria," Veera said. "It's in his blood."

"And the Mathur Financial Group was in our blood, too."

Veera pushed her sweater aside. Her sister's voice was filled with familiar pain, and she hated how much it hurt her to hear Sana that way. "I thought we were done with feeling bitter about what happened to us."

There was a long stretch of silence on the other end of the phone. "I should've known you'd be like this. It's only been a few days since Deepak is back in your life. Are you seriously defending him again?"

Veera pinched the bridge of her nose. She loved Sana, and she knew that this unshakable loyalty to her was a gift. Sana had made up her mind about Deepak, and her feelings were going to make this whole situation so much more complicated. "Can we not fight about this, please?"

"I wanted to lead my family's company with my sister by my side," Sana continued. "But my family doesn't value us beyond who we can marry. Not only are our parents incredibly sexist, but we're in finance. We aren't worth more than what we can do for men."

Veera didn't know what to say. It was so easy for her to feel just as bitter. No one had bothered to come out and support her when she was told to take the severance package. Now that she was fake married, it was as if her value had gone up and everyone was invested again.

"We're just going to have to trust Deepak," she finally said. "This was your idea, too, remember?"

Sana snorted. "No, *you're* going to have to trust Deepak. I'm just going to trust my instincts like I always have. Then I am going to do what I have to so I can protect you, too. Look, I have to go. I'm meeting a potential contract employer—Antonia; she's in the sea trade business—for drinks tonight since I'm here and I'm killing time until Olivia is willing to hear me out."

"Sana—"

"What is it?" The words were clipped, and short. Sana's control on her temper was beginning to fray.

Veera let out a sigh. "Nothing. Just be careful."

"I will," Sana said. "And you, too. I'm just chancing my ego, but your heart is now on the line again."

Before she could say anything else, Sana hung up, leaving Veera alone in silence.

She remembered calling Sana from the bathroom stall of Kareena's wedding reception. Veera had crumpled at the news of Deepak's pending engagement with Olivia Gupta, and her mother and Deepak's mother discussing the potential merger of their companies. That's when Sana had immediately purchased a ticket to come home. She'd been Veera's rock in that moment.

Now Veera was on her own. Except she was stronger now than she'd ever been. She'd reinforced the broken parts of herself with titanium will. If she had to be her sister's strength, she could do it. No, she *would* do it.

Before she could get up and return to her bathroom reorganization, the door chime rang from the hallway. She went to the intercom, the same type that was located on each floor, and tapped the screen.

She was horrified when she saw four familiar faces looking back at her.

"Aunties?"

"Surprise!" they said in unison, and they leaned close enough to the screen for Veera to see up their nostrils to the gold tips of their nose rings.

There was Mona Auntie with her perfect blowout. Then there was Falguni Auntie in her velour tracksuit. She had switched out her Crocs for some sensible white sneakers today that matched the streak of white at her temples. Farah Auntie, with her white wire-rimmed glasses and her laptop backpack, stood off to the side, and then there was Sonali Auntie.

"We've come to bless your house," Sonali Auntie said, adjusting her dupatta over her head. "We need to make sure that you're not living together like hedonistic white people."

FEEBA: Mr. Deepak Datta. Thank you for joining us. You have the entire South Asian community in a dramatic tailspin after your engagement with Olivia Gupta ended. And now, you're married to your long-time friend Veera Mathur. We'd love to know how this happened.

DEEPAK DATTA: Thank you, Feeba, for your time. We love all the work you do at *Indians Abroad News*. In regard to my personal situation, I am normally a very private person, but I knew when Olivia and I got engaged that a part of my personal life was going to become public. I'm here to set the record straight that I'm completely at fault for what happened between us. I didn't give her the appreciation she deserved. My only excuse was that I put the needs of the business before our personal needs, and I'm grateful Olivia realized the mistake we were making.

FEEBA: Are you saying that you've been in love with Veera Mathur this entire time?

DEEPAK DATTA: I wasn't romantically involved with Veera if that's what you're insinuating. But we've been friends for years, and over the last few months she has been working on a global initiative for my division at Illyria Media. After Olivia broke our engagement, the one person I wanted to speak to was my friend, and that was it. That was the moment I realized that I'd been in love with Veera.

FEEBA: How romantic. How Bollywood! Veera, did you feel the same?

VEERA: Yes.

CHAPTER 10

Deepak

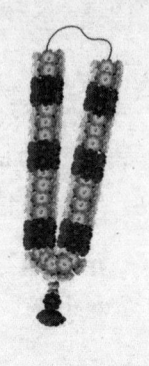

The message flashed on the screen just as he walked into his office.

"Shit," he said. He should've stayed behind and taken another day off. Veera shouldn't be handling the aunties by herself. Not that she couldn't if she wanted to, but it was unfair.

He thought of her surprised expression when he kissed her wrist, felt her pulse jump under his touch, the rich earthy scent of her mehndi hands and the clink of her chuda when he nudged them farther up her arm and out of his way.

Deepak was close enough to see her lashes flutter in surprise, and despite how much he wanted to stay, he had no choice but to head out for the office. And now he had to deal with the board.

He was halfway across the room when he heard the familiar gruff Punjabi. "Watch your language in front of your mother."

The words were said with such a swift delivery that Deepak's spine went ramrod straight to face both his parents, who were occupying the chairs positioned in front of his desk. They glared at him the same way they used to when he brought home a report card that was not up to their standards. Or that time he took his father's Bentley without permission and got into a fender bender at the end of their driveway.

Now, as he faced his parents, his father had been the one to chastise him, but his mother had murder in her eyes. Like she'd told him multiple times before, just because she could only give birth to one child didn't mean that she couldn't borrow one to be her successor if she needed a replacement.

Both of them stood, his father in his elegant charcoal suit, and his mother in her slacks and blouse with a loose cardigan that fell to her knees. His father's hair was still thick and streaked with gray and white while his mother's hair was the same shocking black it had been since she'd found her favorite hairdresser.

In his mother's hand was a silver tray from her home temple. Deepak swallowed hard when she approached him and he saw the om symbol in red powder, the candle, rice, sweets, and the small Ganesha statue.

She began reciting mantras that he had never heard before, but all his years of training by her side had Deepak bowing his head and folding his hands together. When her voice hitched, he knew that he'd hurt his mother's feelings, too.

"Ma, I can explain—"

Without missing a single word of her mantra, she reached out with her free hand and smacked him upside the head.

He rubbed the spot of impact more because of the shock of it than because it hurt. He resumed his silence and waited with his head bowed, refusing to look at his father and mother until finally, she pressed her ring finger into the small well of water on the tray, the raw rice granules, and the deep red vermilion. Then she pressed the tip of her finger between his eyebrows to bless him.

When her mantra ended, she picked up the small chum chum, his favorite Indian sweet dessert. It was oval shaped and bright pink and was like chewing on a saffron sugary cloud saturated in syrup and coated in coconut flakes. He opened his mouth automatically, and with more force than he expected, his mother shoved the entire dessert into his mouth.

Then, she smacked him upside the head again and began to rant in very colorful Punjabi.

You have the brains of an ox.

Why is your mission in life to murder your mother with your bad decisions?

No, you only think of yourself and then you sit on my head and make me deal with it.

He was pretty sure that if he pointed out how she wasn't making any sense, he'd only get reprimanded again. Deepak just swallowed his pink chum chum, the taste sour in his mouth, while his mother finished flaying his hide the way only a Punjabi mother could.

"I'm sorry," he said when her tirade was over. He turned to his father first who stood at a distance with his hands in his pockets. "I know this is a bit of a mess, but I promise I won't lose your legacy over it. I'm going to bounce back."

His promise seemed to calm the old man. He wobbled his head back and forth. "I'm not worried about my legacy, Deepak," he said. "I'm worried about my son. And I'm worried that your mother is going to make me spend that money on a wedding, anyway, when we've just escaped a massive expense."

His mother's string of Punjabi swearing was harsh enough to have both Deepak and his father looking contrite.

"I don't need another wedding, I promise." Then Deepak turned to his mother. "I know your first choice was Olivia, but Veera is special, Mom."

His parents looked at each other, sharing that silent communication that Deepak had come to expect. They had never encouraged the match but when Deepak had asked them for their support and guidance in securing the best partnership for his future position as leader of the family business, they had shared how much they liked Olivia as a person. More importantly, she came with significant leverage on the board. She may have inherited the seat, but she'd been invaluable in providing advice and offering connections. She was a welcomed asset in all the strategy presentations that she'd been a part of.

Because Deepak respected his parents' opinion, he'd done as they'd recommended and contracted with Olivia.

"Deepak," his mother said. "We told you that this decision is yours and if you had feelings for someone, we would embrace them with excitement and love. But Olivia has power on the board. Your goal has always been to lead the company, which is why we encouraged a partnership. We didn't want you to feel like you had to choose between your career and your heart."

"I am responsible for the decisions I've made," he said. "I took your advice, but I now realize that Veera is the best partner for me in my personal life and in business." He swallowed, hoping that he sounded convincing. "We may have acted a little rashly in our elopement—"

His mother scoffed.

"—but once we realized how much we've missed each other and how much of a mistake we made by not being together, we didn't want to waste any more time."

"Have you even seen each other in the last year?" his father asked. "I'm happy for you, puttar, but when we walk into that boardroom, you're going to receive quite a number of questions. Your position is already tenuous, and this rushed wedding made it even more difficult."

"We've been working together since the day we merged Illyria Entertainment with Mathur Financial Group," he lied.

His parents glanced at each other again, then back at Deepak.

"What have you been doing?" his mother asked.

"Ethical lending," he said. "We merged with a finance business to expand our media empire. Ethical lending is a new field, and Veera is the expert. She and her sister have made extensive connections in global marketplaces. I want the board to hear what she has to say, too. I really think that she's onto something and I was working with her to bring her plans to Illyria Media Group as my first big initiative as CEO."

Thank god he'd rehearsed his response with Veera the night before.

Deepak's father stood and adjusted his suit coat. "We're having dinner this weekend where I will hear this plan for myself," he said. "But more importantly, we want to see Veera and welcome her in our home. This time as our daughter-in-law. I'm sure the Mathurs will also want to come."

Deepak shook his head. "I don't think that Veera is ready to forgive her father for what he did. But you can invite her mother. Mom, I'll bring Veera to the Hudson Valley house, and maybe we can stay with you overnight. We already talked about it, and Veera's okay with the plan."

"Good," his father said, as he squeezed Deepak's shoulder, his grip firm and strong. "Badhai ho," he said. There was a sheen in his eyes, and Deepak's throat tightened at the sight.

"I'm so sorry," he whispered. His parents had been looking forward to a wedding, and he hadn't realized until he'd faced them that this would impact them so deeply. Then his arms were full, both his parents hugging him the way they used to huddle together as a trio when he was younger. He felt their strength, smelled their familiar scents of Giorgio Armani and Burberry perfume and cologne.

When they pulled back, his mother was wiping tears, and his father was sniffling.

"Chal, puttar," he said, then squeezed his shoulder again. "If you are going to go into the board meeting and defend your decision to marry Veera, then you have our support."

At that moment, Kim knocked on Deepak's doorframe and cleared her throat. "I'm so sorry to interrupt, but the board is waiting for you in the conference room." Her mop of black hair framed her face and swung back and forth as she popped in and out of his office.

"Okay," Deepak said. Then he cleared his throat again. "I'm ready to face the music."

Minutes later, the Dattas entered the boardroom as a unit, side by side, with Deepak's father in the middle. Around the table were twelve familiar faces; many of them had sour expressions as they focused on him. Behind them, the Hudson River sparkled in the early fall morning.

Although the company had merged with Mathur Financial Group, the offices remained in the original Illyria Entertainment buildings with two new floors added on the lower levels. The board was also primarily Illyria members with both of Veera's parents sitting at the far end of the table, along with two longtime business partners of Malkit Mathur, Margaret Ginsberg and Ming Hsu.

"We're sorry to keep you waiting," Deepak's father said, his voice commanding everyone's attention as it had for years. "Now, as this is an unscheduled meeting that was called by a few of our members, I'm going to open the floor for conversation."

Narinder Patel, an old colleague of Deepak's father, raised his hand. "I am standing in for Olivia Gupta as well."

There was a hush that spread through the room. Olivia was voting by proxy and she'd somehow convinced Narinder Patel to be her eyes in the room? Deepak clenched his hands into fists as he lowered into the high-back leather chair to the left of his father.

Narinder was one of his biggest opponents on the board. He had bright orange hair he dyed with mehndi, and his suits always smelled like mothballs, even though he made millions in early tech investments and could afford a decent suit.

Deepak remembered a time when Narinder would bring lollipops to the office for Deepak. Then he'd taught Deepak how to use the procurement system during his first internship. When had that worn away to this bitterness that now existed between them?

It was obviously intentional that Olivia had selected him as her proxy. She'd known how difficult their relationship was ever since Narinder retired from his executive position to assume a full-time board role.

"There is one more thing," Narinder said. He opened the padfolio in front of him and swiped across the screen. He then cleared his throat and averted his eyes from Deepak's father. "Olivia is calling for section 2168 of the bylaws."

There was a whisper of conversation now. Margaret, a member from Mathur Financial Group, was the first to speak. "Narinder, can you please remind us what 2168 is?"

Narinder leaned forward so he could see Margaret farther down the table. "It's the, ah, it's the need to interview two qualified candidates for any vacant executive leadership position. The board then must have two-thirds approval on the chosen successor. However, if the vacant position in question is the chief executive officer role and the president of the board, then the vote must be . . . unanimous."

The room erupted in conversation.

Manoj, one of Deepak's peers and a colleague with wealthy parents who was a few years older, leaned over to mumble under his breath, "You've really screwed up this one, kid."

Deepak didn't respond. This was exactly what he was trying to prevent with his engagement to Veera. His marriage was supposed to help, not make it worse.

Damn it, Olivia.

No, he thought. No, he couldn't blame Olivia for all this. He was definitely part of the problem.

His father called for attention at the front of the room. "Section 2168 requires a vote. Two-thirds of the board must agree that we're to begin searching for outside candidates." He glanced in Deepak's direction. "I want us to be sure about this. Although Deepak isn't perfect, no one is, are we making decisions based on outdated cultural norms instead of smart business?"

"Please," another board member said. "This is about business, not *diversity* or culture. We're talking about a multibillion-dollar empire. I, for one, would like to be sure the captain of the ship is appropriately qualified."

Deepak's father pursed his lips. At one time in his life, his employees would have trembled, but he was on his way out, and Deepak knew that people felt safe in voicing disrespect because of it. "Let's call a vote. All in favor of initiating 2168?"

Deepak clenched his jaw so hard that he swore his teeth were going to crack. One by one, each of the board members raised their hands. Save for Manoj and two others, every other hand in the room went up. Deepak glared when Veera's parents both raised their hands as well.

If his parents were in their position, they would've done everything in their power to support Veera and her marriage. They would've reached out beforehand to address concerns, but in public, be staunch supporters.

Damn the Mathurs for never seeing the value in their daughter the way they should.

"The truth is," Narinder said to Deepak's father, "looking at all qualified applicants *is* smart business. Deepak has done well for Illyria Entertainment, but competition is a necessity in our world. Deepak, you understand?"

Deepak stood and buttoned his suit coat. He'd had enough of this.

Fine. Announcing his marriage to Veera hadn't worked exactly the way he'd hoped. In the long run, he hoped the board would see how lucky, how incredibly fortunate he was for having Vee in his life.

He remembered she used to wear fitted pantsuits and adjust her reading glasses before she would deliver information in such a deadpan tone, followed by a sweet smile that just flattened her competition. If only she was here now. She'd do the same to everyone in the room.

"I find it interesting that I had most of your support less than a week ago," he said.

"Deepak," Margaret started, "the PR nightmare happened in the last week. We're all wondering if this what we're going to expect from your tenure?"

He looked at her from down the table, and then at the rest of the faces in the room. "Olivia and I were to be married for the betterment of the company. It didn't work out. She chose to make our breakup public. Remember, she's a member of the board, too."

"The CEO position requires a bit more maturity," another member said. "Maybe in a few years, you'll be able to—"

"I have more experience and knowledge about the company than most of you combined," Deepak said, his tone frosting over. "Certainly more than you, sir."

The room silenced again at his hardened tone. "I've prepared for leading Illyria since I was a child. And for those of you who have forgotten, my *wife* had been preparing to lead our corporate partner

Mathur Financial Group before the merger. With her by my side, I am, and always will be, the most qualified candidate moving forward. But if you insist on bringing in an outside candidate, then challenge accepted. Now if you'll excuse me, I have some work to do. I've been away at my wedding and need to catch up."

He turned to walk toward the door, then paused when he gripped the handle. "And one more thing," he said to the room at large. "We're hosting a wedding reception. An invitation will be delivered to you within the week. I hope you can all find it in your hearts to be happy for us."

Deepak stormed out without another word. He dialed Sana's number the minute he closed his office door behind him.

"Hey, brother-in-law," she said, answering the third ring.

"Any luck?" he said.

The humor died in her voice. "No, but something tells me shit went down. What's wrong? Is it Veera?"

"Olivia used Narinder Patel as a proxy."

"I don't know the guy."

"He was a part of Illyria Entertainment's board. With the bad press, the board is now looking for another candidate for the role. They're going to try to take my birthright."

Sana let out a deep whoosh of air. "Olivia is angry at you and now she's playing dirty. But even though she knows I'm here now, it looks like she doesn't want to see me. Not yet anyway. Do you have a message you want me to give her that could change her mind?"

"Just that I'm sorry, and I really want to talk to her."

"Done," Sana said. "And Deepak? Good luck. I mean it."

"Thanks," he said, then hung up the phone. He walked over to his windows, the views similar to the one in the conference room at the end of the hall. What was Veera going to say when she found out the news?

Indians Abroad News

If you are seeking a match for your sons, just remember that should they betray the partner they are matched with, said partner may seek revenge.

That is completely within their right.

Mrs. W. S. Gupta
Avon, New Jersey

CHAPTER 11

Veera

Veera felt like she had been run over by a freight train.

The aunties were like a force that had stormed into the house with bags and boxes filled with temple things that she was supposed to set up in the home. Then they left her with a to-do list a mile long. Veera picked up the note in Sonali Auntie's meticulous handwriting left next to one of the silver trays. The header read "Do this or be doomed to an unhappy life." The first item required a pandit to review star charts.

She looked at the rest of the trays wrapped in red fabric lined up on the dining room table and all over the kitchen. There were lists next to each one.

"Definitely need takeout," she said. She took her phone out of her jeans pocket and was about to text Deepak when the door chime rang from the small unit next to the hallway entrance.

"Deepak?" she called out.

"Yeah." His voice sounded as exhausted as she felt. After a long, heartfelt sigh, he said, "Man, it's good to come home to you."

Her heart did one slow roll in her chest at his sweet words. She walked through the hallway entrance and looked down the stairwell to see him pick up two paper bags and cart them up to the main level on socked feet. His tie hung loose around his neck and the top button of his shirt was undone. What was even sexier was the smell of Chinese takeout.

"Oh my god, please tell me some of that is for me," she said.

"Pork fried rice and beef and broccoli with crab rangoon on the side," he said in response.

She moved out of the way so he could enter the kitchen. "You remembered!"

He shot her a withering look over his shoulder as he headed for the island. "It's the only order you've ever gotten from a Chinese restaurant in all the times we've eaten takeout."

"Okay, fair."

Deepak froze when he saw the trays wrapped in cloth scattered around his kitchen. "Uh, what's going on?"

"Did you get my text message?"

He turned to look at her slowly, bags swinging at his sides, then winced. "The aunties. I'm so sorry; I was jumped the minute I walked into the office, and I haven't had a break since. Was it terrible?"

"I had to fight them with a sword and slay the dragons," she said, as she twisted her wedding and engagement rings. "But I managed. They said because my mom and I aren't on speaking terms, they're, ah, representing."

The sweetness of their gesture, of their kind words as they patted her shoulder and sat her down on the couch, had brought tears to her eyes, and enough lectures about family for a lifetime.

"Did they believe us?" Deepak said, as he opened the first bag. "That you and I are together?"

"They did," Veera replied. They had acted as if they had been waiting for Veera and Deepak to fall in love this whole time.

She knew that she was to blame for making them feel that way. She was probably a bit too obvious in how she'd felt about Deepak when they were in public.

"Good," he said. Then he just slumped against the counter as if that were the last to-do item on a very long list that he'd barely made it through.

She tapped a finger against her chin. "I'm exhausted, but it looks like your day tops mine."

He nodded. "It's been . . . a lot."

Veera strode past him to the small counter space next to his sink so she could wash her hands. That's when she remembered to check to make sure that she was presentable. She still wore her comfiest T-shirt and leggings, but there were no stains. That was always a good sign.

Her chuda set and mehndi were the only parts of her that were a little out of place. But she liked the shocking red on her wrists, the glitter of her diamond ring that contrasted with her casual lounge outfit. Even though they were fake married, she'd committed to keeping the bracelets and jewelry on for the customary time. She heard that some women preferred to wear them for the first year of marriage, but since she wasn't going to be fake married that long, at the most, six months, she thought wearing her chuda for the minimum number of weeks would be acceptable.

Some traditions were worth risking her bruised heart.

"It was really nice of you to pick up dinner for both of us," she said, as she wiped her hands on the towel hanging from the range handlebar. "But I could've done that if you were superbusy."

"You might have to tomorrow," he said. "The company I hire for meal services is going to add some prepared frozen trays to my weekly order." He rubbed his palms over his face and then picked up Sonali Auntie's note next to the silver tray closest to where he stood. "Veera?"

"Yeah?"

"Why does this say that you have to marry a banyan or a peepul tree?"

"Oh, because I'm Manglik," she said. "Farah Auntie got our birth time and date information so she could have her pandit produce our janampatris to see if we're a suitable match. My janampatri—"

"Star chart?" he translated. "Are you talking about the star alignments you're born under?"

"Yup. My janampatri says I am marked and could lead to the downfall of our marriage since you're not also Manglik. There are all sorts of theories behind how some of these religious and cultural rules are designed to be casteist, and Manglik is one of them." She removed two plates from the upper cabinet. "I'm going to ignore it since I'm technically supposed to marry a tree *first*, and a pandit can just do a pooja to satisfy that obligation. Not a lot of peepul or banyan trees in New York during the fall."

"Okay, maybe I should've asked another question first," Deepak said, as he set down the note and walked over to the wine fridge. He pulled out a bottle of white that she preferred.

"What question?" she asked.

"How did the aunties even know you're here?"

Veera shrugged. "I think your mother told them."

"Of course she did," he muttered. Then with hunched shoulders, he began to unscrew the bottle. "She probably planned it this way so that I couldn't come home and interfere."

Veera removed the containers from the bags he'd opened for her, and the kitchen immediately filled with the spicy and sweet scents of delicious Chinese takeout. "What happened today?"

"Olivia sent a proxy to the board meeting. They want to look at other candidates."

Veera paused in the process of picking up a piece of broccoli from her container. "Why in the world would she do that?"

"She's angry," Deepak said. "But of course, she has every right to be."

Veera felt a pang of jealousy. Deepak had chosen Olivia. She had been the undisputed choice. Even if the decision was mostly because of the business, did he have feelings for her? Veera snatched up her phone and was already opening her text app. "Let me tell my sister. Maybe there's something she can do to convince—"

Deepak waved a hand. "It's okay. I already talked to Sana. She's working on it."

Veera paused, then deleted her angry text and put her phone aside. "Fine. Deepak, I'm so sorry that she's putting you through the wringer. But there's no way another candidate from the outside would know nearly as much about the business to compete with you. Even if they have like thirty years of experience over you, Illyria Entertainment, and now Illyria Media Group is *yours*. Everyone knows that."

The corner of his mouth curled but then it set in a straight line again. In a move that delighted her, he grabbed her hand and tugged her across the kitchen until he was wrapping her in his arms and resting his cheek against her temple.

He smelled as delicious as he had that morning. Even better than Chinese takeout, if that were possible. The aftershave was more subtle, but he was still uniquely Deepak. Her hands smoothed over the soft fabric of his button-down shirt. Whenever he hugged her like this, holding her against his chest, she felt the unique mix of both arousal and bone-deep comfort.

"Sometimes I wonder if I really deserve it," he said, his chest rumbling against her ear. "If all this is just because of birthright, and no matter how hard I work, the only reason why I am getting the position is because of my father. I mean, what makes me the perfect candidate over you or your sister?"

"Gender," Veera said blandly as she looked up at him.

"Right. That's my point."

Veera remained quiet for a moment, not sure exactly what she should say to make him feel better in this situation. Then she pulled out of his hug. "So what?"

Deepak looked down at her. "What?"

"I said, So what? Deepak, there is always going to be someone who is smarter or more qualified. You knew from the moment that you were born you had to work for this. But there is a difference between being the most qualified and being the best candidate. Accept the fact that you now have competition, and when you win, make sure that people who aren't as lucky as you are still given a fair shot."

She returned to her food and took one of the crab rangoons before arranging her food on her plate. Then she sipped from the glass of wine that Deepak had poured for her. She felt the cool crisp alcohol linger on her tongue.

They sat on the barstools adjacent to each other. Deepak separated the pair of chopsticks that came in one of the bags and effortlessly twirled them between his fingers before settling them into position.

"I should've fought harder to keep you and your sister in the leadership structure," he said. "But your father made the cut before the merger was finalized."

Veera pushed the container of crab rangoons forward so he could take one. "You have the chance to help me now and that's what matters."

He smiled, and this time it was his genuine, rueful expression.

"Just promise me that whatever happens, you'll talk to me first so we can work together."

"Done," she lied. Veera shifted in her seat and then broached the topic that had been on her mind since the aunties left. "Hey, I was going to ask you. When am I going to see your parents? Are they okay with us visiting this weekend?"

Deepak snapped his fingers as if he remembered something that he was supposed to tell her. "This weekend. They're excited to see you again. We're confirmed for a trip to Hudson Valley."

Veera had to bite her tongue at the thought that the Dattas had a weekend home. It's not like she didn't grow up with a lot of wealth, too. It's just that Deepak's family was on a whole different level than hers.

"That works for me."

"Great," he said. Then he dug into his noodles. They slipped into a moment of awkward silence. Deepak didn't seem to mind, though. He began to methodically devour his food. He topped off her wine and drank deeply from his own glass. The strong lines of his throat clenched and relaxed as he swallowed.

He was so quiet.

What were they supposed to talk about now? They used to always have conversation, but things were different.

Veera pushed around her broccoli floret for another moment before she got to her feet. This was way too weird for her. That meant it was time for her to make her exit. "Hey, I realized that you just got home. I'll take this up and eat in my sitting room. You probably need some space to decompress. I also downloaded this new romance about blue aliens, so . . ."

He looked at her with a puzzled expression. "What are you talking about?"

"Blue aliens? Well, apparently they have—"

"No, not the aliens. Why are you leaving?"

"When you come home, you probably want some alone time and quiet time. You may also want to work. I don't want to get in the way. We both lived with roommates before, but it's been a while since we've had one."

"Whoa whoa whoa," he said, then made a time-out signal with his hands. "We aren't roommates."

She cocked her head as she sat down again, surprised at how swiftly he responded with irritation. She knew that he hadn't had the best day. Maybe that was the reason why. "We have a fake marriage, and we have to live together until your position is secured at Illyria," she said. "Until then, we're roommates."

"No," Deepak said again, his voice even. He set down his chopsticks. "Veera, we're husband and wife."

"Fake husband and wife," she said. She was starting to feel just as anxious, just as tense as he sounded. Didn't he see? Didn't he realize how dangerous it was to even consider that what they had was something real? How was she supposed to protect her heart if he refused to let her keep up the barriers and the walls that she'd erected between them?

He picked up his wineglass and drained the rest of the contents before putting the glass down with a hard clink on the table. "Are you looking for, what, a chore chart?"

She crossed her arms over her chest. "All I'm saying is that when you come home, you probably want some space. I'm trying to be respectful."

He was quiet for the few moments it took him to systematically devoured his meal. Then when his plate was empty and she was still fiddling with a broccoli floret, he dabbed at his mouth with the napkin, and tucked it next to his plate.

"Veera, if I need space, I'll tell you, but I don't want you to think that you're getting in my way. I *want* you here. I *like* spending time with you. And even though you and Sana had been traveling for eight months, I still consider you my best friend and living with you is probably going to be a new adventure every day."

There went her heart again. It thumped heavily in her chest, even as she tried desperately not to read into Deepak's words.

"This feels weird," she said softly.

"Yeah," he said. Then he leaned back in his chair. "Yeah, I know what you mean."

There was another beat of silence, this time the soft hum of the heat kicking on, the early autumn nights cooling enough for the house to require it.

"I have an idea," he said. "Since this has been a truly shit day, and it's our second night as husband and wife living together—"

"Deepak."

"Fine, as *fake* husband and wife. Do you want to watch a movie on the couch, and open up all the trays that the aunties brought over?"

Veera smiled as she fiddled with her chopsticks and cooling food. Deepak knew that despite how old they were, how mature they were when it came to their careers, this was a novel situation, and she was going to periodically lose her shit. He was keeping things light, and she had to meet him halfway. "Yes, that sounds awesome. I'll finish this and clean up while you change, and then I have to tell you about all the postwedding expectations we have to do."

He got to his feet and took his plate to the sink. "I'm afraid to ask."

"It's as bad as you think. Marrying a banyan tree is only the start. Bobbi and Bunty are hosting our fake wedding reception in a few weeks and in addition to the board, the guest list is huge. Then there are three different poojas, and a whole host of married-woman ceremonies coming up now that it's fall. It'll start with Durga Pooja and end with Diwali."

"I hope these trays include dessert to make all this information more bearable," he said.

"Oh, they do. I already started eating some of them. But don't worry, I saved the pink chum chum sweets for you."

Deepak grinned at her over his shoulder, and Veera's heart fluttered.

Hopefully it wouldn't hurt too badly when she fell this time around.

CHAPTER 12

Deepak

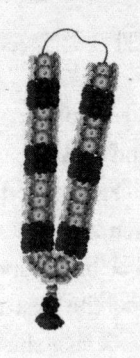

DEEPAK: Any word?

SANA: I'm meeting Olivia tomorrow. She finally agreed to give me five. I know I've asked you this already, but what do you want me to say?

DEEPAK: I don't know, Sana. Literally whatever it takes to get her to come back for the board meeting.

SANA: Fine, I'll do this my way. Just take care of my sister, and I'll handle Olivia.

DEEPAK: Thanks.

Deepak thought it would be way more difficult living with another person than it was. He was all about minimalism and order. The longer he could keep his house the way he wanted it, the more comfortable he felt. But somehow, despite Veera's love of clutter, they'd fallen into a steady rhythm over the last week.

Veera worked on her ethical lending pitch during the day while he was in the office, and they had dinner at night. Twice they went out for a walk like an old Indian couple slowly strolling up and down the same street.

She looked excited whenever she spoke about ethical lending trends in the market, and even though it had been months where they barely spoke to each other by text, Deepak was sure that this was the first time in a while that Veera was thrilled about the work that she was doing.

Hopefully, her pitch was ready to go because he was sure that his father was going to ask a ton of questions.

"Are you sure I look okay?" Veera asked, as Deepak eased off the main highway. The two-lane road cut straight through the hillside to the family home.

"You look beautiful," he replied, without glancing at her in his passenger seat. He was pretty sure that the word *beautiful* was an understatement. No, Veera was more gorgeous than he'd ever seen her before. She was dressed in a deep red sari, with her hair in a loose French braid draped over one shoulder. The color of the outfit matched her chuda set that she continued to wear every day. Her mehndi was beginning to fade, but the designs were still visible enough to prove her new marital status. A small silver bindi winked in the center of her arched eyebrows, mirroring the tiny diamond on her nose, and the subtle, delicate glamour was enchanting.

But out of all the sparkle Veera wore, the ring was the most satisfying to see. She twisted the large diamond solitaire and wedding band on her finger, the symbol of their marriage. He knew that they'd picked out the rings together, and her eyes had gone wide when she saw the size of the diamond. She'd insisted on something smaller and more affordable, but he'd bought it for her anyway. It was worth it considering he'd caught her admiring the ring when she thought he wasn't looking.

"Man, I could really go for a hamburger right now," Veera said wistfully.

He glanced at her, smiling. "What has you craving hamburgers?"

"I always want hamburgers right before I do anything religious," she said. "I know we're not supposed to eat meat before a religious thing, but if you tell me I can't eat something, I'm going to crave that thing."

"Ah. Because my mother is going to probably put you through the ceremony wringer when we get to the house, you're now craving hamburgers."

She dropped her head back against the seat rest. "Yeah," she said with a sigh. "Hamburger with bacon and cheese."

"Wow, that really does make you a bad Hindu."

She burst out laughing, then shoved him in the arm. "Technically as my fake husband, you should accept me flaws and all."

As your real husband.

"I'll tell you what," he said. "If we make it through the weekend in one piece, I will buy you whatever hamburger you want. Even if I have to fly somewhere to get it for you."

Veera turned to him, her eyes lined with sooty black kajal, her lashes long and thick. The tiny gold jhumkas swayed at her earlobes. "Promise?"

"Promise," he said. And because he had a craving, too, he held his hand out, palm up until Veera took it, and laced her fingers with his.

He liked touching her, liked being close after he'd wasted so much time. He knew that he had a lot to make up for, but maybe holding her hand was a nice start on the path to redemption.

Veera left her fingers laced with his as they turned onto his parents' drive and Deepak maneuvered the car through the iron gates at the end of the lane.

The house was smaller than some of the other estates in the

region, with six bedrooms set up like individual suites on five acres of dense forested land. The leaves were just starting to change colors, creating a cottagecore feel to the scenery.

Deepak loved the location. When he was young, he and his cousins would run through the trees and look for animal tracks. After hours of play, they would all come back to a kitchen exploding with mouthwatering smells. His aunts and mother stood around the large butcher-block island working like an assembly line before something delicious was either put on a tava or slipped in a wok of hot oil.

Because this was the first time he was bringing Veera to see his family in an official relationship capacity, Deepak knew that his mother was probably going to cook for her the same way.

He couldn't wait for all of them to spend time together. For his parents to care for her the same way that he—

"Oh my god, this place is like a remote location in a horror movie."

He slammed on the brakes as he reached the end of the driveway and shoved the car in park before he turned his entire body in his seat to glare at her. "Did you compare my parents' house to a horror movie?"

"Well, not the house," she said. She leaned forward to look up at the canopy of trees. "But the surroundings. Sorry, it was the first thing that came to mind."

"*A horror movie?*"

"Deepak, I'm a math girl, so if you're looking for a better comparison for beautiful, wooded scenery, you have to help me do it." She unbuckled her seat belt and slid out of the car just as he turned off the engine and did the same.

They met in the front of the vehicle, and Veera adjusted her sari so the pallu wrapped around her like a shawl. When she shivered, he slipped off his coat and draped it over her shoulders.

"Come on," he said. "Let's go inside. Fall is exponentially cooler here than it is in the city. I'll come back out to get the bags later."

He felt her shiver again, and this time he wasn't sure if it was because of the weather or because of her nerves.

"Don't worry," he said, more to himself than to her.

"I'm not worried," she replied. "Parents generally like me. I'm delightful."

He burst out laughing just as the door swung open and his mother and father stood in the entranceway. They were both dressed up, his mother in a cream-and-pearl salwar kameez and his father in a complementary kurta. They saw the grin on his face, and both of their expressions softened.

"Our bahu is here," his mother said. "Finally! I never thought this day would come."

That's when Deepak noticed the flowers. There were dozens of them.

No, that was an understatement. There were thousands of blooms.

The petals first started at the edge of the doorframe and created a wide path into the house. The curved staircase banister was wrapped in garlands, and strands covered the railing all the way up to the second-floor balcony.

"Okay, now I'm worried," Veera said under her breath.

"Mom, what is all this?" He moved to enter the house through the doorway, when his mother held up a hand to stop him.

"We have to welcome our daughter-in-law first," she said. Then she retrieved another one of her silver trays from a table in the foyer. There was a diya in the center, with rice, vermilion powder, and a small statue. His mother lifted the tray and made two circles in front of Veera, then using her ring finger, she put a dot of sindoor in the center of Veera's forehead. She lifted the pink chum chum sweets to her mouth for Veera to take a delicate bite.

Veera went through the steps, folding her hands at exactly the right moment, but her cheeks had paled, and she kept glancing in his direction.

"Veera, now you have to knock over the rice," Deepak's father said, motioning to a copper urn that was situated just inside the doorframe. "This will mark your first footsteps into your new home."

"Dad, is this really necessary?" Deepak said. Veera was moments away from blowing their cover or running back to the car.

Maybe comparing his family's house to a horror movie was appropriate.

This was her horror movie.

His father ignored him as he set up a tray filled with what looked like red paint in front of the copper urn.

"Veera, you push the urn with your right foot, then you step into the tray."

Veera looked up at Deepak, her eyes wide as she chewed on her bottom lip. This wasn't something they had talked about or prepared for. Deepak's parents had said that it would be a casual dinner and get-together. Additional religious ceremonies only made their marriage seem even more irreversible. These were cultural traditions that solidified their relationship at a soul-deep level. Every rice kernel thrown in blessing was a step closer to their union becoming permanent.

Deepak knew that for his parents, marriage was never just about the two of them. It couldn't be. Their marriage, as Punjabis, was always going to be about community. So, he touched her elbow, hoping that he could urge her along, and they'd deal with the repercussions of their actions later. Much, much later.

"Want to hold on to me so you don't fall flat on your face?" he asked.

The panic turned into irritation in a blink of an eye. Three lines formed between her eyebrows again. "I'm messy, not clumsy," Veera said. "But I appreciate the gentlemanly offer."

With her hand in his, she toed off her heels at the entrance, and in bare feet, carefully tipped over the rice urn, then stepped in the sticky red dye. With his help, she then stepped onto the tile that was prepped for her.

His mother produced another tray, this time with a bride yellow paste that Veera placed her palms in. She was instructed to press her hands against the wall to her right, staining the eggshell color with her prints.

The ceremony celebrating Veera's entrance into the Dattas' home was now complete. No matter what happened after this point, she was well and truly integrated into the history of Deepak's family's home.

"Welcome, daughter-in-law," his mother said. Then she cupped Veera's face in her hands and pressed a soft kiss against her temple.

Deepak saw Veera's eyes brighten with tears as well and swallowed the lump in his throat. When had their plan to fix their careers consumed all the parts of their lives until it seemed impossible to see any individual part without each other? At least that's how he felt about Veera and her presence in his childhood home.

"Now comes the difficult part," his mother said, oblivious to the fact that all of this was difficult for them. "We have to get you cleaned up before I can feed you!"

Deepak removed his suit coat from her shoulders and tossed it over the banister to retrieve later. Then without another word, he scooped Veera up in his arms. With their heads so close together, he whispered in his ear, "Are you okay?"

"Yeah," she whispered back, even as she held her hands to the side so she didn't get the turmeric paste on his clothes. "But I'm tempted to fingerpaint your face like a child."

"Well, we can't have that," Deepak said, amused.

Ignoring his parents' stares, he carried her down the hall and nudged the door open to the half bath. The sensor picked up their presence and the lights flickered on as he set her down on the edge of the vanity countertop.

"What are you doing?" she asked from her perch.

"Just hang on for a second." He retrieved the towels his mother had set out for her on a small console table near the door. He twisted the white stone sink taps and waited until the water felt warm to the touch. Veera watched him as he soaked the first towel before he lifted her left foot to carefully clean the residual red dye.

"You don't have to do that," she said, trying to tug her foot from his hold. "Just leave the towel, and I can—"

"We're in this together," he said, his hold on her ankle firm. He looked up at her from his kneeling position. "And as your husband, I consider it my privilege."

Veera bit her lip and looked away from him. "Deepak, we're getting too deep," she whispered. "This isn't the way it's supposed to happen."

"I know," he said, as he carefully cleaned off the dye. He didn't pretend to misunderstand her.

Veera's ankles were so slender in his hands, her feet had high arches, and her toenails were painted a delicate blush peach. He gently ran the hand towel down the center of her sole. She jerked against his hold, then wiggled her toes.

He wondered what it would be like if she let him touch her toes again like this. If she stretched out on his couch, slid her feet onto his lap, and coaxed him into giving her a massage after they both had worked a long day.

With thoughts of tumbling her back against his throw pillows, of kissing the thin gold anklets that he knew she liked to wear, Deepak stood and retrieved a fresh towel to wash Veera's hands. He stood inches apart from her now, and he could feel the warmth of her breath, the tension in her muscles as he carefully removed the last of the paste from between her fingers.

Then, because he couldn't help himself, he leaned forward and pressed a soft kiss at the corner of her mouth. The edge of his smile touched the edge of her frown. "Are you okay? Want me to make an excuse and take you back to the city?"

Veera shook her head, her dry hands coming up to brush at the spot he'd kissed her. "No," she whispered. "That would be rude, and your mom did so much work to welcome us here. Hopefully, that's the last of the ceremony."

"I think it is," Deepak said. He tossed the discarded towels in the sink where he'd deal with them later. He then helped her off the vanity, so she stood. "Is there anything I can do to make this whole experience less uncomfortable?"

"Baby pictures," she said. Then she smiled.

"You want to see baby pictures?"

"Yup," she replied.

"Yeah, okay, there are limits on what I am willing to do."

She pressed her cleaned palms together and pouted. "There has to be at least one of you sitting in a random bathroom bucket in India. Oh, maybe I can have your mom send them to me so I can set some of my favorites in your living room. I think it'll match that beaded rope you have on your coffee table that you call decor."

He held open the door for her as they walked out of the bathroom. "You know what? Next time you have dye on your feet, I'm just going to let you fall on your face."

CHAPTER 13

Veera

VEERA: HELP. Deepak's mom had a whole welcome ceremony for me when I showed up at the house today. I stepped in red dye, and I marked the house with turmeric paste and everything. I'm currently hiding in the bathroom. Is there anything else I should know that might happen?

KAREENA: Okay, deep breaths. You're going to be fine. You know Deepak's parents. You've met them before.

VEERA: Yeah, at your wedding and at charity events! Never like this.

BOBBI: It's sort of the same thing. All you have to do is be your funny, sweet self, and everything is going to be okay.

BOBBI: You're stronger than all of us, Veera. You always have been so good at shouldering our emotions, your families' drama, and your own feelings. You can do this!

KAREENA: There is probably going to be a chuda ceremony, where your mother-in-law removes your red bangles for you, but that's it. I don't think you have to worry about anything else.

BOBBI: Oh, I remember that Prem's mom also made Kareena a meal.

KAREENA: That's right! When we went out to California, it was a big thing.

VEERA: Wait, where was I during this?

BOBBI: I think that was right around the time the merger talks started.

VEERA: Okay. Good to know.

Veera tucked her phone away into her blouse and adjusted her boobs to conceal it. Then she stepped out of the bathroom with the hopes that she could just follow the voices to where everyone was congregating.

She almost ran into Deepak.

He was leaning against the wall, scrolling on his phone. When he saw her, he looked relieved, and put his cell in his back pocket. "You okay?" he asked.

Veera nodded. Then she held up her hands that were still tinged with a faint yellow color. "I don't think I'll be staining anything in your parents' house, but I had to make sure."

He shook his head. "I doubt my parents would care."

Then he held out his hand as if it was the most natural thing in the world for them to link their fingers together. "Come on," he said, as he tugged her forward. "Mom said that she cooked, and it's been a long time since she worked in the kitchen by herself."

"Is that a good thing or a bad thing?" she asked.

Deepak wiggled his eyebrows. "I guess you'll just have to find out."

They passed under an arched doorway and walked down a small hall that led to a great room. The room was divided by a long dining table with the kitchen on one side and the living space on the other. The ceilings were at least two stories high, and the back of the house was a wall of windows that opened up to a mountain view.

Even though glass separated the riot of lush trees and vegetation, Deepak's parents had brought the outdoors inside. Like the entryway and hall, this space was decorated with fresh flowers, too. The doorways were dripping with blooms in a riot of colors, and the kitchen was bursting with bouquets. The celebration of scents, of color and soft textures were positioned in every corner reminding her that their marriage was no longer an entity that just belonged to them. It was part of a larger community.

"I'm going to see if my mom needs anything," Deepak said against her ear. Then he motioned to his father. "Call me if you need me." He wandered into the kitchen where his mother stood at the island, spatula in hand.

Veera turned toward the living space, twisting the end of her sari pallu in her hand.

"Wow," she said to Deepak's father as she approached the windows. "That's incredible."

"We like to think so," the older man replied. He stood from the couch and put his computer tablet on the coffee table. "You know, your parents came to visit before the merger. They were hoping to get a place up here as well. I don't think they've looked at properties quite yet, but it would be nice to have the extended family close by."

Veera smiled. "That would be nice, but my parents have always loved New Jersey. I can't imagine them going anywhere else."

"But being close to family is important," Deepak's father said, as he approached her side.

She realized then that Deepak got his kind eyes from his father. Her husband would most likely develop the same streaks of white and gray in his hair.

Kaushal Datta was known to have built an empire out of a small production company that his father had started in India. He capitalized on the need for entertainment and news that specifically was marketed toward Indians in foreign countries. However, he was rarely in the news and had little to no press about him. The press that did exist was filled with praise about his gentle demeanor. As he patted Veera's shoulder in a comforting gesture, she knew that the brief interviews were probably all true.

"Come, bahu," he said, using the formal term for daughter-in-law. "Let's sit while your mother-in-law putters around the kitchen. Do you know, she has not puttered in years? But the minute Deepak told us that he was married, she was worried you'd think less of her because she didn't do all the cooking herself anymore."

Veera shook her head. "Trust me, I am the last person to judge."

They moved to the couches, and Veera sat opposite Deepak's father, sinking into the soft, smooth leather.

"So, my son has told me that you've been consulting for him over the last few months."

Veera nodded. "My sister and I were traveling to explore global markets because we were planning on going into business together."

"Equitable finance, right?" he said. Veera had to smile at the casual tone of his voice. As nice as he was, there was definitely a shrewd intelligence in his eyes that she'd be a fool to ignore.

"My sister and I were hoping to build a financial services company similar to what we had at Mathur Financial Group," Veera said. "Sana is an expert in global markets, and that was going to be our specialization moving forward. But my personal interest has always been equitable financial practices."

She figured as long as she stuck as close to the truth as possible, then she could make it through the weekend. That's all she had to do. Veera shifted to the edge of the couch, ready to launch into the pitch that she'd rehearsed during the week, when Deepak's father reached out and patted her hand.

"I admit, I don't know a lot about the field. What got you interested?"

She blinked, trying to compute his question. "How did I first get interested in equitable financial practices?"

He nodded. "Why is it important to you?"

Veera had to think for a moment before she could answer his question. "Well, when I was in college, I learned about microloans. In Bangladesh, lenders were giving women with incredible business ideas and artistic talent a few hundred dollars to jumpstart sales. What was interesting about the microloans was that once the individual paid back the loan, that money would then go to another member in the community for the same reason. This encouraged all the women in the villages to work together so they could all succeed and one by one get the start-up capital they needed."

Deepak's father's eyes widened. "The program was successful?"

"For a period of time," Veera said. "But it wasn't developed for expansion or growth. There was also no financial literacy for the women."

He leaned forward, a glint in his eye. "That's what you want to do with Deepak."

Veera hadn't thought about microloans in so long. When she was in college, she felt like it was almost a no-brainer to invest in the communities her family came from. But once South Asians accumulated the wealth they were constantly searching for, it's as if they did everything in their power to separate themselves from the poverty that they came from.

"My proposal for Deepak is a little more conservative," she said.

"Why?"

This was the second time that she'd been thrown by this man. "Why is my proposal conservative?"

Deepak's father nodded.

"Because Illyria Entertainment, now Illyria Media may not want to explore a space so risky especially if they are just starting in the financial sector . . ."

"Do you think it's worth the effort?"

"Yes," Veera said without hesitation. "What's the point in having money if we can't support the rest of our community? Then we are just becoming part of the problem. We're monetizing off the pain that our ancestors escaped."

His expression softened. This time when he reached out to touch her hand, he gripped it and squeezed. "I hope you don't mind me saying this, Veera, but your father was a fool to let you go. And we were also foolish for failing to stand by your side."

"I don't regret my time learning about global markets," she said softly. "The last year has been good for my career." She meant it, too, she realized. Because without stepping outside the cocoon her father had created for her, she'd have never pushed beyond her comfort zone into spaces that really interested her.

Veera hadn't realized until that moment how much she'd changed. She knew that her friends and family called her soft and sweet, but she'd still managed to survive in the shark-infested waters of her profession. She had carved out a place for herself that felt uniquely hers. That didn't require sweet-Veera, or nice-Veera, or the Veera-with-the-sarcasm.

And maybe, in that moment, being the Veera she was now was the best thing she could do for herself.

"I'm just glad you're here," Deepak's father said. Then he looked over at the kitchen where Deepak and his mother were huddled together. He lowered his voice so that Veera had to lean forward to hear him. "I saw the way you used to look at my son, and I'm so glad he's finally come to his senses and now looks at you the same way."

Oh my god.

"I-I don't know what—"

"We're ready for the last ceremonial event," Deepak's mother called out.

Deepak's father patted her hand one more time, winked, and then sat back against the couch cushions. Veera looked up to see Deepak crossing the room at his mother's side.

There was another silver tray in her hands.

How many thaalis did this woman own?

"I know that it's a bit early," Deepak's mother said, "but according to our pandit, it's been an appropriate amount of time to remove your chuda. Deepak said that you've worn it every day since your wedding, even if you were just at the house."

Veera looked up at her husband and realized that he was

watching her closely. He glanced down at the bangles she was sliding back and forth over her wrist.

"You're supposed to wear them the whole time, right?" Veera said defensively. "I don't have an uncle that I'm close with, so one of our new, ah, friends was the one who put it on me. And I had to google some of the rules."

Deepak's mother sat next to her, hip to hip. She smelled of the flowers that decorated the house, and her smile was just like her son's. Resting the thaali on the coffee table, she took one of Veera's hands in hers and began to remove the bracelets one at a time, exposing Veera's wrist. Then she dropped them onto the silver tray, the sound a musical jingle.

When Veera's wrists were bare, Deepak's mother reached for a small glass jar that she'd left on the tray and dipped two fingers into a pink cream.

With so much care, she gently rubbed the lotion into Veera's wrists. Her breath caught as the older woman massaged her hands. Her eyes were soft and dreamy, as if she were remembering a familiar moment in her history. "Well, even though you haven't had the wedding that a bride deserves, as your mother-in-law, I am going to do everything I can to make sure that you are shown the love that you deserve."

Veera couldn't respond, couldn't speak with the burning lump in her throat that blocked all the appropriate words that were supposed to come out of her mouth.

She needed to put some distance between herself and this woman who was so earnest, so welcoming and sincere. But she couldn't move, couldn't breathe. And standing at a distance, Deepak looked like this was the most normal situation for both of them. With his hands tucked in his pockets, the easy smile on his face, and his relaxed posture, he was acting like this was exactly where he wanted to be.

Deepak's mother lifted a small velvet pouch off the tray and loosened the drawstring. "These bangles were given to me by my mother-in-law. They belonged to her mother-in-law. Over the years, I've repaired them and added some stones. Now they belong to you."

Before Veera could pull back, Deepak's mother held the bangles like she was holding a ball in her fingertips and slipped the bangles onto Veera's wrist.

They were solid gold and embedded with tiny diamonds that spiraled around the circumference in a delicate design.

No, Veera thought. *No, this isn't right.* This wasn't okay. It was one thing for their deception to break her own heart, but it was another to hurt Deepak's parents when they had never been anything but kind to her. They were too emotionally involved in the ruse.

"Welcome to the family," the older woman said. Her touch had the faintest tremor in it as she gently brushed back an errant curl from Veera's cheek. Then she leaned in and cupped Veera's face in her hands. "Now. When are you both giving me grand-babies?"

If I, Mrs. W. S. Gupta, have one piece of advice for all the parents of daughters, it's to hire a personal investigator to make sure that the match you are arranging for your child is not involved with another person. We are responsible for protecting our children from a hurt heart or, even worse, damaged pride.

Mrs. W. S. Gupta
Avon, New Jersey

CHAPTER 14

Veera

Text messages from two years ago:

DEEPAK: Hey, I have a weird question for you.

VEERA: The last time you told me that, I ended up eating the best bagels ever.

VEERA: What's up?

DEEPAK: I have this fundraiser I have to go to this weekend for Illyria. My parents are threatening to set me up with someone.

VEERA: Is that the Gordon Foundation?

DEEPAK: Yes! Are you going?

VEERA: I was going to say no since my father decided not to sponsor this year. He slashed our Corporate Social Responsibility and charity donation budget in half.

VEERA: And yes, I am still furious about it.

> **DEEPAK:** Well, you can always come with me and help me spend Illyria money. These things are so boring and I could really use a friend.

> **VEERA:** Ahh, a friend date?

> **DEEPAK:** Yes, exactly! If you're my buffer for unwanted parental matchmaking, I'll buy you the best New York cheesecake of your life afterward.

> **VEERA:** Consider me your friendly buffer. I will happily dress up for cheesecake.

Veera was overwhelmed, and when she was overwhelmed, she usually reacted in one of two ways: she cried, which was a perfectly healthy response according to her therapist. Or she'd walk out of whatever situation she was currently standing in.

Unfortunately, that was no longer an option for her.

"Are you about to make a run for it?" Deepak asked under his breath. His thigh pressed against hers, sensitizing her entire leg as his fingers brushed over her wrist, tangling with the bangles that Deepak's mother had given her. They sat side by side on the leather couch that was angled toward the kitchen.

"That's what you're supposed to do in horror movies, right?" she whispered back. "Make a run for it? Hopefully there isn't a barn filled with swinging chainsaws and murder items behind the house."

"I feel like I should be offended. My parents aren't that bad."

"No, they're freaking adorable, Deepak. That's the problem. What they're putting us through is pretty horrific though, don't you think?" she replied. Then pulled away from his touch.

The way he was playing with the bangles on her wrist was . . . distracting.

"They're showing us how supportive they are," Deepak replied. He poked her leg now, and she batted at his hand.

"Which only makes this so much more terrible." She looked over at Deepak's parents who were putting away dishes now, and even though Veera couldn't hear them, she knew from the tone of their voices that her presence in Deepak's life brought them so much happiness.

Veera pointed to the bangles then at her fake husband. "The minute we get back to your house, you are taking these and packing them away. I refuse to be responsible for a family heirloom."

Deepak shook his head. "You have to wear them. You're my wife, and my mother is going to expect to see them on your wrists every time you meet."

"Fake wife," she hissed.

Their conversation was interrupted with the sound of Deepak's mother's laugh, and Deepak's father humming a Bollywood tune. They were acting like typical South Asian parents.

Parents that just happened to be billionaires. No big deal.

Throughout the course of dinner, Veera had almost forgotten their money, too. They spoke of Deepak's childhood, of Veera's travels, of the business and the exciting parties that Deepak's mother wanted to take her to.

Veera called out across the room, "Are you sure we can't help you with that, Auntie?"

"Oh please," Deepak's mother said. "Call me Muma." She switched to a mix of Hindi and Punjabi, the same Delhi Punjabi that Veera's mother often spoke at home. "And not at all! We haven't done this in so long. It's nice to feed my family."

"Right," Veera said and swallowed hard. She glared at Deepak.

Her fake husband picked up a grape from the dessert fruit platter and winked at her as he popped it in his mouth. He was enjoying her discomfort way too much.

"We should show you two to your room," Deepak's father said in the same language. He folded the kitchen towel he'd been using and dropped it on the counter. "That way you can get some rest. It's late."

It was so strange to Veera to see a man of his age help with housework. Not that they didn't exist, but her father wouldn't be caught dead in his kitchen, unless it was to throw something away.

Deepak got to his feet. He responded to his parents in English. "Am I using the blue room? I can put Veera in the guest room next door."

His parents looked at each other, then burst out laughing. They responded as if Deepak had said the most hilarious thing in the world.

"Why would you stay in separate rooms, beta?" Deepak's mother asked.

"Because we're sleeping under your roof and it's the first time that you're meeting Veera," he said. He tugged at his suit collar and glanced down at Veera. "When Olivia came to visit, you put her in a hotel room across town."

"Olivia was just visiting as a potential partner," Deepak's mother said. She stepped closer to them, hands on her hips. "You're *married* to Veera."

Deepak looked down at her, panicked. They had a brief conversation about the bed setup before they came to visit for the weekend. He was so sure that they would want to approve of Veera first. He rambled for almost ten minutes about how conservative Indian values could be.

Veera didn't think now was the appropriate moment to tell him *I told you so* but she had every intention of rubbing it in his face later.

"I really think we should give Veera the option to be comfortable—"

"It's fine," Veera said, and she patted Deepak on the arm. She knew that it would've been the right thing to end the farce now. To tell Deepak's parents that they were fake married, and they were so sorry for everything. To give the jewelry back and beg forgiveness.

But at the same time, she didn't want to hurt their feelings. Not until Deepak also agreed to end things so he could manage their disappointment. These were his parents. If she made the choice for herself and Deepak right now and called it quits, then it wouldn't be fair to him since he'd be responsible for handling the fallout on his own.

Her sister's words about defending Deepak came back like a haunted message.

I should've known you'd be like this. It's only been a few days since Deepak is back in your life. Are you seriously defending him again?

"You're *both* in the blue room," his mother said, ignorant of their feelings. "Your bags should already be up there."

"I'd really like to change," she said pointing to the sari that she still wore. "I think getting comfortable is a great idea. It's late, and if you don't mind . . ."

"Go on," Deepak's father said. "You're a part of the family now, so don't feel obligated to stay here if you would like to rest. We're about to go to sleep, too."

"Uh, thanks."

"Okay," Deepak said. He hesitated again. "If you're sure . . ."

"You aren't a teenager with a girlfriend, Deepak," his mother called back as she shut the dishwasher door with a quick hip check. "You're married now."

"That doesn't make this better," he muttered.

"I really appreciate all the decor and the dinner tonight," Veera said over his voice. "If you're sure you don't need anything, then I'll head upstairs?"

"Good night," his parents said in unison. They stood side by side, arms looped around each other, grinning as if their son just won the National Spelling Bee.

Veera stood, aware that every eye in the room was on her as she walked toward the front stairwell. Her bare feet were cushioned by the soft, wilted buds of the flowers that lined the tiled floor even as thoughts of sharing a bed with Deepak flooded her mind.

It was fine. They were consenting adults. They had slept in the same bed together in Goa. Granted, they didn't know exactly what was happening at the time since they were both so drunk, but they could pretend intoxication again if they had to.

Deepak followed her out of the great room, and they climbed the stairs in silence. When they reached the top of the landing, Deepak took the lead toward the left hallway. He walked all the way to the end where there were more flowers creating an intricate design on the floor in front of the door.

"Did your mother do all this herself?" Veera asked.

"No way," Deepak said with a scoff. "Today was an anomaly that you'll never see again. Usually, she has a staff of people who are buzzing around, always working on the house or redesigning some room that she wants to upgrade."

"Well, I'm flattered that she wanted to do it by herself for me," Veera said. She adjusted the bangles on her wrist, feeling the cool metal slide over her skin. "Deepak, this is going to hurt them, too."

"I know," he said, gruffly. "Unless you want to back out, we should just keep following the plan. Then I'll tell them." He gripped the doorknob and pushed. "Let's focus on getting through tonight."

Veera's mouth fell open when she saw the room. If there were a lot of flowers in the foyer and the great room, the bedroom was a botanical garden. A riot of tropical fragrant blossoms in a rainbow of color, all out of season and completely impractical for the Hudson Valley, were situated in clusters in every corner. Pots and urns of different shapes and sizes cluttered tabletops and floor space, creating pathways and focal points. There were gardenias and jasmine, lilies with traditional roses and sweat peas, tulips, daisies, and so many more that she couldn't identify.

"You know," Deepak said casually as he ushered her inside. "They tell you that you're supposed to focus on education. To not get serious with anyone romantically until after you get the degree and the job and the house. Then at the age of twenty-five, they completely change their tune and all of a sudden, you have to get married. You're behind before you get started."

"And the minute you get married, it's this," Veera said motioning to the room.

The king-size bed had a position of prominence on a slightly elevated platform. Recessed lighting circled the bed and was set to a soft glow. From the center of the ceiling, long garlands of flowers created a canopy that surrounded the bed in a halo of yellow, orange, and red buds. A path of flowers stretched from the door to the bed. A wall of windows was closed off by soft beige-and-cream drapes, and in the far corner was a small table with bottled water, and an ice bucket with champagne and flutes.

"It's like a fucking seduction scene," Deepak said, as he stepped into the room.

Veera followed. "All that's missing is the music."

"Nope, we have that, too," Deepak said. He walked over to the dresser. Nestled between two bouquets was a small speaker. He peeled the note off the screen on top of the device. "It says to just press the power button."

He tapped the screen and the in-ceiling speakers began to play an old Bollywood song, "Raat Akeli Hai."

"Deepak, your parents made us a Bollywood seduction playlist. This is the Desi version of Boys to Men."

They gaped at each other for a moment, then began to giggle. Veera didn't know what else she was supposed to do, even as her awareness of him, of his presence was starting to consume her senses.

She watched as her fake husband walked around the side of the bed and picked up another note that was resting on the bedside table.

"'There are herbal vitamins in the top drawer. Tell Veera to take one of each for optimal ferti—'" He dropped the note, as if scalded by the paper itself.

Yup, that was the last straw, she thought. Now it was time to run away.

Veera marched over to her carry-on bag that was sitting near the foot of the bed. She picked it up, and without another word strode into the adjoining bathroom and shut the door. Deepak could either use another bathroom, or he could wait for her to be finished.

As she began to strip, first her clothes, then her makeup and jewelry, she tried to remind herself that this was Deepak. This was her best friend, and even though she'd had feelings for him forever, there was absolutely no reason for her to get hot and bothered over sexy Bollywood seduction music and fertility vitamins. There was no reason for her to dwell on the fact that he'd carried her to the bathroom, or that he'd winked at her when she was trying to get out of the postdinner conversation.

Even as she listed all the facts about their circumstances in her head, her skin felt hot and flushed, the pulse point at her neck throbbed in a thick, steady beat. Her stomach clenched with every desire that threatened to consume her thoughts.

When she finished her skin and hair care in the marble and glass bathroom, complete with pretty gold lotus-shaped sconces and touches of Indian art decor, she straightened her shoulders and realized that she'd just have to deal with her unrequited desire.

"You are thirty-two," Veera said to the mirror. "You are accomplished, and smart, and sexy, and this is absolutely no big deal because you're a mature, experienced woman."

With one last nod at her reflection, she straightened her sleeveless tan top, adjusted her sleep shorts, and strode out of the room.

She came to a halt when she saw Deepak in boxers. His wide shoulders and tapered waist were muscled and honed.

And naked.

Veera slapped a hand over her face. "Oh my god, I'm so sorry, I didn't realize you were still getting dressed."

"I am dressed," he said with a chuckle. He stood back, arms spread, motioning to his naked, firm, and muscled chest. "Veera, you've seen me shirtless before. I slept next to you in Goa shirtless."

Damn it, why did he have to remember that moment?

She dropped her hand and focused her gaze on the ceiling. She refused to acknowledge the fact that she was the one who had been supercasual about their sleeping arrangements when they'd spoken with Deepak's parents downstairs. "Everyone will know if I use the couch, right?"

Deepak nodded.

"Should I sleep on the floor?"

He shook his head.

There was no way out of this, and it was too late to pretend that she wasn't feeling well and to return to the city. Veera looked over at the bed, the warm glow romanticizing the canopy of flower garlands even more. The soft strains of Bollywood music continued to play.

Maybe if she just got into bed, she could close her eyes, fall asleep, and this would all be over in no time.

She should've had more sex in her life. Maybe if she had prioritized dating, this wouldn't feel as awkward as it did. Instead, she was like so many other South Asians her age: anxious socially and romantically.

Hello, generational and parental trauma.

"Hey, so I have something for you that may help you feel less intimidated by sleeping next to my gorgeous bod," Deepak said, as he slapped a hand against his rock-hard abs.

"Oh, no present needed. That sentence did it for me."

"You get to have one anyway," he said. Then he pushed the garland canopy aside and reached under his bed. Veera stepped closer as she heard rummaging and the sound of a lid popping off a box.

"Aha! Here it is," he said. He stood up with a leatherbound photo album in hand. "I present to you some baby pictures of Deepak Kaushal Datta, born thirty-five years ago in New York City."

He faced the foot of the bed and after wrestling with the flower canopy, he lay down on his stomach with the album in front of him. Then he patted the soft sheets and blankets at his side. "Come on. I'll let you heckle me for free."

Knowing that this was an opportunity that she couldn't pass up, Veera carefully climbed on the bed and lay in the same position as Deepak, an inch between them as he opened the album. His lean body, gleaming under the low light, a thick curl of black hair flopped over his brow. Veera looked at the fading mehndi on her hands, the rings they both wore as they touched the edges of the leather album and opened to the first page.

There were tiny black footprints, and a birth card, along with a baby picture of a wrinkly, crying newborn wrapped like a tiny little sausage.

"Wow, you were—"

"An ugly baby, I know," he said. "Everyone tells me that, too."

"Not ugly," she replied. She touched his newborn frown, so serious and ready for the world. "Just . . . sad?"

"I'll take it," he said with a chuckle. His arm brushed against hers, and she had to bite back a shiver. Deepak flipped the page to reveal a collage of family members holding him as a baby. Some of the individuals were familiar. There were Deepak's parents, and a few of the family members who were a part of the Illyria Media Group board.

On the next page, there was only a single centered photo of an older man who held Deepak's sleeping form. He wore a white kurta pajama and a pagadi in crimson red, and he had a shaped beard that did nothing to hide his toothy grin.

"Was that your grandfather?" Veera asked.

Deepak chuckled and she could feel his laugh next to him. "Yes, that's the man I'm named after. Deepak Datta. Everyone said we were exactly alike. He died about ten years ago."

"I'm sorry," she said, softly. "Were you close?"

"Very," he replied. His large hands touched the photo with a tenderness she hadn't seen from him before. "He loved the company he started. He felt like he was some big Bollywood producer. Then when Dad took the company and increased the size twelve times over, he started a scrapbook. He'd clip every mention of the family. We wanted to bring him over to live with us, but he was so happy with the farmhouse in Punjab. He liked listening to the rooster in the morning and drinking chai on his rooftop overlooking the sugarcane fields."

"That sounds magical," Veera said softly. She was leaning closer to him, their bare arms brushing with every breath.

"He's the reason I'm so proud to be a part of our family legacy," Deepak said. "But you have a legacy, too. You get it."

Veera laughed. "No, Deeps. I don't."

He nudged her in the arm, then stayed connected to her, elbow to shoulder. His voice lowered. "What do you mean? You were a senior leader at Mathur Financial Group."

"I was an employee at my father's company," she said slowly. "He even said that he didn't think I had the skills to ever lead his business right before he fired me. We never had a close relationship, no matter how hard I tried to meet him halfway. He always wanted sons, so I was a disappointment from birth." It had taken her a long time to come to that realization, but she was finally okay with it. She knew that going no-contact with the man she'd once idolized was such a strange concept for so many South Asians who thrived on family connections and community relationships. But after years of believing she wasn't good enough, she'd finally understood that she was never the problem. He was.

"He got something special with you, Vee," Deepak said. "He's a fool if he can't see that."

"I know." She flipped the page of his album to reveal another collage of baby pictures. This time, Deepak was a toddler. Right in the center of the left page, there he was, with the same eyes, the same smile, sitting in a bucket.

Veera gasped. "I knew it!" she squealed. She shoved him in the arm. "You have a sitting-in-a-bucket picture in India!"

Deepak laughed and slapped a hand over the picture. "Stop, there is only so much embarrassment I can take."

"What are you talking about? You're so cute!" she said, then pulled the album closer to her so she could inspect the picture.

What would it be like? she wondered. What would it be like to have a family with the man she had fallen in love with? To have babies with bright, carefree smiles and thick curling hair? What would it be like if their relationship was real?

"Come on, Vee," Deepak said and pulled the album away from her. "I think I have some pictures from my high school tennis days in here, too. I was on the varsity team."

Veera grinned, and some of the uncomfortable unnerving feelings from staying with his family slipped away. "Did you have a letter jacket?"

"I did," he said. "But I never gave it to anyone."

"Really? There wasn't a single girlfriend who wore Deepak Datta's tennis varsity leather jacket?"

"No," he said. Then he propped his head on his fist and rolled to his side to look at her. "But you know what? I would've given you my jacket to wear."

Veera arched an eyebrow. "Those jackets are for girlfriends, not for best friends who attend charity events with you to stop your matchmaking mother from interfering."

"I know," he said softly. "I would've still given you my jacket."

Veera felt her heart clench and wished that she could believe him, but she'd known him for over two years, and in that time, he'd never seen her as anyone but a friend.

"Hey, can I ask you a question?"

"Shoot," he said, as he brushed a curl off her cheek. She swatted at his hand.

"Do you have any pictures of Prem and Bunty? I want to know the juicy stuff that I can use as blackmail material if either of them hurt my friends."

Deepak gaped at her. "Veera Mathur Datta! That's just devious. And everyone thinks you're so sweet."

"I am," she said primly. "But I am also smart. So come on. Cough up those college pictures."

Deepak laughed again, then slid off the bed, moving on all fours with his muscles flexing. "I have them saved on an external hard drive. I think they're still in the box under my bed."

"It's a good thing you have your laptop with you," she said.

CHAPTER 15

Veera

They went to sleep at one in the morning after almost passing out on the open albums and laptops filled with moments of Deepak's past. Veera was so tired that she didn't pay any attention to the way that Deepak had cleared the bed and pushed the canopy of flowers out of the way for her to get under the comforter. Her eyes were closed as she felt the soft warmth of Deepak tucking her in.

She woke with a jolt less than two hours later when she felt lips at the base of her neck. They definitely weren't her lips.

Obviously.

Veera shivered delicately at the touch, as sleep melted like mist under the sun and she became more and more aware of her situation. She was still in Deepak's bedroom at his parents' house in the Hudson Valley. She smelled the sweet scent of flowers and could reach across the bedspread to touch the garlands that made a curtain around the mattress.

Then there was the arm wrapped around her waist. She knew that it was Deepak because she had felt the same strength, the same gentle yet firm touch in her hungover state in Goa. He fit against her from shoulder to knee, and one arm tucked under her pillow while the other spread across the slight curve of her belly.

He was so close to her now that she could feel the ridged lines of his muscled pecs and abdomen, the soft thud of his heart against her back. She closed her eyes and took a deep breath. They were still surrounded by fragrant flowers, but there was a rich earthy scent that was all Deepak.

His touch stoked her desire until she was pressing her thighs together, and squirming forward so that she could increase the space between them. The minute Veera moved, Deepak's hold on her tightened a fraction. Then she felt him shift, heard the sound of a yawn, and shivered at the tickle of his breath against the nape of her neck. His hands inched under her shirt until his fingers grazed the bare skin below her navel. He trailed his fingertips upward until they brushed the underside of her breasts.

She closed her eyes and stifled a groan.

"Deeps?" she whispered; her voice was breathy as she gripped her pillow.

"Mm-hmm," he said, the deep gravel of his voice sparking goose bumps down her arm.

Veera shifted again, and this time, her ass pressed firmly against his crotch. She felt Deepak harden and his body fit firmly against the back of hers.

"You're so tense," he whispered.

She knew she should roll away and chance falling on the floor again, but she couldn't. She didn't want to.

Oh god.

He was hard for her. This wasn't alcohol induced or a moment where they had to pretend to be a loving couple. In the darkness of his bedroom, they were alone, and his hands were insistent and thorough as if he were showing her how much he craved her body. The realization had her heart thudding like a drum in her chest. Had Deepak ever been attracted to her like this before?

She squeezed her eyes shut and pushed her ass harder against his bulge, rolling her hips back to hear the deep groan rumble through his chest. She was wet now, thinking of how far his hand would go as he touched her from thigh, over her stomach, and up to the underside of her unbound breasts. His hand climbed higher with each pass until his fingertips grazed over the tightening peaks of her nipples.

"Deepak," she whispered, and in response, he gently pinched the hard buds with firm pressure.

When the arm under her pillow slid down to wrap around her shoulders, she felt her desperation growing as she ached for relief.

She gasped when she felt his fingertips push at the top of her shorts. He waited for a heartbeat before they slipped under the waistband and found her thin, barely there cotton panties. She was embarrassingly damp as she shamelessly pushed her butt against his thick cock.

Deepak pressed an open-mouth kiss on the curve of her neck, just as his other hand slipped farther into her underwear and caressed the top of her mound.

This wasn't happening. This wasn't real. How was this her life that Deepak was touching her in all the delicious, wet places that, a few weeks ago, she only dreamed he'd caress and stroke?

She fisted the sheets, biting her lip and silencing all her moans that she desperately wanted to share with him. This was his parents' home, and even if they were on the opposite side of the house, what he was doing to her was dirty, and hot and private.

His hand dipped lower until it touched her labia, parting her folds and giving her one long, hard stroke with his fingertips.

"You're so wet," he said hoarsely.

When she didn't respond, his hand moved from around her shoulders to grip the front of her neck. He squeezed ever so slightly. "Do you want more?"

"Yes," she hissed, her eyes fluttering shut. "Yes, I want . . . I want more."

"Let me give it to you, Vee," he whispered.

Deepak began circling her clitoris, and because she was so swollen and sensitive, she scooted forward, almost as if her body was trying to escape his touch.

"Nah ah," he whispered and using the hand that currently covered her pussy, he pulled her back against him again. This time, he nudged one knee between her thighs, opening her until she felt exposed.

"Oh god." She was practically panting for him as he began to increase his speed and rhythm, fingering and massaging the hot, swollen clit. He moved his hips in the same deep, gyrating rhythm as his hand until she felt like he was fucking her.

His hold around her neck never relented, and her breasts, tender and sensitive, exposed to the cool bedroom air, throbbed, as he ground his cock against her.

The sounds of her gasps echoing in her ears, his groans, and the rapid jerks of their bodies as they grew damp—the tightening coils of desire wound tighter in her belly.

"Come for me, Vee," he gasped, his words broken as he finger-fucked her, and he thrust against her, with thin layers of clothing protecting the last walls erected between them.

"Just let go."

She felt the orgasm rise in a quick, sudden surge, and when he pinched her clit, she let out a sharp shriek, arching against him until she couldn't breathe, and floating lights burst in front of her eyes. He held her neck firmly, squeezing just as she toppled over the edge. She'd never come so hard before in her life.

Veera collapsed against the mattress and was barely able to acknowledge Deepak removing his hand from her panties and rolling away to the other side of the bed. She heard him get up, and the bathroom door slowly close behind him, as she began drifting into a dream state.

Long moments later, Deepak returned and slid under the comforter behind her. She was half asleep when she felt him lean over her and press a kiss against the curve of her shoulder.

"Good night, Vee," she heard him whisper.

She wasn't sure if it was a dream or reality, but the sound of his voice made her smile.

CHAPTER 16

Deepak

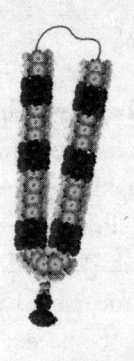

Text messages from one year and six months ago:

VEERA: Hi

DEEPAK: Hi

VEERA: Lunch?

DEEPAK: Am I buying?

VEERA: That's really nice of you to offer!

DEEPAK: Brat.

VEERA: I have been known to be one.

VEERA: Sushi?

DEEPAK: Yeah. Now I have something to look forward to today.

"I'm pretty sure I'm having a heart attack," Deepak said to Prem. It had been two days since they'd returned from his parents' house and he was still feeling chest pains.

Prem was dressed in his white coat and sitting behind a wide oak desk. He rolled his eyes through Deepak's phone screen. "You're not having a heart attack."

"Some doctor you are," Deepak said. "You haven't done any testing."

"I'm looking at your face, asshole, and I know you're just stressed out and overreacting."

Deepak dropped his head to the manila files in front of him. He had so much work to do. He was prepping for quarter four reports, reviewing year-end financials, completing board and shareholder dashboards, scripting town hall presentations, and so much more.

Yet all he could think about was last weekend and the incredible sound of Veera's pleasure. He couldn't believe that he'd touched her like that. That he had the privilege, the honor, of making her come in his arms.

When they woke the next morning, he had every intention to tell her that as her husband, he wanted to do it again. To be there for her for every cry, every gasp, every shiver and release. Except he'd woken to Veera's sunshine smile.

She'd pretended as if nothing happened and let him know that chai was ready downstairs when he got dressed. Then on the drive back, she'd talked about every random subject under the sun from Reagan's administration to climate change to the history of guests that appeared on *Sesame Street*. Every time he'd tried to circle back to their night together, she'd cut him off.

And now that he'd gone back to work, and they'd resumed

living together with even more sexual tension than before, Deepak was losing his mind.

"I have no idea what I'm supposed to do," he said.

"You're supposed to tell her that you want to be with her," Prem replied blandly. "You're supposed to ask her out on a date and tell her that you want to have a real relationship."

Deepak glared at his phone. "You know I can't do that."

"Why not?" Prem asked. "It's obvious that she has feelings, too, if she's still with you after a weekend at your parents' place."

How was he supposed to explain his situation to Prem? Vee's friendship was important to him. If he asked her for more before she wanted more, too, then he'd ruin what they had. More importantly, it was terrifying to think that his growing feelings might not be reciprocated.

Deepak didn't deserve Veera. She'd been kind, and funny, and so patient with him since the moment they met. Even when he'd failed to support her through the merger, she never held it against him like her twin. Now she'd just come back into his life. He couldn't risk losing her again. Not until she was ready.

"I know how Veera will respond," Deepak said. "She has to want this marriage to be a real one and ask me for it, first. If I approach her, she'll just run away."

Prem scrubbed his hands over his face. "Deepak, I think you're overanalyzing this. Remember what you used to tell me when I was on *The Dr. Dil Show*? The simpler the message, the easier it is to connect to an audience. Be straightforward with Veera and tell her how you feel. Assess, address, reevaluate."

That was the worst advice he'd ever heard.

"If she was interested in more, then she wouldn't have pretended that absolutely nothing happened when we woke up in the morning," Deepak said.

"Look, I told you I didn't want details—"

"And I'm not sharing details," Deepak replied. "That's disrespectful to my wife."

"Your *fake* wife," Prem clarified.

"Shut up," Deepak replied. He twisted in his seat so he could lean closer to the screen. "All I'm saying is that this morning, she made me coffee and then waved from her spot on my couch."

"That sounds like something Kareena would do, too," Prem said, a bemused expression on his face. He stroked a hand over his stubble. "I don't know how many times you want me to tell you that you have to stop being a coward and face your feelings."

"Easy for you to say. You literally thought love was a lie, and relationships were built on neurological responses and attraction." His best friend, the cardiologist whose name translated to the word *love*, had been a staunch believer in some wackadoo theory about feelings causing heart problems. That was until he caught feelings himself.

Prem gave him the finger, his wedding band flashing before he delivered the *fuck you* hand gesture. "I'm trying to help you."

Deepak knew that, but he also knew that he was confused, and Veera deserved so much more than his messy, broken spirit.

He heard a ping from his computer and glanced back at his screen to see that Kim had sent him an urgent message.

"Prem, I got to go," he said. Kim rarely sent him urgent messages.

"Good luck, brother," Prem said. "And, no, you are not having a heart attack."

"I'm getting a second opinion," Deepak said, then hung up the call. He spun around in his chair, to read the message more closely.

> **KIM ISHIYAMA:** Your wife is here with your lunch, but she just ran into her father outside your office, and I'm not sure what to do.

> **KIM ISHIYAMA:** Do I leave? This feels intrusive.

> **KIM ISHIYAMA:** Boss, should I hide under my desk or something?

Deepak was up and out of his chair in a heartbeat. He grabbed his suit coat from the back of his seat and shrugged it on by the time he got to his office door.

Since Veera's father was the new chief financial officer of Illyria Media, it was no surprise that he was walking around the executive leadership floor. What was surprising was that Veera was also there and both of them just happened to be in the same place at the same time.

"—I just wanted to help you and your sister."

Malkit Mathur's voice was soft and syrup smooth as he spoke to Veera. His back was to Deepak's door, and over his shoulder, Deepak could see the tense expression on Veera's face. Those three lines formed between her eyebrows. Against the far wall, Kim crouched down next to her desk as if she were picking something up off the floor and got stuck in her hunched position.

"We didn't ask you for your help," Veera said, her voice soft and delicate.

"Of course not," Malkit Mathur replied. His hand made a wide semicircle as he gesticulated. "But as your father, I wanted to make sure that I did what was best by you both. Which is why I helped position you to be the best marriage candidates."

Veera snorted. "By being unemployed? This is not the same generation, the same year that you and Mom got married."

"Oh, don't give me that 'Dad is being sexist' speech again," Malkit Mathur said dismissively. "You don't understand how many sacrifices I made, or how difficult it was to make sure that I took care of you and your sister."

"That's not true," Veera said. Deepak heard the waver in her voice, but he didn't approach them just yet. Waiting from a distance, he watched with pride as Veera continued to stand firm against her father. "Papa, you only made decisions that suited you and the business. You never liked that we were building our own client base, our own methods of working. You never approved. We were paving our own way."

Malkit Mathur tsked at her like he was correcting a child. Deepak fisted his hands at his sides.

"Your sister was paving her own way," Veera's father said. He still spoke in that soft, steady cadence that was subtly condescending. "She was always the risk-taker, the innovative one. But you were wonderful at doing what you were told. I never intended for you to be in the leadership, but it was good for company morale to have someone I could count on to do exactly what I needed and defend my position. To be truthful, I thought Sana would be a good fit for my team in Illyria Media Group because she actually contributed to the company, but she wouldn't accept the position without you. That's why both of you had to go."

There was a long pause, and from his vantage point, Deepak could see the shock and hurt on Veera's face. Then her lips pinched and her chin tilted up in defiance.

"You know what? You did me a favor by firing me. I have never felt happier than I do now without you in my life. You were always the reason why Sana and I never became the leaders we were meant to be."

"Watch your tone with me," her father said. "You're in *my* office, and—"

"No, she's in my office," Deepak said. He stepped forward and waited for Malkit Mathur to turn around.

The older man took his time pivoting on his heels. His expression was a mask of false surprise, followed by a cool smile.

"Deepak," he said, then adjusted his oversize suit coat. "It's nice to see my daughter again, but this time, bringing lunch to her husband. I always told her she'd make a wonderful wife to someone one day. It makes me so proud—"

"She's not here for lunch," Deepak said, cutting off his CFO. "Veera has been consulting for me for almost a year. We're considering different ways to build in equitable finance practices to our business model, and since she's the expert, I wanted to bring her in early."

He turned to meet Veera's gaze, and with a slight tilt of his head, he motioned to his office. "Are you ready to get started?"

Veera nodded as she clutched a brown paper bag against her chest. She didn't look at her father as she said, "Goodbye, Papa," then strode past him. "We have a meeting." She disappeared through Deepak's office doorway.

He was about to follow when Malkit Mathur spoke again. He reached out as if he were trying to grip Deepak's suit coat lapel.

"This is a meeting I should be involved in," he said. "Finance is my division. And I've trained my daughter. I know her methods better than anyone and I can add context to whatever she may be missing. I have the experience."

Deepak shook his head. "I don't think you do, otherwise you

would've seen what an asset she is. I need to work with people who are willing to take risks, at innovating and paving their own way. That is Veera."

He ignored Malkit's stunned expression and returned to his office. After closing the door behind him, he retrieved his phone from his hip pocket and sent Kim a quick message to cancel his next meeting and hold his calls. Then he looked up at his wife.

She stood in the center of the room, bag in hand, tears shimmering on her cheeks, and a fist on one hip.

"Hey," Deepak said softly as he approached her. He felt both a flutter of panic and something more complicated, something harder to identify, when he saw her big, beautiful, shining eyes on the verge of crying. "I'm so sorry that he said those things to you. I'm sorry that he had a chance to talk to you at all."

"I'm only responding this way because I'm mad," she said. Then she put the paper bag on top of Deepak's desk, covering the latest draft of the shareholder year-end reports. With quick, jerky movements, she used the sleeves of her cardigan to dry her face. "Deeps, why is my father such a prick? More importantly, why haven't you forced him into retirement yet?"

Deepak wished he had an understandable answer for her. Instead, he told her the truth. "With his presence, we limited turnover on the Mathur Financial Group side of the business." He wanted to be near to her, so he curled his fingers under her bicep to tug her close. "I'm still sorry," he said and then kissed the crown of her head when she leaned into his embrace.

"We always had a complicated relationship," Veera whispered as she burrowed against Deepak's shoulder and gripped the fabric of his shirt at his lower back. The pressure of her breasts flush against his chest, her electric fingerprints on his skin, reminded him of the night they spent together.

"I really do appreciate the save, Deeps."

"No problem." They stood like that for another moment, holding each other. Deepak inhaled the sweet kiwi scent of her hair, felt the softness of her ponytail curls brushing his fingertips as he stroked her back. He could feel her relaxing degree by degree.

When she pulled away, she was smiling again. "Wow," she said with a deep breath. "Daddy issues by noon. What a way to start a Thursday."

"Since my father is my boss, I have daddy issues every day," Deepak said. Then he cleared his throat and reached for the bag to open it. He almost sighed in pleasure when he retrieved the creamy Thai green curry with chicken. It was their standing lunch order when they used to meet in the middle of the workweek.

"Truthfully, I do want to talk about work," Veera said. As proof of her resilience, she fanned her face with the palm of her hand to dry the rest of her tears, then picked up the utensil packets he'd handed to her while he popped the lids of the containers. "I received a call from Margaret Thakur. We met for coffee this morning."

"Margaret?" Deepak said, as he set her curry in front of her. "From the board?"

Veera nodded. "She was a big supporter of equitable lending when she worked with my father. She heard through the grapevine that you and I are putting together this equitable lending pitch and she wanted to help."

"That's great!" Deepak said. "The more support we have early, the easier it'll be to get it approved and set aside a budget for it." Even though they were using her equitable lending plan as part of their relationship story, he really wanted her to explore whatever career opportunities excited her, and if bringing her proposal to fruition was it, then he would make whatever call, give her whatever resources, she needed.

"There's more," Veera said. She sat in one of the guest chairs opposite his desk. "Before we ended our chat, Margaret told me the board is struggling finding someone for the CEO position because there really is no one else who is qualified the way you are."

Deepak turned to Veera and smiled. "That's amazing," he said. The information was surprising, and he appreciated that she was able to find it for him, but the mention of the board, of his position as CEO, felt like a diversion. It felt like she wanted to re-shift the focus back on him, when moments before, her father had made her cry, and she'd been discussing plans for her equitable lending pitch. He wanted to know more about what made her happy. That was what was important to him right now.

"Amazing? That's better than amazing," Veera said. Then she nudged his knee. "Why aren't you happier about the news?"

"Because I'm still focused on you," he admitted. "I'm still worried about you."

She shook her head, even though the corner of her mouth tilted downward in a half frown. "I'm fine. I promise. I told you; my father and I have always had a complicated relationship."

He hated how quickly she brushed it aside. If he and his father were at odds like that, he wouldn't know what to do. It just went to show how strong Veera was to both grieve family relationships and move on at the same time.

"I still reserve the right to fight him if you want me to."

"Sexist," she said, "but I appreciate you asking first."

"You're welcome," he said. He sat in the chair next to her and used the edge of his desk the same way he used to when they were friends. Colleagues. Their knees bumped companionably, and her bright sunny smile returned as she separated her chopsticks and then rubbed them together to remove any rough edges.

"I'm so glad you stopped by for lunch," he said. "Now tell me more about your Margaret meeting. She's a hard one to read."

Veera took her first mouthful of rice, shrimp, and green curry. "Margaret doesn't want the bottom line. She wants a story. If you're going to sell her on something, make it personal."

"I'll say it again," Deepak said. "Your father was an absolute fool for letting you go."

VEERA: Sana, did Dad tell you that he was firing me, and keeping you on?

SANA: Where did you hear that?

VEERA: Dad told me. Is it true?

SANA: Why are you talking to Dad?

VEERA: I ran into him at Deepak's office. Just answer the question.

VEERA: Please.

SANA: Fine. He said that he may keep me on for the global markets, but I told him hell no if you won't be there.

SANA: I didn't want to tell you because I know he was being an asshole, and he would've probably fired me anyway.

SANA: Please don't be mad.

VEERA: Too late. I'm big mad. You should've told me! What else aren't you telling me?

SANA: Come on, you know that I only want to protect you. I'm the older sister.

VEERA: Don't start that nonsense. And I can protect myself.

Video from Olivia Gupta's website:

Hi guys. By now I'm sure you've heard that my former fiancé, Deepak Datta, married his longtime friend and former business colleague. This video is not about her, because women support women, babes.

This video is about Deepak. How ruthless do you have to be to do that to two women? To lead me along like that, then deprive the other of romance and appreciation?

I have a lot of thoughts, but right now I refuse to talk to any man who crosses my path. I'm on a man hiatus! Screw men.

Let me know in the comments what your thoughts are about this mess. Oh, and check out my blush. Superpigmented, right? It's part of my new collection, and it's giving drama queen. Don't you think?

CHAPTER 17

Deepak

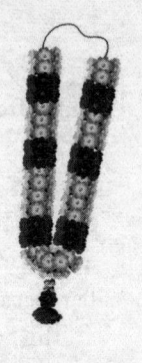

> **DEEPAK:** Hey, any word on Olivia?

> **SANA:** What's the hurry? You still have two months before the board meeting. Do you still have feelings for her?

> **DEEPAK:** Whoa, whoa, whoa. I'm just checking in because I haven't heard from her since the breakup.

> **SANA:** Sorry. It's complicated. I'll share what I can soon.

Deepak swiped past headlines and the financial news on his tablet at his kitchen island, while he remained completely attuned to the sound of Veera upstairs. He was pretty sure that living with her was going to be the death of him. Every time she walked past him in the kitchen or the dining room, he tensed until he felt like his bones would crack. The temptation of her delicious skin, of the way she smelled of floral shampoo and soap, of the delicate clink of her wedding bangles and the way she twisted her rings aroused him to the point where he was masturbating in the shower every morning, and sometimes at night.

He was thirty-five years old, and somehow his hormones did not get the message.

Even though it was the weekend, Deepak should go into work. He still had quarterly reports to finish. A part of him wanted to suffer, though, and stay at the house where he'd have the opportunity to spend time with his wife. Even if she wasn't willing to talk to him about their sexy moment the weekend before, he'd be happy just to look at her.

He heard the footsteps on the stairs a moment later and pretended to read the same article he'd been staring at for the last fifteen minutes.

"Hi," Veera grumbled as she entered the room. The faded Columbia sweatshirt she wore made him smile, but that quickly changed when he noticed the way she was stomping over to the coffee machine to get a mug. The way her hands clenched around the handle, the strain lines around her mouth had him putting the tablet down.

"Uh-oh. What happened?"

"What?" she asked, as she turned to face him. Her thick, shining hair swung down her back in loose curls and settled around her shoulders. "What makes you think something happened?"

"Your face," he said. "Your face is telling me something happened."

She scowled. "It is not."

"It is," he replied. "And you're stalling."

Veera glared at him, then put the cup down. Her lower lip trembled. "I got a text from Sana," she said. Then she cleared her throat. "Apparently, my father *had* offered her a position at Illyria Media Group on his team. She didn't take it because she refused to work for him if I didn't, too."

"Vee, I'm so sorry," Deepak said, as he climbed off his chair. He wasn't sure if he should hug her again when they weren't in the safe space of his office with Kim right outside the door and his parents down the hall.

Veera surprised him by making the decision for him, and wrapped her arms around his waist, seeking comfort from him the same way she had when she'd run into her father earlier that week. Her hands fisted against the small of his back as he leaned his cheek against her temple.

She smelled deliciously like Vee and he brushed at her sweet-smelling air.

"I hate how mad this made me," she said muffled against his shirt. "Sana loved fighting with people. That's in her DNA. But I hated pushing clients. Dad always thought that was my biggest weakness."

Deepak nuzzled her temple, feeling the tendrils of hair catch in his beard. "I know that you've come to terms with the relationship you have with your father, but that doesn't mean his words don't affect you. Sometimes the people we love can hurt us the most."

She was quiet for a long moment. "That's what I'm afraid of," she said softly.

Veera pulled away and adjusted her sweatshirt. His sweatshirt. "Thanks," she said. "But I'll be fine. I know I'll be fine."

She reached for the coffee mug again.

"Wait," he said. "Why don't we go out for coffee?"

Veera dropped her hand. "Go out for coffee? Why?"

I want to spend time with you. I want to hold your hand, tell people you're my wife, and watch you twist that diamond ring you always wear even if we're just hanging around the house. I want to look at your beautiful face across a table.

Deepak shrugged. "It's Saturday, and we should take a break. There is this bakery on the next block where the barista does latte art."

"Latte art?" Veera tapped her fingertips together like an evil genius plotting their next takeover. "What kind of latte art?"

"The kind where the barista does it with a jug of steamed milk. Not the latte art that requires a machine or a little stencil with cinnamon."

Veera wrinkled her nose. "That's not real art."

"That's why you should try this café with me."

Veera looked down at her hoodie and jeans. Then she eyed his shirt and slacks. "Do I have to change?"

"No, you look beautiful."

She flushed.

"Come on," he said, as he picked up his phone. "Live dangerously."

"Fine," she said. "But I am trusting you that I will be getting good latte art."

THE STOREFRONT HAD a dark blue canopy with scalloped edges, white font in script, and a tower of macarons in the window display. Deepak held open the door for Veera as they walked into the small shop with black-and-white-checkered tiled floors, and bistro tables lining the windows and the wall. The display case was overflowing with breads, scones, croissants, cakes, cookies, tarts. Two brass espresso machines sat against the wall behind the counter, surrounded by various syrup pumps and stacks of wide-mouthed coffee mugs.

"This is amazing," Veera said.

"The desserts are great, too," Deepak replied.

They waited until it was their turn to order at the counter.

"What are you going to get?" she asked when they reached the front of the line.

"I'll just have a black coffee."

Veera's eyebrows shot up to her hairline.

"What?"

"Black coffee?" she said. "You're in a bakery, Deepak, not your office kitchen."

"It's really good black coffee," he replied.

Veera shook her head. She leaned against the counter and smiled at the petite French woman who was now ready to take their order. "Hi! We'll get a black coffee, a vanilla latte, a croissant, and a blueberry scone."

Deepak glanced back at Veera. A blueberry scone was his favorite. His mouth was watering at the thought of that crumbly sweet texture on his tongue. He just hadn't eaten one in a while because it had been some time since he'd made it to his gym. He had to pass Veera's room to work out.

Before he could move to pay, she'd whipped out her card and tapped it against the machine.

"Veera," he said in his most aggrieved tone. "How am I supposed to be the doting husband if I can't even buy your coffee?"

She snorted. "I'm sure you'll figure it out."

Thankfully, Veera's back was turned, and she was walking toward one of the empty bistro tables against the window when she spoke. If she had seen his face, then she'd have known exactly what he was thinking.

She hadn't corrected him and called him her fake husband.

Deepak needed a moment to collect himself since her casual acceptance of their relationship rushed through his veins, flooding his brain with euphoria. He walked over to the pickup window and waited for their drinks and dessert. The tray arrived a moment later, and he carried it to the seating area opposite the order counter and placed it on a small, round bistro table in front of Veera.

She looked so happy when she saw the image of the rose on her latte. The sun shone through the window and kissed the curve of her cheeks. Her messy topknot drooped to one side, and her knees pressed against the insides of his thighs as he sat across from her. Her ring sparkled when she adjusted the mug for a picture.

Deepak couldn't deal with the sexual tension any longer. He kept thinking about the night at his parents' house, and how desperately he wanted a redo.

"Vee? We need to talk," he said.

She looked up from her phone that hovered inches above her mug. "Oh? About what?"

He slipped the device from her hand, so she didn't drop it into their drinks. "About last weekend," he said.

Veera's legs jerked against his, and he pressed his knees together, holding her captive, so she didn't bolt.

"What do we have to talk about? I thought your parents liked me."

Deepak shook his head. She was so easy to read, he thought. "You know what it's about. I want to know if you were okay with what we did. I didn't hurt you, or—"

"Oh, is that why you're worried?" She let out a deep breath. "No, you didn't hurt me. We can just—"

"I don't want to forget about it," he said. His heart was pounding so hard that he made a mental note to talk to Prem again about a doctor's appointment. "I don't want to forget."

Veera gaped. She glanced around the café, at the two tables nearby with patrons in conversations of their own. Then she cupped her mug. When her hands trembled, she reached for the croissant again and tore off a large piece.

Deepak knew that this was probably the worst-case scenario. She was rejecting him.

"Never mind, if you don't want to—"

"I do," she said. Her jaw clenched and he saw the muscles in her throat flex as she swallowed hard. "Deepak, I don't know if we should complicate our lives even more than they already are."

She was so damn beautiful with sunbeams on her face. Deepak knew he couldn't go back to just friendship when now he was seeing her as the most stunningly brilliant part of his life.

"This is not complicated," he said softly.

Veera shook her head. "No, sex is always complicated."

They sat in silence, staring at the scone and croissant on small saucers rimmed in a blue paisley design. There were so many things he wanted to tell her, so many regrets he had about wasted time they could've spent together.

Then Veera picked up the scone and moved it forward so that it sat on his side of the tray. "Here," she said. "I ordered too much. You should eat this."

She'd ordered the scone for him. How did she know that he liked blueberry? He'd never eaten a blueberry scone in front of her before.

Deepak stood from his chair and leaned over the table. He touched her cheek with his free hand and waited until her lips parted in surprise before he pressed a kiss against her upturned mouth. It was firm and hot, filled with all the pent-up frustration he'd been holding back. The taste of her was every bit as delicious as a delicate French pastry, he thought as his tongue slowly tangled with hers. He pulled away, scraping his teeth along her plump lower lip, aching for this woman that he wanted to belong to him in every way.

When he sat back, he had the satisfaction of hearing her shuddering breath. Deepak tore off a corner of the blueberry scone, then picked up his coffee. He waited for her to do the same with her latte and croissant before he spoke.

"I'll wait to talk about this more when you're ready."

"O-okay."

"Okay. So how is the reception planning going with Bobbi?"

CHAPTER 18

Deepak

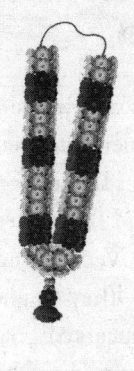

Text messages from one year and four months ago:

> **DEEPAK:** Look, if you steel my Columbia grad sweatshirts every time you sleep over after a movie marathon, I'm literally going to run out of all my favorite ones.

> **VEERA:** Oh no! The bazillionaire is without a sweatshirt!

> **DEEPAK:** LOL. Shut up.

The wedding reception was the distraction Deepak and Veera needed. It had been a few weeks since the visit to his parents' estate, and the feel of Veera's orgasm and their café kiss was like a hazy fantasy that kept Deepak up at night. With the way that Vee grumbled at him every morning, he knew that she was having a few sleepless nights of her own.

Now their party and first major public appearance as a couple had arrived, which meant that they would most likely have a legitimate reason to kiss again.

Deepak looked forward to it as he slipped his diamond cuff links through the small holes of his French cuff button-down and straightened the lines of his three-piece suit. It was in a monochrome jet-black color that matched the shade of his styled thick black hair.

His mother had sent the suit over a few days ago while Bobbi had forwarded a to-do list in a spreadsheet that required two Tylenol to understand.

Deepak glanced in the mirror long enough to confirm that he looked presentable for pictures and his family's expectations. He adjusted his thin gold wedding band, checked the time on his grandfather's watch, and when he saw that they were going to be late if they didn't leave soon, he walked out of his suite and into the stairwell. "Vee? We have ten minutes before the car gets here."

"Just go ahead without me," the muffled reply called back.

Okay, he should probably tell his driver they needed another ten. He sighed, then began climbing the stairs to the guest bedroom floor. He turned left at the top of the stairs and knocked on the door at the end of the hall.

"Vee?"

"I'm decent," came the irritated reply.

When he entered the room, he saw that she was standing in the middle of her chaotic clutter in a state of delicious undress. Her deep maroon blouse with gold detail at the cap sleeves, hem, and neckline was barely fastened at the center of her back. The long tassels that were supposed to secure the blouse in place were opened and fell in long thin ropes to her waist. She wore a voluminous purple-and-red lehenga that was unbuttoned at the hip, and her phone played a YouTube video of a woman trying to fold pleats into a dupatta.

"Uh-oh," Deepak said.

"Uh-oh is right!" Veera replied, as she held up the heavily embroidered fabric in one fist. He realized that she was wearing makeup again. Her face was artfully painted in the same way she'd looked during their staged wedding photos, except somehow, her lashes were now thicker. They fluttered with irritation. There was also a simple round bindi in the middle of her forehead, and her hair was in a loose braid draped over one shoulder.

"What exactly is happening?" he asked.

"I'm supposed to wear this dupatta a specific way and pin it in place, but this is way more complicated than a damn sari," she said in a rush. "My mother used to do this for me when I was younger. Then, I just stopped wearing complicated duputtas."

"As the bride, you have to wrestle with all that fabric, huh?" he asked. He stepped farther into the room and nudged aside a pair of heels that she'd discarded next to the doorway.

"Thank you, Captain Obvious." She tugged at the hem of her blouse to try and cover the small strip of exposed belly skin. He was tempted to reach out and brush his fingers against the soft rich brown color of her abdomen, but he gritted his teeth and focused on the task at hand.

"Do you have something else you can wear?"

Her eyes were bright now with panic. "My mother sent this over for me. She wanted me to wear it, and it's going to be the first time I see her in person since we're back. I've talked to her over the year, but this is going to be different, and I want to make her . . . I want to wear this."

"Ahh," Deepak said, aware that his sound of understanding was probably the most unhelpful response he could give her at that moment. "What can I do?"

"I don't know," she said, her voice beginning to waver.

He'd never met a woman who had an immediate cry response at stress the way Veera did. It was both endearing and panic inducing at the same time. Right now, she was beautiful, and half naked, and he wanted to tell her to strip out of the lehenga and to lie with him.

Which was not a helpful recommendation in the slightest.

Deepak reached for her phone and reset the video from the beginning. He watched as the woman began rapidly pleating the dupatta. The movements were familiar, since he remembered as a child watching his grandmother do the same thing to her chunni right before she left the house. Using her index finger and middle finger, the instructor on the screen pinched the fabric back and forth until it resembled a folding fan.

"Okay, let's do this together," he replied. Then he shrugged out of his suit coat and draped it over the foot of the unmade bed.

He had every intention of behaving himself, of helping her into the outfit, then ushering her into his car, so they could head out to the venue with more than enough time to spare.

But when he stood in front of her to remove the dupatta from her shoulder, she stopped him with a hand on his wrist.

"What is it?"

Veera shook her head, pressed her hands against his chest and leaned into him. Deepak's hands went to her waist, and he felt the soft skin of her exposed hip where the lehenga skirt still needed to be tied.

"Veera?"

"I feel like I'm going to be the runaway wife," she said, as she sucked in air in one hard gulp. "If this was a business meeting, I'd have no trouble at all. But our extended family is going to be there. The entire board. Some of my coworkers I haven't seen since I was let go from the business."

He stroked a hand over her naked back, and his fingers brushed against the barely secured clasp at her shoulder blades. One soft nudge, and it would come undone.

"It's going to be fine," he said. Then he leaned down and pressed a soft kiss to her collarbone, so that he didn't disturb her makeup. "It's going to be okay."

"I-I need . . ."

"What? What is it?"

She let out a shuddered breath. "I'm sorry, it's ridiculous. I'm tense and we haven't talked about it since the café."

"Talked about what?"

Her lashes fluttered again, and the ruby-red painted lips parted with a soft sigh. "What if we need . . ."

That's when it registered what she was asking for. She needed release, and he was the one who could give it to her. His cock swelled, and his fingertips tucked into the waistband of her lehenga. They moved impossibly closer until her breasts brushed against his chest. With every intake of breath her nipples scraped gently over his upper abdomen.

"What do you need?" he whispered.

He could see the color deepen in her cheeks. She averted her eyes, but he pinched her chin and tilted her head up, so she met his gaze.

"Help me, Deepak."

His fingertips unhooked her blouse at her back, and fabric loosened over her shoulders, her breasts were a careless tug away from being exposed.

"Sit on your bed," he said.

With their eyes locked, she followed instructions and lowered to the edge of her mattress. He got to his knees in front of her. "I need you to lie back, Vee."

Without hesitation, she did what he asked. He could see the underside of her bare breasts from this vantage point, her nipples concealed by her loose blouse. Then he slid his hands under her lehenga, and careful to make sure there would be no wrinkles, he folded the fabric back until it pooled at her waist. When she gave him a barely perceptible nod, he bent her legs to rest her heels on the edge of the bed.

She wore payal. The anklets had a tiny cluster of bells that chimed gently when he touched them. His fingertips brushed over her exposed skin, sliding down the insides of her thighs, relishing her trembling anticipation, before touching the crotch of her black lace panties, which were now fully exposed. A damp spot formed between her lips, and he stroked a fingertip down the transparent fabric.

Veera moaned and her knees fell open a little farther.

"You're aching for me, aren't you, wife?" Deepak said softly, and he felt her tremble when he pressed a kiss to her inner thigh. "You're wound so tight."

"Deepak," she said, breathlessly.

He folded up the sleeves of his dress shirt, then he picked up her phone and set a timer. They only had five minutes otherwise they'd be late, but that would be enough. He tossed the phone next to her on the bed so he could see the digits as they began to count down.

Deepak gripped the waistband of her panties and tugged them off. He carefully removed his tie and tossed it next to her panties before repositioning her legs exactly the way he wanted them.

In the bright lights of her room, he could see her plump labia, and the delicious wetness of her sweet pussy. He was starving, and he wanted to eat her up.

Draping her legs over his shoulders, he started at the side of her knee, trailing kisses until he reached the swollen heat of her and gave her one hard, long lick.

Veera gasped, moaning his name. Her fingers dove into his hair as he circled her clit with the tip of his tongue and sucked hard and fast. Then holding her thighs in place, he feasted on her every tremble, every gasp, every quiver as he drank her pleasure and her cries. He felt her tense impossibly harder, then slipped two fingers inside, curling up as he relentlessly focused on the delicate places that made her scream.

He watched her over the curve of her mound, over the bunched fabric of her lehenga, as she exposed her breasts, and her fingertips squeezed her dark, peaked nipples. He heard the chime of her anklet as her feet bounced against his back with every rolling thrust of her hips against his mouth. And then when her body was wound so tight, so impossibly tense, he pushed a third finger inside of her, and, fucking her with deep strokes, he flicked her clit then blew gently on her swollen skin.

Veera screamed so loud that he was sure the neighboring town house could hear as her orgasm crashed through her body, and she shuddered as she flooded his fingertips. He almost came in his pants at the feel of her clenching. Her pleasure was a precious gift and he'd been blessed to savor it on his tongue.

They were both breathing heavily when the timer went off.

Deepak slipped her legs off his shoulders, got to his feet, and walked into the adjoining bath to run warm water over a hand towel he retrieved from the lower cabinet. She was still gasping for air when he returned, her legs spread wide, her lehenga still pooled around her waist. The blouse that had come undone had been gently moved in place to cover her nipples, but Veera's eyes remained closed.

He carefully wiped away the remnants of her orgasm and

folded the towel before he set it aside. Then Deepak gripped her hands and pulled her up to a seated position.

"Are you all right?" he said softly.

She nodded, her expression drowsy, and sweetly sated. Then she motioned to the tent in his pants. "What about—"

He ran a thumb over the curve of her jaw and tilted her face up to his. "One day, I want to fuck your mouth," he said. "But right now, we're running late to our own wedding reception. We should go. I'll be fine."

The crudeness of his words had her eyes opening and her hands holding the blouse over her breasts. "Deepak," she said.

"I know," he said. "Let's get going." He helped her to her feet and turned her around so he could fasten her blouse.

Her body was relaxed and pliant as he turned her left and right to adjust her lehenga skirt, then tied it at her hip. Deepak played the YouTube video tutorial again to watch how to pleat her dupatta, and he was able to quickly make the folds. She held it to her shoulder as he pinned it in place, then draped it behind her back and into the waistband of her lehenga where he fastened another pin.

Neither of them spoke as they finished getting dressed. Veera retrieved another pair of panties from the dresser and stepped into them, and he folded down his sleeves and refastened his tie.

As she retrieved her juttis, he saw the set of baliyan earrings on the dresser and picked one up. He unscrewed the backing and moved to Veera's side. While she began to fuss with her lipstick, he slipped the post in her earlobe and screwed on the backing. Because he couldn't help it, he flicked the small dangling umbrella so the earring let out a musical tinkle sound.

Veera smiled but didn't comment as he reached for the second earring and did the same. Then he picked up her mangalsutra, the diamond pendant he'd bought from Goa on the gold-and-black beaded chain. A symbol of their spiritual marriage and commitment to each other. He stepped around her so that he could loop the necklace over her head and fasten it at the nape of her neck. When he looked over her head at their image in the mirrors, he saw the way the top of her head reached his shoulder blade. The glitter of her bangles on her wrist, and the ring on her finger that said she belonged with him.

Veera was stunning and he'd work every day of his life making up for the time he didn't appreciate her. He'd do his damnedest to show her that he felt so lucky to have her in his life. And if he was successful, maybe he'd convince her that they were good enough for the long haul.

Indians Abroad News

Although I, Mrs. W. S. Gupta, wasn't invited to the exclusive reception for Deepak and his wife, Veera Mathur, rumor has it that Deepak and Veera put on a show. Take note, parents. This is how you convince an entire community that a match was a love marriage.

Mrs. W. S. Gupta
Avon, New Jersey

CHAPTER 19

Veera

Text messages from one year and two months ago:

VEERA: Hey, your parents are here.

DEEPAK: What? Where?

VEERA: At my father's office. They hit it off at the charity event a few weeks ago so maybe they are working on a fundraiser?

DEEPAK: No clue. Let me know if you find out?

VEERA: Yeah, and let me know if you hear anything

DEEPAK: Will do. I'll see you at Prem and Kareena's wedding.

VEERA: Wait, don't we have dinner plans before then?

DEEPAK: I'm sorry, I have to cancel. Work thing came up.

VEERA: Oh, okay. No problem. Talk to you later.

Veera stood in the small office space in the back of Rani's, Benjamin's new luxury dining restaurant, and waited patiently while Bobbi and Kareena fussed over her.

"Are you serious about Deepak being the one who tied your dupatta?" Bobbi asked, as she double checked the pin at her shoulder. "He did a phenomenal job."

"He did," Veera said quietly as she wore the gold bangles, the Datta women's heirlooms, which one day she'd have to give back. She watched the inlaid diamonds sparkle and match the glitter of her wedding rings in the low overhead lighting.

She debated telling them exactly how helpful he'd been. Her friends had always been honest with her about their romances, and she could only do the same. She knew that she'd hurt them when she left, even though they'd been busy with their own lives. There would be some space between them now that they were partnered, but these women would always be important to her.

"What if I told you," she started slowly, "that Deepak kissed me?"

Bobbi and Kareena looked at each other, then back at Veera.

"What kind of kissing," Bobbi said, "the kind to impress a board member, or the kind that impressed you?"

"The kind that was not exactly on my mouth," Veera said slowly.

This time she saw the wide-eyed shock on Kareena's and Bobbi's faces.

"How do you feel?" Kareena said slowly. She hovered at Veera's side, as if she were standing guard just in case Veera stumbled to her feet and needed someone to pick her up.

"I have no idea what we're doing," Veera replied. She tugged on the end of her braid, then stopped when Bobbi pushed her hands aside, so she didn't loosen her hairpins. "Things are getting out of hand, and now we're not only lying to our community, but we're lying to ourselves."

"You have to talk to him," Kareena said, as she ran a hand over Veera's shoulder. "You know that, right?"

"Not yet," she said, turning to look at Bobbi, then Kareena. "I know we have to, but maybe we can just wait until after the board vote. Until after Deepak gets the position he wants, and I get the job that I've been working hard for. I'm excited about a project after so long, and I don't want to lose that yet."

There was that shared look that her friends had again, the one that meant they were having a completely separate conversation without her.

"Why don't we put Deepak out of your mind for now?" Kareena said. She rested her hand on Veera's shoulder before meeting Veera's eyes in the standing mirror that was set up for them in Bunty's office. Her bindi, the same one Veera and Bobbi wore, winked in the overhead light. "Let's focus on the wedding reception. Is there anything you need us to do before we go out there?"

Working a room of business associates was something Veera could handle. She didn't need her friends for that. It's just that not all of them were business associates . . .

"Other than Deepak, my biggest concern is seeing my mother again," Veera finally said, as she covered Kareena's hand with hers, then looked over at Bobbi.

When her father had fired her, Namrata Mathur had made every excuse under the sun for his behavior. She'd always been Veera's staunchest supporter, but for some reason, she'd sided with her father when Veera had been fired.

"Honey, it's too late to uninvite her," Bobbi said.

The three of them stood as a unit, staring at their reflection. Veera could remember the days when they'd all posed in front of a similar mirror before weekend brunches in college. She wished she'd appreciated those moments more when she'd had them.

"If I can't uninvite my problems, then let's just get this over with," she said with a sigh. "I have to face my mother sooner or later, and she's ridiculously punctual. Indian standard time does not exist for her. Once our reunion is finished, I can work my way through the rest of this party."

"You and Deepak have your stories straight?" Bobbi asked.

"You mean our lies?" Veera said. She adjusted her dupatta one last time and straightened her shoulders. "I can't believe that I've become this fraud. Did you know, I pay my taxes early? I have never even gotten a parking ticket in my life. And now, I'm fooling so many people."

Bobbi gripped her arms and positioned her so she could look Veera directly in the face. "You are not a fraud, honey. You are celebrating a real wedding that happened."

"That's a nicer way of looking at it than conning everyone by celebrating a fake marriage."

"Okay, enough procrastinating," Kareena added. "It's showtime." She straightened her flowing lehenga, a bright outfit in colorful prints with a sophisticated design down the front. It matched Bobbi's outfit, which was cut slightly differently but had matching patterns.

They were slightly altered bridesmaids' outfits from Kareena's wedding.

Bobbi opened the door and gave Veera one hard nudge until they were all walking like a unit into the restaurant's dining area.

"It's show time."

Rani's was different from Benjamin's other restaurants. The large space had a domed ceiling with crystal chandeliers that sparkled. The walls were mirrored and hundreds of twinkle lights lined the molding and the walls. The curved bar in the far corner was made of glass and mirror with batik artwork and a pale sandstone backdrop. The tablecloths were cobalt blue with floral sculptures reaching six feet off the table. Waitstaff carried copper trays piled high with appetizers. In the corner, a trio of musicians sat on thick jewel-toned cushions, and with classic Indian instruments, played Bollywood music from a nineties movie her mother used to love when Veera and Sana were children.

In the front of the room was a sweetheart table with a four-tier cake decorated in swirling mehndi designs. The top tier was a mango mousse in honor of their Goan wedding.

Veera smiled at the tropical tribute.

Wish you were here by my side, Sana.

She'd tried to talk to her sister before the reception, but her text messages had gone unanswered.

There was already a crowd of guests milling around in clusters. They smiled in Veera's direction when she walked in. Some were familiar, some were new. She lifted a finger and pressed it over the tiny jewel bindi she'd stuck between her eyebrows to secure it in place, then scanned the room to look for Deepak.

She spotted him right away, standing in the corner with Prem and Benjamin.

His eyes met hers, and like they were in sync again, they gravitated toward each other. When they were less than two feet apart, he reached for her, and she slipped her hand into his. They locked their fingers together. Her continent-size diamond ring glinted the same way the gold band on his left hand was like a beacon.

"Ready?" he asked.

"As I'll ever be," she replied. And swallowed the nauseous feeling of guilt.

As if their words had been put on blast across the restaurant, a line began to form of guests wanting to say hello to the newly married couple. They stood side by side as they accepted congratulations from family friends, members of the community, and business colleagues.

We all knew that you two were meant to be.

It would've saved your parents so much money if you had just admitted how perfect you are together and gotten engaged first.

That poor Olivia. We knew that she never had a chance. Was she invited here?

Veera, your father did the right thing, forcing you to retire. You two can now start your family.

Deepak, what is the secret to getting two beautiful women to agree to marry you? Glad you went with this one. You both always looked like the perfect couple.

Hey, it is open bar, right?

Veera gritted her teeth as she accepted backhanded compliments, posed for pictures, shook hands, and bent down to respectfully touch the feet of her elders, waiting for their blessings.

She saw the tension lines forming around Deepak's mouth out of the corner of her eye and knew that even though he was shaking hands with everyone, he was probably thinking the same thing that was running through her mind.

Would he get married again to the appropriate Mrs. CEO spouse after they were finished?

Would these same colleagues give more of those pretty jeweled cash envelopes with paisley stamps on them as a gift?

Veera had just finished posing for a picture when a familiar woman stepped in front of her line of sight. She was the last one in the receiving line, and looking at her was like looking in a mirror and seeing herself twenty years in the future.

Namrata Mathur was a force. She had chaired multiple South

Asian fundraising and organization initiatives in her time as wife of the Mathur Financial Group's CEO, and she'd raised Sana and Veera with strict love, without the help of nannies or housekeepers like so many of her friends. Now, she was here in the receiving line, proudly standing by herself without her husband at her side.

Even though she wasn't cohosting the party the way that everyone probably expected, she still looked like the mother of the bride in her sequined silver column gown.

"You look so beautiful," Namrata said, her eyes shining with tears.

Veera could feel her own eyes brimming and, on their own volition, her arms opened. The older woman immediately stepped into the embrace. The familiar sent of Chanel enveloped her, and those tight arms squeezed as if Veera was the only person in the room.

Veera *loved* her mother with every part of her, but that didn't stop her from hurting. From wanting something more.

Then, like a pebble in a slingshot, she was snapped back to reality when her mother began fussing with her hair and clothes. "Your lipstick is such a dark color, Veera. Next time, wear something a bit brighter so your skin can glow. You and Deepak should've come to see me the minute you landed. There are poojas to do, you know. Instead, I get a call from Bobbi, and a string of texts from you. Can you imagine how that makes your father and I look?"

"There she is," Veera said with a smile.

As if Namrata Mathur had run out of steam, she sighed, and adjusted Veera's dupatta. "I wish your sister was here, too. Everyone keeps talking about some assignment she's doing. As if that is more important than celebrating your reception."

"Well, she was at the wedding," Veera said.

She winced when she saw her mother's crestfallen expression. "Mama, I'm sorry, I—"

"No, you were always doing your own thing," she said with a flick of her wrist. Her silver bangles chimed. "Marching to the beat of your own tabla, as they say."

"I don't think anyone says tabla, but I get it," Veera replied. She pulled her mother close for another hug, and the rough texture of sequins, the stiff fabric pinned into place was a familiar comfort that she remembered from childhood. With her lips against her mother's ear, she whispered, "I wish you'd been there, too."

They separated to the sound of her mother's sniffle barely audible over the instrumental music and the hum of laughter from neighboring tables.

"Mama, why don't you go sit with Deepak's parents? We'll have Deepak's father give a speech soon, then we'll do the first dance and cut the cake."

Veera's mother nodded and patted her cheek. "Good. I have to go talk to Seema first. That witch is spreading all sorts of rumors about why your father and sister aren't present. I'm going to give her a piece of my mind."

Without another word, she was off in a flurry of sparking jewel tones and Deepak and Veera were alone for the first time since they started the receiving line.

"If we had done this the right way," Deepak said, turning her so she faced him, "we would've probably danced our way out to some incredibly cheesy song and missed the whole receiving line in the first place," Deepak said ruefully. "I'm sorry; I know that wasn't your favorite experience."

"It's fine," she said. She smiled at a guest who passed by with drinks in each hand before she looked back at Deepak. If she could get a short break, she would be able to shore up her carefully constructed facade. If she didn't, then there was a chance sarcastic Veera would come out and feelings would get hurt.

"Any chance you can buy me ten minutes? I just need to not look at people for a moment."

"Yeah, of course," he said.

He glanced over her shoulder and scanned their audience. Because he looked like he was trying to decide the appropriate way to let her go while a crowd of people had their eyes trained on them, Veera stood on her toes and pressed a soft kiss against his jaw. Using the pad of her thumb, she brushed the faint lipstick mark away. The intimate gesture had been more for herself, but it didn't hurt that it sold their image, too.

She turned on her heels and crossed the room. When Veera met Bobbi's eyes, she held up two fingers, and Bobbi motioned to the back hall and mouthed the word *office*.

Walking through a crowded wedding reception was like walking through an auntie landmine. It took her ten minutes, but every time she passed a group of older women, she mentioned that she had to fix her dupatta, which hurried conversations.

She was grateful for the silence when she finally entered Bunty's office and closed the door behind her.

There was a jhoola set up in the corner past the standing mirror that she'd admired when she'd first arrived at the restaurant. Bobbi had mentioned that she wanted the ornate daybed swing to be a featured seating spot in the dining room, but there wasn't enough space after Deepak's parents added an extra twenty guests to the list.

That was fine by her, she thought. She loved having the jhoola to herself. She'd use it during a few minutes of reprieve. People-ing was exhausting.

Veera hiked up her lehenga to midthigh and climbed on top of the swing. Then she crossed her legs and covered her knees with her skirt.

The seat began to sway in a gentle rhythm that had her sighing in pleasure. Just as she closed her eyes, the office door creaked open, and a small head framed by a riot of curls popped through the opening.

There were a few children at the reception, but Veera had no idea who any of them were or who they belonged to. So she did what any normal adult would do in her situation.

She waved.

A small hand appeared and waved back.

"Are you hiding?" the tiny voice said.

"Yup," she replied.

"Can I hide with you?"

Veera shrugged. "Sure, but it'll cost you."

The head bobbed up and down. "Like money?"

Veera shook her head. Then, as if on command her stomach rumbled. She pressed a palm to her abdomen. "Got any food?"

The small little face lit up, then disappeared.

She shrugged. Maybe the fee was too high for the kid.

A few minutes later, when she was sure that she had pulled herself together enough to go back out in the crowd, the door opened again.

This time, the curly-haired kid was holding a wide plate filled with an eclectic array of desserts. He stepped inside the room, and Veera finally got a look at his outfit. He had on pleated black pants, shiny black shoes, a white button-down shirt, and a clip-on bowtie with suspenders.

Damn, tiny clothes were so cute.

Veera held her breath as he bit his tongue between his teeth and carried the plate to the swing. He wobbled back and forth, and for a moment, she wasn't sure if he was going to make it.

"Wow, that looks so yummy," she said softly, before she took the plate from him. She patted the spot next to her on the swing and tried to steady the jhoola from swaying too much as he belly crawled his way onto the seat. He adjusted his red suspenders and crossed his legs the same way she had. The plate of sweets was arranged between them.

"How did you get all these?" Veera asked him.

"I took them off the dessert table," he said. Then held a finger to his mouth and giggled.

"Want to share?" she asked.

The big head of curls nodded. "My mom said I could only have one."

Veera glanced at the door, then back at the plate. "I won't tell if you won't?"

She was met with a bright, happy smile. "Deal."

They both picked up the soft gulab jamuns first. The fried doughballs were sticky sweet and coated in rose syrup.

"Cheers," she said and held it out to her companion. He looked at it with confusion, then pinched his tongue between his lips before carefully tapping his gulab jamun against hers. The syrup dripped everywhere before they shoved them in their mouths.

With chipmunk cheeks and sticky fingers they began to giggle.

The door opened again and they both whirled toward the sound. The boy gasped, as if he were afraid of getting caught, and Veera straightened, her chin lifting in defiance. She was going to protect this child from punishment. This innocent brought her dessert.

When Deepak stepped inside, his gaze went to her sticky fingers, her chipmunk cheeks, the plate on the jhoola, and her companion.

She could tell that he was trying not to smile as he crossed his arms over his chest.

"Raj, you know you get sick if you eat too many sweets."

Veera swallowed the delicious gulab jamun and then held her hand out as if to cover the plate between them. "It's not his, it's mine. He was just, ah, keeping me company."

"Right. If that were true, then why are both of your hands covered in rose syrup?"

"Ah, taste tester?"

The little boy giggled and hopped off the bed. "Bye, Auntie," he called out then ran around Deepak's legs and out the door.

Veera gaped at him. *"Auntie?* And to think I liked that kid."

"Marriage has officially changed your status," Deepak said. He crossed the room and examined the sweets. "Need some more time?"

Veera examined the different offerings and picked up a fruit tart. She held it out to him, and instead of taking it from her hand, he leaned down so she could feed him. His teeth grazed her fingertips and she trembled as his eyes met hers.

Then he gripped her wrist, his hand covering the bracelets that his mother had given her, and slipped her fingers into his mouth. He sucked slowly, deeply, licking off the sugar-sweet gulab jamun syrup until there was nothing left.

She gasped at the feel of his tongue, of his lips closing over her knuckle and the soft suction into his mouth. When her fingers were no longer sticky, he let go of her wrist and slowly pulled her fingers clean.

"We should go," he said gruffly. "People are going to wonder where we are, and my father wants to give his speech. He said it's the most important keynote he's ever had to give in his life, and we have to humor him."

Veera pressed her lips together to stop them from trembling. "Okay," she said. "I'm ready."

When he pulled her to her feet and her lehenga fell around her ankles again, he held her arms to steady her while she put her shoes back on.

"Veera?"

"Yeah?"

"We can just go," Deepak said. "Just say the word, and we'll walk right out."

She smiled, and for the first time since they had gotten married, she truly appreciated that Deepak could see all the strange, jagged facets of her heart. "Thanks," she said. "Thanks. Just telling me that makes me feel better."

"Good," he said. "We're a team."

"We're a team," she repeated. "But if I continue to hide back here, my mother with drag me out by my hair. I don't think I'm safe even if you try to take me away."

The corner of his mouth curled up. "I'll risk it."

She took his hand as he led her out of the office. "Hey, how's the whiskey bar? I haven't tried it yet."

"The aunties are hitting it hard, so I think it's a success," Deepak replied.

CHAPTER 20

Deepak

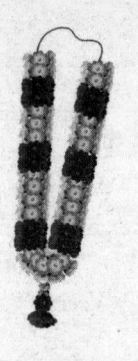

DEEPAK: Any news?

SANA: It's official. She hates you. But do you blame her? It's obvious that she was a means to an end.

DEEPAK: Hold up. Unfair to be judged when you don't know the arrangement we had when we first got engaged.

SANA: Olivia has told me a lot. Who do you think held her phone during her last "get ready with me" video? Look, I'll let you know if anything changes.

DEEPAK: Thanks, Sana.

SANA: You're welcome.

SANA: How is she doing?

DEEPAK: She's perfect. Just like she's always been.

SANA: Yeah, you really need to work on how you show people that you appreciate them.

* * *

PREM: How is it going?

DEEPAK: I am going to crawl out of my skin.

PREM: That bad, huh?

DEEPAK: I'm giving her space so she can make the next move.

PREM: Have you thought about showing her that you care about her? That you think of her as more than a friend now, and that you don't regret marrying her?

DEEPAK: I mean, it's implied.

PREM: I thought you were smart, Deepak.

Deepak walked through the second level of his home, waiting for Veera to finish getting dressed so they could head out to dinner. When he saw the colorful dishes in the sink, dishes that he hadn't owned a few weeks ago, he quickly rinsed them and stacked them neatly in the dishwasher.

He then wiped his hands on the tea towels that had a picture of a cat holding a coffee cup, and a fall-colored scarf, before cutting through the living room.

Somehow, Veera had managed to add clutter here as well. Brightly colored throw pillows and blankets covered his minimalist-design brown leather couch.

Her things were always in the way, breaking up the aesthetic clean lines of his home. He picked up a bottle of her hand lotion from the coffee table and uncapped it to take a sniff. The eucalyptus and mint smelled like her skin, and he smiled at the familiarity of it as he recapped the container. He then put the lotion into a small basket he'd left for her at the base of the stairs. Earlier that day he had added her AirPods and a book that she'd left next to the range.

There were also cords and charging cables everywhere. She had a laptop sitting on the dining table, a phone charger in the kitchen, another draped over the side table and dangling against the arm of the sofa, plus a set of old-fashioned wired earbuds draped over the banister leading upstairs.

As much as he preferred an orderly space, he didn't mind Veera's clutter as much as he thought he would. It was a sign that she was there in the house, and it was oddly . . . comforting.

Deepak glanced at his wrist and noted the time. He had an appointment that he couldn't do alone.

He walked to the base of the stairs and was consumed with a hum of sexual attraction as he thought about approaching Veera's door.

"Vee? We're going to be late!"

Just as he finished shouting, the sound of a door opening echoed through the stairwell.

"Sorry," Veera called back. "I was wrapping up a few things before I had to get ready." She appeared at the top of the stairs in a simple pair of blue jeans and a navy sweater that was perfect for October weather.

He looked down at his tailored slacks, button-down shirt, and fitted sport coat. The words were out of Deepak's mouth before he could stop himself. "Are you sure you want to wear that for tonight?"

Veera froze, her hands pausing on the mangalsutra she'd been in the process of adjusting around her neck. Her face was a study in shock. "Excuse me?" Her tone was arctic.

"I'm so sorry," he stuttered. He climbed the stairs so he could stand on the landing next to her. He held his hands up as if he were already surrendering. "It's not that you don't look beautiful in everything you wear—"

"I know," she said, crossing her arms over her chest. The muscle in her jaw ticked. "You know it hurts my feelings when you don't say nice things about my clothes, right?"

"Veera, Bunty is probably proposing, and I know there are going to be pictures."

The icy expression melted into shock, then unfiltered joy.

"Oh my god!" she squealed. "That's amazing! Bunty is finally proposing!" She jumped him, and he wrapped her up in a hug and swung her around in a circle. When he put her back down, she scrambled away just as quickly.

"Wait a minute," she said, ignorant of how much he craved more of her touch. "I thought we were taking everyone out to dinner to thank them for their help with the wedding reception?"

Deepak nodded. "We were, but Bunty said that a thank-you dinner was the cover story he needed to surprise Bobbi with a proposal. He told Prem and I last night that he's taking Bobbi out today for a romantic date where he'll pop the question." He motioned to his suit. "And now we're all getting dressed up."

Veera rested her hands on her hips. "I mean, obviously she's going to say yes."

"Obviously."

"And Bunty told you this last night?"

"Yes. And Prem. Who I think probably told Kareena today."

"But Kareena never told me," she said, unable to hide the hurt in her voice.

He cleared his throat. "I think Bunty's exact words were 'tell your partners' when we ended the call." Then he winced.

Her sorrowful expression faded just as quickly, and he was beginning to get whiplash from the series of emotions that she was experiencing.

"Why did you wait until this exact moment to tell me?" she told him. She folded her arms over her chest again.

"Probably because I thought you were going to hear it from Kareena?"

She thought about it for a second, then shrugged. "You're forgiven. My friend is getting engaged today and that's all that matters. Since we're running late, you have to help me figure out what I am supposed to wear."

Veera walked back into her room. From his vantage point on the landing, he could see that her bed was still unmade. He made a beeline straight for the left side of the mattress. He'd folded his first hospital corner before Veera returned from the closet. She looked down at the bed, and then back at his face.

"Deepak," she said. "I'm just going to mess up the sheets again. You don't have to make the bed."

He was half erect at the mention of a messed-up bed and visions of Veera naked. He slowly straightened. "If you want to make it out tonight, then it's probably a good idea to avoid mentioning your bed or messing up the sheets."

Veera's jaw dropped. "Deepak!"

"Brat," he said coolly. He kept his gaze locked with hers as he adjusted himself. "Just show me what you're wearing."

Her cheeks were adorably flushed, but she held three demure dresses, all perfect examples of funeral attire, against her collarbone.

"Nope."

"Well, we don't have a lot of time," she said. "In a fit of rage after I was let go, I got rid of most of my pantsuits. This is what I have left."

He straightened. "What? You loved your pantsuit collection." Was that why he hadn't seen any of them since she'd come back to New York? He'd assumed it was because she wasn't in an office anymore or that she just hadn't had time to take them out of her closet yet. She'd had so many that were tailored for her body, cut close to her narrow shoulders, fit against her waist, tapered at her angles, that he'd started to mentally keep track of which ones he'd loved the most.

"You're right, I did love my pantsuits, but I was mad, and I took it out on designer fabrics."

For her to get rid of something that was so intimately tied to the career she'd been forced out of was painful to hear. "Do you need new clothes?"

He wanted to fix this for her, to give her back something that she'd lost. He reached in his back pocket and pulled out his black Amex.

"Keep this with you. Buy whatever you want. Whatever you need."

Veera looked at his outstretched hand and snorted. "Deepak, I was one of your references when you got your black Amex. I already have my own. Why would I want yours?"

"Because I want to be able to buy clothes for you?" he said.

Veera shook her head. "If this is your idea of romance, it needs work."

He looked down at his card then back at her. He tucked it back into his wallet. "I'm listening."

"If you give me your card, I still have to do the work and buy the clothes," she said. "I'm still the one doing the labor."

"You're my wife, Veera," he said. "I want you to be able to get whatever you want or need without thinking about it, but I also don't want to make decisions for you."

"Giving me money is still not helpful here."

Veera crossed the room to stand in front of Deepak. She reached up to cup the sides of his neck, the cool contact of her hands sparking a shudder through his body. She ran her thumb along his jawline, and he met her halfway for a featherlight kiss.

She'd never initiated a kiss between them before, other than the quick hard contact on their flight back from Goa. This one was different. He touched her hips, bringing her close, desperate for the sweet taste of her mouth, but she was already walking back toward her closet.

She retrieved a simple black jumpsuit and held it up. "If you'll excuse me, I'm just going to get changed and then we can go."

"Let's stay in, and—"

"Not a chance," she said. "We're celebrating our friends!"

He pressed his lips together and turned to leave. But when he reached the door, he called her name. "Vee?"

She startled at the sound of the nickname he'd started to use a few months after they'd met. "Yeah?"

She'd pressed the hanger to her collarbone, her eyes flitted back and forth between him and her reflection.

He should've told her when he found out about the proposal.

Instead, he'd been so busy trying to avoid her because of his own feelings.

"Deeps?" Veera said when he continued to stare.

"Nothing. You're beautiful. I'll see you downstairs."

THE TAXI TO THE RESTAURANT was mostly in silence, but when they reached the location, Veera hooked an arm through his and shook her long curling hair back from her shoulders as she led the way through the double doors of Rani's main entrance.

The wedding bangles his mother had given her rested against his coat sleeve. For someone who didn't believe that they had a real wedding, she'd still followed every tradition.

That thought continued to brew in the back of his mind as he pulled open the door to Rani's. Veera stepped through the opening first but came to a halt a few feet into the entryway. Deepak almost careened into her back.

"What's wrong, why did you . . . holy shit."

The restaurant had been transformed into a Punjabi village courtyard. There was a potted tree in the center of the room. Around it was a stone seat that circled the base. In the corner was the infamous jhoola with the iron support beams wrapped in marigold garlands. Stretching from the base of the tree toward the front door was a long table for a little over sixteen guests.

Deepak recognized Bobbi's uncle, aunt, and cousin. They were all talking to Bunty's father, mother, brother, and sister near the makeshift bar that was situated in front of a scenic painted backdrop covering the far wall. The picture was a delicate oil-on-canvas work of mustard fields at sunrise.

"This is incredible," Veera whispered. "Did you know about this?"

"Not at all, but maybe Kareena and Prem did," he replied, as he touched the small of her back. "It looks like they're here, too."

Kareena was the first to cross the room, her slim-fit emerald gown swirling around her calves over chunky block heels.

"Isn't this amazing?" she said, her smile infectious. "Bunty apparently hired Bobbi's best decorator to pull this off today." She held out her arms and hugged Veera first. "You look so chic. I love how you complement each other so well. Sexy power couple."

Veera gripped Kareena's hands and in a low tone said, "When did Prem tell you that Bunty was going to propose?"

"Last night," she said, a grin still plastered across her face. "I was bubbling all day."

Veera's voice dropped an octave. "Kareena, why didn't you call me to tell me?"

Her smile slipped, her eyebrows V-ed. Then she looked over Veera's shoulder at Deepak. "Because I thought Deepak was supposed to tell you?"

"Yeah, if we were *really* married," she said softly.

"We are," Deepak said. The words were out of his mouth before he could stop himself. He leaned between Kareena and Veera and pointed a finger at Veera. "She is my wife."

Kareena raised an eyebrow, almost identical to the way Veera did. "Well then, you should be keeping her informed."

Ouch.

He had been appropriately chided, Deepak thought. He took a step back. "As you were." Then he escaped the two friends and made a beeline for the bar.

"You look like you could use a drink," Prem said. He leaned back against the bar ledge.

"Shut up," Deepak replied. With whatever subtlety he could

manage, he shoved his chuckling friend aside, and ordered a whiskey sour and a whiskey neat from the bartender.

Prem motioned to Kareena and Veera who were still talking in the corner. He made another vague gesture at Bunty's family on the other side of the room, and at the decor that brought the space to life. "Can you believe it? All three of us hitched. I never thought this would happen."

Deepak didn't respond.

"What?" Prem said, his tone growing serious. "What happened?"

"Vee called our marriage fake again," he admitted. "I'm realizing that we're just ignoring the chemistry we have, clinging to our friendship in hopes that sex doesn't fuck things up. But our relationship has already changed."

Prem threw back the rest of his drink and placed it on the bar. "Brother, you need to figure out how you want this to end."

"I just told you," he said. "It's complicated. Friendship makes everything more complicated."

"Yeah? Wait until you fall in love. Then your situation will be a real bitch." He patted Deepak before pushing away from the bar to meet Bunty's father, who had been heading toward them, hand outstretched in greeting.

Deepak felt like he'd just been sucker punched. He'd never thought of the *L* word. He'd just been trying to wrap his mind around the fact that he liked being married to Veera. But love?

No, he thought. He wasn't ready for that yet. He knew that he wanted her, that he respected her, and that she was the woman he'd choose from the start if he had a second chance. But what part of his feelings for Veera was from before their wedding and what part was influenced by the fact that they were already married, and everyone kept telling them how great they looked together?

Hell, he still wasn't sure if Veera could forgive him for his role in fucking up the career that she cherished. Once the board meeting was over, and their fake marriage served its purpose, she could very well want to leave him and fall in love with someone else.

The thought left a sour taste in his mouth.

Deepak picked up the two glasses that had been placed on the bar top in front of him, tipped the waitstaff, and then carried the whiskey over to Veera and Kareena. Without another word, he passed Veera the whiskey sour. He felt the soft brush of her fingertips against his as she gripped the glass. She didn't look in his direction as she tipped her drink toward him. In reflex, he did the same. Their glasses clinked together.

They both sipped at the same time, the ritual centering him more than any words possibly could.

Kareena laughed.

"What?" Veera said. She sounded like she'd been in the middle of a sentence that tapered off in confusion. "What's so funny?"

Kareena pushed her black-framed glasses farther up the bridge of her nose. "Nothing. It's just that you two make a great couple."

Those words again, Deepak thought. *Those fucking words.*

Someone called Veera's name from across the room. Bobbi's sister was waving at her, then motioning for Veera to come over to join her near the windows.

"I'll be right back," Veera said, then with a fleeting glance at Deepak, she left him alone with Kareena.

Kareena turned to stand by Deepak's side so they could both look at Veera together. She was giving Bobbi's sister a hug before she sat on the seat next to her and leaned in to talk. She always did that, Deepak thought. She would get close, her eyes intent, focused, as if the other person's words were the most important thing to her in that moment.

"You really do make a good couple," Kareena said softly.

Deepak was really beginning to hate when people said that to him. But this was Kareena. This was his wife's best friend, and she was one of the few people who knew Veera better than anyone else in the world. Instead of walking away, he stayed to find answers.

"Why do you say that?" he asked.

She looked up at him. "Hmm?"

"Why do you think that Veera and I make a good couple? Because we were friends first?"

Kareena cocked her head. "No, that's ridiculous. That implies that every time two people are friends they should consider a romantic relationship, too."

"Okay, then why?"

"You're just . . . aware of her. You both are aware of each other. It's like you each anticipate what the other needs and you both support each other. Even when Prem and I were dating and you were still friends, you used to do that for Veera. You care for her just like she cares for you. The fact that you're both in sync is incredibly special."

"Kareena, she says the wedding is fake." He couldn't hide his frustration. His confusion.

"God save us from men," Kareena said on a sigh. She leaned in, her heels putting her close to his height. "Deepak?" she whispered in his ear.

"Yeah?"

"Don't fuck this up. Veera sometimes says what she does to protect her own heart, and if she's trusting you with it, then you should treat it as an honor."

Heart. Love.

He needed to see a cardiologist. A good one, since his best friend wasn't taking his symptoms seriously.

Kareena winked at him before she gravitated toward Prem who was still talking to Bunty's father. She and Prem always gravitated toward each other.

Deepak wondered what she meant as he glanced at the daybed. His wife was now alone, smiling as she swung back and forth on the jhoola.

"Fuck it," he mumbled, and crossed the room to be with her, because in a way, he felt like he always gravitated toward her, too.

When he sat next to her on the jhoola, he used the toe of his Armani loafers to push off the floor. Veera lifted her feet and let him take over their gentle swinging without a word of protest.

"Hey, I know I said I had my own black Amex, but maybe you can use your card to buy one of these for your house. I love this thing."

He turned to her and grinned. "Done," he said.

They sat in silence for a few more minutes, watching the crowd move and shift as conversation groups began to form.

"Would you have wanted this?" he asked softly. "A proposal, the proposal party, the full Indian wedding?"

She was quiet for a moment, and then she leaned against his side and rested her head on his shoulder. "I guess I wish I had the proposal part between me and . . . ah, a partner. Something that was just for us. But I can self-soothe as my therapist says. I'm excellent at it, actually."

He felt his chest tighten painfully at the thought that his Veera felt like she was missing anything from him.

"I should've stopped the wedding," he said hoarsely. His words were barely over a whisper. "I should've stopped and none of this would've happened. You should have more than what I can give you, Veera. I stole this from you, and you deserve the excitement with people you love. The planning and the romance."

She sat up and turned to him, her eyes filled with confusion. "Do you regret it, that—"

Before she could finish, the front door burst open, and the glass pane practically cracked against the wall from the force.

Bunty stepped inside wearing a black kurta, his sleeves rolled up his forearms. Bobbi stood behind him in a red Patiala salwar, a look of amusement on her face.

Everyone was silent for two whole seconds before Bunty lifted his arms in the air and roared like he'd just won a championship game.

"I'm getting married!"

Video on Olivia Gupta's social media pages:

Hi, everyone! I just wanted to do a quick "get ready with me" and tell you some fun life updates. For those of you who have been commenting about Deepak's marriage, yes, I know. Good for him honestly.

Because guess what? Your girl is dating someone!

By the way, check out this primer. Isn't the glow, glowing? Like, amazing, right?

Anyway, I don't want to give too much away, but basically, I met up with someone I knew when I was a kid, and we never really got along, but they have this incredible commanding presence that just makes me go, yes, ma'am. You know?

Don't worry about your girl. I swear, I'm coming back from the dead. I'm being the best, baddest bitch I've ever been!

CHAPTER 21

Veera

Text messages from one year ago:

> **VEERA:** Hey, we need to talk

Two days later.

> **VEERA:** It's not like you to ignore my texts. Is everything okay?

> **VEERA:** Deeps, talk to me.

"This is really fantastic material," Margaret said, as she scrolled through Veera's tablet. The reports were a new way of looking at global financial markets that considered marginalized communities, carbon emissions, and sustainability practices in a multipronged approach.

"Thank you. It's still in the early stages, but it's easy to adapt to any global market, and the flexibility is what will make it work for Illyria Media Group." Veera sipped her cappuccino and adjusted her gold bangles as she waited for Margaret to finish. She hadn't planned on pitching her work to Margaret first, but the woman had taken an interest in Veera's project and asked to be involved.

They decided to meet off-site at a trendy Financial District coffee shop with large oak tables and big dome-shaped chrome overhead chandeliers. The hissing sound of an espresso machine and soft, soothing jazz made Veera grateful for the casual ambiance. It took some of the pressure off her for performing in a more traditional setting for their industry.

Margaret tapped the screen once and then nudged the tablet forward. Her smile was infectious. "All that traveling was really good for you and your sister if you both came up with a project plan like this for global businesses."

Veera shook her head. "This was just me," she said. "This is what I was, ah, consulting with Deepak on, actually." She brushed the inside of her wedding and engagement band with her thumb before curling her palms around her quickly cooling mug.

Margaret beamed at Veera. "He was always intelligent. I joined the board because I knew that he could take the business further than his father ever dreamed. And with partnerships like this? Identifying talent like yours, I really do believe it."

"If he gets the CEO position," Veera said gently. She picked up the tablet and flipped the cover over the screen. "I know that it was relatively unanimous to consider an alternative candidate for the position."

Margaret made a dismissive sound, puckering her lips as she sat back with her tea. "He's doing a wonderful job, and I'm sure that his record will speak for itself. There are only a few individuals on the board who are still opposed to him, and we know Olivia Gupta is one of them. For obvious reasons, of course."

"Of course," Veera said with a smile. She turned to tuck her tablet back in her backpack. "Who are the others if you don't mind me asking?" she said casually.

Margaret paused and then shook her head. "No one, really. And they're always changing their minds every other moment, so—"

"It's my father," Veera said quietly. There was no point in letting the unspoken truth sit between them. Relationships in business had to be formed out of honesty, and she and Margaret could be honest with each other about this. "He's Deepak's opponent."

Margaret softened, and she reached out to pat Veera's hand. "I'm so sorry, I don't know what happened between the two of you."

"We've always had a difficult relationship," she said, feeling a sense of déjà vu. How many times had she told people that she and her father had a difficult relationship? How many times had she forced herself to believe that they were both to blame?

"Well, as one of the largest shareholders," Margaret said, "his vote has an exceptional amount of weight. Plus, Olivia and Narinder still doubt Deepak's capabilities. He has some work cut out for him. But like I said, Deepak's successes speak for themselves."

"Right," Veera said. She was going to talk with her father again. She didn't want to, but she might be the only person who could get through to him about Deepak's role as CEO. As for Olivia, hopefully Sana had made some progress.

"You know," Margaret said as she tapped a pale pink manicured fingernail against Veera's tablet cover. "If you present this to Illyria, you're going to have to get your father involved as well. He is our chief financial officer."

Veera nodded. "I guess I was hoping he'd finally retire like Deepak's father."

"I have a feeling Malkit is much more stubborn."

Veera grinned. "That is most definitely the truth."

Her phone rang at her elbow. She'd left it out to keep track of the time, so her pitch didn't run over the allotted hour that

Margaret had available for her. When she glanced at the screen, her brow furrowed. "I'm sorry, Margaret," she said, "but this is Deepak's assistant. She almost never calls me unless there is a problem. Do you mind if I take this really quick?"

"Not at all, dear," Margaret said. She stood and brushed at her pantsuit. "I'm just going to use the restroom."

Veera smiled at her and waited until she'd turned her back before answering the call. "Kim? Is everything all right?"

"Hi, Veera," Kim said, in that hurried voice that she always seemed to use. "I'm actually calling because Deepak wanted me to pass along a request. He's in meetings all day, so he was wondering if you could run downtown to the Kumari Boutique to pick up an outfit for him? He's already ordered it. Your name is on file so you shouldn't have any trouble picking it up. He would've sent a messenger, but he said the package is too delicate to trust to anyone but you."

Kumari was the designer for Veera's wedding lehenga in Goa. Why would he order an outfit from Kumari?

He'd been acting incredibly strange since Bobbi and Bunty's engagement party. She assumed it was because they were now only about a month away from the board meeting and he was busy with work. The hairs at the back of her neck prickled. Something told her that his behavior and the Kumari errand were connected.

Veera looked at her watch and then Margaret's plum-colored peacoat draped over the back of her chair. "What time do they need me to pick it up by?"

"The sooner the better? Within the hour is what Deepak said."

"Yeah, that should be fine," she said. "Just send me the address if you can, and I'll leave shortly and head straight there."

"Great, thanks, Veera."

"No problem, Kim."

Veera ended the call, then waited for the directions to come through. When Margaret came back, they wrapped up their meeting, and Veera hopped in an Uber to go straight to Kumari Boutique.

VEERA WAS STILL UNSURE why Deepak would want her to pick up the outfit in person. With the amount of money he possessed, there had to be someone who was able to do the errand for him. She could only assume it was because of the sensitive nature of the package.

Forty minutes after her meeting, she walked into the beautiful black marble, gold, and mirrored foyer of Kumari Boutique's New York City location. The walls and flooring were black with glittering gold veins that sparkled under the art deco lighting.

She looked down at her beige slacks, maroon silk top, and cardigan. It was the only professional outfit she owned anymore, and even with its tailored fit, Veera was terribly underdressed for Kumari's.

A woman in a sharp black suit approached her on sparkling juttis that her best friends Kareena and Bobbi would've loved. "Hello, how may I help you?" she asked, her accent sharp and clearly from Delhi.

"My, ah . . . well, I'm here to pick up an order?"

The woman's expression didn't change. "Name?"

"Veera Mathur."

It was as if she had said the magic word to get past the dragon. The woman's eyes brightened. "We are expecting a Veera Mathur Datta."

Deepak Datta. Her cheeks warmed. "Technically, that's my husband's last name, so yeah, that's me."

Telling this stranger that she had a husband sent butterflies to her stomach. She'd never claimed Deepak as hers to a stranger in public before. The declaration felt powerful. Like she was stronger because she was part of a unit that she was proud of.

"We have quite a session planned for you," she said. "Come with me."

"Session?" Veera asked, as she walked farther into the store, taking note of the sparkling rows of pastel and jewel-toned gowns, lehengas, and salwars.

They entered a room with rounded ceilings that looked like a birdcage. Gold-colored iron bars curved and arched to meet in the center of the highest point of a domed ceiling connected to an opulent crystal chandelier with teardrop stones and fluted edges.

There, two other women wearing black suits waited for her in the center of the room. Between them was a rack of jewel-toned pantsuits and gowns.

Pantsuits.

"Oh wow," she whispered. She'd always worn gray, blue, black, or beige with the occasional pop of color because it was in her best interest to blend in with the rest of the finance bros in the industry that she'd chosen to work within. But if she'd had a choice, she'd want all the gorgeous floral and royal colors, the bright bling, and the lace trim.

"Hi, Veera, I'm Gurpreet," the woman standing to the left said. She had a small pompadour, and a long black braid that reached the top of her thighs. "I know you wore a sample gown of ours for your wedding. Your husband called us and asked if we could do a custom collection of pantsuits just for you. We were able to get a hold of your sizes from our Goa designers, and this week, the Kumari team created quite the collection. It's one of a kind based on some suggestions and guidelines that your husband shared."

Veera gaped. "Wait, all those clothes are designed for *me*?"

At that moment, her cell phone buzzed with an incoming text. She looked at the screen to read the message from Deepak.

> **DEEPAK:** Surprise. Just go with it.

> **DEEPAK:** P.S. My black Amex beats your black Amex's ass.

"I don't know what this means," she said, reading the message over and over.

"We were told to dress you, have your makeup and hair done, and give you whatever jewelry you like from our collections," Gurpreet said. "Then we have to put you back in the car and send you on your way to your next stop."

Veera scrubbed her hands over her face. "I need a minute."

Had she said something to Deepak about her pantsuits? She couldn't remember. She'd missed them because they had been a regular part of her work routine, of the life that she'd lost. When she had graduated from college, she remembered going shopping for her first work outfit with Bobbi and Kareena. They'd all talked about how a pantsuit was a marker of their accomplishments. Kareena had gone in the direction of high heels and sweater vests, while Bobbi switched up her three-piece suits with the most flair for fashion. Veera preferred comfort and fit.

They'd spent so much money on those first work outfits, but they'd crossed that line between college student and professional together.

Deepak had once commented about her pantsuits, when they met for lunch regularly, and she'd made some glib reply about how clothing was only ever an issue when it was a woman who wore it. Meanwhile, men wore suits every day, and it was never a conversation point.

"Mrs. Datta," the first woman said who'd greeted her at the door. She touched her arm with gentleness. "If I had a man who was trying to romance me with a custom collection by one of the most exclusive designers in the Punjabi community, I'd take the gift."

"Right," she said. As she worked through the reasons why Deepak was doing this for her, she wondered if this was for appearance purposes. Olivia had made another video, and the board vote was soon.

No, she thought. Olivia hadn't said anything that would require a PR response.

Could this be Deepak's attempt at seduction?

"Okay, I guess I'm in?"

As she was ushered through a back door, her pulse quickened at the realization that she may not regain the wardrobe she'd once had, but she was building a better closet that was unique to the person she had become.

Her new stylist led her to a small room and sat her in a salon chair. With flourish, she draped a black cape over her, and fastened it at her neck. "Hair first. Let's keep it simple. A wash, a blowout, and bouncy curls at the ends. We do this every weekend for brides who want us to dress them for their big day, so we're equipped for all your styling needs."

Veera gaped at Gurpreet, who stood off to the side as a supervisor. When the older woman arched an eyebrow, Veera could only respond with a nod.

There were three, sometimes four women who worked on her at the same time. They plucked her eyebrows, filed and painted her nails, and brought her a latte while they painstakingly blow-dried her hair.

Veera was then stripped down to her underwear and told to stand in front of a trifold mirror as an army of women put her in one outfit after another. Each one fit great to her untrained eyes, but Gurpreet and her assistant made alterations on the spot. There was a cobalt blue pantsuit with a pearl trim camisole. Then there was the skirt suit in merlot that had her eyes bulging at the way it hugged her hips and skimmed her thighs.

One by one by one, she was dressed in over two dozen South Asian–inspired designs that brought out her eye color, the shape of her waist, or her jawline. There were half a dozen lehengas and anarkalis as well with delicate detail at the hem or the neckline, but perfect for Veera who preferred the simpler silhouette.

Every outfit also came with a pair of juttis or heels that were for work attire or going out afterward. She was loaded up on simple gold and silver jewelry pieces for her wardrobe.

Veera's eyes filled with tears as she shed the clothes she'd worn during the eight months of travel, during the countless days and nights of doubting herself and her skill. She hadn't thought about her pantsuits, about the clothes that she'd worn in her old life as a critical part of her identity. But now, wearing the bright colors and simple patterns and cuts, she was starting to feel alive again. Less sad, and more . . . Veera.

As Gurpreet dressed her in the last outfit, a slip dress with strappy heels, she said, "All of these will be shipped to your home once we finish the rest of the alterations. They'll arrive Friday at the latest. We're also sending all of the products we used for your skin today. They're vegan, cruelty-free, South Asian–owned brands."

"Thank you," Veera said, as she turned to the side and looked in the mirror. Who would've thought that Deepak had it in him to bring back a part of Veera that she thought she'd once lost with him?

Gurpreet patted her shoulders. "Let's finish you up and send you on your way."

It was another hour before Veera could leave. She'd been offered a selection of leather bags from different South Asian designers that she could choose from to wear on her way out. However, Deepak had purchased the entire collection for her, and the rest of the options would be delivered with her altered clothes.

After hugging the team at Kumari, Veera felt strong and vibrant in her slip dress and heels as she slid into the back of the car that waited out front. She was herself, but better.

It was amazing what clothes could do to her mood, she thought as she twisted her diamond ring.

The car missed the Brooklyn Bridge turnoff, and Veera frowned. "Excuse me," she called out. "Aren't we going back to the town house?"

"No, ma'am," her driver said. "We're going to Midtown. Mr. Datta has asked me to tell you to, quote, go with it, end quote."

Veera grinned. "Thank you, I think I will."

Almost thirty minutes later, they had reached a familiar building on Columbia's campus on the Upper West Side of Manhattan. She stepped out in front of Lerner Hall, a towering building made of glass, cement, and brick.

Veera spotted Deepak immediately. He wore the same suit he'd had on when he'd left that morning and impatiently stared at the street. She saw the moment that he spotted her because he tucked his cell in his pocket. With long strides, he crossed to her car when it pulled up to the front of the building so he could open the door. Veera took his outstretched hand and let him help her out into the chilled dusk.

"Hi," she said, her cheeks flushed at the sight of his heated stare.

"Hello yourself," he said before closing the car door. Her hair fluttered in the wind, and he brushed it off her cheek. "You look beautiful. But you always do."

"That experience was both excessive and wonderful at the same time," she said. And because she couldn't help herself from touching him, from wanting the feel of his soft mouth against hers, she stood on her toes and pressed a kiss on the underside of his jaw.

"I wanted to give you romance," he said hoarsely, gripping her chin between his thumb and forefinger. "I wanted to show you that this isn't about anyone but you and me."

"So you gave me pantsuits and shoes," she said, as she rested her hands on his shoulders and leaned into his warmth. "That's smooth, Romeo. Really smooth."

Veera's eyelashes fluttered and her eyes closed as his mouth came down on hers. She shivered and parted for him when his tongue glided over her bottom lip. She wasn't scared that their relationship would change, that there was no way to reclaim the friendship that they'd once had. Their relationship had already changed, and if this sexy, incredible man with his deep confident voice and kind eyes wanted to be with her, she'd accept him for as long as he gave himself to her. Fake married or not, the way his mouth slid over hers was real and she'd cherish the memory of his taste.

When she pulled back, his eyes locked with hers, intense and focused, while his arms wrapped around her waist, pressing into the silky fabric of her dress.

"Thank you," she whispered breathlessly. She was standing on the precipice of something dangerous and thrilling, nanoseconds from falling.

"You're welcome," he said. Then he maneuvered them both toward the entrance of the building. "Now are you ready for our date?"

"There are more surprises?" she said and linked her arm through his. They walked at a slow, easy pace, with their hips bumping.

"We're going out on the town," Deepak said. "Apparently there is this amazing panel on economic trends in the Global South. Then I figured I'd take you out for milkshakes."

Veera was smiling so hard that her mouth hurt. "I guess you do know romance, Deepak Datta."

He smirked as he opened the door for her. "I'm just getting started, Vee," he said. His hand settled on the small of her back. "There is no going back now."

She had to be careful not to trip, not to show him how his words affected her. That was exactly what she'd been afraid of.

But she knew as he held her hand and they walked into the lecture hall that he was right.

There was no going back.

CHAPTER 22

Veera

VEERA: I have a question but neither of you are allowed to read too much into it.

BOBBI: Okay, strong start. What's up?

KAREENA: I'm already reading into it.

VEERA: Just remember all the times I was so supportive of you two.

VEERA: Okay, say that a guy showed sexual interest and you have one sexy moment.

VEERA: Then you tell him you're interested, too, but it's not the right time.

VEERA: Then he does another sexy thing with you. After that, he totally stops sexy things and starts to romance you instead.

BOBBI: I think I'm following.

KAREENA: Deepak and you hooked up, then you told him you weren't ready. You hooked up one more time, and then you probably said something to him that had him romancing you instead. And now you want to hook up again, but he hasn't made another move?

VEERA: He literally bought me a custom-designed wardrobe with matching shoes, jewelry, and handbags, took me to the greatest lecture I've ever seen in my life, then pressed me up against the wall to kiss me once before he patted me on the ass and went to bed.

KAREENA: Wow, I did not think Deepak had it in him.

BOBBI: Vee, if he hasn't made another move and you're both literally living together, maybe it's because he's waiting for you to make it first? He's probably trying to respect your boundaries so living together doesn't become uncomfortable.

VEERA: Oh.

KAREENA: This is so much more fun when I'm not the one who's having a crisis.

***

VEERA: Hi! I have a favor.

BENJAMIN: Hi, hon. What can I help you with?

VEERA: Can you teach me how to cook something for Deepak?

BENJAMIN: No, sorry. But I can send you some food.

VEERA: What? Why can't you teach me? I want to learn how to do it myself.

BENJAMIN: Because I am a terrible teacher. I'll just get frustrated and snap at you. If I hurt your feelings, both my fiancée and Deepak will kick my ass.

VEERA: Fine. I guess that's fair.

BENJAMIN: Sorry! I'll have one of my guys bring you some cake.

Deepak's kitchen was filled with the scent of frying mustard seeds and curry leaves, simmering onions and garlic, and boisterous conversation in a mix of Hindi, Punjabi, and English. Meanwhile, Veera was doing the only thing that made sense to her and was staying out of everyone's way. She'd perched on the edge of a counter stool at the island, a plate of half-eaten onion pakora and ketchup at her elbow.

"That's the difference between stocks and bonds," she said. She was using a small whiteboard that she'd purchased to help her brainstorm work projects. Because it was bigger than a piece of paper, Sonali Auntie didn't need glasses to see the diagrams she drew.

The older woman tapped the word *bond*. "I like this," she said. "Can you help me, beta?"

"Of course," Veera said.

Sonali Auntie bobbled her head side to side. "You tell me how much you would like for me to pay you for your help, and I'll send you the Venmo."

Veera smiled at her reference to *the Venmo*. "You don't have to pay me," Veera said. "You're already doing so much by teaching me how to cook." She motioned to the rest of the women in the kitchen. "You're all doing so much for me."

She was met with a series of warm smiles. They had been so quick to respond to her text messages.

What they didn't know was that they were aiding her in her plan to seduce Deepak through his stomach.

She'd had enough restless nights, enough tossing and turning and solo orgasms when he was sleeping one floor below her. She was definitely ready to make her move, and it was going to start with an ancient South Asian tool.

Food.

Veera had first wanted to learn how to make sheet pan nachos, which was some sort of magical steak nachos meal that Bunty used to make Deepak when he stayed at the house on his visits east. But he'd completely shot her down and wanted to just send her the food instead.

Thankfully, the aunties were willing and able to come to her rescue.

"Your business services are worth more than making sabji and roti, beta," her mother-in-law said with a smile. She wore an apron that she'd produced from the bottom drawer of one of Deepak's cabinets. Apparently, it was her designated apron whenever she came to visit.

"My daughter was always the sharpest when it came to money," her mother said to Sonali Auntie. "We gave Sona and Veera access to their trust funds at eighteen. The money that their father had invested for them when they were first born. It wasn't much, but Veera tripled the size of her trust fund in two years. Her advice is priceless."

Veera smiled at her mother's praise. She'd always been ready to give it, but Veera hadn't heard it in a while. "I'm good at investing, but, Mom, remember how Sana tripled hers within eight months? Now that was impressive."

Her mother's eyes narrowed. "And who has a larger portfolio now?"

It was without a doubt Veera. She was always the saver. "Sana likes to play the market. Big risk, big reward for her. But at any given time, she can be worth more than I am."

Deepak's mother stood at the stove, ladle in hand. "My bahu, take the compliment when you receive it. It's good for you to boast sometimes."

Farah Auntie was stuffing samosas at the end of the island and passing the cone to Mona Auntie to pinch closed. "You've always been such a sweetheart," she said to Veera. "It's good for you to have some sharp edges."

"Confidence," Falguni Auntie said. "You just need a little bit more of it."

Veera rolled her eyes. "Just because I want to talk about my sister instead of talking about me doesn't mean I don't have confidence. And being sweet isn't a bad thing. In fact, I think there need to be more sweet people in this world." She hated that everyone thought that her nice qualities were hiding insecurities. She was confident.

In fact, she was so confident that she was going to finally master Indian cooking, make some damn food, and have her way with her fake husband.

Her fake husband who was suspiciously starting to feel like a real one.

Sonali Auntie patted her arm. "That's right, beta. It's perfectly fine to be sweet."

The aunties and the moms looked at one another knowingly and continued to work on various dishes throughout the room.

"Now that you're done with your finance lesson, would you like to know how to finish making this sabji?" Deepak's mother asked.

"Oh," Veera said, as she hopped off the stool. "Yes, absolutely."

She rounded the island and washed her hands at the sink before she stepped between her mother and her mother-in-law.

Her mother-in-law by religious ceremony only.

"I'm just so glad that you've taken an interest in cooking," her mother said, interrupting her thoughts. "I tried to teach you as a child, but all you wanted to do was put your nose in a book." She nudged Veera's shoulder, her smile bright.

"We've been ordering quite a bit of takeout lately, and—"

"Hai, hai," Mona Auntie tsked. She stood at Deepak's kitchen counter, and rolled a small ball of dough between her palms and then pressed it on top of a small marble slab before rolling it out with a rolling pin. "One of the greatest joys that we have as family is to be able to feed our partners. To nourish our children."

"Think of it as an extension of breast milk," Falguni Auntie said. Your children need food to survive and your husband needs—"

"That's a clear enough visual!" Veera shouted, her hands up in surrender. "I don't need you to finish that sentence, Auntie."

The older women in her kitchen looked at one another and laughed. She did not care if she missed the inside joke.

"Aunties and Moms, I can sustain my family in other ways," Veera continued, "but I understand. There is something nice about watching someone you . . . care about, enjoying the food that you make."

"You have a sabji recipe now, and you know how to make roti dough," her mother said. "Focus on getting very good at those things, and then slowly, slowly add recipes to your repertoire."

"Okay, I can do that," Veera said. She took the spoon from her mother-in-law and made mental notes about the texture and color of the spinach and paneer.

"I never got to tell you, Veera, but your reception dinner was so nice," Farah Auntie said. She showed her how to properly fill a folded cone for a samosa as she spoke.

"It's so nice seeing my son happy," Deepak's mother said, and she wrapped an arm around Veera's shoulders and squeezed. Her touch was warm and comforting. Supportive. "You know, Deepak's father and I urged him to purchase the town house. When he was looking for a place to live after college, we wanted him to think about finding a location he could grow into. And now, here you are! He looks at you like you're his whole world. Just the way that he should."

"I just wish that your romance would've blossomed a year ago," Veera's mother said, as she cut into a red onion. She sniffled. "Then maybe you wouldn't have left . . ."

The kitchen descended into a deeply uncomfortable silence. Veera shook her head at her mother. Everyone knew that her father wouldn't have changed a damn thing if Deepak and Veera had been romantically involved a year ago. If anything, he'd be more insistent on letting her go. Because in his mind, women couldn't lead his company. They were responsible for the home.

Scratch that. He didn't think *she* could lead the company. Sana had met his qualifications.

As if reading her thoughts, Farah Auntie was the first to speak. "Malkit is a damn fool."

There was a snort, then someone laughed, and a series of giggles echoed in the kitchen.

"I can't argue with that," Veera's mother said. "I've had to keep out of his business; otherwise, I would've lost my daughters, too."

"I think you should've gotten involved," Veera said. Every woman in the room turned to look at her. She smiled brightly and then held up the spoon she'd been using for the saag paneer. "What, did I say something wrong? Mom knows."

Sonali Auntie shook her head. "You're married now, beta. It's important for you to realize that your business is separate from your husband's business."

"No," she said. On any other occasion, she wouldn't have pushed back, wouldn't have argued, and would have let them believe whatever they wanted to, but she was living in this house, and she had a right to voice her opinion here. Deepak would agree with her, too, would support her in correcting these misguided beliefs.

"My husband and I are a team, and the only reason I know that is because all of you raised us to believe that we have the power to be an equal in marriage and life. You can't teach me how to be strong, and then tell me that I'm supposed to hold back once I'm ready to use my strength."

Mona Auntie spoke first. "Yes, but—"

Veera shook the spoon and splattered paneer on the beautiful French designer range. "No buts," she said. "You take on the whole Desi community if you want to, but when it comes to Punjabi men, all of a sudden you have to control yourself and keep out of their business? I don't think that's fair, do you? If the uncles screwed up,

Mom, if *Dad* screwed up in business or in our family, you'd have every right to tell him so."

Veera couldn't believe that after all the chatter, they were so silent now. They stared at her as if she had started speaking French. Not a single one of them moved.

That's when she realized that they didn't understand a word of what she'd said. They couldn't see for a second how important their words of wisdom had been to her and her friends when she was a child, and how painful their rebukes had been in their adulthood.

"You need to practice your rotis," her mother said, breaking the silence.

"The key to a happy marriage is round rotis," her mother-in-law added with a nod.

Veera sighed. She realized that anything else she'd say would only sound like a lecture, and they were only trying to help her. Some battles had to take place over time.

Like a hundred-year war.

"Thank you for helping me," she replied.

Grateful that even though the aunties and her mother didn't see it, they had given her so much more than the ability to make a damn roti.

CHAPTER 23

Veera

Text messages from nine months and two weeks ago:

DEEPAK: Vee, I just heard. Holy shit, I'm so sorry.

VEERA: Where were you? I called and texted you.

DEEPAK: I'm sorry, I got caught up. Fuck your father. Come work for Illyria. I'll make sure that you have a job.

VEERA: If my father is going to be positioned as a CFO, then I would eventually have to report to him. I don't think I can stomach being fired twice.

DEEPAK: Let me do something, anything. You are one of the smartest advisers at Mathur Financial Group. Not only do I know you personally, but I've seen all the financial and employee reports from the merger! How could he do this?

VEERA: Hey, where were you when I called?

> **DEEPAK:** I was with Olivia. She's a member of the board.

> **VEERA:** Oh?

Veera showered and took the time to blow out her hair after the aunties left her kitchen spotless. There wasn't a trace of their presence left.

Even after she lectured them on the patriarchy and again on believing every WhatsApp meme some distant cousin texted them, they'd made sure to help her with the lessons they promised her when they first showed up at her door.

Instead of brushing her aside or reprimanding her for what she lacked, they tried to cultivate her spirit and her knowledge. In her eyes, there was a noticeable shift in the way they treated her now that she was married.

Maybe this was why so many women felt pressured into getting married. Because they were welcomed into a community that they didn't have access to before. They were now part of the "married" group, which meant that everyone understood a different language, a different way of life that was wholly separate from the life they lived as single women.

Veera had to wonder if her friends had that experience as well. Maybe that was why she felt so disconnected from Kareena and Bobbi when they found Prem and Bunty.

She would miss this, she thought. If her relationship with Deepak ended, if they went their separate ways, then she would miss the way she felt welcomed, the way she belonged with the married women in her life.

Veera tried to push thoughts of ending her relationship with

Deepak out of her head as she entered her closet. She wanted to be with him, and she was ready to have him.

Now that she was alone again, counting down the time until he returned from the office, she felt the sexual tension in their house like a fog. She opened the dresser drawer in the walk-in closet and tried to find something sexy in her underwear collection.

"Tonight calls for the best panties you own, babes," she said to herself. She pushed aside the delicate cotton she preferred and settled on the pair of black lace panties he'd taken off her before their wedding reception. "Bingo."

The lace was so impractical, and if she were being honest with herself, uncomfortable butt floss. But she felt incredible in them. Powerful. Immediate vixen.

Veera stripped out of her clothes, brushed her teeth and her hair, and added a sheer skin tint that gave her cheeks a hydrated, healthy glow.

Her thumb brushed over Olivia's name on the tube. She'd purchased it because she felt guilty for how hurt she was feeling from the marriage announcement.

But damn, it was also some pretty good skin tint.

After putting the tube away, she finished getting dressed for seduction in the matching bra, and a thin camisole and sleep shorts.

Veera headed down to the main floor but stopped on Deepak's level. She turned toward his bedroom and decided her plan was worth the breach in privacy. She pushed his doors open and strode inside the meticulously neat and tidy space. God, his obsessiveness was adorable. His bed had hospital corners, and the pillows on his couch in the seating area were plumped and arranged at an angle.

She walked straight into his dressing room and wondered if she should wear one of his T-shirts when her hand brushed something soft. With curiosity controlling her urges, Veera pulled out his Columbia graduate school sweatshirt from the back of the drawer.

It was so comfy looking that she pressed it against her chest and sighed. He had a few and she'd already stolen one. She wouldn't mind a new sweatshirt for her collection.

When she slipped it over her head, the worn fabric enveloped her like a cloud, and she smelled the rich faint scent of musk and evergreen that clung to Deepak's skin.

What would he think if he caught her wearing his sweatshirt? Would he . . . well, punish her for it? Veera's body tingled at the thought.

They'd never flirted with those games before. They hadn't flirted at all until they were married. Then Deepak held her hand, fascinated by her mehndi until the burgundy color faded leaving just the wrist tattoo behind. She usually forgot that it was there, but Deepak touched it often.

Veera hoped that after tonight he'd touch more than just her wrists.

She wrapped her arms around her midsection, enjoying the soft feel of her new sweatshirt, as she walked back into Deepak's bedroom. She didn't want to leave yet. She'd been so respectful of his space when she'd first moved in that she hadn't even opened the drawers in the kitchen. Now she wanted to leave her imprint on his sheets. She wanted him to remember her the way that she remembered him every time she crawled under her covers and touched herself.

Veera strode over to his mattress and untucked his hospital corners at the foot of the bed. Because she was aching for him to the point where she felt a little daring, a little breathless, she pulled the comforter back and crawled onto the bed.

"Oh my, you've been holding out on me," she whispered.

The lights outside were beginning to dim, casting the room in shadows as she rolled onto her back. Did he think of her? Did he touch himself the way she touched her body, late at night alone in her room?

Veera pressed her thighs together as she shifted on the cool, silken soft sheets.

This was insanity and luxury all at the same time, she thought as she slipped her fingers under the waist of her shorts and into her panties. What was she even thinking, touching herself on Deepak's bed?

Her blood pumped hot through her veins as she was consumed with sensation. She wanted to talk to him first, to ask him what he meant when he said there was no going back. She wanted to understand what was happening between them.

Her fingers brushed over her dampness and she sighed, sinking farther into the pillows. This was Deepak's bed, Deepak's sweatshirt, and she wanted so badly to come all over his sheets and leave him with a mess that would remind him of her.

She fingered her sensitive clit, and she slipped a hand under his sweatshirt, under her tank to brush against her nipple.

"Well, this is a nice surprise."

CHAPTER 24

Deepak

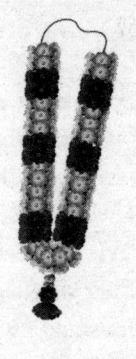

Text messages from nine months ago:

DEEPAK: I'm so sorry I didn't say something earlier about my engagement, but I'm engaged! I think your family knows Olivia Gupta's family, too. I would've told you in person, but I just got so busy with the merger.

DEEPAK: Hey, I haven't heard from you. Is everything okay?

Deepak had had a hell of a day, most of it fighting with the sales team and then the online streaming division about their spring services. Then he'd received a Diwali party invitation that felt like mandatory attendance instead of voluntary.

He planned on working late from the office, giving Veera the time at the house to sort out her feelings until she was ready to come to him and talk, but he'd had enough by early evening that he was willing to risk painful blue balls from seeing his wife.

Except he found her in the same state of arousal that he'd been in.

In his room.

In his sweatshirt.

Lying in his bed.

She must not have heard the door chime as he entered the house, and since the lights were off, he assumed she was upstairs in her room. He'd never expected something like this.

"Well, this is a nice surprise."

He broke her trance, her hand stilling under the waistband of her shorts and her panties. Her eyes went wide when she saw him standing in the doorframe. He could see the embarrassment on her face, the flushed cheeks of arousal when he barked out his order.

"Don't even think about moving."

She froze, her body tense like a rabbit ready to bolt.

He dropped his bag at the door, the dress shoes he'd carried upstairs, and slowly crossed the room toward her.

"Your things are everywhere," he said, as he stripped off his coat and carefully draped it over the edge of the bed. "You never put the throw pillows back where they belong in the living room. The interior designer made it so easy to arrange them in each of the couch corners, too." He began unbuttoning his shirt. "And you never do the dishes at night before bed."

"Th-they're just dishes," she said, her eyes widening as he untucked his shirt and dropped it to the floor.

"After the longest workday I've had in a while, I come in here and now I find out you're messing up my bed," he continued. He unbuckled his belt and pulled it from the loops at his waistband. The buckle made a clinking noise as it fell to the floor. "Wearing my favorite sweatshirt."

Her mouth pursed. "I'm not giving it back."

The room was cast in shadows, but he could see the arousal on her face as she looked over his naked chest. As she traced the lines of his throat to the smattering of chest hair.

"I think you should keep it," he said softly, as he lowered his zipper. "But you have to give me something of yours first."

He gripped her ankles and tugged her to the edge of the bed. Then gripping the collar of his sweatshirt, he pulled her up into a sitting position. Her hand slipped out from her underwear.

"I didn't say you could stop touching yourself," he snapped. "Put your hand back on your pussy." She nodded and immediately returned her hand to the inside of her shorts.

Deepak unzipped his pants and removed them along with his socks, so he was standing in front of her with his tented boxer briefs.

"Take my cock out," he said.

There was a spark in her eyes, a fire that thrilled him. "You take your cock out," she replied.

Deepak didn't respond to her taunt. Instead, he twisted her hair around his fist and tugged just enough to yank her head back in one quick motion. She had no choice but to look up at him. Her fingers began moving in a circular motion under her shorts, and her lips parted, soft and wet.

"I won't say it again, brat," he said smoothly.

Veera raised her free hand and rested it over his bulge. He groaned in pleasure at finally feeling her touch, at the soft, feather-like sensation of her fingertips against him. She reached inside his shorts, and she stroked over his hot, hard length, her thumb brushing over his tip, trailing down the thick vein of his shaft.

Before he could tell her to take him in her mouth, Veera fisted the base of his penis, untucked him from his shorts, and slipped the head of his erection past her lips. His hands tightened on her hair, and he let out a guttural groan as she gently sucked, her cheeks hollowing as she worked the tip, her tongue laving at the underside of his cock.

"That's it," he said softly. "Now take more of me in your mouth."

When she hesitated, he cupped the underside of her face, rough and demanding. "I'll fuck your face, Veera, I swear to god . . ."

Before he could ask her again, Veera tightened her hold on his penis, then she took more of him in her mouth, pushing hard and deep until he sucked in a breath. His groan was guttural now, and Veera began working him over quickly, alternating between using her hands and her mouth to massage his full length.

He held her head between his palms and began pumping in and out of her mouth, his hips thrusting in quick movements that had her moaning with him, her mouth opening impossibly wider, as he touched the back of her throat.

Deepak felt his balls tighten, his breath come faster. "I'm gonna come," he said, his words broken with harsh breath. "I'm gonna come in your mouth or on your tits." He forced himself to slow his thrusting even as he felt her suck off his pre-cum. "Where do you want it?"

When she looked up at him, her eyes meeting his, her mouth full of his cock, her ring sparkling on her finger as she held him, she slid him past her lips even deeper, and sucked hard.

He roared, his head tossed back as he came in hard fast spurts. She lapped up every drop of him in her mouth until his knees were weak, and his back ached with the force of his orgasm.

When he finished, he slipped out of her mouth, and she dabbed at the corner of her lips with the edge of his sweatshirt. He looked down to see that she was no longer touching herself.

"What did I tell you about your hand?" he said quietly.

She narrowed her eyes. "It was too difficult to focus on both—"

"Then it's time for you to be punished," he said. "Strip out of my sweatshirt."

He walked naked toward the Juliet balcony and opened the

doors to let in the air. A soft breeze fluttered through the curtains, the sounds of Brooklyn entering his room. The street was busy below with pedestrians walking by at a steady pace, heading toward the park on one side, or the row of restaurants and shops on the other.

When he turned back around, Veera was wearing a thin knit tank top, her nipples peaked from arousal and from the chilled air gusting through his bedroom. With the streetlamp outside Deepak could see her clearly.

"Get naked," he said. "You haven't been punished."

She glanced over his shoulder. "People can hear us," she said softly.

"Good. I want them to know that my wife is getting fucked."

Veera gaped at him, but she reached for the hem of her tank top and pulled it over her head to reveal big, beautiful breasts, orbs with dusky dark nipples.

How was he already hardening again? He was in his thirties, and he sure as hell didn't bounce back the way he used to when he was a teenager, but there he was, eager to slip into her hot, wet cunt.

"Your shorts," he said, and he waited to see the perfect triangle of her waxed pussy, plump and swollen with arousal. "Then get on your hands and knees."

Veera didn't hesitate to crawl across the mattress, her breasts swaying as she moved. He couldn't wait to suck on her thick, peaked nipples.

He came up behind her, then with a quick tap against her round cheek, he smacked her hard enough to leave an imprint of his hand.

She gasped, then turned to look at him over her shoulder. "You smacked my ass!"

"I'm going to smack it again," he replied, his voice hard. "Spread your knees farther."

She wiggled, then did as he asked, her back arching. He smacked her other ass cheek, and this time, her gasp was accompanied with a groan.

He reached between her legs and ran a finger down her slit, feeling her hot and wet for him. She shivered at his touch.

"Deepak," she whispered. "People can hear." When he ran a hand over the red mark on her ass cheek, she moaned and he knew that this time, her voice was louder, and she was feeling the thrill, the pleasure of a performance.

"Do you want me to close the door?" he said smoothly. He smacked her ass again.

She shrieked, and shook her head.

"I've tested, but Veera, it's been so long because all this time, I've been waiting for you and didn't even know it." He knelt on the bed behind her, stroking a hand over her back. "Do you want me to wear a condom?"

Again, she shook her head, her hair sliding over her bare skin. "I have an IUD, and I tested after the last time. It's been long for me, too. Deepak . . ."

He gripped her hips roughly and put her into position. "As my wife, I want to fuck you bare. Raw. I want to feel you squeezing around me, hot and wet. I want you to feel every inch of my cock until all you'll ever remember when you think of pleasure is me."

Deepak slowly worked his way into her tight pussy, before sliding out and plunging deep. He reveled in the soft muffled shriek as she buried her face in the bedspread. When he gripped her hair again, he used his hold to keep her in position as she rode his dick.

"If you want everyone to hear you like a slut, then everyone should hear you," he said softly, gasping for air as he held himself back. "Scream for me."

He began fucking her, holding her body exactly how he wanted it as he thrust hard and deep into her tight, hot pussy. When she began trembling on the rising wave of her first orgasm, he pulled out leaving her unfulfilled and empty. Her limbs weren't strong enough to keep her upright and she crumpled against the mattress.

"Deepak!" she cried.

"Get on the floor," he said. "Now."

When she was moving too slow, he picked her up in one swift move and knelt with her in his arms until she was flat on her back. Her head lay inches from the iron Juliet balcony bars, and he sat between her spread thighs, stroking the smooth skin of her abdomen that dipped into her gorgeous, pretty cunt.

Her hair fanned around her, and as if she knew exactly what he expected from her, Veera reached over her head, and gripped the balcony bars. The curtains fluttered around her hands, and he was able to see the shadows and shapes of people on the other side of the street walking by. There was no way they wouldn't hear her scream now, he thought.

He bent her legs, hooking her knees over his forearms and plunged into her again. She gasped, moaning, and he reveled at the feel of her delicious heat as the cool crisp night air washed over them. He pinched her nipples, felt every tremble, every cry as he fucked this woman, this perfect other half of his soul, until she was a quivering mess.

He thrust, slow and deep next to the open doors, as they took each other between gasps and cries and pants, drenched in sweat, hands sliding over their slick backs, curls clumping at their temples.

When she orgasmed again, tears on her cheeks from the intensity of it all, her cunt sensitive and swollen, he laid her on her back once more, pressing his mouth against hers, chest to chest, their tongues tangling deep. Deepak's balls tightened, and he began to piston into her. He swallowed her tears, felt the sting at his scalp when she tugged at his hair, and let go until he came apart in her arms.

"Deepak," he heard her say with so much affection that he felt like it was breaking his heart.

"Vee," he said on a broken sigh.

CHAPTER 25

Veera

They spent the weekend in bed, their bodies pressed together until they were glued with sweat and heat. The food that Veera had made for both of them went cold, but they ate it like starving wolves anyway.

At first, they didn't speak about the future. They focused on pleasure, on pushing each other to their limits and exploring each other's wants and needs. But on Sunday morning, there was no escaping it.

"I don't think we have any food left in the house," Deepak said. They were sprawled across his bed, with rumpled sheets and crumpled blankets. The Juliet balcony doors were closed again because of the cooler air. Deepak lay between her thighs, his ear pressed against her soft belly, his thumb brushing the underside of her breasts.

"I feel like we should shower and go out for coffee," Veera said, as she brushed the curls away from his forehead. "There is a new bakery a few blocks down. They do latte art."

Deepak's laughter was a soft rumble against her skin. "I know how much you like the latte art."

"They also have blueberry scones," Veera added, hoping to tempt him into the breakfast date. She loved those quiet moments at a bistro table where his legs would bracket hers, and they'd share pastries.

His lips brushed against the side of her breast before he said, "You always know what I like."

"I do."

They descended into silence, and she felt his muscles tighten against her.

"Veera . . ."

"Deepak," she replied. Then she closed her eyes. *It's now or never*, she thought. She was one to walk away when her life became overwhelming, when she would need time, a lot of time, to process her emotions, but she was never one to run away from the truth.

"When did you first see me?" she asked quietly. "When did you first look at me and think that I was someone more than your friend?"

Deepak shifted against her until he lay at her side, curling her close. She recognized his familiar soft expression, the stubble on his cheek, the disheveled hair, and reached up to run her fingertips over the curve of his jaw. She felt his warm skin, the muscle of his arms as he held her against him.

"I've always seen you, Vee," he said softly. "That was never the problem."

"You know what I mean."

There was a long pause. "I don't know when it happened," he said honestly. "I wish I could tell you that there was a specific moment that I looked at you and I thought that I wanted us to be more than friends. I wish I hadn't been so focused on what I thought I should do, instead of what was right in front of me. After eight months of not having you in my life, when we met in that police station, I knew I had wasted so much time. Then I heard the words we committed to during our ceremony, and I didn't want to say them to anyone else but you."

Her skin cooled from his words, and she shivered as she began to detangle herself from his body. That was what she'd been afraid of, she thought. Because there was a chance that maybe, his attraction to her was rooted in the fact that Olivia was no longer an option for him. She sat up against the headboard and pulled the sheet over her naked breasts.

"What's wrong?" he asked. She saw the look of confusion on his face as he sat naked in front of her.

"I don't want to be a stand-in, Deepak. I don't want to be a replacement for Olivia."

Some of the confusion melted into amusement. "Vee, Olivia and I were never romantically involved. There was no love between us. There was a business deal."

"Isn't that what we have now?"

Deepak shifted so he was leaning at her side, his hands cupping her face. "If you believe that, then I've failed you in so many ways," he said softly. "And I value you so much that I would never disrespect you like that. I swear to you, Veera, I will never take you for granted again. I will never *not* appreciate what you mean to me."

He leaned down and pressed a kiss to her mouth, her lips parting as he pulled her impossibly closer. Veera's head swam. She pressed her palms against his chest and felt the strong beat of his heart.

She wanted to tell him how she felt, how much love she'd stored up for him all this time, but she wasn't ready.

He didn't look like he was ready to hear it, either, even as he asked, "Where does that leave us?"

"We don't have much time until the board meeting," she said slowly.

"This isn't about work," he replied. "This is about you and me. I don't want you to ever think this is about work now, Vee."

"We never had a real relationship, and we can't truly have a relationship until this board meeting is finished. A romantic relationship. I just want to . . . date."

"Date," he said blandly.

"Date," she repeated. "I want more romance." Then she leaned forward and kissed him on his chin. "I want more coffee chats and movie marathons where you fall asleep twenty minutes into a rom-com."

"They're boring," he muttered.

If he still wanted to be with her regardless of the results of the board meeting, then she'd tell him all of it. Her feelings, how frustrated she was with his tunnel vision, and how she wanted to live with him in his Brooklyn house, sign a practical prenuptial agreement, register their marriage at the courthouse, and live and work together.

But right now, they'd be together the way she'd always wanted, the way they needed, before they jumped six steps ahead into marriage.

She saw the tension in his face, the disagreement reflected in his eyes, but he pressed his lips together in a thin line. "Fine," he said.

"Fine?"

"Fine," he replied. "I can date. We'll date, we'll go out, we'll sleep in my bed, and when you see that we're just as good as ever, then I hope you decide to stop saying the word *fake* in front of the word *married*."

She wouldn't, couldn't until they spoke of love. Until she told him that she loved him more than tradition and culture and ceremony. Until nothing mattered but what they felt for each other.

Veera nodded. She used the edge of his expensive sheets to dab at her eyes. "Yeah, that sounds good," she finally said.

He settled back with her wrist in hand, a thumb brushing over her tattoo with the pad of his thumb. "Good," he said. "You know what is so important to me?"

"What?"

"The fact that you're my best friend," he replied. "It's so ridiculous to say at our age. Best friendship. Friendships now are about giving each other space, or accepting cancellations and knowing that life has come up. But with you, when I use the words *best friend*, I think it's about always being there in my life, every day, always within reach. With you, we aren't Veera Mathur, Mathur Financial Group, or Deepak Datta, Illyria Media heir. We're whoever we want to be. Cheesy, right? Your face is telling me it's cheesy."

No, it wasn't, she thought. Veera brushed another tear off her cheek and cleared her throat. "I'm so glad you're cheesy," she whispered.

"Oh, yeah? Good," he replied, eyes brightening. "Then if we're dating, it's time for a morning-after coffee run. Let's get that scone."

"You mean latte art," she corrected.

Then she laughed as he dove on top of her, covered her face in sloppy kisses, then scooped her up to carry her into the bathroom.

Maybe, she thought. *Maybe this will work out after all*. She just hoped that when the board meeting was over, he'd still choose her.

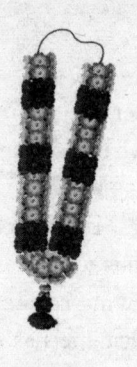

CHAPTER 26

Deepak

Text messages from seven months ago:

> **OLIVIA:** Hi, handsome. I think it's important that fiancés have each other's numbers, don't you? I can't believe we waited this long. We've already been engaged a few weeks.

> **OLIVIA:** Would you like to go out to dinner tonight? I was invited to a new restaurant that's opening in Brooklyn. It would look good for both of us to be seen in public together for Illyria Media Group.

> **DEEPAK:** Hi, Olivia. Unfortunately, I have a work engagement. Let me connect you with my assistant, Kim. She'll coordinate the best time for us to connect.

Deepak spent the rest of the week walking around in a perpetual state of bliss.

He was dating his wife. When he held her hand it was because he wanted to. When he twined his fingers through hers and kissed her knuckle right above the ring he'd given her, it was because he wanted to taste her skin. And when he laughed with her, it was because they had joked about something that was just for them.

He sat staring out of his office windows, looking at the clouded skies over New York City, the depths of fall rolling in like another storm, when there was a knock on his office door. He was about to tell his assistant that he needed another moment before he hopped on his next call when a deep baritone voice, thick with an accent, interrupted his thoughts.

"If this is what you plan on doing as the next CEO, I doubt you'll be able to convince Narinder on the board that you're a good enough candidate for the job."

Deepak whirled to see Veera's father standing with his hands tucked in his suit pockets. His thick white hair was combed back, and he wore a gold Rolex the size of a baseball.

"Mr. Mathur," Deepak said smoothly as he got to his feet. "I have a call in a few minutes, but I'm happy to make time if you need to review something with me."

Malkit Mathur stepped inside the office and closed the door behind him. "No need to be so formal. I am your father-in-law now."

Too bad the man hadn't acted like much of a father.

Deepak simply waited, legs spread, watching this former CEO peruse the shelves in Deepak's office. He stopped in front of a picture of Deepak with Bobbi, Bunty, Kareena, Prem, and Veera standing in their Taylor Swift shirts in Vegas at Prem's and Kareena's joint bachelor and bachelorette party. They were re-creating the opening scene from *Friends* in front of the Bellagio fountain, and someone was kind enough to take a few of the shots for them.

"When was this taken?" he asked casually. His fingers lingered on the edge of the frame, next to Veera's face.

"A little over a year ago now," Deepak said.

"Hmm."

Deepak waited for him to come around until the old man stood in front of his desk. "Is there anything you need? Documents for the board?"

Malkit shook his head. "I just came to tell you the news that we found a candidate that we're interviewing for the CEO position. They're a former Mathur Financial Group employee, and I believe they'd be an excellent fit for the role."

The news was a sucker punch. He'd hoped after all this time that the board wouldn't be able to find someone before his father's retirement. That they'd all just let it go.

"Anyone I know?" Deepak said casually.

Veera's father smiled, and it took on a sinister edge. "Possibly."

"Well then, I look forward to the competition," Deepak said. He made a mental note to ask his father about it later.

"There is one more thing," he said. Deepak didn't like the way his lips curved in a smile that was as slick as an oil spill. "I saw the little presentation my daughter put together. The equitable lending practices project? I ran the numbers, and it's not going to work for Illyria. Feel free to tell her that we won't be hiring her, or adopting her plan in the near future."

This time, Deepak had to school his features. His hands fisted at his sides. "I don't believe I asked you for your input or permission."

"You didn't have to," Malkit Mathur said. "I'm the CFO, and I work directly with your father. End of discussion."

Just as he turned to leave, Deepak leaned forward, resting his fists on the surface of his desk, the same one he'd had since he was promoted to director of the marketing department.

"We missed you at our wedding reception a few weeks ago," he said casually.

The other man stopped halfway across the room. He turned slowly. "Yes, I heard from some of the other board members that it was a beautiful affair. Unfortunately, people are still wondering about your intentions, Deepak, considering how fast you married another woman when you were engaged to Olivia Mathur."

"Because I was engaged for the wrong reasons," he said. Although this man didn't deserve the truth, Deepak gave it to him. "Now I have a question for you. Why did you encourage your daughters to work for Mathur Financial Group if you were never going to give them an opportunity to lead the company?"

"Excuse me?" Veera's father gaped at him, his face turning ruddy.

"You heard me," Deepak replied, as he rounded his desk. "It sounded like you were looking for a buyout opportunity with a larger business for a while."

There was irritation in Malkit's eyes, an arrogance that had hurt Veera in the past. "I don't see how this is relevant."

"I married your daughter," Deepak replied. "I'm thinking about hiring her back. In fact, I want to give her your job. I can see how incredible her work is. I know that her proposal has merit, and it's worth investigating. If we're expanding our operations, that makes it my business."

"My job?" The words exploded from his mouth in fury. "That would be the biggest mistake Illyria could ever make! As one of the largest shareholders, there is no way I will let you try to bully me into retirement."

"Oh, I don't need to bully you," Deepak said softly. He stepped even closer until he could see Malkit's pupils shrink. "Your numbers speak for themselves. I have been reading them as I put together the year-end reports for the board."

"That's *preposterous*!" Malkit stumbled two steps back and

straightened his lapel. "I see what this is. You're throwing a tantrum to get your way. Puttar, it's clear to me that as CEO, you'll just drive what your father built into the ground."

Deepak closed the distance between them again, looming over the older man who was beginning to perspire at his temples.

"Why are you so against Veera succeeding?" he said in slow, measured words.

"Because she isn't qualified to lead an organization," he said, his words taking on a hard edge. "She will never be qualified. She's too soft for this business, and she should be home like her mother."

Deepak wanted to believe in the selflessness of this man's comment but he had a feeling that it wasn't quite honest. There was something else there, under the surface, that had Deepak pausing. Then it all started to click into place.

"Are you threatened by your own daughter?"

The man sputtered. "You are out of your mind, Deepak. You, just like my daughter, have an inflated sense of self-worth."

That was it, Deepak thought as he rocked back on his heels. That was the real answer behind what was going on. "You *are* threatened by her. Because she is better than you. She calls you out on your bullshit. What kind of man is afraid of his own child's success? Malkit, you haven't seen her in so long. Doesn't she matter to you more than business?"

"That is none of your concern—"

"It absolutely is," Deepak said. "We're talking about my wife, and I will not stand for anyone hurting her. If you want to come in here and threaten to pull support because you think I'm unfit, fine. But if you're doing it to get back at Veera, at your incredible, intelligent daughter who has only wanted your love and your respect, then you're going to have a fight on your hands. Do I make myself clear?"

He saw Veera's father swallow, then take a step back. "Have you no respect for your elders?" he said in Punjabi. His voice wavered, thick with anger and disgust. "Have you no appreciation for what we've done to give you what you have?"

"I have plenty of respect for my parents," Deepak said. "But for you? Because of the way you've hurt Veera? Absolutely not." He absolutely hated when people demanded respect simply because they had aged past a certain point. Silent obedience was not in Deepak's DNA.

There was that glint in Malkit's eye again even as he backed up a step. "What makes you think you are so much better than me?" he replied. "When you've done nothing but hurt my daughter, too? We're no different, Deepak Datta."

"We couldn't be more different."

Malkit removed a handkerchief from his pocket and dabbed it at his forehead. "You're hurting Veera, too, are you not? After all, she was your *second* choice. My wife told me that Sana is still looking for Olivia. I specialized in strategy, Deepak. What are you hoping to do, pass one wife up for another when she comes back? Whatever is the most beneficial to you to get Illyria?"

"You have no idea what you're talking about."

"I don't?" he said, eyebrow raised. "As far as I know, your religious ceremony still hasn't been formalized yet. There is no marriage license. How long do you think that people are going to let you enjoy your little show before they start asking questions?"

Deepak clenched his jaw. No, he thought. He refused to put up with this shit. "Your absence from Veera's life, both personally and professionally, means that you've lost the right to talk about her in any way. Your little intimidation visit today is proof that you've gone too far."

Malkit opened his mouth to speak, but Deepak cut him off.

"Enough. Just know this, that whatever happens with the vote, I'll make sure that should you breathe wrong in my wife's direction, I will do everything in my power to wipe you out so that people won't even remember your name. Are we clear?"

The lines around Veera's father's mouth deepened into worn grooves. He adjusted his shirtsleeves while slowly retreating toward the door.

"I think your father and your family have taken Illyria as far as it will go," Malkit said. "Your father is at least smart enough to know that and step down."

Before he opened the office door, he stopped and faced Deepak. "Just know that I am waiting, as is the rest of the board, for you to leave Veera and go back to Olivia when it suits your business interests. Regardless of what the media says about how you look like star-crossed lovers, I'm not buying it. Whatever you think, I hope I'm wrong."

Then he was gone, leaving Deepak alone in his office, the light on his call comm flashing with his waiting conference line. Except all he could think about was whether Veera's father was right. Were people expecting him to leave Veera for Olivia?

Is that what Veera believed, too?

No, that wasn't possible. He paced the floor of his office, walking back and forth along the same worn carpeted space. Despite the very serious threat of losing everything he'd worked for, all he could think about was the woman who was currently littering his house with her charging cords and cables. The woman he flew halfway around the world to find and to be with.

His chest was pounding so hard that he had to bend over at the waist and prop his hands on his knees to breathe.

Damn it, he was having a heart attack again. Sweat formed at the base of his spine, and he closed his eyes and tried to breathe through the incredible pounding in his chest, his thoughts flooded with Veera. He stuck two fingers between his collar and his tie and pulled, trying to suck in more air.

In that moment, he didn't care about his legacy for shit, and all he wanted to do was make sure that his wife was okay.

He stumbled back to his desk to call his assistant. He had to cancel his calls for the day. He needed to plan. He needed a well-developed strategy.

CHAPTER 27

Veera

> **KAREENA:** Bobbi and I are planning for the fall festivals. Video chat this weekend?

> **VEERA:** What, like, planning trips to a pumpkin patch or getting apple cider donuts? I'm in.

> **BOBBI:** Not quite as "fall." Navratri, etc.

> **BOBBI:** We started doing it last year. Now that you're with Deepak, we can all do it together!

> **VEERA:** I mean, I could've done it when I was single, too, but yes. Sure, let me know when.

Veera knew that once her friends had partnered up, they would be a part of a world that was wholly different from her own. That they'd spend time together without her because they'd want to do couple things, and she wasn't a part of that.

But now, even in her fake marriage and real relationship, she'd started to see the extent of what she'd missed. And somehow, that made her feel even more alone than ever.

"Do you have your shopping list?" Kareena asked, as she looked at Veera through the video chat screen. "I sent it over. It's in a spreadsheet format. Plus, there is a Diwali cleaning list in there, too, so you know what you have to do for your first event."

Veera looked at Bobbi's face in the corner of her screen. "Do you have this, too?"

Bobbi nodded. "We built it together after Bunty and I moved in. This way, the aunties aren't breathing down our throats with last-minute reminders."

Veera knew that it was childish to think that she had a right to the information just because she was their best friend. Knowing Kareena and Bobbi, they probably thought they were saving her from a massive headache by keeping her out of it.

"I feel like I need to sync this in my Google Calendar. Is there a Hindu events Google calendar thing?"

"You'll get the hang of it," Bobbi said. "Durga Pooja comes first. To welcome her into your new home. But you don't really have to do much for that."

"Then comes Navratri, which is nine nights," Kareena added. "But you don't have to go dancing all nine nights. The aunties probably want to see you either the first or the last night."

"There is Karva Chauth after that, but it's patriarchal and up to you on whether or not you want to fast for your husband," Bobbi replied.

"Followed by Diwali," Kareena said.

Veera dropped her forehead to the table and then began banging it against the surface in a slow, steady rhythm.

"Oh, come on," Bobbi said with a laugh. "It's not that bad."

"What happened to the days when all we had to worry about was whether or not the groceries we bought a week ago are going rancid in our fridge? Or where we're going to go for a boozy brunch that isn't going to charge us by the glass?"

"Gone, my friend," Kareena said with a laugh. "We've traded it for cultural obligations and domesticity."

"And sex," Bobbi said. "Access to both sex and love. And five-course meals every day."

"Or sessions of playing doctor," Kareena replied.

"Good god, make it stop," Veera said.

"Come on," Bobbi said. "It's probably a nice break from worrying about Sana, or your future business. By the way, what is the deal with that?"

Veera wished she knew. She had showed her plan to two other Illyria board members who were former Mathur Financial Group employees, and she was met with a ton of positive feedback. Deepak's father had also asked for her pitch deck, which she provided. Since then she hadn't heard from anyone. She'd been working on a framework for how her equitable financial practices model would fit within multiple industries just in case she wanted to consult on the subject and Illyria didn't work out, but it felt like busywork.

"Let's just say that this board meeting can't come fast enough. Four weeks is too many."

"Has Deepak offered any support?" Bobbi asked. "I mean, he's getting what he wants from your relationship, but you should also feel like you're getting something out of it."

Veera shrugged again. "I am getting . . . it."

"Wait a minute." This time it was Kareena who leaned into the camera, her glasses framing her wide eyes. "You're getting . . . it?"

Veera debated keeping the information from them, but she couldn't. Her friends hadn't been malicious when they did couples things together without her. Treating them the same way she felt would be an asshole thing to do.

So, expecting a total meltdown and freak-out, she blurted out what had happened the weekend before. "I made Deepak Indian food, then I stole his sweatshirt, which I'm never giving back, by the way, and then he pulled my hair, and oh my god, it was the best sex I've ever had."

There was deadpan silence before Bobbi spoke.

"This happened four days ago, and you're telling us now? Thirty minutes into this conversation?"

"It hadn't come up," she said, weakly.

Kareena burst out, "Veera! You've been weird since you came back. No, you've been weird with us since you left on your trip. Why won't you talk to us? Ever since you've been away, we've had to find things out like they're just random facts when this is huge!"

She could feel her spine stiffen at the tone. "Hey, you guys have been busy. I haven't processed all of it yet and sometimes I need space to do it. I'm telling you now, aren't I?"

"That's not good enough," Bobbi said firmly. "You haven't had sex in what, years? Since that guy who was so happy that he cried every time he took his shirt off."

"I thought we weren't ever going to talk about Dan again."

Bobbi leaned forward until her nose practically touched the screen. "This is such a big commitment for you, and we want to be there for you. Now we don't know if you haven't said anything to us because there is something wrong and you're not happy, or because it's us."

Veera cocked her head at Bobbi's tone. Her friend *did not* just speak to her like that. "There is nothing wrong, guys. I haven't slept with anyone in a long time because I didn't want to. Then Deepak came into my life, and I didn't want anyone else."

Her friends were quiet on the video conference screen, as if they weren't sure what to say to her now that she'd effectively told them to mind their own business. She crossed her arms over her chest and waited.

"I'm happy for you," Kareena said. "I really am. But, Veera, we want to be there for you, and we can't if you don't feel like you can trust us with what's going on in your life."

The bitterness bubbled in her throat like acid, and the feeling burned. "I know that I left you both to travel with my sister, but I have always been here. I reached out every other day to share pictures and tell you where I was. And all that time, you two were traveling together, and making lists, and having parties. And not once did you tell me that you were doing those things and that you missed me. So excuse me if I think twice about telling you what's been happening in my life, too."

"Oh, no," Kareena said softly. Her mouth fell open. "I'm so sorry that you felt that way, Vee. We never—"

Veera sniffled, and she tried desperately to swallow her tears. "It's fine. Our lives are different now."

"But we're not different," Bobbi said. "We have partners, but we are still a unit."

"No, we used to be a unit," Veera said. "Now we're friends who are married."

"You don't mean that," Kareena said with a gasp.

"Vee, what are you even saying?" Bobbi added.

Veera's computer started flashing with an incoming video call from her sister, and she practically jerked out of her seat. Other than the odd text message, and the random voice recording, she hadn't had a chance to sit and talk to Sana since she'd first left.

"I'm sorry," she said. "I have to go. Sana is calling and she probably has news about what's happening with Olivia."

"Wait," Bobbi said, holding up her hand to the camera. "Veera, you know you can tell us anything, right?"

Veera wanted to believe that was true, so she nodded while she pressed a hand to her clenching abdomen under the table. "I'm sorry," she said. "I really am."

"We are, too," Kareena replied. "Love you, Vee."

She waved before ending the call and switching to Sana's window. Her sister's face filled the screen. She wore a knit cap, and her cheeks were rosy with the cold weather. Sana was obviously standing outside on some sort of a porch.

"Hey, where are you?" Veera asked.

Sana pointed the camera to rolling hills in the distance. The sound of wind whistled through the phone speaker. "It's gorgeous, isn't it?"

"Yeah," Veera said, when her sister's face filled the screen again. "Sana, what is going on over there? You're supposed to talk to Olivia and ask her if she's willing to come back for the board meeting the week before Thanksgiving. I haven't heard from you in a month other than something about you and Olivia getting to know each other."

"Things have been hectic," Sana said, as she looked out in the distance. "I got a call a couple days ago from Dad, and I've been doing recon to cross-check his story."

"From *Dad*?" Veera gaped at her. She always thought that she'd be the one who failed to hold firm on her boundaries first. She was always so eager to forgive. For Sana to talk to their father was huge. "I thought we were no-contact with him. What did he say? What did you tell him?"

Sana's jaw clenched, then she looked back at the screen, her eyes narrowing. "He said what I always knew would happen.

Deepak is fucking you over. He's lying to you, Veera. You're just not seeing it. I'm calling you to tell you that the deal is over, and you should go back to your apartment."

Veera understood the words that Sana was saying, but she couldn't believe her. Together, they didn't make any sense. "I live with him. We talk every day, multiple times a day. What could he possibly be lying to me about?"

"Your equitable lending plan," she said. "Dad said that somehow it got on his desk, on Deepak's father's desk, and it turns out that Deepak was the one who didn't recommend it. He shut it down. You don't have a chance of working at Illyria Media Group after all."

Veera collapsed back in her chair.

How was her equitable lending program rejected before she even had a chance of presenting the full pitch?

No, she thought. *No, there is no way this is true.*

"Dad is lying to you, Sana."

"Look, I normally wouldn't believe him," Sana said gently. "But he's the CFO. He gave me details that were so specific about your equitable lending plan, there was no room for doubt."

She rattled off some of the highlights that Veera had wanted to make.

"Oh my god, he did read it."

"I knew it," Sana said, her voice cracking like a whip. "I knew Deepak would fuck you over. I told him that I'd only bring Olivia back if he upheld his part of the bargain in supporting you, and he cheated. Just like he's cheating his way into the CEO role—"

"Stop it, Sana," Veera snapped. She leaned so close to the image of her sister that her nose practically touched the screen. "No one cheated anyone into the CEO role. I know you're angry on my behalf and I love you so much for always being there for me, but let me figure out what's going on. If you don't want to stay with Olivia and convince her to come back, then just come home. We would be happy for you to stay here with us."

"We?" Sana said, her voice incredulous. "You're a *we* now? You don't think he did it. Oh my god, Veera, you're defending him again!"

"I'm defending myself," she shouted over Sana's voice. "Why do you think I don't have any common sense of my own?"

"Because right now you don't, you *chute*. Why don't you fly out and come see me? Maybe with some distance, you can—"

"I got married, Sana," Veera snapped. "There is no turning back for me now, and you need to stop trying to dictate my life. I love you, and I can't tell you how much I appreciate you wanting to protect me, but this is too far. Believing Dad after all he's done is too much."

"I'm trying to *help* you."

"Well, stop it!" Veera snapped.

Before Sana could respond, her phone was snatched from her hand, and a beautiful face filled the screen. Olivia Gupta was a natural beauty with flawless skin, healthy, thick curls, and a pouty mouth with a shiny pink tint. "Hi, darling."

Veera's anger cut off like it had disconnected from the internet. She gaped for two seconds in silence, her hand falling to her lap, before she found her voice. "Oh. Uh, Olivia?"

"Yes, it's me," she said, then flipped her hair at the perfect moment for the British breeze to waft over her skin and flutter her curls. "Look, I know that you and I don't know each other, but it looks like we're sort of in this mess together. The four of us."

"The . . . the four of us?"

Olivia nodded. "You and Deepak, me and Sana. Since, you know, Sana and I are together."

"You and *Sana*?" Veera knew she was repeating everything that Olivia was telling her, but this was harder than her Kumon comprehension homework. "Are you two in England together-together? Like *together*? Wait a minute, you wrote about someone on your website. Were you talking about Sana?"

Olivia's eyes brightened. "Oh, you're so sweet! You read my website. Sana was right, you're adorable."

"Ah, thank you?"

Olivia nodded, her hair bouncing with enthusiasm. "I haven't told my followers yet, because we want to do a big announcement. Maybe at a pop-up venue in Miami. Surprise! Olivia has fallen in love after all."

"Olivia," Veera said. She cleared her throat. "We should probably talk to Deepak—"

"Oh, I agree," Olivia said with a smile on her face. "In fact, we're going to come back to the States soon. Sana has some meetings, and I think you two need to figure out who you trust."

Veera gripped the edge of the table. "Sana and I have always trusted each other."

"Are you sure about that?"

"I don't want to sound mean, but none of this is your business."

Olivia's eyebrows jerked up before her expression cooled. She looked away from the screen, and then the sound of a door slamming came through the line. "I think that's where you're wrong. And since Sana has stormed off, I'm going to assume this conversation is over. I have to soothe my baby now. Toodles," she said.

The screen went blank. Veera pressed her fingertips against her eyeballs. This could not be happening. None of this could be happening right now.

How did she end up in a position where she had to choose

between supporting her twin sister, and supporting her husband? The man she'd been friends with before she fell in love?

If one thing was certain, Veera was done sitting around and waiting for this ridiculous board meeting to happen. She had to do something, and she had to do it now.

She needed a whiteboard.

And maybe a latte.

Readers! Never underestimate the power of family when matchmaking your children. Your prospective match may be influenced by their siblings to pursue a relationship or reject one. Present as a united front as a whole family when you find the perfect jeevansathi!

There is no shame in bribing your other children, either. Sometimes incentivizing them to comply can also go a long way.

Mrs. W. S. Gupta
Avon, New Jersey

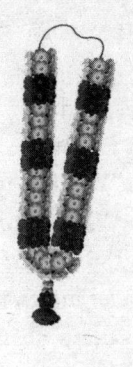

CHAPTER 28

Deepak

Draft email from six months ago:

> **Veera,**
>
> **I miss you. I think I made a mistake.**

It had taken Deepak the rest of the day to find a paper trail of how Malkit Mathur was able to get his hands on Veera's proposal. Apparently, Margaret had sent a glowing email with the proposal attached to another member of the board. That member had been open and receptive and forwarded the message to Malkit, urging him to reconsider working with his daughter.

The son of a bitch hadn't even spoken to Deepak's father regarding the matter.

Deepak knew he had to tell Veera what was going on. She deserved to know the truth that her father was behind sabotaging any plans she had of coming back to work as part of the Illyria Media Group empire.

He walked in his front door, toed off his shoes, and dropped his bag. He was about to call out Veera's name when he heard the dramatic start of Darth Vader's "Imperial March."

Veera did not like *Star Wars*. It was the only franchise she despised. For her to be playing the "Imperial March," something had to be up.

"Vee, honey?" he called out, his voice hesitant.

When he didn't get a response, Deepak took careful steps up to the main level. The kitchen was empty, but he heard the Darth Vader march getting louder and louder. "Vee?"

That's when he saw the chaotic mess on his dining table. There were papers strewn everywhere. Veera's laptop was open, and her screensaver was a picture from their staged photo shoot in Goa. They faced each other, and the sun shone behind them, illuminating their profile.

Seeing the picture made him feel safe enough to take a breath.

"Vee?" Deepak called out again.

That's when he saw the giant whiteboard in his living room. It stood on a metal frame attached to four wheels. From underneath the board, he was able to make out a hot pink pair of suit trousers and hot pink heels.

He also could hear the sound of furious writing, of dry erase marker on board.

Deepak walked over to her computer, then wiggled her mouse so the screensaver dissipated to reveal her playlist titled "Fuck Everyone" that she'd connected to his Bluetooth ceiling and wall speakers. Debating his chances of survival, Deepak paused the playlist.

The music died immediately.

"Hey!" Veera shouted. Her heels clicked against his hardwood as she took two steps to the left and popped out from behind the whiteboard. "That was my inspirational music."

"Well, hello to you, too," he said, amused. He took in her attire. The suit was definitely a new addition from Kumari's. It was vibrant, and she came alive with it hugging her curved frame. The shoulders were boxy, the coat cut high on her waist, and the pant legs flared over shoes in the same shade.

But it was her face that got to him. He knew that he would never tire of seeing her at the end of the day. He'd never stop wanting her to be the last person he talked to, the last person he touched before he went to bed, and the first person he laid his eyes on in the morning.

Crossing his living room, he bent to press a quick kiss against her pursed lips. "What happened?"

"What makes you think something happened?" she asked.

With his hands on her waist, he pulled her flush against him. "You look like a woman on a mission. You hate *Star Wars* but you're listening to the 'Imperial March.' My dining room is a disaster, and instead of one of my sweatshirts you've stolen out of my closet, you're wearing a hot pink pantsuit."

Veera sighed. She held up a finger. "First, I got into a fight with Kareena and Bobbi. That's . . . I don't know. We're in a weird place. Then my sister called and told me something that I need to talk to you about. It has to do with Illyria."

She looked wary now, like she wasn't sure how to tell him. Deepak could sense that her news was going to be the same as what he'd learned today, too.

"Yes," he said slowly.

Her brow furrowed, and she took a step back. "Yes to what?"

"Yes, your father canceled your equitable lending plan. I spent all day trying to figure out how he got his hands on it, and then I tried to rally enough support from other members on the leadership team to override his decision. My father loves it, but he won't be CEO for too long, so he doesn't really have a say."

Veera's mouth dropped open. "My father was the one who nixed my idea?"

"Yeah, he came to tell me himself," Deepak said. His hands dropped from her waist. "Why, what did you think happened? Wait, was that not what was bothering you, too?"

"Oh my god," she said, then capped her marker and put it on the silver tray behind the whiteboard. "That bastard! My sister called me today and told me that you had been the one to recommend that Illyria Media Group reject my proposal. Sana obviously believes that version of the story."

It was Deepak's turn to gape. He sat on the arm of his sofa in front of her. "What the hell? Why would I do something to sabotage my wife's work? Not only is it good, but it's designed by someone I trust."

Veera began pacing, her arms crossed over chest. "My plan is not just good, it's fucking fantastic!" Veera shouted. "I can't believe he'd lie and try to play all these political mind games! He's so determined to make sure that I never have a chance at getting back the job he took away from me. And you know what? I've had it. I don't want it anymore. I'm pivoting."

Deepak's head was spinning. "I'm so confused," he said. He reached out and caught Veera's hand and tugged her forward, so she stood between the V of his legs. "Did you believe your father? Did you think for a moment that I was the one who betrayed you?"

"What? No, of course not. Obviously, I trust you over him." She leaned forward and planted a quick, impatient kiss against his mouth, as if she knew she had to reassure him, but also had no time for his feelings.

Her impatience only made him smile.

"So what do you want to do? If you are done trying to work with Illyria, which isn't a dead deal, by the way, what's next?"

"I'm glad you asked," Veera said, her eyes brightening. She went back to the whiteboard stand and took care to remove the silver tray stacked with colorful markers before she carefully turned the board around. On the other side was a chaos of color and text. There were charts, diagrams, and math that added up to a sizable number.

Deepak pushed off the edge of the couch and approached the board. He started at the top corner and was able to figure out the way she worked through the information, her flow of logic as he got to the section where she'd done some quick back-of-the-napkin-type math.

"I realized that I am trying to capture a part of my life that I didn't even know if I liked anyway," Veera said with a shrug. "I worked for someone who obviously didn't appreciate me. Most of my colleagues were finance bros, and my sister and the work were my favorite parts. I thought I'd changed because of the trip I took, but I changed long before that moment. I somehow became this passive worker bee. I'm not a worker bee. I'm a Queen Bee, dammit. My proposal proved it, and if Malkit Mathur doesn't realize that, then someone else will."

Deepak ran a hand over her hair and down her back. Then he motioned to a large number at the bottom corner of the board. "That's it?" he asked. "That's the dollar amount you need to start the business?"

"That's it," Veera said. She shifted to stand next to him and crossed her arms. They were shoulder to shoulder, and he could feel the quick zing of electricity course through his skin. "I have half of it," she continued. "The orange is my contribution. The red is what I would need to raise. I think I have the contacts that can help me do it."

"I can help," Deepak said. "For most of it anyway. You have family and friends who can do the rest."

"Who?" The thought that she had family or friends who would be willing to fund her business start-up seemed to surprise her.

Deepak began listing off names as they came to mind. "My mother has quite a few of her own investments and would appreciate this. Then you have Bunty and Prem who would be happy to support you any way they can. But you wouldn't need that much from either of them. I can do the most."

Veera hummed. "I never recommend borrowing from family."

"You wouldn't be borrowing from me," Deepak said. "This is your money, too. We're married."

"Not legally," she muttered as she looked at the diagram and tapped her lower lip with a pink-painted index finger.

Deepak went rigid at her side.

Not legally. They had been married in culture and custom. They had performed all the rites and services. But to Veera, they still didn't have a real marriage. They were just dating.

Well, damn.

Unaware of Deepak's spiraling thoughts, Veera stepped closer to the board to look at some of the small text that she'd written on the right side along the edge. "I just want to do the work that I'm passionate about," she said softly. "I can't believe my father is so angry I won't fall in line that he's trying to hurt me to prove a point."

Deepak had to remember to unpack his feelings about making their marriage legal later. "You don't need his approval, and you never did. I'm here to support you. So many people will support you."

Her eyes brightened as she turned to face him. "Promise?"

Deepak pulled her into his arms again. "Of course. So, you're no longer mad about your father?"

She rolled her eyes. "Of course, I'm still mad at him, but I'm madder at my sister who is trying her best to protect me when I don't need it. She refuses to see beyond her feelings and think about all the times Dad has lied to us in the past. This is a power play a few weeks before your board meeting."

"I feel like I let you down," he said honestly. "I'm yet again part of the reason why you're facing this career hurdle." And if this was the reason why she wanted to leave him . . . Well, he couldn't blame her.

He'd fight for her, but he wouldn't blame her.

Veera rested her cheek against the soft fabric of his suit lapel, oblivious to his spiraling thoughts. "You didn't do anything. My father is the one who let me down again. And if I'm being honest, my sister is letting me down, too. She's hurting and she's doing what she thinks is best, but that doesn't mean it's okay."

"Where do we go from here?" he asked quietly.

"Straight to my own company," she replied. Then let out a long, heartfelt sigh. "If Kareena and I weren't arguing, I'd ask for a best-friend discount and ask her to start working on some business filing documents."

She propped her chin on his chest and looked up at him. Her eyes wide and clear of the animosity he'd expected. "Whatever guilt you're feeling, you can make it up to me by ordering takeout."

Deepak's heart filled with so much want and need for her that he was bursting from it. This time, he didn't need a cardiologist. He didn't need a checkup or a therapist. He wanted this feeling, this all-consuming joy when he looked at Veera.

Without another word, he stepped out of her embrace and un-buttoned his suit coat. He shrugged out of it before tossing it on the back of the couch.

Veera turned to him, a questioning look on her face. "What are you doing?"

"I just realized something," he said calmly as he undid his vest and laid it on top of his coat. "This is the first time that I'm seeing you in that pantsuit, and I haven't shown you how much I love it on you."

Veera's questioning expression morphed to humor. "You've seen me in pantsuits before."

Deepak loosened his tie and tossed it aside. His cuff links were next. "But not this one. Not the one I bought you. With heels and that ring on your finger."

She held her hand out and looked at the sparkling diamond before she spoke again. "Deepak, we are having a serious conversation about my future here. I'm plotting how I can get around my father, and what to do with the rest of my life."

He placed his cuff links on the coffee table and unbuttoned his shirt at the wrists. "Some exercise will help you think clearer."

She snorted, then motioned toward him as he began unbuttoning his shirt. "And you know exactly what exercise we should do."

"Obviously," he said smoothly.

"Fine," Veera said, her tone prim and professional. Her pink tongue wet her bottom lip and her cheeks flushed with rising anticipation, at his increasing nakedness. To his delight, she shrugged out of her own suit coat and tossed it next to his. It was followed by her camisole. "I'll agree to some exercise, but we have to turn the music back on. 'Imperial March.'"

Deepak paused as he unbuckled his belt. "You're joking."

"Not at all," Veera said, as her pants slid to the floor. She stood in the living room in a pair of basic chocolate brown high-waisted panties and a satin bra. "I'll have sex with you as long as it's to the 'Imperial March.'"

"Of all the ridiculous things, Veera." He was surprised that his erection didn't soften right then and there, but she was standing in her underwear in their living room. Now all he wanted to do was fuck her on every inch and surface of his town house. He'd neglected his duties as her partner to mark all their shared spaces with her orgasms.

"Fine, if you don't like the terms . . ." Veera went to pull her pants back on but there was no way that was an option.

"Wait, wait," he said, hand outstretched. Then debating his options, he groaned. "Fine, turn on the 'Imperial March.'"

Veera clapped like a seal and jogged across the room to her laptop. Her breasts bounced, her ass jiggled, and he was momentarily distracted when she bent over her laptop.

That was until his speakers began blasting *Star Wars* again. He rubbed his hands over his face as she returned to his side.

When they faced each other again, one foot apart and wearing only their underwear next to the sofa, Deepak started chuckling. "This is fucking ridiculous, Veera."

"Kareena loves Taylor Swift. Bobbi and Bunty are more of the Punjabi music couple. I love soundtracks to movies. This is my mood today, and this is how we are going to conquer what I can while I'm here."

"Nerd."

Veera shrugged. "I put it on repeat because we know that you're not a three-minute kind of man."

This time Deepak couldn't control his laughter. He reached for her, and they tumbled on the couch together. His hands coasted over her tight nipples and her round waist as he kissed her between smiles and chuckles. She straddled his lap, and he cupped her breasts. Then he slipped inside her and Veera's laugh turned into a sigh.

They moved together, falling in a familiar sink that filled him with joy. His hands cupped her hips, her hair fell around her shoulders to curtain their faces, as he sipped from her lips. And because he knew he could have fun with this woman, he could laugh with her, he pulled back, holding her still, even as he was desperate for more.

"W-what?" she gasped.

"You have to ride me to the beat," he said.

She almost fell off his lap, laughing so hard. Her inner muscles squeezed him, and he nearly came. Then Veera pressed her smiling mouth against his while Deepak squeezed her ass, slapping it hard enough to leave the imprint of his hand.

As Veera managed to create some sort of rhythm to the "Imperial March" and he lost himself in the feel of her taking her pleasure from him, Deepak knew that he couldn't wait to have thousands of moments just like this.

With Veera.

CHAPTER 29

Veera

The board meeting was fast approaching, and Deepak was acting like everything was just fine and dandy at home. He held her at night when they slept. They walked down to the bakery in the morning, he bought her lattes, and he asked her for her opinion about Illyria Media Group investments. He stood in front of her whiteboard and helped her figure out a business strategy so she wasn't relying on Illyria Media Group to continue. Veera also had told him about Sana and Olivia's relationship. They both had to come to terms with the fact that the couple was a permanent fixture in their lives.

And now, it was finally Karva Chauth.

As a holy day where women fasted for their husband's prosperity, it was an incredibly patriarchal practice, but Veera wanted to be a part of the ceremony, just once, for herself. Their marriage was a religious and ethnic one, which meant that it was completely reasonable for her to do it.

So she got dressed before dawn and followed the instructions the aunties had texted her about the morning ceremony. Deepak had been so sweet to her and climbed out of bed as well so he could help her get ready for the day.

Then her mother-in-law had showed up at her door at four a.m. from their New Jersey home. She'd carried bags filled with food and ritual things Veera didn't know she needed. With Deepak's help they had set plates for her, helped her with the pooja practice, and ate before sunrise.

"This is your first Karva Chauth," her mother-in-law said simply as she ran a hand down Veera's hair. "Married women take care of one another today, and as my daughter-in-law, you are my responsibility. My suggestion is to sit and watch *Keeping Up with the Kardashians*. They never eat on that show, so it won't tempt you, and there are enough seasons to get you through the day."

Veera laughed, then hugged her mother-in-law as tight as she could, appreciating every moment with her.

After she left, Deepak nudged Veera back into bed, cupping one hand over her breast as he wrapped around her and slept.

At noon, he left her side to get dressed for the office. He had to go to work for a few hours because of how close they were to the board meeting, and his father's impending retirement. But he gave her a long, lingering kiss and a promise for late-night cheesecake after she broke her fast.

When he returned at seven, he helped her carry her thaali out to the garage so he could drive them into New Jersey.

The end of the night celebration for Karva Chauth was going to be at Kareena and Prem's house since that was the most convenient place to meet for family and friends. That was what Kareena always wanted, Veera thought. She was happy her best friend was surrounded by so much love and community like she'd always dreamed.

"Whoa," Deepak said, as he pulled the car up against the curb in front of the house. The driveway was packed with at least four cars. "This is a lot of people, Vee."

"I told you that you didn't have to come," she said softly.

He put the car in park and turned in his seat. His eyes were full of warmth as he cupped a hand behind the back of her neck and squeezed. "It's your first Karva Chauth," he said. "Of course I want to be here with you. Technically, I *should* be here for you, since you're supposed to look at my face and then the moon before I feed you with my own hand."

"I haven't eaten all day, and you want to make smug alpha-hole jokes right now?"

Deepak grinned, unaware of how his life hung in the balance. "You really didn't have to fast for me."

"No," she said. "I'm fasting for myself. I needed some time to find clarity."

"Clarity?" he asked, as he unbuckled his seat belt. "From fasting?"

"Monks do it all the time. Pandits, too. And our aunties."

"Yeah, they're not the best example, Vee. Is that the kind of clarity you're looking for?" There was a questioning tone in his voice.

"Let's just go," she said. Then she got out of the car and when he met her on the sidewalk, they linked hands and walked side by side up the walkway.

The door was open, just the way that Kareena and Prem usually left it for parties. Upon entering the foyer, the thick aromatic smells of chickpeas, curried potatoes, and sweet semolina and raisin halwa filled the air.

There were string lights over the doorways and as they walked down the short hall into the large open space that now held both the living room and the kitchen.

When the aunties saw her, there was an echo of cheers. "The bride is here!"

As they swarmed around her in red silk fabrics, their mehndi hands waving in welcome, Deepak whispered in her ear, "Why are they calling you the bride?"

"Because it's my first Karva Chauth," she replied. That was why she'd opted to wear the same red sari she'd worn when they'd gone to Deepak's parents' house. She also had her gold bangles on, her mangalsutra, and the ring that Deepak had bought for her in Goa.

She was pulled forward, separated from Deepak like two pieces of Velcro ripped apart. The irony wasn't lost on her that a celebration of womanhood, of marriage, was more about the community of women that celebrated and less about the men that claimed they were a central figure in the practice. She followed the aunties and her mother-in-law as she carried her thaali to the living room.

Kareena and Bobbi met her next to the Pooja platform with silver trays in hand, as they leaned forward to press kisses to her cheeks.

"Hi, bride," Kareena said, before she touched the small gold baliyan at her ear. "I feel like I haven't seen you since Bobbi's engagement."

"That's because I don't think you have," Veera replied.

"I'm glad you were there," Bobbi said, as she wiggled her finger to show off the pear-shaped diamond.

They descended into a brief awkward silence.

Had that ever happened to them before? Had they ever had awkward silences between them? Their texts had been strained, and no one addressed the argument that had unfolded on their last video chat.

"Bobbi, are you fasting, too?" Veera finally asked, as she admired the palazzo pants and kurta Bobbi wore.

"Nope. But last year, Prem asked Bunty and Deepak to come and keep him company," Bobbi said. "I tagged along. Same deal this year."

"Where was I last year?" Veera blurted out.

Bobbi cocked her head. "I think at the time you had just flown to Madrid. It was right after the merger."

"I didn't even know this was going on."

Maybe they should have taken the time to talk about their feelings, Veera thought, because she definitely sounded bitter now. Dammit. She was so sick and tired of this bullshit. Of the secret plans that weren't intentional but hurtful all the same.

To Bobbi and Kareena's credit, they looked regretful.

"We need to talk," Kareena said.

Before Veera could say anything else, Mona Auntie called Bobbi's name from across the room. "I have to go help with the setup." Then she was gone, and Veera was watching her look just as comfortable as Kareena in this community of women.

"I should probably help, too," Kareena said. "Why don't you join us?"

Veera nodded. "In a minute."

She just needed a minute.

When she was alone in front of the pooja platform, she debated her options. Outside or downstairs into the basement where Deepak and the guys had escaped? No, people would notice she was missing.

An arm looped around her shoulders before she could take another two steps toward the kitchen, and she was pulled into a familiar embrace. "You look beautiful," the woman said.

Veera turned to look at Deepak's mother and gasped in relief. "I didn't know you were here!"

"I was just freshening up in the bathroom. I saw my son skulk away into the basement with the other spouses. So? How are you feeling?"

"Hungry."

Mrs. Datta laughed; her firm grip on her shoulders was an anchor that Veera hadn't known she'd needed. "Don't worry, darling. You'll have more than enough to eat soon. Will you come with me for a second?"

Veera looked at the room, the flurry of women cooking and setting up their silver trays. "Sure."

She held Veera's hand and led her back toward the front door until they were in the foyer, and the sounds of conversation were muffled. When they were alone, the older woman took a small silk pouch out of her shoulder bag and handed it to Veera.

"It's your shagun," she said quietly.

"Shagun?"

"It's a gift that a mother-in-law gives to her daughter-in-law. Some mixed nuts and dried fruit. There is some money for you as well and a coffee shop gift card. New lip gloss, too." Deepak's mother wrapped her hands around Veera's folded hands, her expression serious. "I know it's not a day for me to ask something of you, but I feel like I should."

"Sure, what is it?"

The woman looked over her shoulder and Veera realized she was thinking about Deepak.

"Your father is going to vote against my son at the board meeting."

Veera nodded. Even as Deepak and Veera had worked on her business plan, they'd talked endlessly about what Deepak could do to position himself as the strongest candidate and win some of the naysayers to his side. She'd called her old contacts, she'd spoken to Margaret, and she'd even reached out to a few team members who worked for her father to ask if there were any weaknesses they could explore on the board.

"Deepak has been . . . worried," Veera finally said.

"My son doesn't have a shot in hell," his mother said bluntly. "I know when we spoke in your home that we advised you not to get involved. There is one exception and that is when your children are impacted. Deepak will lose the vote if Olivia, your father, and Narinder and a few of the other staunch supporters of Malkit vote against my son. I know you and your father haven't been on speaking terms, but if there is any way you can convince him to think about Deepak in an objective way," she said softly.

"He'll never listen to me," Veer said, her laugh humorless and broken. "He didn't even listen to me when we were working together. He tried to sabotage my proposal before I had a chance to even propose it to the company formally."

"All I'm asking is for you to try." She reached out and squeezed Veera's hands over the shagun pouch. "This may be the only way to change his mind. As Deepak's wife, and your father's daughter, I can't imagine how difficult this is for you. And because of the way your marriage began, I'm sure there are a lot of people who are doubting my son's sincerity and honesty about how he's going about getting this role."

Veera gaped. "Excuse me?"

Deepak's mother's eyes sparkled, and they looked so much like her son's. "We all know that there was a bit of sharab involved. We know that it wasn't intentional. But both of you look so happy now, and that's all that matters."

Veera could barely speak, but she managed to get out, "How long have you known?"

The older woman laughed, her head tossed back in gleeful joy, before she straightened the pallu on her sari. "Darling, we've known from the beginning. We kept waiting for one of you to crack, but you've fallen in love, which is exactly what we hoped for."

She leaned forward and pressed a kiss to Veera's forehead. "You're stronger than all the men in that office," she whispered. "You're stronger than your father. And no matter how it happened, I'm grateful that you're my new daughter." Then with one pat on her arm, she turned to reenter the living room.

Veera sniffled back the tears and pressed a hand to the ache in her chest. Her fingertips brushed her mangalsutra. She remembered when Deepak had first tied the priest's beads around her neck during their ceremony and how much she wished it was real. Somewhere along the way, it had become so much more than a fantasy, than a wish.

She looked over at the hallway that led to the kitchen and took a moment to open the shagun pouch. Inside, she found the lip gloss, the gift card, and the dried nuts, as well as a small box of luxury chocolate, a ridiculous amount of cash, and a tiny jewelry box with a card.

She read the card first.

> *These were my first Karva Chauth gifts from my*
> *mother-in-law. She was a witch, but she had great taste*
> *in jewelry. Now these are yours.*

She wished her sister was there to see how happy she was. To know that Veera was finally finding her place.

Her phone buzzed at that moment, and she saw a message from Sana. Veera's hands tightened on her phone.

SANA: Where are you?

VEERA: At Kareena's house for Karva Chauth. Where are you? You haven't answered any of my calls for the last week!

SANA: It's a bit of a story. I'll tell you soon.

Veera stared at the text. Well, that was ominous, she thought.

"It's almost time!" Kareena's voice echoed throughout the house. Someone began singing an old folk song and other voices joined in.

Veera peeked out the window and could see the faint shadow of the moon through a stray cluster of clouds.

A full moon was the sign that it was time to eat, but it was also a time for people to lose their common sense.

Praying for the best, Veera reentered the living room and walked over to the small table that held every married woman's thaali. There were flowers on it, along with a small diya, the flame burning bright and hot. Uncooked rice, symbols in wet red tikka powder, a coconut on a bed of palm leaves. It looked exactly like all the pictures she'd found online and included all of the elements that the aunties and her mother-in-law mentioned.

"Come sit with me," Kareena called out from across the room. She motioned for Veera to join her on the floor. The couches had been pushed to the edges of the space, and the coffee table had flowers and a statue in the center. The women all spoke at once while they adjusted their saris, dupattas, and salwars as they formed a circle facing one another.

"I will lead the pooja again this year," Sonali Auntie said from her position as she put her tray on the floor in front of her.

"You will do no such thing," Falguni Auntie snapped. "You take your time, and we're all hungry here." She'd given up her Crocs but she still wore fuzzy socks on her feet that clashed with her red salwar kameez.

"This is not about food, but about spiritual fulfillment," Sonali Auntie responded.

"I'm too hungry for this," Mona Auntie replied.

"You're all weak," Farah Auntie added from her spot on the

couch outside the circle. "Haven't you ever heard of Ramadan? Now try that fast." She held a camera as if to take photographic evidence of the event.

Veera listened to their fight with amusement, enjoying the way that everyone was together. Her mother-in-law sat next to her and began explaining what would happen next.

Then Mona Auntie began to sing, and Veera was told how to pass her tray to the right and take the tray from the left. After she was able to pick up the words, or at least what she thought they sounded like, her voice joined those around her, melding with the aunties', with her mother-in-law's, and with Kareena's.

This was for herself, but also for the part of her that wanted to claim a space in a community that didn't make room for the single thirtysomething woman she had been. She had a right to be here, even though she hadn't gotten legally married. Her cultural marriage was a real one. She belonged.

Right?

After they finished telling the story of Karva Chauth, Veera went outside with the rest of the women and held her mesh channi up to the moon, then she turned to look at Deepak, who stood fidgeting in front of her as his mother took pictures of them together with her giant iPad.

When he came into view through the mesh sieve as she held it up between them, he smiled at her. Then in true Bollywood fashion, he pointed at the moon and gave it a thumbs-down. Then he pointed at her face and nodded.

This was the charming side of Deepak, the part of him that had rarely come out to play, the part that she had fallen in love with.

Veera put her sieve down, and Deepak took her to a corner where he held the tray between them and fed her the first bite.

"Now me," he said, smiling at her before opening his mouth wide.

She giggled. "Deepak, this is for those who fasted."

"I did fast," he said.

Her eyes went wide. "What? What are you talking about?"

"I fasted," he said. "If you weren't going to eat and drink all day to bless our marriage, then I was going to do the same thing. We're in this together. We've always been."

Veera looked over at the couples, including a laughing and loving Prem and Kareena before she turned to Deepak again. She felt that every moment they'd had together over the last couple months meant more to her than he could ever realize. She didn't want to wait until after the board meeting anymore, she didn't want to see if he'd choose his company or make a decision about their relationship over her.

Because she knew that she could trust him to always choose her.

"Deepak, I have something to tell you . . ."

"Looks like I got here just in time."

Deepak turned first and the shock on his face was enough to have her whirling around, juggling the tray in hand.

Olivia stood holding a Fendi bag in one hand and wearing a red close-cut dress that made Veera think she was there to commit murder.

And she was looking right at Veera's husband. "Hello, ex-fiancé. I think it's time we finally talked."

CHAPTER 30

Veera

Veera hadn't eaten or drunk anything all day and now she was sure she was being tested because she wanted to kill everybody.

And probably cry.

"Olivia," Deepak said. "What are you doing here?"

"I came because I had to talk to you," she said. "I'm sorry, it looks like you are in the middle of something, but this was really the only time that I could get away." Olivia waved to the aunties who were standing in the back making no secret that they were staring in open curiosity. "Is there a place that we can talk?"

Deepak looked over at Kareena and Prem who had crossed the patio to stand at Veera and Deepak's side. Prem was the first to speak. "We have an office upstairs. Why don't you both go ahead and have your conversation up there?"

Deepak turned to Veera and rested his hand on her lower back. "Are you okay with this? Do you want to come upstairs to hear what Olivia has to say, too?"

She wanted to roll her eyes. Of course, she wasn't okay with this, but at the same time, she was mature enough to know that Deepak and Olivia had some unresolved issues they had to sort out. "I'll be fine. You can share the highlights."

He pressed a kiss at the corner of her mouth. "Yes," he said. "Promise."

"Veera, there is someone waiting out front that I think you

should talk to," Olivia said quietly. She glanced up at the aunties and then back at her. "She didn't want to come in because she knows everyone here."

Veera straightened. Her sister. Sana was here.

"Should we all go around to the front?" Deepak asked Veera quietly.

"No, I'll talk to her myself," Veera said.

"Okay, call me if you need me." With one last look in her direction, Deepak motioned for Olivia to follow him through the sliding doors, into the house and down the hallway out of sight. If Veera was a stronger woman, maybe it wouldn't bother her so much to see Deepak with his ex-fiancée.

Or the fact that he once thought Olivia was the better fit for him for Illyria.

Because Illyria was still his first goal. His first love.

"What's going on?" Bobbi said in a low voice when she reached Veera's side. Bunty had also walked over, a small bowl of kheer in his hand that he was steadily devouring. If Veera wasn't so distracted, then she would've probably found the sight of him eating rice pudding out of a tiny bowl in his brawny hands amusing.

"Olivia is back," Kareena said to Bobbi.

"I saw that," she said. "But is there anything we can do to help?" She turned to Veera, her gaze always so perceptive.

"I honestly have no idea," Veera said. "I have to talk to my sister."

She slipped past her friends, and after one small, forced smile toward the aunties and her mother-in-law, Veera walked the front of the house. She found her shoes from the pile that had accumulated next to the front door. She paused at the base of the stairs, straining to hear voices, but when she was greeted with silence, she had to close her eyes and move on.

This was Deepak. This was her friend and the man she loved. They were sleeping together, and he had earned her trust and respect. She had to trust him now, too. He would never hurt her, even if he hadn't told her how he felt yet.

Veera quickly put her shoes on and walked out the front door.

Her twin stood at the end of the walkway. Sana Mathur leaned against a cherry red Audi parked right in front of the house. Her hair was slightly longer and curled at her nape. Her clothes were fitted dark pants, a tucked-in button-down shirt, and a long thigh-length coat.

"Hi, sis," Sana said slowly as she straightened. She held out her arms for a hug. "After eight months, you'd think I would be sick of seeing your face."

Veera's throat burned. "Same," she said and quickly made her way down the walkway in her sari and heels, bracing herself against the chilly night air, until she hugged her twin.

The soft warmth of Sana's familiar body, of her fierce hug, was a soothing balm. Deepak was the other part of her heart, but Sana was the other part of her soul.

"Sana," she said, as she pulled back, "why are you and Olivia crashing a Karva Chauth celebration in New Jersey?"

"We wanted to warn you before you both found out on your own. Thankfully, I still had Kareena's address from the last time I visited with you a few years ago."

"Warn us about what?" Veera said. She had a feeling she was not going to like this.

Sana shifted from one foot to the other. "We're not going back to the city. We're staying at Mom and Dad's house."

Veera gaped. "Mom and Dad's? You're seeing Dad? Sana!" The betrayal felt like a knife in the gut. "Why would you even consider letting him back into your life after all that he's done to us? To you!"

"It's more because Mom wanted to meet Olivia," Sana said. "And, ah, Dad and I are working on an announcement for my candidacy for CEO of Illyria Media Group. I've decided that I'm applying for the role. I have a really good shot at it, too."

Her sister, Sana, was the other candidate. Her sister was going up against Deepak and the board. Veera stumbled back a step. The wind whipped down the sidewalk chilling her to her bones.

"What the hell are you doing, Sana?"

"I'm taking an opportunity," Sana said, her voice hardening. She shoved her hands deep in her pockets. "Mathur Financial Group was our legacy. After running around the UK with Olivia, I realized that I didn't want to just consult with random clients. I didn't want to have to spend most of my time selling my services. I want the life that I had, and this is the best way to take it back." Her lips flattened in a thin line. "Working with Dad is like working with the devil, but he's better than trusting Deepak."

There was that bitterness again, that hatred her twin had developed for the man she loved.

"Deepak is not the person who is trying to hurt me," Veera said. "Dad was the one who canceled my proposal presentation. He nixed it before it even made it to Deepak's father's desk."

"There you go, defending him again," Sana said evenly. Her voice was the same condescending tone that she used to use when they were kids. It was often applied when Sana said, *Oh, Veera. There you go again, being so optimistic or nice to people.*

"You said you did recon," Veera replied. "What did you find out?"

Sana didn't answer her.

"You are such a chutiya."

"Hey! Don't call me a chutiya!"

"How can I not when you are literally a chutiya," Veera shot back. She wanted to strangle her sister. "You couldn't find any evidence that Deepak turned down my proposal, could you? You're trusting Dad."

"It doesn't matter," Sana said, chin tilted up, hands on her hips. "The board isn't going to support Deepak, which means the job has to go to someone else. Dad said that with my candidacy, we could run Illyria—"

Veera gasped. "You are kidding me!" she shouted. There was the sound of a car alarm going off, of a door slamming, of a dog barking down the street, and Veera counted to five, desperately trying to keep her temper under control, otherwise she was going to shove her sister's face in Kareena's manicured lawn the same way she beat Sana after her twin cut off her Indian Barbie's hair when they were seven.

"Sana," Veera said, trying to sound as calm as possible. "Dad is taking advantage of a situation. He sees you as a way to get that power and take over Illyria Media Group."

"He won't take advantage of me," Sana said.

Nope, there was no way she was staying calm. "This is why I will always be smarter than you are."

"Shut up, Vee!"

"Come on, Sana, be realistic," Veera said. "I mean, Dad is already getting you to do what he wants! You've never been the kind to write press releases about your intentions. Not until you've won whatever you're after."

"The press release is not just about the candidacy," Sana said slowly. "It's about your wedding, too."

Everything that she'd come to love about her new life was going to fall apart and shatter. "You wouldn't," she whispered, her voice barely louder than the wind.

"Vee, he's taking advantage of you," Sana said. She stepped forward, hands outstretched. "This is the only way. Then it'll be easier for you to untangle yourself from him and move on."

Something about her tone had the hair on the back of Veera's neck prickling. "This isn't about the job at all, is it? It's all about Deepak. It's about hating him because he gets the support you want."

"Fine, maybe it is about Deepak," Sana said, her eyes filled with rage. "You were taking his side again, defending him whenever I made a comment about the way he did business, the things he said, or his history with Olivia, and I could see you changing. I could see you moving further away from me."

"I'm not an object to belong to you or anyone else," Veera snapped.

Sana rubbed the back of her neck. "Look, when Dad approached me, I saw a way to the life I was promised, a life that was gifted to Deepak while we fought tooth and nail for half of what he received. He shouldn't get everything he wants while you're still unemployed. That's not fair. He doesn't deserve your loyalty. Hell, he doesn't deserve your love, either."

Veera wrapped the end of her dupatta around her ice-cold arms. "Can't you see that what you're trying to do is just going to hurt me in the end?"

"God, no. I love you! You're my sister. This was never against you." Her eyes filled with tears, and like it had always worked between the two of them, Veera's eyes immediately did the same.

Sana used her sleeve to swipe at her cheeks. "You may have forgotten, but I still remember when you called me, crying in that bathroom at your friend's reception party, devastated that he couldn't see you for how beautiful you really are."

"Can't you see beyond your rage?" Veera asked. "What happens if you win? What happens if this ridiculous plan of yours works out? That press release would ruin any chance I have of getting a job in this city when it's done. And that job you think you want? That life you are envisioning for yourself? It isn't anything like what you had with Mathur Financial Group. You got to travel the world and explore market areas, but I was here, doing the grunt work and dealing with Dad every single day." She jabbed a finger against her chest with every word. "It was fucking miserable, and I have way more patience than you do."

"I'll take my chances with the job, and I'll protect your reputation." She stepped forward to grab Veera's shoulders, to pull her into an embrace, but Veera shoved her sister's hands away.

"I don't need you to protect me," Veera said, as she walked backward toward the house. "I never did. I just wanted you around for your support."

"Veera? Wait, Veera, hold on a minute. Vee, he took everything from us!"

"Go see Mom and Dad," Veera said, as she spun around to yell back at her sister. "I hope you realize that his love is conditional and you stop this nonsense before you lose me, too."

"Fuck you," Sana snapped. "How dare you say that to me?"

"I'm your twin, jerk," she shouted. "I'm saying it about myself, too! *He failed us, Sana*. He failed us and it sucks, but being just like him isn't going to get you anywhere. And you're doing exactly what he'd want by hurting Deepak. By hurting *me*."

There was a sniffle and another gasp. "No, I'm not! We're twins. Twin-tuition! This isn't about hurting you—"

"Sana," Veera said, her voice firm and in a tone she rarely used toward anyone unless she was truly upset. "I am so disappointed in you that you can't see the truth. You should be ashamed of yourself."

This time, her sister's tears were audible, but Veera didn't stop. She refused to let Sana decide what was best for her. Veera had let her get away with it in the past because she truly didn't care about the outcomes, but this was her future. This was the man she loved.

Without another backward glance, Veera stepped inside the house and shut the door. The warmth enveloped her with such intensity that her entire body shivered. She looked up the darkened stairwell and wished that Deepak were with her.

What was she supposed to do now? Go back with the aunties and celebrate womanhood like her twin didn't just betray her? Go back outside and risk seeing Sana again and fighting some more with her twin?

After another moment of silence where she stood in the stairwell on wobbling heels, she realized that she had to leave. Between Karva Chauth and Olivia returning, between her sister going back to their father and Sana's bid for CEO, Veera needed to get out of there right now so she could breathe. She wasn't going to disappear like she had almost a year ago, but she wanted to go back to her house, the same one she lived in with Deepak, and get some air. Then, when he was done with Olivia, she wanted to tell him how she felt, lay it all out there for him so that there were no secrets between them.

She loved him, and she wanted to know if he loved her enough to support her, too.

Just as she turned for the door, a familiar face entered the hallway. Her mother-in-law's expression was painted with concern. "Beta, are you okay?"

Veera's eyes welled with tears. She felt strong but, damn, a good cry would definitely help her feel stronger. "I don't think I can wait for Deepak. I really need to go home right now and get myself together," she said, her voice cracking. "I'm fine. Really. Deepak and I are fine. But I have to figure out what to do with my sister."

The older woman nodded. "Then we'll get you home." She had her phone in her hand a second later and texted by tapping the screen with her index finger. "My driver will take you back to Brooklyn. I'll send your things with Deepak. Why don't you slip out now before the rest of your aunties come to check on you?"

Veera nodded, and before she could turn to leave, she wrapped her arms around her mother-in-law and squeezed. "No matter what happens, thank you for being in my life."

"Beta," the woman said, sighing. "Go take a few deep breaths and drink some water. You and Deepak will figure this out. The important thing to remember is that you have a whole village behind you."

CHAPTER 31

Deepak

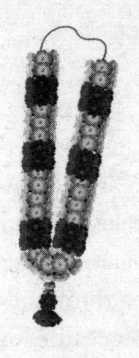

KIM ISHIYAMA: Boss, incoming! Attached are some surveillance photos I took.

KIM ISHIYAMA: Olivia is back in the country! She is traveling with your sister-in-law, Sana Mathur.

KIM ISHIYAMA: Both of them look so cool, don't they? Like you either want to be them or be with them.

KIM ISHIYAMA: I am not going to get fired for this, am I?

When things went to hell in his life, they ended up doing so in the most spectacular way possible. Here he was, under a moonlit sky, celebrating his marriage with this incredible woman, and the ex that he'd been trying to speak with the whole time to convince her to come back for the board vote shows up at his door.

Thank god for friends, he thought. The office upstairs in Prem and Kareena's house was the perfect place to have a cordial business meeting. There was a large standing desk in one corner, and two armchairs facing each other against the opposite wall. It reminded him that his and Olivia's relationship had been about business this whole time.

"What are you doing here?" he asked, as he switched on the light next to the desk and closed the door behind them.

"You know how I like the drama," she said smoothly. Olivia looked around the room, then crossed to the armchairs. Her long, manicured fingers brushed over the soft fabric of one of the matching throw pillows. "Your friends have good taste. I would've liked to get to know them better. Not like it matters now that you're married."

He'd rehearsed this a dozen times, and the only words that came out of his mouth were weak, and not nearly enough. "I'm sorry."

She raised an eyebrow. "For what?"

"For saying yes to marrying you knowing I was in love with another woman," Deepak replied. He knew that now. Veera had always been the one, but he'd been so stubborn about wanting to marry the perfect person for the business, not the perfect person for him. "You deserved so much more than me."

"Just tell me this," she said quietly. "Sana said you and Veera hadn't spoken since the day we got together, but I want to hear it from you. While we were engaged, did you—"

"No," he said, quickly. "No, not at all."

She cocked her head, as if she were genuinely curious. "Then how did you get married to her twenty-four hours after leaving me?"

"Didn't Sana tell you?" he asked. If they were together romantically like Veera had said, then Sana would've told Olivia all their secrets. The drunken night in Goa, and all the scheming that happened afterward.

"Deepak, she's not exactly your number one fan right now," Olivia said. "She is upset that you hurt both me and her sister. Anytime your name comes up, it's usually followed by the phrase 'fuck men.'"

He cocked his head to the side. "Hurt Veera? Because of her job?"

Olivia clucked her tongue and shook her head. "Sana is right about one thing. Fuck men."

"Olivia . . ."

She adjusted the throw pillow on one of the chairs, taking her sweet time. "From what I heard, Veera was in love with you when you were still friends. Practically from the beginning. She wasn't hurt that you didn't tell her about me. She was heartbroken that the man she was in love with was marrying another woman. A woman that he thought was perfect for him when she was right there."

He gaped at her. "Veera had feelings for me, for that long?" He pressed a fist to his chest. Some of the throbbing pain from the past few weeks seemed to ease. Wow, he really was an ass. How could he not see it? How could he not know?

"For being so smart, you developed a one-track mind, sweetie, and became way too concerned with Illyria votes and not enough with the person right under your nose."

His head still reeling with the truth about Veera, Deepak thought about Goa, about stepping onto that mandap, and smiled in memory of Veera's drunken exuberance. "I don't know how I missed it this whole time," he said quietly.

To love and be loved by his best friend felt like . . . magic.

Olivia sat in the armchair and crossed one leg over the other in one smooth move. "Once you catch your breath, what do you plan on doing about it?"

"Make it legal," he said immediately. "I want the second time around to be something that she'll remember even more than the first. I love her, Olivia." The words were so easy to say now. They felt as natural as breathing.

Olivia nodded, her mouth pursed, her legs spread as if to brace herself. "I'm not a bad person, Deepak. I'm glad you're happy. Just know that I don't know if I can forgive you. Not yet, maybe not ever. But I can be kind to my girlfriend's twin."

"I understand that," he said. "I can even respect it. And you didn't owe me your time, either, so I appreciate that you gave it to me so I could explain myself."

She nodded, her eyes shifting to the side as if she were thinking of what to say next. Then she added, "And I'm sorry, too. For the videos, and all the moments that I hated you. The truth is, if it wasn't for you, I wouldn't have spent time with Sana."

Deepak tilted his head, smiling. "How did you and Sana end up together? Veera told me, and I still couldn't believe it. Did she find you and then you saw her and thought 'yeah, she's the one'?"

Olivia shrugged. "We've known each other for years. Traveled in the same circles. We were always like a match and flame. And finally, we ignited." Olivia sighed, her expression relaxed and peaceful, as if she'd finally found her calm spot in the chaos that was her life. She was always so intense, and it was only fitting that she fell in love in such an intense, chaotic way.

"I'm happy for you, but what's with showing up at Karva Chauth?"

"Oh," she said. She blinked in rapid succession. Her long lashes fluttering. "I didn't want you to be caught by surprise. Neither Sana nor I thought you two should see it in the news."

"News?"

"Sana is the other candidate the board is considering for CEO. Because of her connections, her experience, and the fact that she's a queer Indian woman in an industry that needs change in the C-suite, she can unseat you."

"Shit," Deepak said. He had wondered if Sana was the candidate. His incredibly efficient assistant had been keeping him up-to-date on office gossip, but no one could figure out the details. "I was afraid you'd say that."

Sana would be amazing at the job, no doubt about it. And she had just as much of a claim over Illyria as he did when it came to legacy.

Olivia checked her coffin-shaped nails, a term he'd learned from reality TV that Veera had made him watch the week before. "The board meeting isn't for another week, but Malkit wants to do a big press release and announcement. The intention is to create some chaos. His plan is to accuse you of setting up the wedding with his daughter as a way to distract from the fact that you aren't fit to be the next leader. That you lack maturity and knowledge to be the head of a global organization."

Deepak sat heavily in the desk chair opposite Olivia. He braced his forearms on his knees. This news kept getting worse and worse. He scrubbed his hands over his face.

"How can Sana not see what her father is doing?" Deepak said. "He's *using* her."

"I know," Olivia said gently. Her sigh was heavy. "I don't agree with any of it, so I convinced Sana to stop here on the way to her parents' house. I told her she should warn her sister first. She's not listening, Deepak. Hopefully Veera can talk some sense into her. But my baby is hurt and she's trying to protect both her sister and herself. Not that she wouldn't make an excellent CEO, but she doesn't want it. She would hate leading Illyria Media Group."

Deepak could understand why Sana was lashing out. The way Veera talked about her twin bond was something special and different from what he, as an only child, ever knew. But from a practical perspective, he also knew that this was a PR nightmare about to happen.

Deepak's thoughts raced with all the potential pitfalls a message intended to create chaos could do, especially if that candidate was a Mathur daughter who had been ceremoniously kicked out of the company before the merger. That kind of gossip would impact their stock prices, and there was a chance they would lose advertisers over it. Right before their big holiday season.

His goal should be to squash any plans for Sana's candidacy and protect Illyria Media Group. He had spent his entire career determined to cultivate the company that his grandfather and then his father had built. He was set to lead an empire.

But if the press release referenced his marriage, questioned Veera's intentions and character, then he'd give up his career, the company, and his dream in the blink of an eye to protect Veera's heart.

"I have to go," he said and got to his feet. He needed to be with Veera. He needed to tell her how much he loved her, and that everything would be okay. He wanted to tell her that if she wanted to support Sana, he wouldn't ask her to choose between her twin and her husband.

And he needed to tell her that he knew. He knew that she loved him and that he felt the same way. That he wanted to do more than date. He wanted to make their marriage permanent.

Legal.

Forever.

Seven lifetimes with Veera Mathur would never be enough.

"Thanks, Olivia," he said. He held out a hand to help her to her feet. "This means a lot to me that you're here."

"You're welcome," Olivia replied. She placed her clawed fingers in his, accepting his offer of assistance. Then he let her go, the cool, professional connection between them the same as it ever was. She crossed the room but paused when she touched the door-knob. Her smile was enhanced with a shiny peach gloss. "It's so strange, isn't it? That the Mathurs have these incredible daughters, but their father is an absolute prick. And you're an absolute prick, and you have these incredible parents."

Deepak grinned at her. "You're hilarious. Absolutely hilarious. Why don't you save it for your column instead of trying to dish out terrible auntie advice in person? It doesn't suit your influencer role."

Olivia winked at him. "I think it's time for Mrs. W. S. Gupta to retire anyway. What started out as a joke has become way too serious for the rest of the Indian community.

"I remember when you gave me the job all those years ago, and we planned it out to be more of a farce, but there are WhatsApp chats dedicated to that column now. Way too creepy. Besides, it's only a matter of time before the rest of the board realizes who I am."

"I can protect you," Deepak said simply. "Even with all the passive-aggressive digs that you've made over the last few months, I'll shield the information personally. After all, I've kept it a secret all these years when you first started working freelance at *Indians Abroad News*. Even when you were tearing apart my best friends, Prem and Bunty, and I wanted to fire you for the stunts you pulled. If you want to keep writing . . ."

Olivia shook her head, her smile deepening. "Mrs. W. S. Gupta has caused enough problems in your life over the years. And Prem's love life was hilarious content. I had no choice but to write about him."

"You're just lucky it turned out okay," Deepak said dryly. He would've immediately told his best friend about the columnist, but after all these years, he honored the nondisclosures he had signed with a young, eager Olivia who had just wanted to make content and heal from the grief of her father's sudden death.

"It always turns out okay, Deepak." With a salacious wink, she said, "It'll turn out okay for you, too. Let me know how I can help. I'll gladly work with you to get Sana out of her father's clutches." She was out the door in a flourish of big hair and perfume.

Deepak smiled, and he knew that if their circumstances were different, they could still be friends. But right now, he needed to talk to Veera.

He left the office and walked down the stairs to the foyer. He half expected Veera to be waiting for him, but instead, all he found were his mother, Kareena, and Bobbi.

"I had my driver take her back to Brooklyn," his mother whispered when Deepak reached her. "She left almost ten minutes ago. She said she didn't want to be here. My daughter-in-law is upset, Deepak. Go fix it."

He wasn't sure what Sana had said to Veera, but knowing that she left on her own, that he wasn't there to support her . . .

Deepak kissed his mother's cheek. "Do you think you could—"

"I'll handle everything," she said, then motioned for Deepak to go.

He didn't waste any more time, and with a quick "thank you" and kiss on her cheek, he was out the door. He had a runaway wife to catch.

CHAPTER 32

Deepak

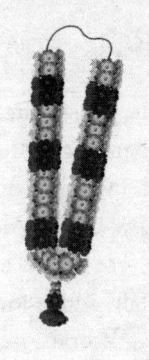

> **DEEPAK:** Mom has the aunties. Hold the fort.

> **PREM:** Got it

> **BENJAMIN:** Done, brother.

"Veera!" Deepak called out as he burst through his front door.

Heart pounding, he locked the entrance, then jogged up the stairs to the main level. The kitchen was dark, empty, with discarded dishes in the sink, exactly as they had left it that morning.

"Vee?" he called her name again, as he strode past the dining room where Veera had left her laptop and charging cable, through the living room, which was clean for once, with the throw pillows in their appropriate corners, positioned at an angle. The shadows of neighborhood vibrancy pulsed through his sliding doors, muted by his curtains.

He took the stairs two at a time to their bedroom, the one that they had shared since they'd first had sex—since they'd first made love. The lights were on, the bed unmade, but Veera was still missing.

He spun in a circle, unsure of what to do with himself, when he heard footsteps through the ceiling. They were coming from the guest suite. When was the last time she'd gone up there other than to get dressed? To store her things? His stomach knotted at the thought of her wanting to sleep in a separate bed than him now that she'd spoken to her sister.

He turned and ran up to the third floor, cursing the number of stairs in his town house.

"Veera?" he called out again. This time, he saw light from under the door at the end of the hall. She was here. She was still in their home. He was going to knock and tell her that he wanted to give her whatever support she needed. Deepak was going to be rational and calm about this, even as his heart began to pound at the thought of losing her.

Assess, address, then reevaluate.

As he approached her bedroom, all common sense flitted out of his brain.

He busted the door open.

She stood in front of the bed, an empty suitcase on top of the comforter. Half her clothes were folded and placed neatly inside. Her face was blotchy, her mascara smudged as if she'd recently cried. She wore his Columbia sweatshirt and the leggings that he loved because they cupped her butt.

"Deepak?"

Why was she packing? Why had she been crying?

If she planned on leaving him, there was no way he was going to let her go without a fight. Or without some serious begging on his part.

"No," he said, his voice so cutting that she jerked back at the sound of it.

She gaped at him. "No? What do you mean *no*? You can't just barge in and say no."

"I can, and I did," he said. Then in a fit of panic, he strode over to her suitcase, scooped up the folded piles she'd made, his arms overflowing with jeans, T-shirts, and blouses that she'd neatly packed in the bag, and walked out the door.

"Deepak, what are you doing?" she said, her voice reedy and high-pitched. "Where are you going?"

He stormed downstairs, across the landing, and into his bedroom. The sensor lights flickered on as he walked into his closet and turned toward the built-in dresser. That's where he'd cleared out space for her things a week ago. He managed to open one of the drawers and dropped the pile of clothes inside. Deepak shoved the drawer closed, then turned around and headed back upstairs, with Veera following at his heels.

"Wait," she called after him, even as he went straight to the closet in the guest room and grabbed all of her new pantsuits in a bear hug, yanking them off the wooden rod, before he walked past her again.

"Deepak, stop! I need those!"

"You are not packing," he said then practically raced back down to his suite where he came to a halt in the middle of the closet and scanned all the meticulously designed shelfing units. Shit, he hadn't thought about where her clothes would hang. He'd have to build out an extension so that she had ample room.

Veera stormed in after him and stood in the middle of his suite, hands fisted at her sides. "Let go of my clothes, Deepak! I can't believe I'm saying this, but you are making a mess, and you need to stop right now!"

"You're not going anywhere," he shot back. Then he dropped the armful of soft fabrics between them, the same fabric that smelled like Veera. Silks, satins, and cottons fluttered to the floor. He stepped over them and reached for her.

Some of his anxiety abated when she didn't shy away from his touch. As careful as he'd ever been in his life, Deepak stroked his hands over her shoulders to her wrists, touching her cheese tattoo, the diamond ring, and tugging her closer so he could lean down and kiss her puffy eyelids.

She let him do all those things, remaining pliant in his arms. Was she mad at him? Was she so angry that she was packing up to go? If so, why wasn't she raging now? Why wasn't she telling him to leave?

"Married spouses live together," he said, looking down at her upturned face.

"Fake married," she said, like the world's worst broken record.

"We'll go to city hall tomorrow and we'll get that fixed, then. I was planning on taking care of the marriage certificate soon, anyway."

Veera tugged her arms out of his grasp, then stepped back. "Before I yell at you for messing up my clothes, tell me what Olivia said to you in the upstairs office. Did she mention my sister?"

"That's what you want to talk about?" he asked, incredulous. He was losing his mind in fear that she was leaving him, that at best she was moving back upstairs and at worst she was going to stay with Sana and Olivia.

"That's what I want to talk about," she said.

Deepak scraped a hand over his jaw, a small stubble forming where he'd shaved that morning. "If you're asking whether I know about Sana's CEO candidacy, I do. I don't care."

Veera gaped. "What do you mean, you don't care?"

He shrugged. "I don't care. I did for a moment, but then I realized that if I fought back, you'd be stuck in the middle and I'm not doing that to you."

She held up her hand again to stop him. "You almost married

Olivia Gupta to secure your legacy. What happened to wanting to honor your grandfather or something like that?"

"I want you," he shouted. "I want you! I *love* you, Veera. Why the fuck didn't you tell me that you loved me, too?"

His roar lingered in the room, and then there was silence. Veera's eyes went wide. "Y-you know."

"Olivia," he said, breathing heavily.

He'd assessed, addressed, and reevaluated his life over and over again, and the truth had been there right in front of him from the very start.

He realized now that he'd been so afraid that she wouldn't love him in the same way he loved her. That if he kept quiet, there was hope they could hold on to whatever friendship they'd begun their relationship with, even if it was false hope.

His heart pounded in his ears hard enough that he could barely hear his own voice. His palms sweat, and his breath came out in ragged bursts as he looked at his very serious best friend, his partner, his wife, who was stunned into silence. "Vee, whether you're in the middle of the office, or you're in my home wearing my clothes, leaving your cords and cables everywhere, I love you. I want to be with you. I want to show you how you are the most important person in my life, and I swear I will never take you for granted again."

Veera's eyes filled with tears. "You . . . you love me?"

"Until I'm mad with it," he whispered. He felt like he was toppling over an edge and falling had never felt so breathtakingly beautiful before.

When she didn't say anything, when all she could do was stare at the clothes on the floor, he had an idea.

"Don't move," he said. Then he ran out of his room to the small hallway pantry next to the stairs. He rarely opened the single pane closet door since he only used it as a way to honor his parents. The motion sensor lights flickered on, and at eye level was a tiny shelf decorated with statues of Hindu gods and goddesses. In front of the statues was a small, mirrored tray holding a few essential vials and containers.

Deepak retrieved a red flat plastic container the size of a dollar coin. Then he ran back to his room, careful not to spill the vermilion powder.

Veera was still standing next to the pile of her clothes that he'd dumped on the floor, and he approached her while carefully opening the container.

Veera's eyes widened. "What are you—"

"From the moment we walked around that fire on the beach, you've been my *life* partner. My jeevansathi." He pressed his thumb in the powder, and in one firm flick of his wrist, he streaked it along her hairline, marking her as his wife.

As a married woman.

That's when she let out a loud, wet sob.

"I've loved you from the beginning, Deepak," Veera said, her voice cracking. "And you never saw me as anything more than a friend until you couldn't have the woman you wanted."

He was so stunned that this brilliant incredible woman could ever believe she was his substitute when all he'd ever wanted was to be with her, knowing that he was the one who was never good enough for her.

"How could you think that you could ever be second best to anyone?" he whispered.

Veera sniffled, then spun on her heels. "I need to go upstairs," she said. She reached up to touch the powder, then her hand dropped at her side as she began to walk out the door.

No, he thought. No, she was leaving him. She loved him, but she was still packing to go.

"For god's sake, will you stop running away from me?" he shouted, panic a fist in his gut. "I thought you needed space, but this is not just space, is it? You're leaving again. You ran away to Europe—"

Veera gasped and turned to face him again. "Because I lost my job! I lost my *father*."

"You ran away from us," he shot back. "I was a fool, but so were you. And now you're running away again! That's cowardly for someone as resilient as you. I'm sorry it took me so long to figure out that I was afraid of how much I loved you. We're together now, and I don't want to let you go. Don't let me go, either. Please."

Then, because he knew he was begging for his life here, he crossed to her and got to his knees in front of her, before he wrapped his arms around her waist and pressed his face into her abdomen.

"Please," he said into her shirt, the pounding in his ears growing impossibly louder. "I swear, I will show you how much I love you every day for the rest of our lives together. I need your cords everywhere, your throw pillows, and our movie marathons. I need to go to the bakery at the corner and know that you'll order the blueberry scone for me, but you'll eat half of it. I need to know that we'll always toast with a whiskey at a party, because we've decided that it's bad luck if we don't. I need to watch those healthy cooking YouTube videos with you knowing that we'll end up ordering out anyway. I need you by my side like I need air because just being in the same room with you makes me feel like I'm the strongest man alive even if I lose Illyria."

He buried his face in her stomach, and then felt the tentative touch of her fingers in his hair, stroking over his shoulders, and he shuddered. There was the sound of a sob, and Veera fell to her knees in front of him, so that they both were caught up in each other's arms, holding on like they'd finally found each other, even though they'd been right there the whole time.

"I can't believe you called me a coward," she whispered, as she cupped his face in her hands. "Then you acted like some Bollywood movie hero and put sindoor in my hair."

"Desperate times," he whispered back.

"I can get my own scone," she replied.

He pressed a kiss against her wrist. "I love you even if you don't, Vee. I love you for all of it. Just please don't go."

There was a long pause, until finally, she giggled. She giggled and hiccupped. "I wasn't going anywhere," she whispered. "I wanted to move my clothes down here into your suite because I had no intention of letting you miss out on what we are together. We're partners. I won't get between you and my sister. And you aren't going to ask me to choose. But we're permanent fixtures in each other's lives."

He felt like he was having one of those heart attacks again, the ones he'd been telling Prem about. He shuddered, pulling her closer into his arms.

"Vee, I'm sorry it's taken me so long to catch up," he mumbled against her throat, his arms banded around her back, while she circled his shoulders and neck.

"You're forgiven," he heard her whisper.

It was a while before they pulled apart, separating inch by inch, each added degree of space punctuated by kisses and tentative touches. They caught their breaths, and Deepak knew the rush of almost losing each other was an adrenaline spike they needed to process.

He looked at the mess he'd made and sighed. "I'm going to have to pay for dry cleaning, aren't I?"

She sniffled and nodded. "Yes. Do you really not care anymore about the CEO position?"

"As long as I have you, then, no."

"That's ridiculous," she said, then blotted at her cheeks with her sleeve. "If you're as smart as I know you are, you should be able to figure out how to love me *and* keep the company. I've never asked you to sacrifice Illyria for me, to sacrifice the legacy that's so important to you, and you wouldn't be the man I loved if you were so willing to give up bazillions of dollars."

He chuckled and helped her to her feet. "Is that an official financial adviser term?"

She raised an eyebrow, managing to look haughty despite her botchy swollen eyes. "Want me to calculate your net worth to figure out to the decimal point how expensive your sacrifice will be?"

"No, I trust you," he said, before he pressed his lips firmly against hers, kissing her until he felt his knees weaken and his chest swell.

When they came up for air, he said, "Love you, wifey."

Veera sighed. "We're going to have to work on that."

CHAPTER 33

Veera

> **VEERA:** I'm sorry I ran out on you both.

> **VEERA:** We need to talk.

> **VEERA:** Can we meet in person?

> **KAREENA:** Clearing my schedule tomorrow.

> **BOBBI:** Me, too. Come to my place.

Veera knew that even though she had been so mad at her friends for feeling left out, for the way that their relationship was changing because of how their lives had shifted, they were the first people she wanted to talk to after she found out about Sana's plan. They were the friends that despite their differences, she knew she could count on.

Two days after Karva Chauth, she sat down on Bobbi's couch in the large Jersey City loft space that used to be Deepak's apartment before he sold it to Bunty. It was exceptionally designed with high ceilings and a gourmet kitchen. The space was also beautifully decorated, featuring jewel tones and floral flourishes, just like Veera expected from Bobbi's home.

Her friend, now with a diamond of her own winking on her left hand, sat next to Veera and handed her another tissue.

"I'm going to kill her when I see her again," Veera said. "She's always been the more perceptive person between the two of us, but now I'm not so sure. Did you know she somehow convinced me to go on this strange German's boat and it almost sunk with all of us on it? And now this! At Karva Chauth, we were yelling at each other so loud that I'm sure we were the reason the neighbor's car alarm kept going off."

"I bet it was because their son was trying to sneak out again and pressed the alarm instead of the unlock button," Kareena said from her spot in the armchair across from the coffee table. "He's done that before."

Bobbi shook her head at Kareena. "Vee, it sounds like you have every right to be that angry."

"I know, right?" Veera cried. Then she noisily blew her nose into a tissue.

"What does Deepak say?" Bobbi asked.

That was the last question Veera wanted to hear. "Why does it matter?" she said. "I don't need him to tell me how to murder my twin. I can make my own decisions."

"Honey, I'm not talking about murder. I'm talking about Sana's chances of being the alternative candidate at Illyria."

"He's not happy about it, but he's more worried about me," Veera said. She dropped her head against the back of the couch and closed her eyes. "He won't talk to me because he thinks that I'll feel like I'm taking sides. To be fair, I told him I didn't want to get in the middle, but that doesn't mean I won't be a sounding board if he needs me. He's just . . . shut down all conversations about business the past couple days."

"You two are stronger together," Bobbi said and patted Veera's leg. "You'll think of something."

"And we're stronger as a group of six," Kareena added. "If you need more help, we'll get together and we'll sort it out."

The reference to friendship had Veera's anger subsiding, and guilt taking its place. She'd called her college roommates, her ride-or-die besties, begging for a moment of their time because she wanted to talk to them, and without a moment's hesitation, they dropped everything to come and see her.

She sat up in her seat and dabbed her eye again with the tissue. "Kareena, I'm sorry if we ruined your Karva Chauth."

Kareena waved a hand in dismissal. "Are you kidding me? The aunties loved every moment of it. They'll be talking about Olivia's entrance for *years*. I'm just glad you and Deepak are okay. And maybe now, you'll stop acting like a weirdo around us."

Veera thought about Kareena's words and nodded. "I guess when we were all single, I assumed that we'd go through all the stages of our lives together. I thought that we'd find our loves together, we'd get married and have babies together so there wasn't a moment where we didn't know how the others felt or where one of us was left behind. And I was so happy for both of you. So happy," she repeated. She looked at both Bobbi and Kareena, then back.

"But you were moving on, and I was stuck in the same place that you'd left me. I was the single friend with married friends. Always the bridesmaid, never the bride." She remembered the first time Kareena and Bobbi had canceled on her because they were with Prem and Bunty. She'd sat alone on her couch with takeout, old episodes of *Buffy* playing on her TV, while she tried so hard to convince herself that loneliness wasn't allowed. That marriage and dating and men weren't the answer.

She knew that marriage didn't work for everyone, and companionship could come into her life in so many different ways. She was going to be the single friend with lovers.

Except that wasn't what she wanted, and she was so ashamed of her unhappiness.

"I'm not going to tell you how ridiculous you were being, because we've all felt that way," Bobbi said softly. "I'm just sorry if we were a part of why you were in that position."

Veera nodded. "I was the person who chose work over love, and who people assumed was too picky or not attractive enough to find a partner, when it was really that I fell in love with a man who didn't see me. When I came back months later, both of you had this language, these moments that you shared that didn't include me, either."

Bobbi shifted so that her back was against the couch, and her side was pressed to Veera's. Kareena crossed the room and sat on Veera's other side and assumed the same pose. Then they all slumped in their seats and linked hands, staring up at the ceiling together.

"Just because we found people we want to have in our lives," Kareena said, quietly, "didn't mean we were going to leave you behind. It didn't mean we intended to leave you out of messages and texts that should've included you."

"I know it wasn't intentional," Veera said. "But it happens. We get older. We have our own families. It's not possible to do margarita brunches every weekend. And even if you don't want it to be that way, that's just . . . life."

Veera felt Kareena squeeze her hand. "Please tell us that you didn't leave and travel with your sister for eight months because you felt like we were leaving you out."

"Not really, but I'd be lying if I didn't say that it was a part of my reasoning," Veera said honestly. "Making plans with both of your schedules was hard enough. And then? It just felt . . . lonely. I live in a city surrounded by people, and I was lonely."

"And when you found Deepak," Bobbi said slowly, "you thought we'd intentionally kept you out of these couple moments. Oh, Veera, I'm so sorry."

"It's okay," Veera said. "It hurt, but I know it wasn't on purpose. Truthfully, I should've just talked to you about it instead of keeping secrets and acting like a jerk."

"Yup," Bobbi and Kareena said at the same time.

Veera had so many happy moments with her friends, so many joyous occasions. And then she remembered the times she sat on the couch next to them, talking about everything from their hopes and dreams, to heartbreak and loss. "I should've come to you sooner," she said again. "I love you both, and you're so important to me. I should've come to you sooner."

"That's obvious," Kareena said.

"Agreed," Bobbi added.

She giggled and squeezed their hands. "Good god, both of you are going to be insufferable if you have children."

"Not me," Bobbi said. "Bunty and I are happy to be the family that takes care of others."

"Prem and I are waiting for another year or so," Kareena said. "Even though my father is increasingly concerned about my aging egg reserve."

"Did I tell you guys my mother-in-law set up Deepak's bedroom in their family home as a seduction suite?"

Bobbi gasped.

"No," Kareena said, her tone willed with horror.

Veera grinned at the memory. "She had sexy Bollywood music, and fertility supplements for me next to the bed."

Veera's best friends both burst out laughing.

Kareena dropped her head on Veera's shoulder, then Bobbi did the same.

"Now I want a margarita before I hear in excruciating detail what this seduction suite looked like," Bobbi said.

"You can add that as a design service, Bobbi," Kareena said.

"Not a bad plan."

The conversation was silly and so familiar to who they once were. It felt like coming home to be with them, to feel them by her side. No matter how busy they got, how hard it would be to make time to see Kareena and Bobbi in her life, she'd always love them.

Kareena got to her feet. She straightened her sweater vest and held out a hand for Bobbi and Veera. "Come on," she said. "We've sorted out why Veera was acting like a butthead, and we've apologized for being assholes ourselves."

"And?" Veera said.

"*And*," Kareena replied. "We still have one huge problem that we have to figure out. Are we planning a murder? Or are we going to figure out how the Mathur sisters, Deepak, and Olivia fit into this new Illyria Media Group?"

"I guess we're having margaritas after all," Bobbi mused. "I refuse to talk about your business things or seduction suites without margaritas."

Veera grinned at her friends, then clapped her hands together. "Are we plotting?"

Kareena and Bobbi grinned at her then nodded.

"Bobbi, I hope you still have the whiteboard! I think we're about to make a pros and cons list."

CHAPTER 34

Veera

> **VEERA:** Bobbi and Kareena helped me whiteboard a plan
>
> **DEEPAK:** Why does that sound ominous?

"I can't believe you bought a pie," Deepak said. They stood side by side in the black marble and chrome lobby of Olivia's building. An attendant in a black suit sat at a wide circular desk, eying them as he held a receiver to his ear and spoke in hushed tones behind his cupped hand.

Veera looked up at Deepak, tempted to touch the smooth, freshly shaven jaw, to muss the styled black hair combed to the side and back, revealing the strong angles of his face. "It's almost Thanksgiving," she said and wiggled the wrapped pie plate that she held in front of her with both hands. "We can't show up to someone's house without pumpkin pie."

Deepak kissed the corner of her mouth, then rubbed her back in a smooth circular motion. She felt it through the thin insulated coat she wore on their trek from Brooklyn to the Upper West Side. "Let's hope we get a chance to try it before your sister kicks us out. Then we can go get some lunch before I head into the office."

"There is a second pie at home," Veera said and smiled when he kissed her again, a quick peck that she knew he delivered to show his gratitude and love. It was powerful to be able to touch him, to be touched by him in the way that she'd once dreamed of.

"Do you think your sister would move back to New York?" Deepak asked.

"Only time will tell," Veera said. She glanced at the gold fixtures that reminded her so much of the Kumari boutique. "This is a nice place. If both she and Olivia are serious, I can see her living here."

"You can head up," the attendant called out. He stood and leaned over the front of the desk. He pointed two fingers at the elevator bank. "Last one on your left. The panel is preprogrammed, so just step inside and it'll take you to Ms. Olivia's floor."

"Thank you," Deepak and Veera said. They followed the directions and entered the steel-and-glass elevator, which took them up twenty-five stories in a smooth, easy ride.

Every floor they ascended had her heart beating just a little bit faster. *This was it*, Veera thought. This was her moment to hash out a compromise with her twin.

The night before, Olivia had called Deepak and asked for a few minutes of their time so they could talk. She'd assured them that they wanted to work together, to come up with a solution that was right for both Mathurs and Dattas.

As they walked down the hallway, Veera thought that enough time had passed that her anger had cooled, even though she still disagreed with Sana's motives. But that's how it had always been between them. Burning hot and fast before snuffing out, leaving a thin tendril of smoke as the only remnant of their argument. They were sisters, and they brought out the ugliest in each other but also the strongest parts, too.

Before they could ring the bell for the last apartment on the left side of the hallway, Olivia was yanking the door open for them.

"Hello, you two," she said, draping her curvy body against the door jam, a sultry smile on her glossy mouth. "Come on in." She stepped back to allow both Deepak and Veera to enter the small foyer.

Veera noticed Olivia's casual attire, and she couldn't recall her ever looking so approachable in her videos. Her loose T-shirt, her hair tied up in a messy bun, her face devoid of makeup was just as beautiful as all the polish and glam. But definitely just as intimidating.

"This is for you," Veera said and handed over the pie. She took off her low pumps at the entryway and set them next to Deepak's dress shoes.

"Pie," Olivia said, her face brightening as she inspected the wrapped dessert in her hands. "I love pie. That's sweet of you. Damn, I wished you weren't as kind as your sister says."

"I'm sure that's not what she's saying right now," Veera replied blandly.

"She is, even though you called her a chutiya."

The voice came from the end of the hall. Veera turned to see Sana in a similarly casual outfit as Olivia's. With her leggings and oversize sweatshirt that dipped off one shoulder and exposed her *cash money* tattoo on her collarbone.

Veera ignored her twin's entrance. "Olivia, you have a beautiful home, and I appreciate you letting us come by."

"Sure," she said. Her smile was amused. She set the pie plate down on the gold-and-white console table to her right.

"Vee," Sana said, with a sigh. "Don't be like that when you just walked through the door."

"Be like what?" she asked, even though she knew that she sounded bratty.

She *had* called her sister a chutiya.

More than once, if she remembered correctly.

Veera squared off in front of her twin. The woman who looked just like her, except not. Sana's hair was still that short, curled mop that draped effortlessly over her brow compared to Veera's carefully coifed bun. Her soccer body versus Veera's dancer's form.

"I'm sorry," Veera finally said to her sister. "I will refrain from name-calling in your girlfriend's home, as long as you do the same."

Sana nodded in one quick jerky movement. "Agreed."

Veera felt Deepak's warmth as he wrapped an arm around her shoulder. She immediately looped hers around his waist and leaned into his side. She saw her sister's stare zero in on the contact, but instead of irritation, Sana looked . . . guilty.

"Sana, I promise, I won't hurt your sister," Deepak said, slowly. "And I don't want her in the middle of my business, especially if it forces her to choose between us."

"I know."

"You . . . know?" Veera asked. She gaped at her twin. "What convinced you?"

Sana looked over her shoulder at Olivia and then back. "I, ah, talked to Margaret. She found out that I was the other candidate. She told me pretty much the same story. That it was Dad and that he's playing a power game. He's trying to use me as his puppet."

"Sana, I'm really sorry." Even though she told her sister the truth first, Veera knew it had to hurt even more when it came from a neutral third party.

"I'm so sorry I didn't listen to you," Sana said. She glanced again at Olivia and tugged at the neck of her shirt. "I was just so angry on your behalf that I actually trusted Dad and could've ruined your relationship."

"It's okay," Veera said. Then she crossed the room and wrapped her sister up in her arms. They fit together like always. Sana's hug, her warmth, was the only consistent affection she needed in her life next to Deepak's. Feeling her twin close, even though they had seen each other only a few days before, chipped away at some of the tension in her shoulders. "Thank you so much for always wanting to protect me," she whispered, as she pressed her cheek to her twin's. "For giving me the chance to travel and to get away from the city."

"But then we didn't go into business together," Sana said quietly.

"It's not what you wanted, but it's what I needed to hear." Veera truly believed that, too. She just needed some hope, and her sister gave it to her.

Veera held on tightly as Sana did the same, and the last piece in her life seemed to slide into place. Her spirit was in equilibrium again.

"That's so beautiful," Olivia sniffled from behind them.

Sana chuckled and sniffled as well. Veera wasn't finished yet, though.

"Sana," she said, leaning back in the embrace, her arms still wrapped around her sister's waist. "You know this is not about Deepak, right? This is about you and me and Dad. This is about him not believing that we'd ever be good enough."

"But we are," Sana replied, eyes rimmed with tears. "Damn it, we are. And I hate that I fell into his trap."

"I feel like there is something to be said about trying to be more American in business while becoming more toxic Punjabi at the same time," Veera mused. Or maybe her father just hadn't evolved the way that so many of their community were finally starting to do.

"Son of a bitch played me when he said that Deepak was the one who turned down the proposal," Sana said, as she squeezed Veera's hand. "We asked you here so I could tell you in person that I'm going to drop out of the running. I don't want to be a part of this. I don't want to be a part of his plan."

Her sister had always been there for her. And to a fault, she tried to fight Veera's battles as well. But now, it was Sana who needed her. It was Sana who was still grieving all the years that they worked so hard under their father's mentorship, only to have him use them and brush them off like they never mattered in the first place.

Veera realized that while she had been traveling, she had been able to process a lot of her fears and doubts. She had contacted her therapist and done remote counseling. She had been working on herself, which is why it had felt like such a betrayal when she was ready to start the next phase of her life. Her sister wasn't ready then.

But now, they had finally gotten to a point where they could lean on each other and move forward together.

Veera brushed her wet cheek with a pad of her thumb. "I think I have an idea on how we can all get what we want, but, Sana, you can't tell Dad yet that you're pulling out of the race. We're all going to have to work together."

"Just tell us what you think we should do," Sana said. "You were always the strategist, so I'm happy to follow your lead."

Veera rubbed her palms together. "Perfect. We'll start with Olivia."

"Me?" Olivia said, pressing a palm to her chest. Her long, painted fingernails added flourish to the simple move. "I'm happy to help, but what can I do in this situation?"

"Two things," Veera said, the gears in her head turning rapidly as she started to envision the parts of her plan working in sync. She'd already brainstormed so much with Deepak, and then again with her best friends. All she needed this whole time was Sana's and Olivia's cooperation.

Deepak beamed at her, his smile so confident in her.

They were going to be okay.

"Olivia, the first request I have from you is for you to use your personal platform. Then . . . your Mrs. W. S. Gupta column."

Olivia's eyes went wide. She whirled to face Deepak. "You told her? You know that's a breach of contract."

Deepak shrugged. "Sue me. It's one thing to keep secrets from my friends and family, but I'm not going to keep secrets from my wife."

"I won't tell anyone, I promise," Veera said, as she made a scout's honor gesture. "But both your identities could really come in handy."

Olivia looked at Sana, then back at Veera, and to Deepak. "Fine," she said, her shoulders slumping. "What would you like me to do?"

"We'll start with eating that pie," Veera said. "And take a selfie." She turned to her sister. "After that, we're going to have a long conversation with Mom."

CHAPTER 35

Deepak

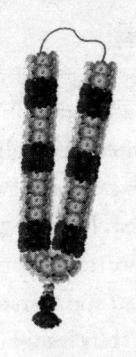

> **DEEPAK:** I need help.

> **SANA:** Look, we're still not best friends yet, so every request is going to be reviewed with scrutiny.

> **DEEPAK:** I want to make my marriage with Veera legal.

> **SANA:** Fine. Favor granted.

Love was the one emotion that made Deepak feel exposed.

Unsure.

Insecure.

The sensation was exhilarating, but at the same time he felt like he was punted into New Jersey traffic.

He loved Veera Mathur Datta, and she loved him back. They were tied together for seven lifetimes, even though he was still afraid that the lives they'd wanted, his career and her work, were standing in the way of their happiness.

But Veera's plan gave him hope, and when he committed one hundred percent of his feelings, emotions, and trust in the woman who was meant for him, he could finally see that they might have a future clear of Himalayan-size hurdles.

To keep his mind occupied and to stop from worrying, he threw himself back into his routine. On Monday, he'd finished the financial reports for the quarter four meeting before breakfast. He'd negotiated a contract for programming in Asia Pac that morning over his first cup of coffee, and he'd approved invoices and sponsorship proposals by his second.

His leadership team who had taken the bulk of the work off his plate over the last few months, specifically since his trip to Goa, were all given early quarter four bonuses that would be gifted prior to the Holiday Gala.

Kim was also promoted and given two headcounts as a support staff because she deserved the opportunity to grow and expand her skill set.

It would take him some time to stop leaning on her as his sole point of contact, but he knew his assistant would make the transition easy for him.

"Kim?" he called from his office. "Let me know when Mrs. Mathur is here."

"She's here," a voice said from the doorway.

Deepak looked up to see an older woman in an oversize white collared shirt, a floral oversize cardigan, and a musical assortment of jewelry on her hands and wrists. Her eyes were exactly like Veera's and she had glossy, styled hair in the same shade of black.

Namrata Mathur was, without a doubt, beautiful, even though she was married to a heartless bastard.

"Auntie," he said, as he came around the desk to greet her.

"Muma," she said warmly. "You are, after all, my son-in-law now."

Funny, he thought. She hadn't done a single thing, participated in one tradition, event, or celebration to welcome her daughter and Deepak as a couple into her life. Sure, she'd attended the reception and visited their house when the aunties had driven out to teach Veera how to cook, but she'd done nothing else to share her excitement in the way that Veera thought she would.

He pressed a soft kiss to her cheek. "Muma then. Come in, have a seat."

She looked over her shoulder to see Kim quietly close the office door behind her. "Aren't we waiting for my daughters? For Malkit?"

Deepak winced. He'd lied to his mother-in-law, but under the circumstances, he hoped that she'd forgive him. "I'm sorry, but it's actually going to just be us."

Her smile faded, and he saw the marks of disappointment. "Oh," she said. "So, we're not going to have a family meeting? A TV intervention?"

The fact that she thought an intervention was possible was so out of the realm of understanding for him. She'd been married to Malkit for so long. Didn't she know what he was like? Didn't she see the way that he had treated her daughters?

"Why don't we take a seat?" he said gently, then led her to one of the two chairs in front of his desk.

"Is everything okay with Veera then?" She sat and crossed one foot behind her ankle, placed her bag on top of his desk next to his computer monitor, and folded her hands in her lap.

"Not really," Deepak said, as he sat across from her. He leaned forward, forearms braced on his knees. He was sweating. God, why was he sweating so much talking to this woman?

He knew that what he was going to say would break her heart, and he couldn't stand hurting one of the most important people in Veera's life.

"Auntie," he said gently.

"Muma," she repeated.

"Muma," he said, the word sounding thick in his mouth. Awkward. "Did you know what happened when Veera and Sana's father decided to sell the company and merge with Illyria Media Group?"

Namrata Mathur was usually a sharp, intelligent woman with wit. That's what his mother had said about her in the past, and that's what he'd witnessed with his own eyes at cocktail parties and in conversations she had with her daughter. But there was something about her fragility in the moment that made him want to apologize for even asking the question.

She had sadness in her eyes. Like she'd sacrificed family for money and greed, and she knew that she'd never be able to regain what she once had.

"Malkit did what he thought was best," she said simply. "I know the girls aren't happy with that decision, but he supported them, gave them an education and a job."

"Then he fired them," Deepak said. "Told them they'd never be good enough."

She flinched, her knuckles whitening as she gripped her hands together. "They argued, but fights like that happen, beta. It was something said in the heat of the moment. He doesn't really mean it."

"If he doesn't," Deepak said slowly, "then why is he trying to pit Sana and Veera against each other? That's malicious, Muma."

Her eyes went wide. "I don't know what you're talking about. I don't really get involved in business."

This time, Deepak reached out and placed a hand over hers. "You're a member of the board because Mathur Financial Group belonged to both you and your husband. Whether you like it or not, you have no choice but to be involved. And if you don't support Veera, you're going to lose her, too."

"Veera wouldn't—"

"Yes," Deepak said firmly. "She remembers everything about the people she loves, from what they've said to her to what they've done. She's always been generous, but Veera has limits. You know this now that she no longer talks to her father."

Her face was as expressive as her daughter's. He watched her lower lip tremble. Her eyes went glassy, and she began to squeeze his hand as if she needed his strength.

She took a deep breath, and then let go.

"What did Malkit do now?" she said, her voice harder.

Deepak smiled. "It's quite a story, but you promise you won't tell him?"

"For my daughters, I'll carry this conversation to my next life."

DEEPAK WALKED TO THE BAR two blocks over from Illyria Media Group. The establishment with a wineglass decal in the window was an unassuming popular spot because of its convenience between a towering finance conglomerate and a luxury hotel. He ducked under the canopy, out of the brisk wind, and stepped inside. There was a bar top to the left side of the narrow space, and a few high-top tables in the back. It took him seconds to spot the woman he was meeting.

Sana sat at one of the high-top tables, her tablet propped up in front of her and a wineglass the size of a small globe in one hand.

"Hey," he said, as he approached the table. "You're drinking wine?"

Sana nodded. "Olivia thinks I need to expand my palate so I'm trying this out. Want some?"

"If that's a Château Lafite Rothschild that Olivia prefers to drink, then no. Not to my taste." He motioned to the bartender and asked for his usual whiskey order.

The bartender filled a tumbler one third of the way full with deep amber liquid from a bottle on the top shelf and slid it into his hand just as Sana closed her tablet.

"My father called me this morning," she said and leaned back in her chair, her pose relaxed and tense all at once. "He wanted to know if we could reschedule the meeting I'd canceled yesterday. I think he was fishing."

"What did you tell him?" Deepak asked.

"All the things we had rehearsed. I told him that I found some new dirt on you which is why I couldn't make it to finish the draft on our press release. I was double checking that my facts were straight."

"Nice save," Deepak said.

He held up his whiskey glass to tap against her rim. She looked at his outstretched hand, then with a smile, she complied. "Veera does that, too," she said.

"I picked up the habit from her. I feel like I'm going to have bad luck if I don't now."

Sana nodded, her smile pensive. "Is Mom on board then?"

Deepak thought back to the conversation that he had with Namrata Mathur. She was horrified at the detail in which Malkit Mathur had tried to screw over his own daughters.

"He doesn't hate them," she'd said, patting Deepak's arm. "He wants what's best for them. He thinks that they should settle down and have families, that's all."

Deepak took another sip of his whiskey, feeling the comfortable burn as it traveled down his throat. "Let's just say that she'll support us as long as she doesn't have to do anything directly to hurt her husband. She insists that Malkit is determined to love you in his own way, but he can't see how the way he wants to love you is hurting you, too. I told her that he's just threatened by his daughters' success. It's the twenty-first century, and if he can't see how lucky he is to have you both, then it's his fault."

Sana gave him a half smile. She stared into her wineglass, as if she were looking for all of her answers in the merlot. "If Mom follows our plan and she votes for you," Sana said slowly, "then you'll have a chance to win. There is your father, Narinder, Olivia, Margaret, and Charles from Mathur Financial."

Deepak froze. "Charles was a no a few months ago."

"I just spoke to him," Sana said. "He didn't know my father was trying to game the system. Charles is a rule follower. Doesn't even jaywalk."

Deepak felt a small sigh of relief. "That's it then. I'll get the CEO ticket."

"You will," Sana said quietly. She leaned back in her seat. "And Veera is starting a company. She was always the brains behind the operation. I was really just the closer. But if we're being honest, she could do that job, too. She just preferred not to."

"She's going to become a CEO after all," Deepak said with a smile. "And she'll be incredible at it. Now she can pick and choose what kind of work she wants to focus on, too."

Sana nodded as she continued to tilt the wineglass side to side, watching the way that it rolled back and forth. Deepak had to work to hide his smirk behind his whiskey tumbler.

She pouted just like Veera.

"Hey, after the board meeting, are you going back to England? Veera said you had some interest from a start-up out in Oxford to consult."

Sana glanced at him, then back at her glass. "It depends on the second phase of Olivia's makeup launch, but I think that's the plan."

"Is that what you've always wanted, too? To consult with flexibility?"

Sana shrugged. "I honestly don't know if that's the direction I want to go anymore. Maybe I'll ask Veera if she needs some help. I just don't want to be stateside forever. I enjoy traveling."

Deepak pursed his lips to keep from smiling. "You know what? I heard there was a job opening recently. President of Global Operations. A huge part of it is finance, but there is a lot of travel required."

Sana's head jerked up. "What's the pay?"

"You'd have to name your price," Deepak said.

"Bullshit," she scoffed. "There isn't a single company that is going to look at me and tell me to name my salary. I'm in my early thirties, and I'm a queer woman of color in finance. Outside of the South Asian business universe, I'm up against even more nepotism and dude-bros."

"Fine," Deepak said. He lifted one hip to remove his phone and typed a number in the text box before he sent it to Sana. They both heard the ping at the same time.

Sana glanced at her screen, and her eyes bulged. She barely managed to set the wineglass on the table without spilling the liquid over her tablet. "What the hell is this?"

"It's your offer," Deepak said. "And it's at the top of the pay scale, so if you want more, it would require board approval."

Sana's brow furrowed. "Deepak, I don't understand."

"You don't want to be CEO," he said gently. "And frankly, you haven't run a business of the same size and scale as Illyria Media Group, so you're not qualified for the position. You also don't know the media space, which is seventy-five percent of Illyria's business and what most of the leadership manages. But you know how to make money almost as well as my wife. And you're family.

The CFO position won't give you the travel you crave, but our global division is suffering, and we need to put leadership on the ground."

Sana's mouth fell open, and in a rare moment of affection, she slipped out of her chair, rounded the table, and wrapped her arms around his neck for an embrace.

He held her in a bear hug, lifting her boots off the floor to the musical sound of her twin laugh. It was like Veera's but different. He pressed a brotherly kiss to her cheek before he set her down. "See? I'm not such a bad guy," he said.

"No," Sana said, as she returned to her seat. She was grinning at him, her cheeks flushed. "I guess you're not. Is that why you wanted to meet me for a drink? To offer me a job?"

"Partially," Deepak said. He finished his whiskey and put the empty glass on the table in front of him. "But I wasn't kidding about what I had texted you last night. I want to legally marry my wife. I ordered the marriage certificate, but we just need to sign it and file it with an officiant. We'd really like that officiant to be someone we trust. They can just get a license online."

Sana grinned. "Yes," she said. "Yes, I'll be your officiant."

"And the job?"

"I'll work for you, too, brother-in-law. You have yourself a deal."

She held her hand out to shake and he met her firm grip over their glasses.

"Now are you going to give me a rundown on the team?" she asked. "The responsibilities? The benefits? What are your top three priorities? What kind of budget am I working with?"

He laughed and was tempted to tease her by withholding all the answers she wanted. Just to see how irritated she'd get. He'd never had a sister before, he realized. It wasn't half bad.

CHAPTER 36

Deepak

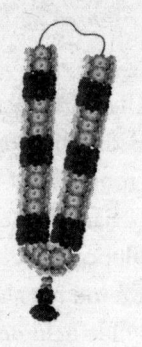

DEEPAK: Lunch?

VEERA: Yes! One?

OLIVIA: Who eats at one?

SANA: One works for me!

PREM: I can do one. It'll take us a beat to get to the city.

KAREENA: Omg, Halal Guys?

BUNTY: Immediately yes.

BOBBI: I love Halal Guys.

OLIVIA: Are they organic?

Deepak dressed with his wife the morning before the board meeting. They stood in their closet, slipping on underwear between kisses, buckling their belts, and selecting shoes. He helped her into her suit coat and she straightened his tie.

After gathering the paperwork they needed, Deepak held her hand, feeling her fingers rub against his gold wedding band, as they walked to their favorite bakery with the blue awning. He bought her the latte that she loved, while she picked out the blueberry scone and tore half of it off for herself. At 6:25 a.m., they sat at the small table with their tablets, reviewing their notes before the meeting at Illyria. Veera was going to come in with him, because it was finally time to present as a united front.

When they finished their breakfast, Deepak ordered them drinks for the road as Veera packed their bags.

"What are you thinking?" he asked. They stood outside the bakery just before seven a.m.

"It'll be nice going back into an office like this after all this time," Veera said. She adjusted her suit coat and purse before she retrieved the mint tea she'd asked him to hold. Unlike Deepak, who'd opted for another coffee as his second hit of caffeine, she'd switched her to-go beverage of choice. "As much as I liked traveling with Sana, I was never going to be happy doing global accounts the way my sister wanted. I think that was part of the reason why I was so desperate to get back to the way things were. Before the merger."

He leaned down and pressed a quick kiss to her lips. "But there is no going back now," he said softly.

"No," she replied. "We're moving forward." Veera used the pad of her thumb to wipe away the remnants of her lipstick that had transferred to his mouth. He'd never stop craving her soft touches, the brushes of her fingertips against his.

At seven, they slid into the back seat of a luxury black sedan. Veera wanted them to start using the subway, thought that it would give them more time together, but it was the week before Thanksgiving and the weather was starting to get chilly during the day.

The drive was also an opportunity for him to rehearse, just one more time.

At 7:25, they pulled up in front of the Illyria Media Group building. Deepak held her hand, feeling the hard metal of her wedding bangle brush against his wrist, as they took the elevator up to the executive floor. Their conversation had since quieted, but Deepak knew Veera was as sure, as confident, as he was about the rest of their plan.

The elevator opened with a soft swoosh, revealing a stylish Olivia and Sana, who were already waiting for them. The women were dressed in matching hot-pink pantsuits, which looked absolutely devastating in completely different ways. They complemented Veera's custom royal-red Kumari pantsuit as well.

Deepak had to wonder if they'd done it on purpose.

As if on cue, Kim strode into the lobby with a tablet tucked under one arm. "Mr. Datta, your parents and the Mathurs are waiting for you."

"Thanks, Kim."

"Of course," she replied, and took their coffee cups and bags after Deepak retrieved his laptop.

"This is fun," Olivia said cheerfully, as they walked as a unit past rows of open seating and empty offices. "It sucks that our villains aren't spicier than your parents, though."

"This is spicy enough for me," Veera said with a snort.

When they walked through the conference room doors at 7:30 a.m., four sets of eyes turned in their direction.

Olivia went over to the glass wall and pressed the button so it frosted over, giving them the privacy they needed. "Isn't this wonderful?" she said cheerfully. "We're a group of South Asians standing in an office building, talking about accumulated wealth. What a time to be alive!"

"What is happening here?" Veera's father blustered. His eyes went wide when he saw both Sana and Veera at the front of the room. He looked over at Deepak's father. "Do you know what the children are up to?"

"They're not children, Malkit," Deepak's father said smoothly. "I think they have a proposal they want to share with us."

Deepak stood next to the presentation board and docked his laptop. The board flickered so that his computer screen appeared, and a copy of the presentation he'd worked on with Veera popped up.

Leadership Assessment. Illyria Media Group. RIWF.

RIWF. Reduction. In. Workforce.

"Do you know what all of us have in common in this room?" Deepak said, as he began. "We all wanted to be better than what our family expected of us."

"Dude, that's the line you're leading with?" Sana whispered behind him.

He ignored her. "You've never asked us what we wanted for our vision of the future that you expect us to lead."

His mother sniffled, and Deepak had to stop himself from rolling his eyes. She always cried when he presented during Illyria Entertainment town hall meetings, too.

Veera stood next to Deepak's side. "I was thinking the other day," she said. "None of us—Sana, myself, Deepak—were consulted at all for the merger. The decision was made for us, and about our futures, when this was something that we had been fighting for since we were children."

"You can't expect us to hand you everything on a silver platter,"

Veera's father said. Then he chuckled, as if he had made a joke that no one else in the room laughed at.

"We didn't expect anything, especially from you, Papa," Veera said with a serene smile. "We earned it. We fought for it. And we helped the businesses grow."

"Now that the companies have merged," Sana said, as she stepped forward to stand next to her sister, "Veera and I no longer have any stock in the business. That ended when our employment was terminated."

Malkit guffawed, then readjusted the lapels on his suit coat. "Which is why I don't understand why we're giving you the time—"

"Chup kar, Malkit," Namrata Mathur said. She smacked her husband's arm in a quick tap of rebuke. Her eyeballs bulged and with a clenched jaw, she spoke in Punjabi. "You cost me my daughters for eight long months. You didn't listen to them earlier, but I swear the god, you'll listen to them now. You've eaten so much of my head, I'll walk out, I swear the god."

Malkit Mathur's face turned a deep crimson red under the dark brown of his skin. He pressed his lips together and focused his attention on Sana. The embarrassment must've been brutal, Deepak thought.

Good. He deserved it.

"Here is the plan," Deepak said. Then he switched the slide to show the growth by department, compared to Mathur Financial Group growth in the three-year period before the merger. "Both Dad, and you, Malkit, are going to announce your retirements at the board meeting."

Malkit Mathur rushed out of his chair. The leather high-back office chair rolled back and crashed against the wall. "Like hell!" he snapped.

"You will," Deepak said, calmly. "Otherwise, you will be fired. Your department has done the worst during the merger period, and your projections aren't looking that great, either. Dad? Do I have your support?"

"You do."

Malkit turned to Deepak's father. "I trusted you with my business!" he roared. His skin turned splotchy and spittle flew out of his mouth. "Haramzadhe! We were supposed to create an empire together!"

"Malkit, we already have. Now we're supposed to give that empire to our children to run." Kaushal Datta leaned back in his chair, an expression of casual disgust on his face. "You're the one who is not following the plan."

"I will vote against you, Malkit," Veera's mother said quietly. "You've worked long enough, made more money than our parents could've ever imagined. I want to go back to India, and I want to spend more time with my family. Buss. Enough. It's time for us to enjoy our lives."

"They aren't qualified, Namrata," Malkit said. He motioned to his daughters with his palms up as if to say, *See? Look at these women before you.*

"We're more than qualified," Veera said. "And if you don't think we are, then that still reflects poorly on you since you're the one who trained us all these years."

Fire burned in his eyes as he glared at her. "And I suppose you'll take over as CFO?"

"No," Veera said. "I'm opening up my own financial business, but Illyria Media Group can be my first client. With the help of Margaret, and a few of the other senior staff, I'm developing the first equitable financial practices division in a South Asian–owned business that supports entertainment sectors. I'll also partner with companies like Bharat Inc. in the tech industry and specialize in B2B corporate lending."

"You're too soft," her father said. "You'll never make it. Now your sister—"

"Doesn't want to be in New York," Sana said. She touched Veera's shoulder. "Instead, Deepak has asked if I'd be interested in leading the Global Ops division and I've applied. Olivia can work from anywhere, so if I am offered the job, I'll be restructuring the India office first. Mom, maybe you can come south and visit us."

Veera's mother brightened. "Oh, wonderful! I'd love that, beta."

"No, no, no," Malkit Mathur said. He rested his hands on the table. "If you try to get rid of me, you have to pay a massive severance fee."

"Unless you don't hit your corporate goals," Deepak said. He tapped the keypad on his laptop and another slide popped up with a snapshot of contract language. "Then your fee is reduced by every percentage you're short. And the rest? Well, I'd gladly pay that out of my own pocket."

"You should be happy your daughters are succeeding, Papa," Veera said. "You can't teach us to be leaders and then tell us we're not ready when it's time for us to lead."

Malkit Mathur straightened his jacket. "I still have a significant percentage of shares, and—"

"And if you use it to hurt my daughter-in-law or my son," Deepak's father said, as he slowly got to his feet, "then you're going to have a bigger fight on your hands than you might be ready for."

Deepak's mother wiggled her fingers at him. "I will also be supporting my daughter-in-law and my son. Malkit, when you approached us with the plan to merge, you sold us on our children working together. You're the one who is going back on your deal."

"I agree," Namrata Mathur said. She turned to her husband. "Malkit, stop this nonsense."

Deepak held his wife's hand as she saw the proud man she'd once looked up to, the person that she had always cared for and loved, turn on his heels, and walk out of the conference room without another word.

Veera squeezed his fingers, once, twice, then let him go.

There was an audible release of breath from everyone around the table.

"I have to apologize on his behalf," Namrata Mathur said, when the door closed behind him. Her voice began to tremble as she slowly got to her feet as well. "He never used to be like this. Then a few years ago, he started to act so much more controlling. As if he were worried that Sana and Veera would change everything the way that he wanted it, and their vision was a bad thing."

"Namrata, you don't have to apologize for him," Deepak's mother said. She reached across the table and tapped the surface with the palm of her hand. "Everything worked out the way we wanted it to, nah? You and I dreamed of our children finding each other and look what happened?"

"Wait, you wanted us to get together?" Deepak burst out. He bounced back and forth between his mother and mother-in-law. "Me and Veera?"

Both the older women shared a look, then burst into giggles. The tension diffused in the room.

"Of course, we did," Namrata Mathur said, smiling at him. "Silly boy. When Veera was with you, she glowed."

"And when you were with Veera," his mother added, "you relaxed! You laughed. You were yourself. And Olivia, I'm so sorry, I never thought that my son would rope you into his insanity."

"That's okay," Olivia said. She wrapped an arm around Sana's waist and leaned into her side. "Everything happens for a reason, and I know I've found mine."

Deepak's father clapped and stepped back from the table. "Good, now that Olivia is here to vote, I think the only person we have to concern ourselves with is Narinder."

"Don't worry about him," Olivia said. "He's been a wonderful friend, and he'll be supportive."

"Thanks, Olivia," Veera said.

Olivia winked as she leaned her head against Sana's shoulder. "No problem, sweetie."

The parents began asking about the weather and chai, as if everyone hadn't experienced an adrenaline rush seconds before.

As if their children weren't moments away from starting a coup.

They were speaking over one another in a mix of languages, recommending the best chai restaurants, as they walked out of the room together.

When Deepak, Sana, Olivia, and Veera were alone, Deepak moved on impulse and pulled all three women in for a group hug.

His face hurt with the force of his grin. "How badass are we, huh?"

"Did he really just say badass?" Olivia asked, tucked against his side.

"He did," Sana replied from her spot under his other arm.

"He's a nerd," Veera agreed. Then she stood on her toes and kissed his jaw.

With a rallying cheer, they separated at once, replaying the meeting in various degrees of exaggeration. Within minutes, they were laughing and the weeks of stress and anxiety passed. There was no doubt in anyone's mind that Malkit Mathur was going to retire at the meeting, and Deepak would be voted in as the next CEO.

CHAPTER 37

Veera

Veera loved the crisp feel of winter weather, the cool breeze as it whipped between skyscrapers. She held Deepak's hand as they left the office that afternoon and made the long walk through midday pedestrian traffic and early holiday tourists to the popular food cart on Fifty-Third Street.

"Is this what smugness feels like?" she asked.

Deepak chuckled, the warm sound escaping his mouth into the cool air with puffs of white. "I need more context."

"I feel happy. Ergo, smugness."

"Happiness makes you smug?" he asked, as they stopped at the end of the line that snaked down the street. He turned to face her, then with his hands on her waist, tugged her close. She burrowed against his chest just as a brisk wind rushed by them.

"It's been a long time since I've been happy," she said. "I earned my emotions. Don't you feel smug?"

He dropped a quick kiss on the tip of her nose. "I would if you signed the damn marriage certificate instead of insisting on a prenup."

She patted the lapels of his wool coat. "Prenuptial agreements are like marriage insurance. They're smart business. Look, Kareena is drafting them this week. I'll sign the certificate as soon as they're done."

They moved a few steps forward and resumed their close

embrace, enjoying the anonymity that came with the hulking city that surrounded them.

"I still don't like it," he muttered.

For a man who was supposed to head an incredibly profitable, incredibly successful media conglomerate in a few months, he wasn't exactly making sound investment decisions in his personal life.

That was okay, Veera thought. She loved him anyway. She loved the life they were starting for themselves, too. And if he was too emotional about money, then she'd have to be rational for both of them.

When they were next in line, Veera stepped out of his embrace and tucked an errant curl behind her ear. Knowing her man, the friend she'd grown to love more and more each day, she decided that he'd earned a break from her teasing. "I'll take care of the paperwork with Kareena, and you handle the trip for our next marriage ceremony."

"I can do that," Deepak said, his smile brightening. "I want the full wedding experience."

Veera worried her ring with her thumb, watching it twinkle in the cold late-fall sunlight. "If you're sure, but Deeps, do we really need any more ceremonies?"

"I'll marry you a hundred times over," he said and gave her a smacking kiss that made her giggle.

"Next!"

They stepped up to the food cart and ordered two chicken and rice platters with red and white sauce. Deepak paid in cash, then they moved to the side until their containers were ready.

"Hey, we're here!" Olivia called out. "Sorry we're late! I had a brand meeting." Her singsong voice was like a beacon for tourists walking by. With her faux-fur-lined coat, she was the picture of flamboyant fashion, which was only accentuated by her swirling cloud of shining black curls.

Sana walked at her side wearing lace-up heeled boots and a thick black peacoat. A style icon in her own right.

They could appear in magazines together.

Veera motioned to the cement ledge that surrounded the office building behind them. "We're going to sit and eat over there," she said to her sister. "Come and join us when you have your food."

Just as Veera and Deepak sat hip to hip on the ledge, Bobbi and Bunty arrived. Shortly after, Prem and Kareena strolled down the sidewalk in their direction, hand in hand.

Less than ten minutes later, all eight of them were sitting on the ledge in front of the food cart, their containers open, carefully balanced in one hand, while they ate with plastic forks in the other, hunched over their steaming food. They were hip to hip, talking all at once.

"You know, guys, we can enjoy our food somewhere with heat," Kareena said from the far end of the ledge. "We don't have to suffer like this."

"And miss out on chicken and rice when it's steaming hot and fresh?" Bunty called back from the other end of the row. "No, thank you."

"Deepak and Vee, are you going to tell us how the board meeting went, or should we not talk about it?" Bobbi called out.

Deepak smiled at Veera. She winked in response.

"It was anticlimactic." He had to shout so everyone could hear him. "But you're looking at the next CEO of Illyria Media Group."

There was a resounding cry of cheers and Veera watched with

pride as their friends got up to pat her husband on the back and give him awkward side hugs while they made sure not to drop their precious takeout containers.

"Are you all friends now?" Kareena asked, as she motioned to Sana and Deepak.

"Considering I'm working for him," Sana said with a smile, "I have to be nice to the boss. I'm going to lead Global Ops for Illyria Media Group. Still unconfirmed, but I doubt the CEO's wife is going to put up with any bullshit obstacles."

Veera nudged Sana's arm. "You're just lucky that your background check won't have the shenanigans in Madrid on it."

"What happened in Madrid?" Bunty called out. "The food in Madrid is the best."

Veera glanced at her sister and saw that Sana was smiling back at her. There were memories of drinking way too much alcohol and then trying to appear professional during stakeholder meetings, all while covering up their new *cash money* and *paneer* tattoos. They were thirty-two but hadn't quite lived until they had traveled the world together.

"Nothing," they spoke in unison.

There was another round of laughter.

Olivia stood up and held up her phone. "Hey, can I get a picture of all of us?"

There were grumbles, complaints about hair and wanting to finish their food, but when Olivia began to whine, they all squeezed closer together, tilting their heads one way or another.

"Let's do this right," Olivia said, as she ran into the middle of the sidewalk and set up a makeshift tripod faster than Veera had seen anyone move in their life. Mindful of the foot traffic, she waited until there was a brief break in flow before she ran back to her spot on the ledge between Sana and Bobbi.

"Say 'samosa'!" she shouted.

"Samosa!"

Olivia pressed a coin-size remote and there was a tiny flash, and then another, and then a third.

"Got it!" Olivia called out. She disassembled her tripod, then passed her phone down the line so that everyone could see the picture.

When the phone reached Veera, she leaned closer to Deepak so he could see it as well. It was a perfect snapshot of their friends, of their growing family.

Deepak pressed his lips against her ears, warm enough to trigger a shiver down her spine. "Should we tell them?" he whispered.

Veera nodded. Then whispered back, "I love you."

"I love you," he said. He stood and set his lunch container on his ledge seat. He took a few steps back and motioned to his friends like a conductor.

"Can I have your attention, please?"

"Already bossing people around," Prem shouted.

"This isn't your boardroom, asshole," Bunty added.

"Let the man talk," Sana said with a laugh.

"You're just saying that because he's signing your checks now," Bobbi commented.

"Truer words were never spoken."

Veera tucked two fingers in her mouth and let out a piercing whistle loud enough to have half the block looking in her direction.

"Thanks, Vee," Deepak said, grinning.

"You're welcome." Her father had given her two gifts: trauma and the ability to whistle like a drunk Punjabi uncle. At least one of them came in handy.

"We are planning a trip," Deepak continued. "January is going to be busy as we transition into our new roles, so we're leaving right after Christmas."

"Where are you going?" Prem called out.

"To Goa," he said. With his eyes fixed on Veera, his face full of love, he added, "In fact, we're *all* going to Goa. For one week."

Everyone was stunned silent.

"Look." Deepak held his hands up in surrender. "I am not the greatest best man, and I'm terrible at wedding planning, but I can spend money. So . . . I'm paying for all of you to come with us to Goa for another wedding." He smiled at Veera. "I want to marry my wife properly this time. Not with a traditional ceremony, because the one we had was special to us, but with a marriage certificate. And a few parties . . ."

Olivia was the first to scream. Then they were leaving their lunch containers and tackling him with a hug.

Veera stayed back, watching their joy as pedestrians shook their heads and muttered curses about blocking traffic. She met her husband's gaze as he accepted slaps on the back and gentle embraces with kisses on the cheek.

Mostly from Bunty.

Come here, he mouthed over the chaos of their friend group.

Veera shook her head and pointed at her chicken and rice with her fork before she took another bite.

Brat, he mouthed again. Veera shivered. She knew she was going to get deliciously punished later, and she didn't mind at all.

Not one bit.

EPILOGUE

Two weeks after Veera and Deepak returned from Goa with their friends, Veera cut out a Mrs. W. S. Gupta article and fit it into a frame that she'd purchased in India. Ignoring Deepak's exasperation, she set the frame on their mantel in their home. Whenever their friends came over, the article reminded them of the love stories that altered their lives forever.

To my loyal fans and loved ones. This is my last Mrs. W. S. Gupta column, and I'm so sorry to have to say goodbye to all of you. I've had the privilege of writing to you for over five years now, and I've enjoyed each and every chance I've had to share wisdom.

The intention of this column wasn't to trick your children into marriage, but to think critically about the way we encourage our children to live lives better than the ones we've lived ourselves.

My last advice to you is this: Your children are the product of the insecurities that you carried when you raised them. Your children are the hopes that you had. Your children are more complex and deserve the opportunity to make their own mistakes. You've made yours. It's time for them to have a chance.

If they make a mistake, that's their problem.

Wishing you many happy matrimonies and joyous unions in your lives.

Mrs. W. S. Gupta
Avon, New Jersey

AUTHOR'S NOTE

Every time I sat down to write a book in this trilogy, I thought I was wrestling with the hardest Shakespeare play out of the three that I'd chosen. But now, after finishing *Marriage & Masti*, I'm sure that this last one was the most difficult to finish.

For hundreds of pages, I laughed and cried with parts of myself that I crushed like mirror dust and poured into these novels. Now, I'm finally saying goodbye to the characters that have truly become friends to me. When Deepak and Veera first appeared on the page in *Dating Dr. Dil*, I knew that their love was going to be a complicated messy one. I also knew that they belong together. Because let's be honest, friendship will always be a strong foundation for a romantic relationship.

Veera was so sweet and kind, but she also had this acerbic sense of humor that periodically burst through. Deepak, on the other hand, was incredibly rigid and serious, and I knew that he was the perfect foil for Veera's chaotic quiet sweetness.

Putting both of them in the context of *Twelfth Night* was an easy decision for me, because Deepak didn't see Veera for the romantic heroine she could be until he realized that Olivia was never the right choice for him. Veera is also a woman operating in a male-dominated industry, where she is succeeding at her job. She has a sister who is on this quest, too. Sana is this chaotic, fiercely protective character that everyone falls in love with, including our drama queen, Olivia. Then Deepak, as Duke Orsino, is in love with the idea of marriage as a vehicle for something he believes is just out of his reach. When really, he's in love with the person in front of him the whole time.

I also think part of the joy of writing as a member of the diaspora is straddling two different cultures such as South Asian Punjabi experiences, and the American experiences that are a more direct mirror of Shakespeare. In a way, adapting these narratives was a form of decolonization for me.

I'm so glad that all of you have stuck with me through three books of chaotic love and friendship and have enjoyed my Shakespeare reimaginings as much as I've enjoyed writing them. Your support has meant the world to me and has truly given my career life.

Thank you, besties.

Mrs. W. S. Gupta signing off for the last time.

ACKNOWLEDGMENTS

I have written nine other acknowledgments in my life, and every time, it's more and more difficult to capture the names of all the people who have helped me get to this point in my writing career. This book was hard to write. Most of my drafting and revisions occurred during a really difficult health crisis, which is why I want to thank the people who not only helped me get this novel to the finish line, but who held my hand while I cried.

To my family, specifically my partner, who has always been so incredibly supportive, a loving and true cheerleader even when my writing had to take priority over our time together.

To my agent, Joy Tutela, who will always be such an incredible partner in this wild industry. To Susan and the rest of the David Black Literary team as well.

To Ariana Sinclair and the Avon team. This is for the individuals within publishing who go above and beyond to not only listen to marginalized authors but try to deconstruct systems where marginalized stories are designed to fail. Thank you for all your support.

To my friends: Smita Kurrumchand, Jordan Reiser (and Manfred and Debby!), Namrata Patel, Mona Shroff, Katee Robert, Sierra Simone, Nikki Sloane, Ali Hazelwood, and Morgan Elizabeth for your incredible love and support.

To my sensitivity readers, who have requested anonymity: Thank you for helping me craft Sana in a way that became both powerful and deeply human. *Twelfth Night* is incredibly difficult because of the way both trans and queer identities are depicted. I wanted to be respectful to my queer community friends, and with your incredible support, we balanced a delicate tightrope where Sana pushed hard on Veera but was never her villain. The Rapinoe reference is for you!

To Sanjana Basker and Debra Akins. You both were the real MVP.

And to the friends I've lost along the way to marriage and children. Our friendships are frozen in time, and I think about our moments fondly. Thank you for the history that we share. Your friendship has taught me so much about myself and has helped shape the writer I am today.

DISCOVER THE IF SHAKESPEARE WERE AN AUNTIE SERIES BY
NISHA SHARMA

Nisha Sharma's hilarious new romantic comedy inspired by *The Taming of the Shrew* features a love-phobic TV doctor who must convince a love-obsessed homebody they are destined to be together.

"Nisha Sharma's *Dating Dr. Dil* is what would happen if you put all my favorite romantic comedy tropes into a blender: a frothy, snarky, hilarious treat with a gooey, heartwarming center. The perfect addition to any rom-com lover's shelf."
—EMILY HENRY, #1 *New York Times* bestselling author of *People We Meet on Vacation*

"What a joy! *Dating Dr. Dil* is further proof that Nisha Sharma is a mega-talent who can do it all. Anything Nisha Sharma writes is an auto-buy for me."
—MEG CABOT, #1 *New York Times* bestselling author

"Bursting with character, spicy tension, and laughs, *Dating Dr. Dil* is the enemies-to-lovers dream book!"
—TESSA BAILEY, *New York Times* bestselling author of *It Happened One Summer*

In the hilarious follow-up to the breakout rom-com *Dating Dr. Dil*, Nisha Sharma adds shakkar and mirch to Shakespeare's iconic comedy *Much Ado About Nothing* for one sweet and spicy love story.

"Red-hot. . . . This exhilarating rom-com hits all the right notes."
—PUBLISHERS WEEKLY (starred review)

"In this fun and flirty contemporary romance steeped in South Asian culture, author Sharma will delight readers with playful banter, steamy scenes, and a love story that will leave readers eager for more."
—LIBRARY JOURNAL

"[In] Sharma's latest delectable rom-com... their chemistry sizzles. . . . Her fans will be thrilled to welcome back the large cast of colorful characters that are so realistically drawn within this privileged Punjabi community."
—BOOKLIST

DISCOVER GREAT AUTHORS, EXCLUSIVE OFFERS, AND MORE AT HC.COM.
Available wherever books are sold.